S0-BSW-273

GONE
THE
SUN

Other Books by Winston Groom

Better Times Than These

As Summers Die

Conversations with the Enemy
  (with Duncan Spencer)

Only

Forrest Gump

WINSTON GROOM

GONE THE SUN

 Doubleday

NEW YORK LONDON TORONTO SYDNEY AUCKLAND

Published by Doubleday, a division of
Bantam Doubleday Dell Publishing Group, Inc.,
666 Fifth Avenue, New York, New York 10103

Doubleday and the portrayal of an anchor with a dolphin
are trademarks of Doubleday, a division of
Bantam Doubleday Dell Publishing Group, Inc.

Library of Congress Cataloging-in-Publication Data

Groom, Winston, 1944–
　　Gone the sun.

　　I. Title.
PS3557.R56G6　1988　　　813'.54　　　88-382
ISBN 0-385-23576-3

Copyright © 1988 by Perch Creek Realty and Investments Corp.
All Rights Reserved

Printed in the United States of America
August 1988
First Edition

BG

To
Theron Raines

Day is done, gone the sun,
From the hills, from the fields,
From the sky.
Rest in peace, soldier brave,
God is nigh.

—"Taps"

GONE
THE
SUN

BOOK ONE

Soundings

A destiny, you might call it, began—according to the weather report in a yellowed newspaper clipping—on a drizzling February afternoon in 1943, when James Payton "Beau" Gunn II officially arrived on earth and was certified a human being of American citizenship.

This event occurred in a small hospital in Washington, D.C., while the bitterest war in history raged on both sides of the world. The first of the two most important documents that circumscribe our lives attested that Beau was a white male weighing a respectable eight and one-half pounds and that he had a small triangular birthmark on his rosy bottom.

The second document, recently signed by the county coroner, revealed, among other things, that in four intervening decades Beau had grown to a height of six feet two inches and a weight of one hundred eighty-four pounds; he had acquired an inch-long scar on his right hip just below the waist and suffered from mild liver enlargement—none of which had anything to do with the official cause of his death. Of course, there's more to it than that. Sometimes I think we should be issued another paper, a Life Certificate, if you will—which could contain some brief statement for historical purposes that could explain how a person lived and what they accomplished and where they failed and why.

Because I was his friend, I followed his life pretty closely; still, there are gaps and shadows and voids where he flashed in and out over the years. There were times, you see, when Beau's path was as bright as that of a comet burning its way through darkness to the stars. He always returned, however, as though a siren compelled him to come home; pulling him back to earth,

3

even though he knew—must have known—the atmosphere would vaporize him. I guess it was partly my fault too.

He called me "Pappy," and had since we were boys, because I was six months older and that counted for something in those days. Later, when we were men, I became fascinated by his success and by the demons that tormented him. I was responsible for his return to Bienville and, in a way, I was responsible for his death. We engaged in long talks the whole time we knew one another. He told me things he didn't tell other people, so it seemed natural to me that I should be the one to piece together the real story of Beau Gunn's shortened life and violent death.

I've been at this project more than two years now and I've interviewed most of the principal actors at length—even Sheilah Price and Dan Whittle, two of the most difficult. Where there were holes in the story I have taken license to fill them. The large body of information I've collected is my Life Certificate to Beau Gunn.

Beau's memories of his early years were fragmented and vague. He remembered a hole burned in an awning someplace, and an impression of snow, which he would not see again until many years later because at the age of sixteen months he was bundled up and taken by his mother to the Deep South shipping port of Bienville, Alabama, to wait out the war while his father was overseas.

These were not extraordinary times. After the war, Beau's family moved into their first home and his father resumed his practice of law. Beau and I used to play in woods that lay around our houses, climbing white slatted fences covered with honeysuckle, lying for hours in clover fields and hiding up in a large mulberry tree in his backyard. At various times he had a dog, a cat, a rabbit, a parakeet and a turtle. His mother, who had a theatrical voice and a flair for drama, would read him *The Wind in the Willows* and *Winnie the Pooh,* as well as heavier fare such as *Julius Caesar* and *Macbeth;* in fact, the first motion picture Beau ever saw was a film version of *Macbeth,* and even at the age of eight, he knew the scenes and most of the lines before they came on-screen.

How he got to be known as Beau tells something of the way he was raised. When he was little, his father took to calling him "Bo" and it stuck. When he was old enough to read and his mother could leave him notes with instructions, "Bo" came under scrutiny. Mrs. Gunn wasn't a pretentious woman but she felt "Bo" wasn't dignified enough; smacked too much of "Bubba" or "Buddy"—those kinds of countrified names associated with uncultured folks—and so when she sat down to write him his first note, she scratched out "Bo" and wrote "Beau." She thought it a handsome-looking name and was proud of her inventiveness. And so it was.

At the age of six he was remitted to a venerable military academy in Bienville to be educated into something resembling a gentleman. Twelve years later he was graduated, and entered the state university—the scholastic reputation of which lay somewhere between a moderately energetic liberal arts institution and a country club. But he did well there, was tapped into a number of honor societies and received his degree just in time to take part in the Vietnam War.

Yet for all the apparent normality of Beau's early life, he was always different from the rest of us; he was often a loner and never really aspired to the same things we did. Even in the little things he was different. When, for instance, everyone else had a Chevy or a Ford, Beau owned an old MG sports car. He dabbled secretly in watercolor painting, played the piano and taught himself to play the guitar long before it became fashionable. He read books without being told to, tinkered in the sciences, collected stamps and coins and once sculpted a huge butterfly (no one knew exactly why) out of a piece of wood. He excelled on the playing fields too, which mattered a great deal in those days, but sometimes he seemed strangely elsewhere.

There was a little group of us back then who were close friends, and we formed a secret society called the Five Funny Fellows. Some of what happened to us was, in fact, funny, but there was tragedy too. Through it all, adolescence and adulthood, we never really lost touch and some of us did pretty well, considering.

Beau was a good-looking man; tall with lean muscles, an angular face, high cheekbones and a dark complexion that set off his cobalt-blue eyes. He had fine, light brown hair that sometimes fell over his forehead, but even when it began to turn gray he never looked more than twenty-five or thirty. His nose was straight and narrow until it was broken in a football game our senior year at Singer Academy, after which it seemed to suit him better. The old nose was too aristocratic. He needed an imperfection.

Just when he finished college, the Army got him. Beau wasn't ideally suited for the job, but he nonetheless found himself commanding first a rifle platoon, then a company in the treacherous jungles near the Cambodian border during those peculiar and enigmatic early years of Vietnam. At the time he viewed his duty with the resignation of a young man consigned to a summer of manual labor between school terms. He had been raised as a patriot—"my country, right or wrong"—and could vividly remember Nikita Khrushchev proclaiming on national television, "We will bury you," which he took as a personal affront. Once into the fray, there wasn't time to do

5

much philosophizing about it, though toward the end of his tour he became consumed by a deep and inexpressible rage that he was unable to direct toward anything in particular, except perhaps life itself.

And then he was wounded. It wasn't a very bad wound, or a heroic one—he had been standing on a hillside eating from a can of C ration peaches when an incoming mortar round sprayed the area with shrapnel, a shard of which penetrated his hip, shattering the bone and leaving him with a slight limp, and that was the end of his war.

Beau returned changed, of course, but it would be years before he could admit how much and how profoundly. He worked at a few odd jobs before becoming a reporter on a large daily newspaper in Washington, D.C., where his own life had begun more than two decades earlier. He wrote about everything from the farmer who grew a twenty-pound squash to the troubles in Northern Ireland before concluding that journalism was a bleak career. Following a long-suppressed dream, he took a stab at playwriting.

His first play, *Such a Pretty Girl,* was sold and opened in an Off-Broadway theater, where it ran for a week to very good notices. Beau gained self-confidence and a certain amount of prestige, so he moved to New York City, did a few television scripts to earn money and fell in with a fast-moving, artsy society crowd. He wrote another play that had a successful run on Broadway . . . two that had a lukewarm reception and another that simply, politely flopped. Meanwhile, he had spent the last several years working on what he felt was going to be his magnum opus; the subject—Vietnam—was one he now felt enough distance from to write about sanely, more or less.

But things weren't going well.

Beau was forty years old and by most standards a success, though he didn't really feel like one. He didn't consider himself a failure, either, but he knew the weaknesses of his work and the loneliness and uncertainty and craziness that went along with a writer's life. He had begun to have money problems and was restless about the idea of settling down and having a family. He had started asking himself the old simple questions: Is it worth it? Where does it lead? How will it end? Each time he attempted a new play he'd stretched himself further and, as in an aging athlete in some pain, there was a point where the elasticity was going to fail him. He knew it and he was becoming a little frightened—relying a little too much on whiskey to ease his contests with the specters and angels.

One fall day he packed up and came home to Bienville; retreated to a ramshackle hunting and fishing camp at Still River about twenty miles north of the city, up in the delta swamps, and there he spent his time trying to make last-minute fixes in the Vietnam play.

6

By this time he had also met Sheilah and discovered the concept of impossibility.

I realize now that he loved her, but as with DiMaggio and Marilyn Monroe, there were too many differences, the expectations were too great; fire and ice—it was too right and too wrong. I believe that she loved him too, in her way, but Sheilah was a little bit crazy—maybe more than a little—and there was a side of her that was cold and angry. Still, things surely would have turned out differently for Beau if they could have put it together. Who knows? As I said, he talked to me and I tried to be a good listener. We were friends from childhood. I think he told me things he wouldn't say to anyone else. I wish I could have helped him more.

Sometimes I wonder how much it all matters now, except to those of us who cared for him. We roll it around from time to time and we try to see the different shapes it takes and how it worked and how it didn't. Beau was a good man; decent, but regrettably unfinished. Regarding what happened in the end, I think he'd been honest with everyone but himself. Of course, he made his mistakes, but needless to say, we all do, which is why they put a rubber mat around spittoons.

Still River

November 1, 1983

Beau couldn't remember exactly when he began to contemplate shooting the old bear.

The thought had crossed his mind several weeks earlier when he saw the bear rummaging painfully through his garbage, but for the past two days, there had been no sign of it. He had turned the idea around from every angle he could imagine, including what might have been the angle of the bear; then, some hours ago, he fished out two twelve-gauge slugs from the make-shift gun case, cleaned their corroded brass casings with a penknife, wiped them with an oily rag and set them side by side on the mantel above the fireplace. Now the slugs looked almost new; in fact, they were probably older than the bear and possibly older than Beau himself.

I had picked this night to go up and see him. I knew he planned to break camp the next day and return to New York and I calculated he might be in a good mood for what I wanted to discuss. Over the years, I'd learned that Beau's moods had to be anticipated. There were times when he was recep-tive and others when he was tight and closed off.

I had brought up the subject I was coming to discuss once before. That time he was in one of his unresponsive moods, but it had been a month or so earlier, just after he arrived, and he was visiting with his father. I needed him and I thought he needed me. I knew his playwriting career was at an ebb and I sensed everything was not right with Sheilah. Besides, I had another reason to visit; I had Tommy Brodie's trouble to tell him about.

Earlier in the evening, Beau had caught a trout and cooked it for supper, and after he scraped the bones into the garbage and washed the dishes, he stepped out into the cool October night and walked down the little path from the cabin to the pier on the lake. The smells were of the lake and the river and the surrounding swamp, the damp-sweet aroma of cypress and hyacinth and the musky odor of the swamp grass and the tepid, tea-colored delta water that barely moved in the tidal pull of the bay, fifteen miles to the south. He thought of Sheilah and thought, too, of how she wouldn't like it here.

Beau took out a cheroot and licked the end of it; suddenly he caught the scent of the bear: sour, moldy and pathetic. Most of its teeth were long gone and its claws broken. It had been reduced to scavenging Beau's garbage heap, supplementing that diet with washed-up fish or carrion or an occasional mussel. Even the bear's scat reflected these odors as it piled up around the shallow den it had dug for itself in a hummock not far from the cabin.

Lately, the bear itself had begun to reek. Beau had observed that it didn't go into the water anymore and its fur was mangy and tangled and rank.

A three-quarter moon was halfway into the sky, pasted against the millions of hard autumn stars, and Beau struck a match to the cheroot and braced himself against the railing of the pier. A fish burbled in the lake—preying or preyed upon—and an owl made a noise somewhere far off in the swamp. For a few moments it became utterly still, and then the bear began to grunt forlornly in its den. Poor old feller, Beau thought, poor old gent.

He puffed on the cheroot and a sweet wisp of bluish smoke hung momentarily in front of him, then drifted out slowly over the water. The cigar was one of the last of the Cubans he had brought with him; a reminder of the days when he could afford to buy them by the boxful—a hundred bucks a crack. The smoke reminded him again of Sheilah, who detested his cigars. No, she wouldn't have liked it here, he decided with renewed conviction. A lawn party, sunbathing on the Atlantic beaches at Southampton or possibly driving through New England to look at the foliage was about the extent of her interest in the Great Outdoors. Sheilah didn't like what she didn't know. It led Beau to another reflection.

In an idle moment a few years back, even before things started going wrong, he had sat down and filled two entire pages of a legal pad with Sheilah's idiosyncrasies. In addition to his cigars, she didn't like horses or dogs (they scared her), going to museums or exhibits (they bored her), expensive cars (they embarrassed her), country music (tacky), Shakespeare (pompous) or public displays of affection; nor did she like men opening doors for her or helping her on with her coat, or Southern men (you can't tell what they're thinking), or being called on the phone late at night, or drinking liquor, or being kidded . . . and so on . . . such an inconsistent and complicated chorus of peeves that Beau often stumbled over himself trying to avoid them. Looking back, he wondered why he had.

Once, during a minor spat, he had taken out the list and showed it to her, stupidly thinking that it might have a positive effect. She received this gesture with such a hail of vituperation that he stormed back to his desk and made one final, sour entry, "doesn't like criticism either," and crammed the document back into its drawer. Standing on the dock now, thousands of miles from her post-Freudian anxieties, savoring the bittersweet mingling of the woods and the pungent odor of the crazy old bear, Beau was reminded of the conversation they'd had after a friend of hers remarked that by the time Sheilah was thirty she was going to be a "certified battle-ax." The irony, he thought, wasn't that it was true, but that she'd told him the story as though she were actually proud of it!

Beau blew a smoke ring from the cigar and watched it dissipate against the light of the moon. Well, he thought sourly, I almost married a battle-ax. He drew on the cheroot and held it away so he could see the orange glow of its tip, wondering how he'd got himself into a predicament, the very idea of which made his palms damp. The situation was all the more aggravating since he'd been the one to initiate the engagement in the first place *and* there was still a large and baffled part of him that missed her terribly, perhaps still loved her. He knew he wanted her, wanted to possess her—she who could never be possessed entirely. He wondered if he'd ever know how he really felt about her.

Beau probably heard the drone of my motorboat about then. We move by boat up here; there are no roads in these swamps and man has still made few inroads among the cypress and the reptiles.

My mission was clear now. I had just become the principal purchaser of Bienville's newspaper and I wanted Beau to run it for me. When I spoke with him last, the idea hadn't quite taken shape. I and the little syndicate I put together had concluded a year's negotiation to buy the *Courier-Democrat*. I had inherited a nice sum of money from my family and believed the city deserved better than what it was getting—furthermore, the paper enjoyed a virtual monopoly on advertising, and was thus the equivalent of a gold mine.

From his days as a journalist I knew Beau had the background; he grew up in the city, and he could add class to the paper. I was confident that if I could persuade him, he wouldn't let me down.

There was the other thing too. Something that had happened since I had seen him last. It was a horrible thing and involved us both to some extent, and the newspaper and the Five Funny Fellows. It was not good news, yet I was somehow elated that I could tell Beau because it was the kind of news that might sway him in the direction I wanted. His conflict was lost on me then; I was single-minded. All my life I'd been a businessman, and business was business. But I meant well, and Beau was my game that night.

The big engine of my boat throbbed like a toothache. The water ahead was shallow and black. It was an open boat, with a handcrafted mahogany-and-glass windshield. I stood at the wheel and eased the throttle forward, kicking a plume of white spray behind me in the starlight. I was feeling good then, almost immortal, and I thought Beau might be feeling that way too.

It was just before nine o'clock and Beau had decided to have another go at the script before he turned in. He reached for the walking cane he'd fashioned from a gnarled piece of hickory a few weeks earlier. For the first time in years, the hip was bothering him again. He thought it might just be the climate, but the pain was different than he'd remembered. He'd never had much of a limp, actually, but for now, with no one else around, the cane would do. He went back up the path to the cabin and took two logs from a pile outside the door and threw them onto the fire. In the far corner of the room was the table he used for his desk; neat, as he'd left it, as he left everything.

After his experience at the Academy and college and the Army and the little apartments in Washington and New York, he had cultivated a need to have things reasonably straight. From time to time he had lived with women and found them to be far more disarrayed than he, and often as not he'd wind up cleaning their messes as well as his own. Once, long before Sheilah, when he'd been going with Courtney, she'd remarked on his fastidiousness and it set him thinking that perhaps he was neater than most people. Then, later that night, Courtney said she knew why: it was because his mind was so chaotic, that he needed to have his surroundings in order so as not to go nuts. He didn't much appreciate that interpretation at the time, but later he realized it was also the night he'd fallen in love with Courtney.

On the desk was a kerosene lamp, which Beau fired up, illuminating his working tools: an old stationery box containing half a dozen sharpened pencils, several erasers, a pad of three-by-five slips of paper for making notes and a packet of paper clips to attach them to the manuscript. A dictionary and a stack of fresh legal pads lay next to this and on a smaller table was the typewriter, an old Smith Corona upright, and a stack of pulp draft paper. Nothing fancy.

Centered prominently on the tabletop was the manuscript itself, his working copy. Beneath the smudges and coffee stains on the cover sheet it was barely possible to make out the title: *In Fields Where They Lay,* and beneath this: "A Play by James Payton Gunn."

Beau poured himself a brandy and sat down. Brandy was good for this type of work—idea work—and what he needed most was an idea. Everything else was fixed. He turned to the second scene, second act, where the idea was needed. In less than three weeks the play was scheduled for a reading at the Kennedy Center in Washington, and Burr, the producer, had given him an ultimatum that unless some improvements were made, their chances weren't good.

He began reading the scene through. The setting was the interrogation tent of an infantry encampment at the base of a mountain called "the Fake" because it did not appear on anyone's map. A nameless North Vietnamese soldier was being questioned by two men. One of them was holding a knife and barely touching the prisoner's navel with it when Lieutenant Roth, the company commander, entered the tent. What happened next? Burr didn't like the rest of the scene as Beau had written it originally, and neither did Herb Warren, the director. For that matter, neither did Beau. He felt he'd fudged it somewhere, but wasn't sure where or how. It troubled him like the dream. He closed his eyes and ran his fingers through his hair front to back in a single motion. He still kept his hair a little long with a slight curl in the back. It was a style he'd adopted since coming back from the war. Even after more than a decade, it was a comforting reminder that he wasn't in the Army anymore.

He heard the faraway sound of my motorboat and got up and looked out the door. Seeing nothing but the glassy waters of the lake shimmering in the pale light, Beau settled into an ancient overstuffed chair—his father's lone capitulation to creature comfort in this wilderness—and picked up a copy of *Best Plays of the 1920s,* marked at the beginning of Act II of Maxwell Anderson's *What Price Glory?* Captain Flagg and Sergeant Quirt seemed as handy as any excuse for not dealing with his own second act.

Beau was so engrossed in the play that he wasn't even aware I had drawn the boat up to his pier until I flashed the big power spotlight across the windows of his cabin.

"Who's there?" he called. He had come out onto the porch and I noticed he was using a cane again. I hadn't seen him with one since just after the war.

12

"Could you please turn that damned light out," he said, shading his eyes. I flicked it off and the light faded down slowly.

"It's me, Pappy—Pappy Turner," I hollered back. He waved then, and began to make his way down the path. As he approached I said, "Hope I'm not interrupting anything."

"I'm shacked up with fifteen Egyptian belly dancers, that's all," he grumbled casually. "But you might as well come on in anyhow.

"To what do I owe the honor?" he asked, bending to shove another piece of wood onto the fire. "Want a drink?"

"No, thanks," I told him. "I ran into your old man on the street a few days ago. He said he had some mail for you that came to his office, so I picked it up," I said, handing him a packet.

"So now I have the world's highest-paid mailman," Beau said absently. He was examining the mail. "Obviously you have other fish to fry."

"I'll get around to it. In my own time," I said.

Beau laid the packet on the table. "How's my old man?" he asked.

"Seems fine. God, how old's he now?"

"Eighty. How're Peggy and the kids?"

"Fine except for Cory. She's become permanently attached to the telephone. I believe it's sucking her brains out through the earpiece."

"That age, huh?"

"Drives me crazy. I even gave her a separate phone line all her own, but she's on it all the time so they call my number and want me to go get her. Like I was the maid or something."

"You sure I can't get you something to drink, Pappy?"

"Well, a beer maybe."

"I got some chilled out behind the house in that little spring. I'll be right back." He left, taking the cane with him. The old place hadn't changed much. I remembered the time we'd gotten stuck up here with Tommy Brodie and three college girls and the motor wouldn't start and the roof leaked and the girls squawked all night till Beau blew his stack and said we'd paddle back; in the middle of the night in a pouring rainstorm, he had us paddle downriver right through till the next afternoon.

He came back with two bottles of beer, handed one to me and sat in a straight-backed chair with the other. He reached for a quart of brandy and poured himself a tumbler. I asked how his work was coming.

"They sort of took the wind out of my sails after that last one," he said complacently.

"Yeah, I heard they came down hard."

"That's a mild way of putting it," he said. "I wasn't the only one attacked either—the cast, the director, the set—hell, I'm surprised they didn't complain about the programs and the price of the tickets. . . . Lord," he said after a pause, "these days every critic thinks he's Edmund Wilson. There ought to be a law."

I knew how bad it had gone for him with the last play. There'd even been a local story giving some of the critics' uncharitable comments. Beau was a proud man. I think it bothered him most that they were so unkind. Almost as though they were personal enemies. Beau had always wanted to be liked. I could see that the recent defeat had affected him deeply. Finally I got around to one of the things I wanted to tell him.

"Beau, Tommy Brodie's in a lot of trouble."

He put down his glass and looked at me. "What's wrong?"

"They've charged him with murder. A girl was killed, a secretary—nobody we know. She was found knifed to death about two weeks ago outside some sleazy restaurant. They picked up Tommy. He's being held without bond and the lid's on so tight we can't find out a thing. I got in to see him yesterday for about fifteen minutes. He wouldn't tell me much. Just sat there chain-smoking cigarettes. Said he didn't do it, but that was about all. Said if the time ever came, he could prove he was innocent."

"Jesus," Beau said. He fumbled with the brandy and took a swallow. "You don't know how he's connected?"

"Not the faintest idea. Nobody's talking. I put two of our best reporters on the case but they aren't getting anyplace. Of course, even our best people aren't worth a piss in the rain, but the district attorney and the cops have sealed everything that leaks."

"What about a lawyer?"

"He didn't have one, and didn't have the money to hire one, so they appointed this guy named Melcher. I don't know anything about him. I spoke to him after I left the jail. He says Tommy told him the same exact thing he told me—nothing, except he didn't do it and could prove it if necessary."

"Well, they have to have something on him. Of course, that other thing, it might not help too much . . ."

"I think it's the reason they're holding him with no bail."

"Oh, for heaven's sake," Beau said, "that was twenty-five years ago. He was a kid. They know that."

"It looks like they're using everything they can," I said. "I phoned Evan Roche myself—he's the D.A.—and he wouldn't say anything."

"Evan Roche is the D.A.? That little shit? Good Lord, in itself that seems like a crime." He paused a moment. "Is there anything I can do?"

"Nothing I know of," I said, "but I thought you'd want to know."

14

I stayed a while longer and we talked about old times. Both of us had reached an age where memories mean more than they used to. We discussed poor Tommy Brodie, who was one of the original Five Funny Fellows. He'd become a sad case in recent years, but he was still our friend. In a way, I think both of us felt responsible for him; felt his predicament was somehow ours too. In a way it was, because of the other killing that had happened long ago.

I noticed that Beau had drunk a good bit of the brandy and was getting mellow, so I decided to make my pitch.

"How'd you like to be editor-in-chief of the Bienville *Courier-Democrat?*" I asked, leaning back in my chair to let it sink in.

He smiled at me like I was a crazy person. "I left that business a long time back, Pappy. I told you that before."

"Look," I said, "I'm talking two years maybe. Nothing permanent. At least let me make my case."

He got up and fetched two more beers and sat back down looking skeptical. I delivered the speech I'd rehearsed on the boat ride up, but in the back of my mind I worried a little. Brandy, then beer. That was serious drinking. I knew Beau liked a couple of drinks, and could hold his own with anybody, but he seemed to be going at it with a vengeance tonight.

When I paused, he didn't say anything, so I told him I wanted someone who knew what he was doing to come in and kick ass. I said Beau was ideal because he was a hometown boy, well respected, and already knew the ropes. I reminded him that years ago he'd told me he'd like to come home and run the paper one day, and that now was his chance. We'd give him a free rein.

"Pappy," he said slowly, "there've been moments I've thought it was time to chuck it and come back down here for good, but I don't know if I'm ready yet. I've still got a couple of weenies to roast up in New York."

"Hell," I said, "you can still roast them!" I was starting to get excited. I told him he could work on plays in his spare time. Told him he'd be free to go up North anytime he needed. I said I wanted a paper that was going to win a Pulitzer Prize.

"There isn't going to be any spare time for whoever sits in that editor's chair," he said. "He'll be busier than a one-legged man at an ass-kicking contest."

"Look," I offered, "why don't you think it over, let me know?"

"You really know how to work on a guy when he's down, don't you?"

"If I didn't, I'd be a bad businessman."

"Pappy, you sure ain't that." He poured some beer into my glass and we sat staring into the flames. I didn't want to leave it at that.

"Beau, this city's changed a hell of a lot since you left. For the better and for the worse. I know you've noticed some of it. We've gotten big—nearly three-quarters of a million people. Folks are calling us the next Houston. Buildings are going up thirty stories tall; interstate highways surround the city. The oil has a lot to do with it. You wouldn't believe all the Mercedes-Benzes and Rolex watches and swimming pools. But there's an ugly side too: people digging slant wells, double-selling, cheating and swindling. If that's not enough, Bienville's become a haven for dope smugglers."

"You don't say?" he offered curiously. The brandy was working on him.

"I do say. It got too hot for them in Florida, so they've been showing up here. Half the people who've got boats are probably in the smuggling business, cocaine, marijuana—illegal aliens. They picked up a boatload of Mexicans just the other day being brought in by smugglers. And it ain't limited to just the fringes or the scum either—you'd be amazed at the rumors of who's involved—politicians, businessmen, city officials."

"Sound's tailor-made for a Pulitzer, Pappy. Maybe I can recommend somebody for you. I worked with some pretty fine editors in my time."

I let that last statement pass without comment. "No Pulitzer the way we're set up now. We got to clean up our own kitchen first. One of our chief political reporters, for instance, is in a business venture with a convicted felon. An assistant managing editor owns a bar that's so shady you can't see in there at high noon and it wouldn't surprise me if some of the staff are on the take."

"Who's the editor now?" he asked.

"It gave me great pleasure to fire him last week. Fellow named Dooley. He'd been on a trip to Las Vegas with none other than Fletcher Cross, all expenses paid."

"Fletcher Cross"—Beau chuckled—"that old swindler?"

"That 'old swindler' is a member of the Bienville Country Club, owns a big estate in town and, until we took over a couple of weeks ago, managed to get his mug in the paper two, three times a month for performing good civic duties."

"Kiss my ass!" Beau laughed.

While we spoke, Beau sorted once more through the mail I'd brought him. There was a letter from England in a television network envelope. He tore it open and glanced through it, then fingered it absently for a while. I could tell he wanted to read it closely. He seemed distracted. I think he might have sensed he was on a collision course with his own life, but wasn't sure why or what to do about it and the uncertainty was grinding away in his mind.

"How's Sheilah?" I hadn't met her then, but he'd told me several months earlier that they were getting married. I probably shouldn't have asked, but curiosity got the better of me.

"Fine," he said unenthusiastically. "She's in London now—on assignment. The network sent her to the U.K. bureau for a month or so as a sort of training program—assistant to the bureau chief. I don't think she'll get many stories on the air, but it'll be good experience."

"Have you two set a date?"

"Nope," he said. "Not going to be any date. We sort of broke it off and she went to London and I came down here."

Then he began to tell me some of what was on his mind.

"You know, Pappy, I used to think you had to pick between brains and beauty, and I've certainly wasted enough of my time on the latter, but Sheilah's got both. Damned extraordinary woman. She's interested in ideas—mostly her own right now—but that's probably just a phase. She's reached the age where she's beginning to deal with seriously complex issues."

I nodded and Beau took another sip.

"And she doesn't give a hoot what she wears, like a lot of women do—hell, if it wasn't for her job at the network, she'd go around looking like her clothes were thrown on by a pitchfork. And even then she looks better than three-quarters of the women you've ever met.

"Doesn't make a fuss about what she eats either, like some of them do—all that *stuffed* this and *sautéed* that. And she ain't all caught up with houses and jewelry and fancy cars, even though she easily could have been. She comes from a fairly hoity-toity Philadelphia family. But she's really something of a rebel. I think that was part of what attracted me to her."

"So what's the problem?" I said.

He got up, put another log on the grate and stood with his back to the fire. He was twisting his hands and I could tell he was becoming agitated.

"Well, like I say, brains *and* beauty—it's a lethal combination. You think you've found it all, but there's something missing. She's unpredictable—she has moods. I don't think I've ever come up against anything like it."

"Well, you've got moods too," I offered as a joke, but Beau ignored me as he picked up the poker and stirred the fire. Then he turned, as though he wanted to ask me an important question that wouldn't quite come out. So I tried to help. "Are you still in love?"

"I don't know," he answered. "I'm not sure if I know what it means anymore. I think I'm obsessed in a way. She's still got this hold over me."

"Obsessions are a bad thing," I told him. "I had one once myself."

"You?"

"Sure did. Over race cars. About fifteen years ago. First it was those little formula things, and then I decided I was going all the way to Indianapolis."

"Oh yeah, I remember something about that."

"It was consuming all my time and my thoughts. I'd go to bed thinking about race cars and get up in the morning thinking about race cars. And all day long, and all night. Peggy was pregnant with Cory, and Susan was two years old, and all I'd ever talk about was race cars. It damned near drove Peggy crazy and she finally made me go to a shrink."

"You go?"

"Yep. Shrink said there wasn't much he could do. Said an obsession usually fades in time. He told me to hang in there and ride it out."

"How much time?"

"Four to seven years—depends on the circumstances."

"Four to seven years!" Beau groaned.

"It's a lot quicker if you can figure a way not to indulge yourself in thinking about whatever it is. In my case, I started thinking about something else, and in about a year I'd forgotten all about race cars."

"What'd you start thinking about?" he asked.

"Sailing," I said.

Beau laughed halfheartedly and shook his head. "Four to seven years," he repeated. "That's . . ."

He let the words trail off. I felt sorry for him just then. He seemed bone tired, almost weary. When I look back now, it was probably just the opposite. He was keyed up; smoldering like paper about to burst into flames. But I could tell he was ready to close the discussion.

"Pappy," he said finally, "I want to ask you about something." He took a swig of beer to chase his brandy. "There's an old bear that's taken up house-keeping just behind here. You remember where the ground drops off, where we used to shoot at tin cans?"

"Bear? The hell you say!" I leaned forward in my chair.

"Yeah, and this one's on his last legs too." He told me about the bear and its scavenging and its sad behavior.

"I thought they'd all been run out of here after they put in the other railroad bridge and the interstate," I said. "Hell, I read a story a few years ago

18

that the bears had all migrated up to Cole County or someplace—and you got one living in your backyard?"

"If you can call it living. I don't give him much longer. When I leave, and there's no more garbage for him to eat, you know what's going to happen . . ."

"Yeah," I said. "He'll probably wander over to Harville to one of those garbage dumps and some kid'll shoot him with a twenty-two."

"Exactly. And wound him or something, or he'll just starve to death here. Either way, he doesn't stand much chance . . ."

"So what are you going to do, take him back to New York with you?"

"I think I'm going to put him down," Beau said.

"Why don't you just call the game warden?" I asked. "Might be simpler."

"They'd screw it up," he said. "Probably wouldn't even bother."

I nodded. "Can you find him?"

"Yeah. He'll get into the garbage sometime after midnight. I finally just started throwing the edible stuff on the ground. I don't know what he does the rest of the night, but about daybreak he wanders down to the water and I can hear him moving in the cane near the boat landing, looking for washed-up fish, I suppose. Then he goes back to his den and sleeps. Last few days, I haven't even seen him leave the den."

"Is that when you'd do it?"

"Unless you'd like to volunteer."

"I would not," I said charmingly. "It ain't my bear."

Half an hour later I was on my way home, after promising that my secretary would make Beau a reservation on the next afternoon's flight to New York. I also agreed to call his father and arrange a lunch date for the two of them. The moon was low in the western sky and a few wispy clouds sailed overhead. I watched him standing on the pier as I pulled away in the boat. The little cabin behind him was glowing like a jack-o'-lantern. He had promised to give me an answer about the editor's job in a week or two. I put the odds at fifty-fifty.

Back inside, Beau picked up the letter from Sheilah and studied the large, eccentric handwriting and the British stamp. "Dear Beau," it began. Not "dearest" or "darling" like in the beginning—a signal that she was dissatisfied, but not enough to close all her options.

She told him about her latest accomplishments. She'd been introduced to the head of the Labour party and to Prince Charles's second cousin. She'd attended several sessions of Parliament and worked on numerous stories, including the big coal strike in Wales. She wrote that she was ready to come home and try her hand at getting on the air. Her patience at being merely an off-camera *reporter* and not a full *correspondent* was wearing thin.

Beau put the letter down and poured more brandy. He had to give her credit, she'd come a long way in the past four years.

They had met at a cocktail party when he was a newspaper columnist in Washington and she was a research assistant for a local television station. It was, among other things, sex at first sight. Beau took a large swallow of brandy and wondered what she was doing now. There was a six-hour time difference, so it would be nearly 5 A.M. in London. Sheilah liked to be in bed by midnight. He wondered if she was alone. The brandy was working on him; had taken control, and was assisting him, in his drunkenness, in torturing himself.

She's probably with somebody, he concluded sourly. He knew who it would be if she were in Washington—one of those aging preppy bankers or stockbrokers she attracted—guys who never accomplish more in life than expertise with money and ballroom dancing. Of little interest for Sheilah, except she could control them. She liked to have control . . .

He tossed the letter into the fire and watched it turn to ashes. Then he lay down on his iron cot, along with thoughts of his play, the newspaper offer, Tommy Brodie's trouble and the bear. He concentrated on the bear.

Out there in the night the creature was gathering itself; probably in pain, hungry, left behind, doomed—not meant for interstates or garbage piles.

Beau's eyes were closed and he was breathing gently. In the morning he would have to deal with the bear, one way or the other. Sheilah entered his mind again, only to be joined by Tommy Brodie, but before long sleep came, and with it came the dream.

The Dream

Great red gouts of fire flashed ahead of him and the world shook in the gray dawn. Reds, greens and yellows pulsated like strobe lights; primary colors that slowly changed shades and shapes, then settled, but there were stupendous, inhuman roars and the howls of men. The sounds drifted to a distant, constant growl. Sharkey was in front of him, running toward him, his face a mask of deep-red anger, his mouth a black hole. He was waving Beau back, screaming some unintelligible words. A tree beside him splintered and cracked, and ahead automatic weapons began their horrible chatter. Bullets fell like soft rain over Beau's position; millions of little silvery pellets that floated gently down like ashes; then they passed overhead in a sweeping arc, covering the ground behind him like so many fallen stars.

An enormous red sun appeared above the mountain and hung motionless, until Beau felt he could not bear to look at it. When he finally did, it rose before his eyes into the gray sky and began to move around one side of the mountain, then behind it, reappearing on the other side. Finally, like a huge, vulgar balloon, it slowly and deliberately seemed to sink and begin to roll down the little valley until it filled its space entirely and stopped and cast a sour orange glow over everything except the silvery twinkling bullet-stars on the ground. Beau watched himself stand up, watched the spectacle of the sun as the silhouetted men appeared; stark and black, like cartoon characters. They filed up the mountain, the strange sun glowing behind them; tiny men, far away, with stiff movements. They began to fall out of sight, as if swallowed by a hole in the earth.

Beau felt himself falling, falling, sliding down the hillside and hollering

21

something he couldn't understand. He finally stopped beside a dry creekbed with the awful red sun squatting above him. Bullets made *whews* and *pings* but none of them seemed very close. There were sharp, splintering cracks too, like the sound of large falling trees. Pacer, the radiotelephone operator, was holding the handset and Beau was yelling something into it but he knew no one was listening. Suddenly the whole scene cleared. The sun moved into its proper place in the sky and the colors returned to normal. Beau could see part of his company clawing their way up the hillside into a hail of murderous gunfire. Occasionally one of them would jerk spasmodically and fall down. Others, whom Beau could not really see, were crawling, sweating, cursing. He was alone, as isolated in his little pocket as a man sailing above the ocean in a blimp.

Suddenly, three men came crawling fiercely up to Beau's rock, their faces dirt-smeared, uniforms sweat-stained. Their eyes were brooding and intent; one of them, Hooker, was pleading with Beau to pull back. The other two simply looked at him and said nothing. Beau knew they could not actually be there because they were dead men; he had seen them killed himself at the counterattack in the forest. Hooker, who was not dead, continued to plead, but slowly and rhythmically, with the certainty of a man who had nothing more to lose. But Beau really wasn't listening; he was more interested in the faces of Howe and big Lieutenant Donovan—dead men who seemed to be nodding in agreement with what Hooker was saying. He was thinking how odd it was that only last week he had looked down at big Donovan's chest stitched across with machine-gun bullets, his head resting peacefully in some creeping vine, his face blue-white. And Howe, with the one little hole at the base of his neck, his lips parted in a grimace, the medics preparing both of them for the body bags.

The scene changed, the red-orange colors returned and the three men were gone. Beau was alone again except for Pacer, the RTO. He was gripped by an indescribable panic and felt that he was going to do the wrong thing; felt like he was skidding on an icy surface, felt out of control.

Things ahead of him moved very fast; the silhouettes on the hill had reappeared and were climbing higher. There were savage, silent explosions among them. Beau saw the men branch off, as if in a flanking movement, and this was the *envelopment*. The one he called the "butterfly" envelopment, because if it could have been seen from above it might have resembled the shape of a butterfly. Beau had dreamed this part before and so he floated in time and skipped forward.

Katherine drifted into the dream, ridiculously dressed in a pair of college-girl walking shorts and a madras shirt tied above the waist, her long legs tan and inviting. She sat on a rock in the dry streambed, oblivious to the carnage up on the hill, and smiled at Beau as though everything was going to be all right. Her presence pulled him back several years to the quietness of the University campus, to the football games on Saturday afternoons, the fraternity house and going out into the woods on Sundays on picnics. It was all so far away from this, so comforting, yet Beau was still aware of the horror around him.

He became both the observer and the subject of the dream, watching himself motioning for Katherine to come to him and for God's sake to *get down*, away from the incoming fire, and then she was gone, simply vanished. The battle flared up again on the slopes; the line of black silhouettes was slip-sliding downward again; then there were others around him—Whitley, his executive officer, Sergeant Trewes, runners and others, watching intently as the men continued their slip-and-stumble withdrawal down the hill.

"It ain't workin', sir," Sergeant Trewes said calmly.

"Sir, Battalion's on the horn," Eric Pacer said, holding out the handset, "and the weapons platoon wants to know what to do."

Beau looked at Whitley, who was observing the situation through his field glasses. "What about the weapons platoon? Why not have them move up here and let's call it a day? I'll do it," and he took the handset and spoke quietly into it.

The growling and banging seemed to grow around Beau and he suddenly saw himself floating above it all, high above the battle area; looking down, he could see plainly where he had gone wrong. The line of attack that was meant to get behind the enemy fortification had run into a wide series of flanking bunkers and was stalled and hit from both sides and above. The enemy had accomplished exactly what he himself had hoped to with his own little variation of the classic double envelopment which had been so often cited in classes at Fort Benning as the great maneuver at the Battle of Cowpens in 1781. But it hadn't worked, because he hadn't thought it out properly. He knew he was probably going to swing for this mistake.

"Battalion's still on the horn," Pacer said.

His brilliant planning, *his* damned original idea, turned into a slaughter. They had never made the outer loop of the butterfly's wings; they had been cut down on the inside line, next to where the thorax was located. Back at the command post, the first of the two platoons from the hill came streaming past, a confused and frightened mob, wild-eyed, grime-covered, some with fresh field dressings out of which seeped bright red blood, sweating and cursing in the heat. Beau's mistake! *His* fault! *His* brilliant idea!

Pacer was extending the handset toward Beau, pleading only with his eyes.

"Trewes, see what Battalion wants!" Beau shouted, near panic.

"What do you want me to tell them?" the sergeant asked.

"Tell them to go fuck themselves for all I care," Beau shrieked.

Murderer, I'm a murderer, Beau thought, wondering how the rest of his people were going to fare during the night.

Suddenly it was pitch dark and a tent had been set up to interrogate prisoners and Beau was again the invisible observer. Two men, one with a knife, were interrogating a prisoner. The prisoner was wearing only shorts and sandals and he was rain-drenched from a prickly wind-driven storm that had begun just before nightfall. Out in the rain two other prisoners squatted in the mud, roped together hand and foot. They couldn't have been more than sixteen or seventeen years old and they were trying to light a cigarette. Beau wondered how the hell they were going to do it in this downpour.

Inside the tent, the men continued to interrogate their prisoner. The man holding the knife had it extended waist high, the blade barely touching the prisoner's navel. The other man, seated at a table next to the prisoner, was asking questions in Vietnamese and pointing to positions on a map lying on the table. Every so often the man with the knife would gingerly flick it deeper into the navel so that a thin trickle of blood had begun to run down over the lip and into the prisoner's shorts. Each time the blade touched the prisoner he would give a little yip, almost like a puppy. Outside there was disgruntled cursing and the sounds of soldiers slogging to get in out of the rain. There was the hum of a generator and the distant thuds of artillery.

Inside the tent everything changed. The colors became primary again, mostly bright red and orange. Watching this, Beau seemed to have two simultaneous perspectives: he was as tiny as an atom in a room of infinite size with everything else huge; but then he also became a giant, and the forms of the four of them—himself, the interrogators and the prisoner—were crammed into an indescribably small space in which they could still function.

Then, wraithlike, Courtney appeared, just as Katherine had earlier, her beautiful peaches-and-cream smile silently pleading with him to stop this. She was bare to the waist and he wanted to touch her wondrous soft breasts. Beau tried to reach for her, but she backed away. The man with the knife seemed to pay no attention and continued his grim work.

Then the faceless interrogator reached across the table for a holstered pistol and in one swift, almost casual motion, removed it from the holster, drew back the slide with a metallic click that both armed the chamber and cocked the weapon and, as part of the motion, casually and deliberately pointed it directly at Courtney's forehead and fired. Beau screamed as the head exploded with the impact. The eyes rolled up and blood flew out of the ears; the body sailed into a field desk and slammed to the floor with such force that it might have been struck by a baseball bat. Suddenly it was not Courtney's body lying there, but the prisoner's. The man with the .45 put the gun on the table as Beau's scream died in his throat.

At once Beau was totally, wholly awake! His heart was jumping and his head throbbed. Outside the moon shone through the cabin window just above the trees. He propped himself on his elbows, breathing heavily, and stared across the moonlit lake until he was convinced that it was only the dream again. After a while he stuffed a pillow between his trembling legs and drew them up, fetuslike, against his chest, willing himself not to dream.

Moorings

At daybreak Beau lay with his eyes closed, still shaken by the night's visions. After the dream, which had been more disturbing than usual, sleep had been elusive and his mind had swirled in and out of it with needlelike electricity. A few birds began to chirp in the grayness and Beau summoned the fortitude to swing his feet onto the floor and sit up. He put on coffee, rinsed his mouth and got into trousers and a green wool shirt.

He began to pack a few of his things while he waited for the coffee to boil. He put the typewriter in its case and the dictionary and office supplies into a small handbag. Outside, invisible crickets chirped and a pink glow began to light the sky.

It was the introduction of Courtney that added a new and sinister twist to the dream. There had been other out-of-place people in the dream before —his father, for instance, and Sheilah and, of course, Katherine—but never Courtney. There was a wistful part of his heart that reserved a special place for her, despite the fact that she was gone forever.

Beau sat at the table with his coffee and decided against breakfast. His gaze fell to the two shotgun slugs on the mantelpiece. Outside, dawn had given way to bright light and Beau could see it was going to be a brilliant clear day. He took his coffee and walked into the crisp calm of a Deep South autumn morning. A bream, or possibly a bass, burbled to the surface of the lake, spreading rings of water. At the dock his sturdy Dauber-built skiff drifted lazily against the pilings. In the silence, he had an impulse to start talking to himself, just to take his mind off things, when, with no warning, the old bear ambled out of the marsh twenty yards from where he was standing.

Beau was startled; there had been no sound, not even a rustling of cane. The bear moved straight to the water's edge and looked in both directions. Beau stood motionless, expecting it to see him at any moment and bound off into the thicket. Instead, it took another step and tested the water with its paw.

Somehow the bear seemed different. It still moved stiffly, painfully, and its fur was as filthy and matted as before, but it carried itself in a positive way. Three or four more steps and the bear was up to its chest in the lake. It shook its head in the water like a swimmer preparing for a workout, then turned directly toward Beau. For an instant their eyes locked. The old bear's mouth was open and its thick tongue was hanging out; it suddenly plunged into deeper water and began to swim along the far bank. Within a hundred yards it came ashore, shook itself, looked at Beau again and lumbered back into the forest with the dignified gait of an aging thoroughbred.

"Can you beat it!" Beau exclaimed. "Can you beat that!" A surge of relief flowed through him as he went back to finish his packing and get on with the day.

He locked the cabin and carried his gear down to the skiff and started the engine; the first leg of a long journey. He cast off the line, gave the piling a shove and turned the boat toward the slough that led to the river. He took a long backward glance at the little cabin and the placid lake and woods where so much of what he was now had been formed. This trip he had come to realize that much, much more of himself had been left behind here than he ever would have admitted.

Several hours later, Beau used a pay phone at the fishing camp to call a taxi, and within half an hour was riding toward Bienville.

Rafts of coot had already begun to form in the waters on both sides of the causeway; the larger ducks would come later, in December. It fascinated him the way they would feed right up in the shallows until exactly the opening day of hunting season, then move instinctively from the shoreline and just out of shotgun range. Years earlier, driving along across this same stretch on his way back to the University, Beau had nearly killed himself watching a duck hunter in a blind about a hundred yards offshore.

He looked at his watch and calculated he would arrive at the restaurant about the time he'd said. He didn't want to keep his father waiting. He wondered if he should tell him about the newspaper offer. The old man would get excited because it would mean Beau might be coming back home. He decided to play it by ear and again his gaze wandered to the ducks on the bay and the time so long ago when he'd had his brush with death.

27

The hunter in the blind had been decoying a lone canvasback. Beau could see the man crouched behind the strips of cane with a duck call in his mouth. The bird circled lower and lower. As he had driven past the blind itself, the duck made a sensational glide over the decoys and Beau got a final glimpse of the hunter rising with his gun. He remembered his own heart beating in anticipation—then he looked up suddenly to find a gigantic tractor-trailer barreling straight down on him from ahead. Beau had absently strayed into incoming traffic while observing the little drama being played out between hunter and duck. He swerved across the road at what would surely have been the final moment of his life, and wound up hubcap deep in bog, shaking, but thankful to be alive. Also, he never did find out if the damned duck lived or died and to this day he sometimes wondered about it.

The taxi glided smoothly through the late-autumn morning, passing small fishing boats, abandoned duck blinds, other fishing camps; on past the shipyards and then the downtown skyline came into view.

Pappy's observations of the evening before sprang to life. No more a historic little port town harboring fruit company ships and cotton from upstate, Bienville was a city now, with all of a city's problems. Perhaps it had grown too fast—leaped up, like Houston, in twenty years. There was fast money to be made in Bienville now. Oil, shipping and commerce money; booming real estate and transportation terminals and a banking center for the region.

They reached the town proper and drove down an oak-lined street near the waterfront. A few unsavory-looking characters lounged against a building housing the bail-bond company. A midday drunk lurched out of an establishment known as the Port of Call. Minutes later they passed the big gray Gothic building that housed the Bienville *Courier-Democrat*. No one was going in or out; it almost looked closed. Beau had been inside once, years before, and remembered how staid it had been. The newsroom might as well have been a morgue. A few old men sat at desks in white shirts and loosened neckties, pecking away at ancient typewriters. Several editors bent over typed pages, scrawling with pencils. There were no copy boys, no teletype machines, no ringing telephones—in short, no energy, no urgency—a world apart from Beau's own newspapering days in Washington, where even at 2 A.M. a frantic staff kept pace with events unfolding around the world.

Thinking about the *Courier-Democrat*'s offices had caused Beau's chest to tighten. Many years before, an old editor in Washington had told him that no matter how far he strayed, newspapering would always be in his blood, and that much, he thought, was true. There was something about being inside a newsroom while a big story was breaking that was like no other feeling in the world—people charging up the aisles, a nervous hum of conversation, reporters standing in clusters, editors yelling, phones ringing.

Suddenly he reined himself in. He was too old for all that crap. Newspapering was a young man's game. He sat back in the cab and began to think about his play, but something inside him quickly sank. He really didn't know if he could pull it off. He didn't know if he could make this play work. And what about the next one and the one after that?

One institution in Bienville simply refused to acknowledge the rest of the modern progress, and remained perhaps the last vestige of local charm. It was a fish house so eclectic and bizarre that a stranger, upon entering its doors, might wonder if he hadn't arrived in Bedlam.

Danatreux's began fifty years earlier as a shack that backed up to the river. It had a wharf in the rear where shrimping, crabbing, oystering and fishing boats could tie up and deliver an amazing selection of fresh seafood. Oysters were the specialty of the house: raw, fried, stewed, baked, served on buns—whatever. Over the years the shucked oyster shells had formed a sort of grayish marine landfill beneath the original shack, on both sides of it and down to the bank of the river. Whenever old Felix Danatreux had felt he needed more space, he simply built an adjoining shack and painted it a different color. By now there were more than a half dozen of these, all somehow preposterously connected in an architectural mélange that looked like the result of an earthquake or a low-speed collision of freight trains.

If the outside looked bad, the inside was worse. There were hundreds—perhaps thousands—of hand-lettered signs, each bearing some slogan or political punditry. These had expanded haphazardly over the years like the added-on shacks. Each time Danatreux heard a saying that amused him, he would paint it on a sign and nail it to the wall:

We have an agreement with the bank: they don't sell no oysters and we don't cash no checks.

If you're drinking to forget, please pay in advance.

The trouble with the public debt is that private individuals have to pay for it.

And so forth. This was the setting Beau had chosen for lunch with his father.

29

The old man was waiting for him at the oyster bar, drinking a tall glass of iced tea. Beau gave him a warm handshake, but not the hug they reserved for longer absences.

The elder Gunn sized up his son. "You look fit," he said. "That leg bothering you?"

"A little. Must be the weather," he said.

There was a wistful look on the old man's face. He had become an octogenarian not long before. "Did I tell you Enos Cunningham died?" he asked. Enos had been one of his father's friends.

"Yes," Beau said, remembering his father mentioning it several weeks before.

Mr. Gunn nodded. "You want some oysters here, and then we'll sit down?"

"No, just a scotch and soda," Beau said.

The old man looked at him but said nothing and ordered half a dozen oysters for himself. "You know," his father said, "the hell of getting to my age is that your friends keep dying off and it isn't easy making new ones."

Beau was caught off guard by this. He nodded again. The oysters were served up by a thickset albino black man named Eddie. Eddie had been opening oysters behind the bar at Danatreux's for twenty-five years. He smiled when he saw Beau.

"Lemme see the hand," Beau said. Eddie proudly extended his left hand, the one he held the oyster in when opening it. It was an enormous paw with calluses built up in heavy grayish layers.

"You know Pappy be comin' in here all the time now that he own that newspaper," Eddie said.

"I figured as much," Beau said. He sipped his scotch.

"Folks talking 'bout you gonna be the editor."

Beau nearly spit out his drink before recovering and gulping it down. He looked at Eddie, then at his father.

"How in hell did that get around?" he said.

"Not many secrets in this town," the old man said.

"Folks say you gonna be startin' a *crusade,*" Eddie said.

Beau screwed up his mouth. "Don't count on it." His father was beaming as he led him to his regular table in the corner. Beau was proud of his father, and proud too that the old man hadn't developed a stoop or a shuffle and that his hawk-nosed face did not show his years.

At the table, Beau looked around the room and didn't recognize any familiar faces. He did, however, notice a number of Rolex watches on the wrists of polyester-suited men who did not have the look of Bienvillians. He wondered if the parking lot was full of Mercedes-Benzes.

Beau could tell the old man was dying to ask about the newspaper job, but he postponed the inevitable by asking a question himself.

"Pop, what about Tommy Brodie?"

"It's a terrible thing. I can't believe he would do such a thing. He was always a nice boy, wasn't he?"

"Yes. Do you have any idea what they've got on him? How they're connecting him to this?"

"None whatever. But they must have *something*. I hear they arraigned him in the middle of the night so there wouldn't be any reporters around. Got the magistrate out of bed, I'm told. I don't believe I've ever seen a case where people were so closemouthed. Usually you hear something."

"Who was the girl?"

"Don't know, really. I remember seeing her around a few times. A real pretty girl, a brunette, young. I think she was the receptionist at the title company. I wonder if he was dating her."

"Maybe, but Tommy's been pretty much a drunk for twenty years. He's been living by himself up in a garage apartment. Had that little clerking job at the lumberyard. I haven't seen him in a year or so, but I can't think of him as anything but harmless—harmless as he was back then, when the other happened."

"Maybe so," the old man said. "I gather the girl wasn't sexually molested."

"That's what Pappy told me. That much is known."

"Or robbed."

"Pappy said her purse was untouched."

"So there must be some other reason."

"It's impossible to imagine Tommy Brodie doing anything like that. Of all the things, he just wasn't that way."

"He used a knife once," the old man reminded him.

"That was a long time ago. And you know as well as I do what happened."

"The law has a long memory," said the elder Gunn.

The menu at Danatreux's was as varied as the creatures of the sea, but a bowl of gumbo was de rigueur and each ordered it to start.

"What about your girl—Sheilah? Have you thought any more about the future?"

Beau put down his spoon and drained a last swallow of scotch. "Yeah, a

31

lot. But my mind still hasn't changed. I'm afraid we'd tear each other apart," he said.

"Oh?"

"And also, now that the cat seems to be out of the bag, there's the question of whether or not I take this *Courier-Democrat* position. There isn't any way Sheilah would leave Washington and move down here. It would mean quitting her job."

"So you're thinking of taking it?"

"I'll get to that in a minute." Beau waved at the waitress to get another scotch. "Maybe it's the coward's way out. Maybe I just don't want to face the real issue."

"Which is?"

"That Sheilah and I wouldn't be good for each other," he said.

He hadn't really discussed Sheilah with his father, simply because he felt the old man wouldn't understand. After all, Sheilah's neuroses, if indeed that's what they were, were grounded in the late twentieth century. Such things as her inability to resolve the conflict between having a career and a relationship at the same time had no real meaning in his father's world. The issue simply didn't exist, even today, in a town like Bienville, where to his father's mind the "career woman" was still just a girl who couldn't find a husband for herself.

"I tried to sort it out up at the camp, but I didn't get very far," Beau said glumly.

"What's the problem?" The old man was studying the menu for the second course.

"Might be me, might be her—maybe both of us. Like putting a lion and a tiger in the same cage. You see, Sheilah's, well, I suppose *difficult* would be one way of saying it."

The old man smiled and drank some of his iced tea. "I knew a girl like that once," he said.

Beau raised his eyebrows. "Really?" Never had his father spoken of a woman other than his mother.

"I was a little younger than you," he said. "It was about 1938, just before the war. She lived in New Orleans and I'd met her at a dance after a sailing regatta. Beautiful girl; smart, too, and she had some family money.

"I'd go over there on weekends or she'd come over here. But she'd have these moods. Whatever you wanted to do, seemed like she'd want something else. Just contrary, was what it was. But when she was feeling good, she was great."

"What happened?" Beau asked in amazement. His father might have been describing Sheilah.

"If we were all going to a dance or out to eat, like as not she'd just announce she wasn't going. Or if she did, she'd be sullen and later have unpleasant things to say about my friends. Made people uncomfortable. When things weren't going well for her, she'd usually find some way to blame it on me. One minute she'd say I was paying too much attention to her, the next that I was ignoring her. That's the trouble with the crazy ones, Beau, they make you feel like it's *you* who's crazy."

Beau nodded in agreement. "How long did it last?"

"On and off for a couple of years. I guess I finally figured out that what she really didn't like was herself. One day she just broke it off, stopped coming over."

"I was awfully hurt," the old man said. "I don't think I've ever felt as bad. I must have thought about calling or writing her a hundred times, but I never did, and the next year I married your mother."

"Were you in love with her?"

"Your mother?"

"No, the other one."

"I suppose so. I used to think about her, even after your mother and I were married. But then the war came along and so did you and it just sort of faded away."

"Do you know what happened to her?"

"She died a few years ago, I heard. Not long after your mother. She sent me a letter once, to my office. It was just after the war, maybe 1949 or '50. Didn't say much, just what she was doing. She'd gotten married and gone to San Francisco and then got divorced and was running a bookstore there."

"She wanted to see you again?"

"I suppose so, but she wasn't the type to ask. I considered writing her back, but I never did. Funny, for a while it all came home again. And that was after ten years. I found myself wondering if she'd gotten it all out of her system by then."

"You think she had?"

"My guess is no." The old man had begun fingering his napkin, folding and unfolding it in a nervous way. He was looking out the window across the water.

"I suppose," Beau said darkly, "that even when all the hollering is over, it's still never easy."

"Just don't let them outsmart you," the old man said.

33

Beau ordered red snapper and excused himself to go to the rest room. He was washing his hands and looking at himself in the mirror when a man who had come in after him suddenly spoke up.

"Bet you don't remember me, do you?"

Beau had barely noticed him. He was short and bald, about Beau's age, wearing soiled khaki pants and a flannel work shirt. He might have worked in a service station or as a plumber.

Beau gave him an embarrassed smile. "I'm afraid I don't. I've been gone a long time." There was something vaguely familiar about his face.

"My old man used to run the garbage service across the bay in the summer," he said. "Spinker's Sanitary Collection."

It suddenly clicked for Beau. He remembered the narrow-eyed boy of fourteen or fifteen who'd come each day to pick up the garbage.

"Of course, of course," Beau said, fighting to recall the boy's first name.

"Loyd Spinker," he said. He zipped up his fly and stuck out his hand. "I remember all you guys," Loyd Spinker said, "you and Eric Pacer and Chord Lewellen—and Brodie too."

Recollection piled on remembrance for Beau. Loyd Spinker had once tried to sell them some pornographic photographs and another time he got them some bootleg whiskey.

"It's good to see you again, Loyd," Beau said, somewhat uncomfortable with these occasional brushes with the past.

"Too bad about Brodie," Spinker said.

"Yes, it is."

"Brodie ain't done it, though. And that's a fact."

"Really?" Beau asked.

"I work at the terminal—on lift maintenance. I see things all the time. That's why I come in here when I saw you. You're a friend of his, right?"

Beau nodded.

"And Turner too. You was all friends back then."

"Yes," Beau said, "we were all close."

"Turner, he owns the newspaper now, right?"

"That's right," Beau said.

"Well, Brodie ain't stabbed that girl. He ain't stabbed nobody. I know Brodie a little. He might have knowed her, but he ain't killed her."

"You seem pretty certain," Beau offered. "What makes you so sure?"

"Like I told you, I hear things, I see things."

"Loyd, I think you should talk to Pappy Turner or to the police."

"Nope, I ain't talking to no newspapers or cops. Get my ass in a world of shit."

"Pappy Turner wouldn't do anything like that," Beau replied. "He's a friend of Tommy Brodie's just like I am."

"Well . . . if you ain't interested . . ." Spinker didn't finish the sentence. He looked off into the mirror.

"Look," Beau said, "I came here to have lunch with my father, and I've got a plane to catch in about two hours. If you know something about this, I'd like to hear what it is, but you really should talk to Pappy Turner."

Spinker made a disdainful face. "I can't prove nothin' anyway. Nice seein' you." He walked out of the rest room.

Beau followed, but Spinker was halfway across the room as Beau emerged. He watched him walk out the front door, then returned to the table where his father sat.

"I just had the most astonishing conversation," Beau said.

"In the men's room?"

"Do you remember the Spinkers, the people who used to collect the garbage in the summer across the bay? Well, a guy followed me in there and it was Loyd Spinker, one of the kids who used to come around on the truck. He works at the ship terminal now."

Beau related Spinker's assertions about Tommy Brodie while the old man listened patiently.

"But the last thing he said was that he couldn't prove anything—right?"

"Some such as that. But it sounds like he knows more than most people. I'm going to call Pappy when we're finished."

"What about the newspaper?" the elder Gunn asked. He seemed determined to get a reading of Beau's intentions.

"I haven't agreed to anything yet. I'm going to think about it."

"What kind of salary is he talking about?"

"We didn't get to that. I'm sure it would be pretty good."

"From what you've told me recently, it might be a good idea to have some financial security for a while."

"That's God's truth," Beau said dismally, watching the shapely rear of a waitress walking past. "I've been doing some things for television to pay the bills, but it's a jungle up there." He decided to change the subject slightly. "Pappy tells me there's a lot of shady stuff going on around here. You hear anything?"

"Rumors."

"Such as?"

"I don't repeat rumors."

"Yes, you do." Beau chuckled.

"Not this kind," the old man said. Beau noticed that his fingers were clenched tightly around his iced-tea glass. He knew the old man well enough not to hound him about it.

They talked around the subject of the *Courier-Democrat* for a while and then the bill came. Beau reached for his wallet but his father waved him off, so he excused himself, went to the pay phone and called me.

I interrupted a conference to talk with him.

"You're coming to work for us," I said jubilantly.

"I said I'd let you know about that—there's something else." He told me about Loyd Spinker.

"I'll have somebody on it right now," I said. I remembered Spinker too— he'd once sold me some firecrackers that turned out to be duds.

"I'd handle this one with kid gloves, Pappy. He's skittish about the press. I've seen his kind before. It's probably going to be a one-shot deal—either he talks or he doesn't. Be careful who you send and how they play it."

"That," I replied, "is precisely why you ought to be down here running this paper and not me."

Beau had planned to take a taxi to the airport and tried to decline his father's offer to drive him until he realized the old man actually wanted to spend the remaining time with him.

They drove down St. Mary's Street, a wide, oak-lined boulevard. Each spring for twelve years Beau and the six hundred cadets of Singer Academy had marched down St. Mary's to the little Confederate cemetery and stood for hours in the hot sun, suffering would-be orators paying homage to the dead of a century before. The old man recalled it too.

"Remember the time you unveiled the monument to the Confederate Army?" he asked. "You were about seven and all dressed up in a tie and jacket like a little man. We still have the picture from the newspaper at home."

It suddenly came to Beau that his father always said "we," even though his mother had died nearly ten years before. He needed a companion, Beau thought, but there weren't any now, except in his memories.

They drove on and the old man chatted about things long past, as though the present world was an alien place. They passed Singer Academy. Cadets were at play on the athletic fields and the place looked much as it had when Beau graduated twenty years earlier. In the distance, beyond the parade ground and the playing fields, he could see a handful of cadets marching off demerits on the gig grounds. Beau had completed a considerable number of penalty tours himself. There had been the "court-martial" episode, and then the business with the Five Funny Fellows. Tommy Brodie had been a part of it too.

Soon they were on the airport highway, passing the shopping centers, fast-food joints and used-car lots that mark suburbanization gone wild. In five miles they must have passed thirty fast-food restaurants. No one seemed to eat at home anymore.

His mother would have called all of this "tacky." He thought of her briefly and sadly, lying on her deathbed, ravaged by cancer.

Once, alone with her in her room toward the end, Beau had lamented that he was sorry not to have come sooner but work had been pressing and his life did not seem to be his own. She responded by revealing a bit of herself to him that she had silently carried with her over the decades.

She had once been a beautiful and elegant woman with long black hair and green eyes and she had aspired to become an actress. A professor of drama at the University, a man of some reputation, had hailed her as "the new Sarah Bernhardt." After graduation she headed to New York and the Great White Way—all this in the depths of the Depression.

She had managed to get into a few productions, the most notable being *The Philadelphia Story,* with Katharine Hepburn. Her role was that of a maid who pushed a teacart across the stage and, at some point, said a line which got a nightly laugh. But that was as far as her career had gone. That chill February afternoon in the hospital room she said, "You've got to do what you're doing. Don't let anything stop you," and she smiled through the pain.

"I'd rather be here with you," he said, holding tightly to her frail hand.

"Now let me tell you something," she whispered. She looked away for a moment, out the window where the afternoon shadows slanted across the green hospital lawn. It had been a weekday, but it felt to Beau like Sunday.

"One time I was an actress. I was in New York. I was in *The Philadelphia Story . . .*" Her voice seemed to fade.

"I know you were, Mom," he said, pressing her hand.

"And I think I could have gone on to be very good, you know. But there were other things too. It was not easy in those days. There was literally no money . . . And then on a trip home I met your father. We got married and I came back here and lived a humdrum life . . ."

"That's not true," Beau said falteringly. "Look at the work you've done—with the Little Theater, setting up the actors' workshop, raising money for . . ."

"When you *know* you have your chance, you mustn't walk away from it."

"Do you regret it?" He felt his eyes welling up.

"Sometimes," she said, "sometimes." And then she drifted into an unsettled sleep with Beau still holding her hand. After a few minutes he was still sitting there with a tear drying on his cheek.

They made the turn into the airport, where a DC-10 sat on the runway. Beau dealt with the ticket counter and the luggage and by that time the plane was boarding. He gave his father a long hug.

"I'll call you Sunday, usual time." The old man nodded and watched him go up the ramp. He was still watching as the plane taxied onto the runway, and even though he couldn't possibly have known on which side Beau was seated, he gave a final little wave just before the plane passed out of view.

Beau saw him and waved back through the tiny porthole. It suddenly occurred to him that the Wright brothers had not yet made their flight at Kitty Hawk the year his father was born.

The plane climbed and banked into wispy clouds, and below, the western sprawl of Bienville gave way to patchwork fields and rivers. Beau settled back and thought of his father and the girl from New Orleans and also of that day in the hospital room with his mother; each with their secret little disappointments in life, which, toward the end, they wanted to share with him.

They were flying higher now, leveling out, crossing Bienville Bay. Far to the south the great Gulf of Mexico shimmered in the afternoon sun and to the north and beneath him was the tangled green delta swamp. From this altitude, he could even see the mixing of the tides. Somewhere down there was the grunting old bear and Beau silently wished him well.

The pilot turned northeastward and a great blue maw of sky appeared before them as though a tremendous mouth had opened up. North toward New York City, the play, his future. Beau had a sudden surge of emotion; a feeling that things were reaching a critical mass in his life. What was he leaving behind here? The little dots that connected him: the cabin at Still River, the Academy, his father, the Five Funny Fellows, old loves, sailing on the bay, steamy nights in drive-in movies, long spiral passes on damp green football fields. Maybe the man was wrong; maybe you could go home again.

Beau's heart raced for distance against time like the crackling whine of the jet's engines. He was gearing himself for the uncertainty and change that lay ahead.

VICISSITUDES I

The Court-Martial of
Cadet Corporal Gunn

September 1953

It is easier to get a feeling for the man Beau became by dipping into his past. A good beginning might be the day when he was promoted from the Primary Battalion at Singer Military Academy to what was then called the Senior Battalion. He was ten.

This event occurred during the first week of school on the first day of organized parade drill, and there was a certain amount of ceremony attached to it. It was a very hot day, which in Bienville is saying something. The city is located just above the Tropic of Cancer at about the same latitude as Cairo, Egypt, and it sits at the edge of a great swamp near the Gulf of Mexico. At high noon it can be about as oppressive as any place on earth, and even on a normal day from May through September it was not uncommon to see some child frying an egg on the sidewalk just to prove that it could be done.

The graduation to the Senior Battalion was considered some kind of milestone for us Singer cadets. We were all in the same class—Beau, myself, Tommy Brodie, Eric Pacer and Chord Lewellen. Now we would be "real men." Never again would we lug around the small wooden "dummy" rifles. We would be issued real Army M-1s, plugged, of course, so they wouldn't shoot, but the idea of feeling the real thing, a 9.1-pound heavy metal weapon that might actually have been used to kill somebody in the war—to feel its weight and balance, to open the hard-spring slide and feel the tingling, scary sensation when the bolt cracked back barely missing the thumb (occasionally it would not miss, and the unfortunate rifleman would for the next few days

39

walk around with a severe case of what was called "M-1 thumb")—all of this was looked forward to by us boys in grades one through five with a growing sense of awe and nervous anticipation.

There were initiation ceremonies of a sort, inflicted on the new recruits mostly by the sophomore cadets who, in their turn, were brutalized by the third- and fourth-year cadets.

A pitiless sun baked down on the parade field that day. It was eleven-thirty when the bell sounded for us to assemble and six hundred-odd toy soldiers scampered down stairways and halls to the armory to pick up our rifles and double-time it into the heat. Word had been put out that the last man in each squad to meet assembly would be made to run around the drill field with his rifle over his head. As the rumor spread, the punishment became darker and darker.

The cadre was ready for us "new boys" when we arrived. Stand at attention, mister! Suck in that chin! Shoulders back! Drop down—give me ten! You little asshole, you gonna wish you was anyplace in the world but in my squad! Most of this hazing was done in mock severity but there were, of course, as in any walkway of life, a few truly mean souls and Beau had the misfortune to inherit one of them.

The boy's name was Hogan. He was a sophomore, not particularly large for his age, but to Beau he looked huge. Hogan was a pasty-faced unathletic character with puffy cheeks and cruel green eyes and none of us liked him. Tommy Brodie called him "Hog Breath" behind his back.

"You there! Where's your name tag!"

Beau looked down and to his horror he'd forgotten to pin it on. Usually in the mornings his father gave him a preliminary inspection to make sure he was properly uniformed, but this day his father had been out of town.

"*What's* your *name,* mister?" Hogan hissed.

"Gunn, sir, Beau Gunn," said Beau shakily.

"Gun!" Hogan hollered. "That's your *gun,* in your goddamn hand! I want to know your name!"

Scenes like this were being repeated all over the company and in other companies as well, but for Beau and the rest of us, it was an awful experience. None of us had ever been yelled at like this before and we felt weak and terrified.

"My name, sir, is Beau Gunn."

"What kind of candy-ass name is that!" Hogan spat. "Beau—that's a girl's name!" He said it as though he had a mouthful of ashes.

Beau trembled in front of this superior.

"Get in this squad here!" Hogan shouted. "All you little shits get in this squad here! Dress it up! What's that you're doing there, Gunn? What the hell are you doing?"

Hogan positioned himself directly in front of Beau, looking down into his sweating face; Beau could smell his foul breath.

"Dress it UP!" Hogan shrieked.

"Sir, you want me to come up or go back?" Beau asked weakly.

"UP!" Hogan roared. "*UP* is *that* way!" he said, pointing to the sky. "I want you to come FORWARD, numbnuts!" Beau inched forward and dressed right to the boy next to him. "Ten-hut!" Hogan shouted and they all snapped to. Hogan then got into his position as squad leader and the rest of the platoon came to attention and became silent.

Because they were the first platoon to organize themselves to attention, they had to stand that way until the other platoons in the company did the same, which took nearly five minutes, and then another three or four minutes while the other companies got it together. Beau, because it was his first time at serious drill, had made one major mistake. He had locked his knees in order to stand straighter and this was cutting off his blood circulation. The heat was almost unimaginable: gray shirts inside wool uniforms were soaked through like dishcloths; sweatbands inside hats were slicked through; feet sweated through socks into shoes; the battalion staff, standing across the field in formation, shimmered in the midday sun like a desert mirage. Beau suddenly felt weak. He did not know what was happening to him, but he felt his throat close up and a wave of dizziness swept over him, passed, and then he saw his rifle fall from his hand and heard a loud clatter as it hit the ground just before he followed it, crumbling into the boy in front of him.

He was not really out, or if so, it had been for only a few seconds. But he was totally weakened. People helped him up but he was unsteady.

"Okay," Hogan said. "Go inside and wash your face and pull yourself together and then get your little ass back here." Beau teetered off, trailing the big rifle behind him, feeling nauseous, embarrassed and alone. He put his gun back in the armory—as was the rule, since guns weren't allowed in the main building—and went into the downstairs washroom. He loosened his tie and looked at his face in the mirror. He was white as a sheet of paper.

He turned on the water; then for a moment felt he couldn't catch his breath, and at that same moment realized he was going to be sick. He rushed to a stall and threw up in a toilet. After a minute or two he felt a little better and went back to the washbasin and tried to clean himself.

Suddenly the door burst open and through it came the object of much fear and loathing among the Singer cadets in the person of one Major Carl Otto, an enormous bald and hairy former college football lineman who had a

41

reputation for handing out swift and immediate punishment to any cadet, young or old, whom he suspected of trifling. The means of Major Otto's punishment were somewhat unique, consisting of a sharp rap on the head with a huge ring of keys that the major carried around with him as part of some custodial duties. Instead of getting demerits, they got "the keys." It was more expedient—the swiftest justice of all—these dreaded keys.

"What are you doing in here?" the major demanded. "You're supposed to be on the parade field."

"I . . . ah . . . I . . ." Beau stammered. Major Otto was the most fearsome character he could imagine.

"I said, what are you doing in here?" Major Otto growled.

"No . . . no . . . nothing," Beau croaked. His throat felt closed, his tongue wouldn't work.

"Confound you!" Major Otto shouted. "I said, *what* are you *doing*, boy? I know you're doing something. Nobody does nothing!"

"I . . . I . . ." Beau could not get a word out, and as he tried, he saw Major Otto reach into his pocket and take out the enormous ring of keys.

Beau was collared and keyed in the same instant. He saw stars and felt a numbness before the pain and for a moment thought he would black out again.

"Now get out of here and get back to your company!" Major Otto roared. Beau stumbled out the door and down the hall toward the armory to retrieve his rifle. He was too stunned to cry; too stunned to do or say anything. He could only move reflexively with Major Otto's instructions ringing in his ears.

Luck was against Beau that day, however, because in the armory he encountered the most awesome figure of them all—Colonel Walter ("Fat Man") Swaggert, the commandant himself! Colonel Swaggert had previously been an instructor of physics, and when he was teaching, no kinder or more jolly man could be found, but when he was promoted to commandant his demeanor changed entirely and the cadets were so fearful of him that some of us, myself included, would occasionally walk around the outside of the building to get to class just so we wouldn't risk running into him in the halls. Swaggert had his own version of Major Otto's "keys of justice"—a huge paddle which he used with relish on the bottoms of mischief-making cadets.

When Beau entered the armory and suddenly saw Colonel Swaggert before him, the expression on his face must have resembled the way a person might look having just come across a large savage animal in the woods.

The colonel was walking up and down studying the rifle racks and writing on a clipboard. When he looked down and saw Beau he must have noticed the mixture of fear and guilt on his face and naturally suspected chicanery of some sort.

"Why are you here?" His icy voice cut through Beau, whose head still reeled from "the keys."

"I . . . I . . ." he stammered. He still could not speak. He wanted to, but it was so much to tell he couldn't think where to start exactly.

"You're late, aren't you?" the colonel snapped. "Where've you been?"

"In . . . in the . . . bathroom . . ." Beau replied faintly. He wanted to tell the colonel about being sick, and getting "the keys," but then he thought that if he mentioned "the keys," the colonel would think . . .

"You *are* late, then!" said Colonel Swaggert. He sounded delighted. "Come here, boy."

Beau followed the colonel's beckoning fingers around the gun rack and saw the fat man reach on a shelf for an enormous three-foot wooden paddle.

"Turn around and bend over," the colonel said sweetly. Beau was too frightened to do anything but obey. He could not believe what was happening, and he was not prepared for it when it did.

The paddle hit him with such force it lifted him off the floor and sent him to his knees. The stinging was utterly dumbfounding. Crying was out of the question; he could only gasp and flush with pain.

"Now," said the colonel, replacing the paddle on the shelf, "get your rifle and get out to your company."

Beau picked up his rifle and got outside the door before reaching back to clutch his stinging behind. Never, never had he been beaten that way. Spanked when he was younger, perhaps, but nothing like this. He was around the corner of the building when the tears came. He couldn't hold them back. He looked around desperately for a place to hide before anyone could see him crying.

A clump of small trees and flowering bushes looked like a good haven. He darted in among them and was rubbing his eyes when he heard somebody call his name.

"Tommy?" Beau said. "Is that you?"

Tommy Brodie's face appeared from behind a shrub, tear-stained and dirt-streaked.

"What are you doing here?" Beau asked.

"They told me to run around the field with my rifle over my head. I did it once. I just couldn't do anymore. I . . . I . . . came over here." He began to cry again.

"You'd better get back out there. We both better had."

"No—I can't," Tommy said. "I can't do it. I'm scared . . ."

"Tommy," Beau said, "we got to. We'll be in trouble if we don't."

"Please," Tommy pleaded.

"Well, I'm going back. You don't know what happened. I'd better . . ."

"Please don't," Tommy whined. "Please stay. I'm scared."

Beau went over to Tommy and sat down beside him. He tried to per-suade him to get back to the drill, but Tommy was beyond persuasion. He must have stayed there for another fifteen minutes, and then he saw the first people returning to the armory from the parade field.

"C'mon," Beau said. He took Tommy Brodie by the sleeve and pulled him to his feet. "C'mon," he said again, and the two of them fell in behind the vanguard from the drill. "Maybe nobody'll notice," Beau said without any conviction.

In the hallway outside the armory Beau felt a rough hand on his shoulder. He turned and saw the pasty face of Hogan, his squad leader.

"Why didn't you come back like I told you?" Hogan said.

"I . . . well . . . got sick," Beau said, glad at least that he'd regained his speech. "And when I was finished, I . . . ah, the drill was over . . ."

"No, it wasn't," Hogan said slyly. "Wasn't that you coming from behind that clump of trees out there? There was somebody else in there with you. You were loitering, weren't you?"

"No . . . I . . . told you . . ."

"That's lying," Hogan said. "Jackson saw you too. We were coming in and I said to Jackson, 'That's Gunn, isn't it?' and he said, 'Yeah.' "

"It wasn't," Beau protested.

"That's lying, Gunn. You know what lying means around here."

"I'm not," Beau said. But Hogan had waved down Dan Whittle, a third-year man and the battalion executive officer. Whittle was everything Beau aspired to be: nice-looking, bright, athletic, popular. In fact, the irony of what happened between them years later is that they were really so much alike.

"Sir," Hogan said, "Gunn here was supposed to come back to the drill field after he fell out, but he didn't. Jackson and I saw him loitering in the trees out there and now he's lying about it. There was another guy with him."

Dan Whittle frowned. "Well, what were you doing? Are you lying?"

"No, sir," Beau said weakly. He'd been through so much already he didn't know what to do. Hogan would gig him for sure if he admitted he'd been behind the trees. Lying, he knew, was the gravest offense of all. But he just couldn't face any more today.

"No, sir," he said again. "I was sick. I was in the bathroom."

"Who was this other boy?" Whittle asked.

Beau stood with his mouth closed. He knew, vaguely, that Dan Whittle was an important character at Singer. That he was not to be trifled with.

"You say you were in the latrine the whole time?" Whittle said.

"Yes, sir," Beau said, but it didn't sound convincing. It was his story, though, and he was going to have to stick to it now.

"Sir," Hogan said honestly, "I'm telling the truth and Jackson will tell you too. We saw him and that other boy in the trees."

"You know the penalty for lying, don't you?" Whittle asked.

"Yes, sir . . . I think so . . ."

"It's an Honor Council offense. You understand that?" Then Beau remembered. Dan Whittle was on the Honor Council. Suddenly he became terrified. An Honor Council offense was by far the worst thing a Singer cadet could have happen to him. And yet he was too far in now. If he told the truth, then he would have already lied and would get the Honor Council anyway.

"I want you to tell me the truth one more time," Dan Whittle said. "Were you or were you not under the trees?"

"No, sir," Beau said. He had a sinking feeling that he was making a big mistake.

"Okay," Whittle said, "you cadets go wherever it is you're supposed to go. I'll handle this now."

Two days later the full might of Singer military justice swooped down on a frightened Beau Gunn and dragged him into a maze of recrimination and guilt which would haunt him for the rest of his days.

Two days after the run-in with Hogan and Dan Whittle, Beau was summoned to the commandant's office. There he was given a letter and instructed to read it before proceeding to a bench outside the Honor Council door.

Charges had been preferred against him for lying to a superior officer and a trial was to be conducted. If he was found guilty, he could be expelled from school. I heard about it later that day, from Tommy Brodie, who had seen Beau just after he got the letter. We would have helped him, but there was nothing we could do.

No one is as scared or lonely as a small guilty boy sitting in a chair outside the doorway to some official office, waiting to learn his fate. In Beau's case he might have been lonelier than most, because there were no ifs, ands or buts about truthfulness in the Gunn family.

The door to the Honor Council chambers opened and a tall boy, wearing the black armband of the sergeant at arms, stepped out.

"Come inside," the boy said. Beau entered the chambers to see six stern-faced upperclassmen sitting behind a long, glass-topped table. They were wearing their blouses and Sam Browne belts and behind them hung the American flag and the flag of the Academy. The president of the council was Cadet Captain Dan Whittle. A chair was arranged in front of the table, facing it, and Beau was led to it. Off to the side were Cadets Hogan and Jackson.

"Gunn," said one of the senior boys who was acting as prosecutor, "we have taken testimony from Hogan and Jackson and also from Cadet Whittle. There is obviously lying going on and we want the truth from you."

Beau felt a sickening ache in the pit of his stomach. He nodded.

"Now," the boy said, "Hogan and Jackson said you were under the trees when you should have been at drill. They say you told Cadet Whittle—and he confirms this—that you were not under the trees, you were sick in the latrine. What is the truth? Were you under the trees or were you sick in the latrine?"

"I . . . ah . . . was sick in the bathroom, sir," Beau said. "But then after . . ." He suddenly decided not to mention the run-in with Colonel Swaggert and Otto, because somehow he thought that would get him into more trouble. "Well, then I went out under the trees. I was there too."

The members of the council looked at each other incredulously. "So then it *is* true that when I asked you if you were under the trees, you were not telling the truth?" Dan Whittle asked.

Beau simply looked ahead and gulped.

"Is that correct, or not?" the boy acting as prosecutor asked impatiently.

"Yes, sir, it's true," Beau said.

"That you lied?"

Beau nodded.

"And who was with you?"

"Nobody," Beau stammered.

"You were alone?"

"No."

"Then you were with somebody, weren't you?"

Beau sat silently, looking at the stern faces confronting him. Then he looked down at the floor and slowly shook his head.

After a long, quiet pause, Whittle and the others held a whispered conference.

"All right, you can go now," Dan Whittle said. The sergeant at arms came over to Beau and escorted him out of the room. He stood in the hall for as long as he could, until he heard footsteps, and then he quickly made his way back to the classroom because the offense of Loitering in the Foyer was punishable by three demerits.

46

"This is one of the most appalling things I have ever heard!"

The voice belonged to Beau's father, and he was standing in the office of the commandant, red-faced, looking down at Colonel Swaggert, who was seated behind his desk.

"Please, Mr. Gunn, sit down for a moment, will you?" Beau was standing at his father's side, at attention. "And you too, son," the colonel said.

Beau's father was livid. "You have given this boy fifty demerits! Fifty hours of those penalty tours when, he tells me, he passed out from heatstroke, went into the bathroom to be sick to his stomach, was cracked on the head by some bozo who carries a big set of keys around, then beaten with a board by yourself—all in the space of twenty or thirty minutes—and then, because he was too humiliated to let the other boys see him crying, you send him up in front of some kangaroo court to face charges that could get him expelled! What kind of place *is* this!"

"Please, Mr. Gunn. Let's just talk about this . . ."

"I will do the talking here, Colonel. I am supposed to be in federal court at this very moment. So it is my nickel and I'm going to have my say. Now what about this so-called trial, or court-martial, or whatever you call it? Was he represented by anybody on his behalf?"

"It doesn't work that way," Swaggert said.

"Did he have an opportunity to tell his side of it?"

"They are given that opportunity."

"Were you, son?" the senior Gunn asked. "Did anybody ask you what happened that day, like you told it to me?"

"Not, not . . . no, sir. They just asked me if I'd lied."

"You people sound like a bunch of Communists here!" Beau's father said in disbelief. "And what were you doing hitting him with a board? And who, pray tell, is that bozo with the keys?"

"It was a paddle, not a board, Mr. Gunn. And the man you refer to as a bozo is Major Otto, a member of our teaching staff," said Colonel Swaggert defensively.

"It's astonishing," said the elder Gunn. "Does he always roam around whacking people over the head with those keys?"

"I don't know, sir. I intend to ask him," the colonel said dejectedly.

After Beau's father had threatened to remove his son from school, file a lawsuit and go to the newspapers with the story, Colonel Swaggert agreed to suspend imposition of the fifty demerits, but stated that he would have to place a warning in Beau's file concerning the gravity of not telling the truth.

Beau was sent off to class after that. Under most circumstances the incident would have been promptly forgotten. But not at Singer and not in Bienville.

First off, Beau's father's defense of him, eloquent and effective as it was, earned Beau a position high up on Colonel Swaggert's shit list, and he held this position for the remainder of his days at the Academy. Worse still was the stain on his character and reputation for having been officially branded a liar. Bienville was not a small town even then, but neither was it a big city, and the cadets of Singer were the ones who eventually ran the town, and no one ever forgets when one of their number commits a sin as indefensible as lying. So, for weeks after the incident, Beau was shunned by many of his classmates. There was, of course, one exception, Tommy Brodie, whose skin he'd saved and who took to following him around like a puppy. In all the years that followed, the incident at Singer haunted Beau a little. It worried him, too, that anyone checking into his past might stumble across such an ignominious piece of information.

VICISSITUDES II

The Last Buffoon

October 1955

Two years later, Beau sprouted up so fast it recalled one of those time-lapse films in which the frames are speeded up and a seed becomes a plant before your eyes. By his twelfth year he was nearly six feet tall and still growing. This fact was noted by practically everyone—from his platoon leaders, who awarded him demerits every month or so for too short trousers; to his mother, who was responsible for getting the trousers let out; to his friends, myself included, who gave him the nickname "Stork." Of course, he became as sensitive about his height as a young girl becomes self-conscious about her growing breasts. Last but not least, Beau's size was noticed by the athletic coaches at Singer Academy.

In those days there were only a few schools in Bienville and the athletic rivalry among them was fierce. We Singer cadets were particularly conscious of this because, being a private institution, we were often reviled as snobs by public or parochial school students and we were only about six hundred strong, including the primary grades, so it was almost impossible to compete with the huge public schools, which had thousands of students.

The competition was so great, in fact, that one entire wall of the gymnasium was enshrined with life-sized photographs of the last Singer football squad to have beaten Hamilton High, our arch public school rival—and that by only two points, twelve years earlier.

Still, we were proud to be Singer cadets. It was a good school and it taught the regimens and disciplines meant to produce the future leaders of

49

the community as well as polish them into gentlemen. I remember an incident, for example, at cadet chapel one Monday morning following a Saturday football game during which some of the cadet corps booed a referee's call. After prayers, the school supervisor marched sternly to the podium and the corps was called to attention. He said only four words, drawing them out very slowly: "Cadets—do—not—boo." And then he left the room. We stood at attention for the remaining ten minutes of chapel to ponder this proclamation each in his own way, and to this day I have never booed anyone or anything again.

In any case, so that our confidence might not be totally annihilated, the Academy scheduled games with small country teams too, in places like Orange Grove, Ten Mile and Ozona, where the thirty-yard line was marked by a foul-smelling chicken coop and one entire half of the football field sloped downhill. During one night game there, an errant field-goal attempt struck an overhead electric wire, raining a shower of sparks on the terrified players and fans alike and blacking out the field for a good twenty minutes.

Football was so important at Singer that while we were there they hired a former professional player as head coach.

This gentleman, who had once been a fullback for the Detroit Lions, decided that what we lacked in size (we were outweighed forty pounds per man in the line and twenty-five per man in the backfield) we must make up in cunning and guile, and so he issued a playbook of nearly a hundred professional-style plays so complicated that the team spent most of its practice time just trying to remember what to do. Worse, on the field in competition no Singer cadet possessed the ability to execute what was expected of him. That year we won only one game and that by default, and the Monday after the final game, while the coach was summing up the season to the team, which had been called together in the bleachers, a bird flew over and crapped on his bald head. A week later he was dismissed.

But we were game and we were hopeful at Singer and athletics played a major role in the life of every single cadet. And if football was the most important sport, basketball ran a close second and the searching eyes of the coaches soon singled out Beau as a prime candidate for that sport.

The junior varsity was, of course, the proving ground for the "big time" and engendered almost as much fervor and spirit as the varsity games. Beau was only twelve (going on thirteen) when the coaches approached him. He'd played basketball on and off for years but it did not much impress him as a sport. His father had installed the requisite hoop on the garage at home and Beau spent countless hours playing "horse" or other games and practicing dribbling. And he had played in Little League games in the parks. But now they wanted him for JV, and the first week or so of school the coaches gave him drills and exercises to prepare him for the beginning of official practice in October. The rest of us were in awe of him because of this.

In those days Beau was on the cusp of becoming a young man, but he was still a boy. In the locker room, the first day of practice, he observed with acute embarrassment the body hair and genitals of the older members of the squad. And the way their muscle tone had begun to develop and the way the veins stood out in their forearms, hands and calves. These were boys fourteen and fifteen, only a year or two older than himself, but boys who dated girls, boys with deep voices who drank beer, boys who were allowed to go out on weekends to ride around in cars and do who knew what all.

But most of us, myself included, were still basically children and we played children's games and lived in our children's world away from adult things. But for Beau, all that was about to end.

On the first day of basketball practice, the competition was ferocious; an hour of wind sprints, calisthenics, drills, and then practice games that seemingly went on forever. Beau thought he would never draw another steady breath. The elbowing and shouldering from the stronger, older boys had left him sore and bruised and, finally, he was singled out by some sadistic assistant coach to shoot twenty-one straight baskets from the foul line and each miss set him back to the beginning. By the time he was done, it was dark outside and Beau was alone in the shower room, painfully putting on his clothes.

He had to hitchhike home because he had no ride. He was picked up by a nice man who had attended Singer himself years before and who questioned him prodigiously about the upcoming basketball season. Suddenly, through the side window of the car, Beau saw a group of perhaps half a dozen children dressed as ghosts and spacemen and Indians and other creatures.

"It's Halloween," he said to the man driving. "Is it Halloween?" Beau was stunned. It hadn't occurred to him. Halloween!

"Yeah," the man said, "the little vandals will be at it tonight."

At home, Beau sat at the dinner table and barely touched his plate. He was too tired to eat and painfully sore in his legs, arms and back. He excused himself early and went to his room. Two days before he had purchased a record by Buddy Holly, the currently popular rock-'n'-roll singer. He set the arm of the record player so the song would repeat itself and lay down on his bed. Halloween! he thought. How could he have forgotten? Every year he went trick-or-treating with me and our friends. At first our mothers had taken us around, and later we'd gone alone. Beau knew the route well and he knew that we'd all be out there tonight—myself, Chord Lewellen, Tommy Brodie, Eric Pacer. In some ways, it was Beau's favorite day of the year; the eerie jack-o'-lanterns, the cutouts of ghosts and goblins, the free candy and fruit and trinkets, a different tribute at each door; being allowed to go out on a school night without supervision, to laugh and play tricks and huddle secretly in the nighttime.

Yet something was gnawing at him, something he couldn't quite put his finger on. Somehow JV basketball had propelled him forward in a leap that left such things as Halloween behind, along with Santa Claus and the Easter Bunny. The practice session that afternoon had been a rude awakening to the adult world, and as he lay on his bed stiff and aching, some incomprehensible impulse deviled his twelve-year-old mind to skip back to the old tricks, to sink back into Halloweens past. Halloween is truly a children's holiday—an occasion when roles are reversed and children have power over grown-ups, can wreak havoc, be aggressive and "bad."

The Buddy Holly record stuck, so Beau got up to fix it—but then, as if drawn by the force of his desire, he went out into the hallway and up the stairs and into the attic. Below he could hear his father and mother, still at the dinner table.

There was a cedar bureau he hadn't been inside in almost a year. It contained an old space-suit costume and a Pied Piper outfit his mother had made for him years before.

He took out the space suit and examined it. It was made of cotton, grayish with red piping, and was really sort of a one-piece jumpsuit with a plastic bubble helmet ordered through the mail. He removed his pants and shirt and tried stepping into the space suit.

Immediately he realized it wasn't even a question of a tight fit; he simply couldn't squeeze into the thing. This came as a surprise, of course, and a disappointment, but Beau had always been a determined child. He was good in his studies for that very reason—he did not like to be stumped by problems and he usually found his way through them or around them and was not to be undone this night merely by the weird growing process that had afflicted him.

He stood in his underwear and rummaged through the bureau. He could not wear his father's military clothes, and besides, he had been in his own military uniform all day. He knew better than to wear his mother's things. There was a pair of satin breeches that had belonged to some long-forgotten Mardi Gras outfit but he couldn't find the top to it. And then, in a far corner of the bureau, he stumbled onto a clown suit he barely remembered. It was something his father had worn to a masquerade years before. It was pale white with big polka dots in red and green and ruffles at the cuffs, sleeves and shoulders and an authentic-looking plastic mask with a big red nose and an orange fright wig. To top it off there was a big green dunce cap that stood nearly two feet high.

Beau slipped into the costume and it seemed to fit him. He stole into the kitchen and found a brown-paper bag, then fled out the back door, on his way to catch up with the rest of us.

He bounced along the sidewalk until he was two or three streets from home, figuring we would have worked our way there by now, but all he encountered was a tiny witch and some other small child of unidentifiable gender with a sheet over its head. Both of them seemed to give him a wide berth as he passed by. Not seeing us, Beau decided to go ahead and start collecting his loot. The first door he knocked at was answered by a pleasant woman whom he had seen before in the grocery store. Naturally, she didn't recognize him in the clown suit, and she was slightly taken aback.

"Oh," she said, looking him up and down, "my goodness," and offered him his pick from a tray of candies. Beau accepted a few, put them in his bag and went on his way. But he had a sudden and strange feeling that somehow he was out of place.

He went to three more houses, where the reception was the same. Everyone seemed startled to behold a six-foot—no, with the dunce cap, an eight-foot—clown standing there with a bag in his hand. He began to feel foolish, but wasn't quite ready to give it up. He thought that if he could just find the rest of us, it would be all right.

Beau skipped the last four houses on the block and turned down another street that was quiet and dark, except for the moonlight. There was still no sign of our ghostly party. He walked along, almost grateful now for not running into anybody else, and when he came to the end of the street he'd just about decided to call it a night.

But there was a big Victorian house that sat back from the sidewalk and was surrounded by overgrown azalea and camellia bushes and big oak trees. There was only one light on in the house and, realizing that his bag was almost empty, he figured to take one more crack before packing it in. He walked up the steps and rang the bell. When nobody answered he rang again. He finally heard footsteps in the hall and a light came on. The door opened a crack and he had a glimpse of an elderly gray-haired woman just before she jumped back with a shriek of fright. The door slammed shut. An instant later it opened again, wider, and the lady, obviously trying to compose herself, said, "Oh, I'm sorry. I'd forgotten it's Halloween—and you . . . you . . . well, wait just a minute." She went toward the back of the house.

Beau had an impulse to tell her he'd forgotten it too, but didn't, and just then he noticed a man sitting in a chair partially turned away from him. The man had been reading a newspaper but had stopped and was staring at him. He seemed kindly enough, with white hair and wire-rim spectacles.

"My, my," the man said cheerfully, "you're a *big* one, aren't you?"

It was in the long moment after the last word was spoken that Beau realized he was a ridiculous sight; that time had passed rapidly by and he had yet to catch up. One thing was certain, he could never, never do this again. His first impulse was to run away, but he was too polite. The old lady was walking toward him now with an apple in her hand, polishing it on her apron. She handed it to him, this big, red, shiny apple, and said, "Well, happy Halloween," as her hand nervously closed the door.

"Yes, ma'am, thank you," Beau almost whispered as he turned and went down the steps into the dark yard and put the apple in his bag. He was beginning to sweat and his heart was beating rapidly. He did not quite understand all of the implications of the realization he had just reached, but he sensed it was part of a greater change. He hurried toward home, anxious to rid himself of his silly costume and get into his bed.

He had just turned the corner of the main street leading to his house when he saw three boys coming toward him. He immediately recognized them as first-teamers on the basketball squad. They were wearing their letter sweaters and laughing and cussing and coming his way. Beau dove headlong into a clump of shrubbery and tried to bury himself in the thick leaves, hoping they hadn't spotted him.

They hadn't, but one of the boys stopped to light a cigarette inches from the bush in which he was hiding.

"Damn!" one of them said. "Did you see the ass on that Caroline West! I bet she's a rabbit!"

"And Sally Faulk," chimed in another. "She's built like a brick shithouse! Gimme a cig, will ya?"

Beau was close to panic. They were under a streetlight so he could see the boys plainly and he realized that if any of them looked down they'd see him too. One of the boys, Tom Grove, who'd given him a particularly hard time that afternoon at basketball practice, took a beer can he had concealed under his sweater and handed it to one of the others to hold. Then he took out a piece of candy, unwrapped it and tossed the wadded paper into the bushes about an inch from Beau's nose.

This was too much. Beau, unable to contain himself, leaped to his feet and bolted out of the shrubs like a gazelle, dashing as fast as he could across the street into an alleyway between two houses. The basketball players were nearly scared out of their wits; someone yelled an obscenity after him, but he kept on going, hoping, praying he hadn't been recognized. If anyone had been watching that night, here is the specter they would have seen: a huge clown, loping down alleyways and across fields, silhouetted against the moonlight, leaping fences with long innocent strides as he made his way toward the sanctity of his room.

After sneaking back into the house around nine and hiding the humiliating clown suit in the darkest corner of his closet, Beau lay in bed with the lights out, playing the Buddy Holly record softly and munching on the apple the old lady had given him. It was only after long hours of the voice on the record intoning "Peggy Sue" that Beau began trying feebly to comprehend what had happened to him and to his life. In fact, it was simply what happens to all boys, though each comes to it in a different way. Beau knew he had passed a threshold, or at least was passing over it, a passage deeper and more disturbing than anything he'd experienced before, both exciting and scary, from which he would emerge a very different person.

After a while, his thoughts wandered to what one of the boys had said about that girl, Sally Faulk, whom Beau knew, or at least had seen, because she was the older sister of Katherine Faulk, who was his own age. Katherine was a pretty girl and blossoming into a young woman. Beau had known her from Sunday school and church, but never thought about her as anything but a "girl." It was undeniably true that her sister, Sally Faulk, was "built," though previously he had subconsciously not noticed because he had not wanted—nor was he ready—to deal with it. But as he lay there thinking, he began to dwell on her, and began to feel a new, strange tingling in his loins which, he had already discovered, would go away after a while if you let it alone. Suddenly he didn't want it to go away and he somehow realized that an entirely new vista would occupy much time in his life to come, for better or worse.

VICISSITUDES III

The Five
Funny Fellows

By the summer of Beau's fifteenth year, his physiology had worked out for him. He was a strapping six-foot-two-inch athlete, lean-muscled and good-looking, and he involved himself in most of the things young men of our age did: girls, beer drinking, parties, good-natured troublemaking and other indulgences. But by the end of that magical summer Beau had become embroiled in a foul and senseless incident, the impact of which would nettle his mind for the rest of his days. In some ways it had a great effect on his behavior in the final chapters of his life.

Like many teenagers, Beau was a member of a clique. It was an ordinary clique of five close buddies who ate their school lunch together, talked on the phone and ran with each other on weekends; yet it was more than that, because we had formalized it; made it secret. And Beau, in a very short time, established himself, more or less, as our leader.

We called ourselves the Five Funny Fellows—Beau, myself, Tommy Brodie, Eric Pacer and Chord Lewellen. It was, incidentally, the summer they began calling me Pappy. There were no meetings as such, and no real rules, except that we would never divulge the membership of the Five Funny Fellows, or what we did, which was basically a kind of mild vandalism and joke playing. People became aware of our existence after a while, because we left our emblem—FFF—in chalk, at the scene of whatever crime we perpetrated in order to confuse and baffle our victims and enemies.

The summer of 1958 was in many ways a magic summer for Beau and the Funny Fellows; it was the last summer of freedom before we would be expected to get jobs between school terms and earn some of our own keep; we were entering the upper classes at Singer Academy and would have rank and privileges after so many years of being at the mercy of the senior cadets. We would graduate to varsity sports and would soon be eligible to get driving licenses, with all the wonderful mobility cars afforded.

It was a good summer in general. The weather, though hot and muggy, was mostly clear, and even when it rained, the Five Funny Fellows were not deterred. We would secrete ourselves away somewhere, usually in Beau's room in the big summer house his family kept across Bienville Bay, and smoke cigarettes and swig beer, which we ingeniously kept hidden in the cool water of the toilet tank in Beau's bathroom. Once, when Beau's mother was entertaining her bridge club out on the porch, three of us huddled behind the closed shutters which opened on the veranda and heard ourselves being discussed by, among other people, our own mothers.

One dour old woman was complaining about the despicable vandals who had caused a big vulgar word to appear on her lawn by carefully placing large amounts of salt on the grass.

Beau's mother was heard to say loudly, "I know who it is—it's those damned three F's, or whatever they call themselves."

"It's a disgrace," my mother said. "I wish the police would catch them!"

"I wish I knew who they were. I know they're responsible for setting off the driftwood fires the day before the Fourth of July—they even drew three F's in the sand by each pile!" This last exclamation came from an unidentified voice.

Tommy Brodie's mother sighed. "They're probably some of those local boys. Our boys wouldn't do such things."

We could barely contain ourselves. Tommy was pounding the bed in hysterics and Chord Lewellen had to go into the bathroom to keep his laughter from being overheard.

The Five Funny Fellows never did anything really bad. About the worst was the night we turned a big valve near the huge swimming pool at the Oak Hall Hotel and let out all the water. We only realized how bad that was a few days later, when the local paper printed an item saying that it cost the hotel nearly five hundred dollars to refill it. Most of the time, we engaged in simple pranks: lighting the Fourth of July bonfires on the third, hiding someone's boat so they'd think it was stolen, setting off firecrackers or spying on college kids making out in the big oval upstairs room at the Oak Hall Hotel.

One of our favorite pranks was to torment the tollbooth man at the road that crossed the bay. The usual method was to heat up the quarter toll by holding it on the cigarette lighter with a pair of tweezers and then deposit it in the poor devil's hand, speeding off in the hail of his profanity. We once worked out an elaborate trick to drill a hole through a quarter, attach it by means of piano wire to the bumper of the car and then drag away the whole cash register before the man realized what was going on. Somebody among us did in fact drill a hole in a quarter, but that's as far as it got.

We used the old "purse trick" and several variations of it—where a discarded purse is filled to overflowing with costume jewelry or some such and left on the road at night with a string tied to it. The driver of a passing car, if he was gullible enough, would slam on the brakes and start backing up, by which time, of course, the purse had been hauled in and we would get a good laugh from the bushes as the driver paced back and forth trying to find the thing. On a slow night we would simply go out to a pear orchard by the roadside and throw fruit at cars. It was *that* sort of mischief.

But then there was the incident that would cast a pall over all of us—not only the Funny Fellows but our families and, in fact, the whole summer community. And, of course, it shadowed back to Bienville, to Singer Academy and other institutions of the city. Afterwards the Funny Fellows disbanded and it was the end of enchanted summers.

We had all decided to spend the night out. It was a Friday and the weather was clear and warm and we were going to stay out in my parents' boathouse, since they were in the city. We knew we could drink beer, say dirty words and smoke cigarettes with impunity. In the afternoon we gave an old Negro man some money and got him to buy us a case of beer. We bought hot dogs and rolls and potato chips, and when we assembled near dusk, there was a lot of good-natured ribbing. The beer was opened and things began to get silly.

Adults tend to forget just how cruel teenagers can be to each other. The cruelty is not necessarily vicious or mean-spirited; sometimes—perhaps most times—it's just intended to incite a response, to get someone's goat. And the cruelty, or "teasing," as we called it then, went on almost constantly. Occasionally one of us would get angry, but there was never a fight or even lasting hard feelings. There were times, though, when it got tense, when one of us, in learning just how far he could go in provoking the emotions of another, went beyond the bounds.

This particular night the object of the teasing was Tommy Brodie and his principal teaser was Chord Lewellen. It was really ironic that Chord and Tommy should get into it, since they had been lifelong friends and even their parents were close friends. They went to the same church, shared secrets, money and, when they were small, even clothes. They were close enough to have been brothers, and with the perspective of an adult, I realize this might have contributed to what happened.

A year or two before, Chord Lewellen began to fill out almost as Beau had. He was a tall, good-looking, athletic boy and had a way with girls. His family was so proud of him that his father, a wealthy cotton broker, even hired a special photographer to take pictures of him in various athletic contests. Chord was sought after for various student offices at Singer, and we all knew that his family planned to buy him a brand-new car when he reached sixteen.

All this adulation seemed to affect a darker side of Chord, and there were times when he could be conceited and something of a bully.

Tommy Brodie was almost the opposite. His Cajun ancestry left him dark-skinned and instead of growing up, he grew out. At the age of fifteen he weighed in excess of two hundred pounds, most of which was around his waist and thighs. He was a jolly boy, with a shock of curly black hair and dark watery eyes, but he was most definitely a follower, not a leader. His family didn't have as much money as the parents of the other Funny Fellows and so he tended to be stingier, which, of course, earned him the reputation of being "cheap." If there was one thing you could not be if you went to Singer Academy, it was cheap.

No one could remember how it started, but at some point Chord Lewellen began teasing Tommy Brodie. He was on his case about bumming cigarettes, then chiding him for not repaying a two-dollar loan, but the teasing seemed good-natured enough and Tommy took it with an embarrassed smile and a hurt look in his eyes.

More beer was opened and Chord's teasing became harsher. It was amusing in a way, because Chord was good with words and images and he jokingly, but too precisely, described Tommy as a "beached whale" or a "human icebox" and all of us chuckled. Finally, though, Chord pushed Tommy too far, and Tommy snapped, "All right, maybe I ought to just go home."

"You'll never fit through the gate," Chord said. "Hell, you might fall through the wharf and drown yourself 'fore you could get there!"

The gauntlet was thrown. Tommy slowly got up and began to collect his things.

"Aw, c'mon, Tommy," Beau said. "We're just kidding. Don't be a sourpuss."

"Sometimes it's not funny," Tommy said.

"It's only supposed to be funny," Beau replied.

"Not to me," the fat boy said, but he put down his things and sat again, this time in a dark corner of the boathouse, so that all you could see of him was the orange glow from his cigarette. It was after sunset and the charcoal was ready and we began to cook the hot dogs. Then, for no reason, Chord started in on Tommy again.

"Well, we'd better eat up before two-ton gets to the food," he said.

Tommy, who was approaching the fire, froze in mid-step, turned suddenly and went back to his corner. None of us really noticed, what with all the beer being drunk, but he didn't eat at all that night. It was nearly ten o'clock when somebody suggested we go for a swim. The tide was out and the tepid bay water was only waist deep. Beau was the first to strip off his clothes and jump in.

"Hey, where's Tommy?" somebody said. We looked around and he wasn't there.

"He's up on the dock," someone else said. "Hey, Tommy, c'mon in!"

"Nah," Tommy said, "I don't feel like it right now."

"He's probably whacking off," Chord yelled merrily. He reached down into the shallow bottom and picked up a handful of wet sand.

"Hey, blubber-butt," he shouted, "use this to whack your carrot." He flung the sand in Tommy's direction, but there was no response, so Chord repeated the act, the sand stinging the sides of the boathouse and wharf. "Let's get him!" Chord said. "C'mon, Eric, let's run him in." He flung another handful of sand. Eric too picked up some sand and threw it in Tommy's direction. Then I threw some at Beau's back, stinging him, and Beau returned the shot and Chord hit Eric and so on. But then Chord got two big handfuls of sand and climbed up on the wharf and approached Tommy, who was cowering in the corner.

There was a little platform landing on the boathouse with steps down to the water and when Tommy saw Chord coming he climbed down it and backed away.

"Now stop, Chord," he said plaintively. "Okay?"

But Chord kept on coming, moving slowly, weighing the sand in his hands. "Into the water," he said. He was giggling.

"No, Chord—I don't want to."

Chord fired some of the sand at Tommy's legs and big fat Tommy turned his back, facing the rest of us, who were in the water.

"C'mon, Tommy, just get in here," Eric said. Then he took a wide sweep with his hand and sprayed Tommy with water.

"Nooooo!" Tommy cried.

Here, there might have been a touch of compassion; some impulse from one of us to put a stop to the teasing because it had become pathetic and mean now, but perhaps because it *was* just that, because it aroused some dark, animalistic instincts in us to fall on our prey, we did not, not any of us. And also, Tommy's behavior inspired this feeling; it was babyish behavior and possibly to us an uncomfortable reminder of how close we all were to being children. After all, it was only teasing, only playing, only a game . . .

I was the one to start the splashing in earnest, and the others, including Beau, followed; we sailed great arcs of water at the cringing Tommy, drenching him, stinging his eyes, laughing and shouting for him to jump in.

He retreated to the steps of the landing, only to be met by a hail of sand from Chord. Caught in this cross fire, Tommy Brodie lapsed into an uncontrollable panic and bolted onto the dock and toward the wharf and the safety of land.

But here fate played its hand. Lying on a rail around the dock was a rusty old oyster knife. Someone, long before, had probably left it after shucking oysters for an evening's meal. The weather and salinity had rusted it beyond use for oysters or really anything worthwhile. But as Tommy backed along the rail, his hand stumbled on the knife, and grasped it, blade down, in the plunging position. Chord still had one remaining fistful of sand and he was stalking him, catlike. As Chord reared back to sling the sand, Tommy, perhaps out of nothing more than fearful panicked reflex, lunged with the knife, crying, "Nooooooo!"

We boys in the water heard this, but nothing else except footsteps bolting down the wharf, and then a slight groan; it might even have been a sigh.

Beau was the first one out of the water. He had no reason to feel alarm, but he did anyway.

"What? He run off?" Eric asked.

"Hey, Chord, what'd you do to him?" I hollered.

Beau found Chord sitting on a wooden bench on the dock, under the roof, close to where we'd cooked our hot dogs. Because it was dark, he only saw Chord sitting there. He could not see the stream of blood that had shot across the deck out of his burst heart and splattered on the wall fifteen feet away, nor could he see the pool of blood in Chord's naked lap and on the bench and dripping between the cracks in the boards into the water. When he switched on the overhead light, Beau was suddenly able to see the dead-glazed eyes of his friend and was drawn up in such horror that for a long moment he couldn't speak a word; he could only stare.

An hour later we were assembled in the living room of Tommy's house. Beau had called his father and told him what had happened, so he was there. Tommy had run home, which was only a matter of a mile or so down the beach, and had hidden in terror in his bedroom. Even he was not prepared for the news that Chord was dead. The police and an ambulance had arrived, but Chord was obviously beyond help, and so they covered him with a blanket and drew chalk marks where he had sat and left him in the upright position on the bench.

An old country sheriff was questioning us boys. Beau's father had persuaded him, at least for the moment, not to take us up to the county seat at this hour of the night, and suggested to the sheriff in his most lawyerly way that what had happened was more in the nature of an accident than a homicide.

But somehow in the course of all this, somebody—it could have been Eric—blurted out something about the Funny Fellows, and when the sheriff pursued this line of questioning, probably more out of curiosity than anything else, he learned we were the perpetrators of the local pranks and, of course, all of this got into the newspapers later. Beau and the rest of us were in a lot of hot water with just about everybody over that.

The next morning, accompanied by his parents and by Beau's father, Tommy was taken up to the county seat and booked on a murder charge. But by afternoon, after reading the statements of the rest of us and talking to Tommy and Beau's father, the sheriff reduced the charge to manslaughter.

We were all allowed to go to Chord's funeral, except, of course, for Tommy Brodie, whose presence would have been conspicuously inappropriate. In fact, we soon discovered that none of us were welcome. At the gravesite, after the burial ceremonies, we went up to Mr. and Mrs. Lewellen, but our condolences were not accepted. Mrs. Lewellen sobbed and turned away, but Mr. Lewellen scowled and said, "We don't think Chord would have wanted your apologies."

The aftermath of Chord's death was felt for a long time. Tommy went before a judge, who put him on five years' probation, and a few weeks later his parents sent him away to a boarding school in Michigan. Eric's folks sent him off, too, to a very strict military school upstate.

For Beau, it was a strange and sorrowful episode in his life. Riding back across the bay with his father the afternoon of the funeral, he barely spoke. He looked out the window at the vast expanse of water and the few fishing boats, and his old man apparently figured it wasn't the time to console him, and so he left him alone.

Just before dark, Beau changed his clothes and went for a walk in the woods. There he tried to grapple with the events of the last week. How much was he responsible? How could it have happened? For the first time he came

face to face with his own mortality and the question of whether there is really fairness in the world.

Looking back, I don't think it had as great an effect on me, either because I was too young or because there was something in my system that let me blot it out. But Beau was different. It troubled him. He felt guilt, and an inability to deal with how swiftly and surely all our lives had changed.

Over the years, he managed to adjust, but he never really got over it. Somehow, I think it became *his* burden and it set him just a little more apart, made him a little more alone.

The Broadway Blues

November 2, 1983

There was darkness in the dream this time, green, stinking darkness; the pale shapes of trees and undergrowth and death in the quiet, soft darkness. Over the years the dream was never quite the same, though some things in it remained constant: there was always the hiss of a radio between transmissions. And no one smiled out of pleasure; it was an ugly dream—colors were either too vivid or too dull; faces often seemed waxy, poulticed. New characters drifted into the dream, some finding permanent places, some never to return; the visitors worked their way in so they seemed to belong, though Beau knew they didn't. Always there was the dark foreboding.

There were times when Beau seemed to be able to control the dream, either to guide it or at least to stop it when it became too terrible. Other times he simply had to ride it out and let the dream carry him. Whichever the case, Beau had become as accustomed to it as a hunchback is to his hump, and in a strange and perverse way, he even became fond of it.

There was water in this dream—a variation; shallow mucky water that sucked on boots and legs. Suddenly the men came on a scene that was unspeakably grisly: mutilated bodies, most without clothing, lying in unnatural positions, almost as though they had been dropped into the forest from the sky. In the soft green darkness no one spoke, but some of Beau's men moved through the bodies looking for things. Beau—as a participant now,

64

rather than the observer—couldn't remember what they were looking for, but he knew he had the answer somewhere. The radio hissed.

Beau's father was in this dream. He was standing next to a preposterously gnarled tree, talking with someone, paying no attention to the dead men. In fact, he ignored them so completely he gave the impression he didn't know they were there. Beau went up to him and they shook hands, as old friends who hadn't seen each other for a while, and then Beau pointed to the dead men and said to his father, "They must have been caught here by artillery." The old man paid no attention. Beau began to feel anxious, and took his father's arm and led him to the bodies, but his father seemed intent on other things and was oblivious to the carnage.

Then Beau began to shout, but the old man remained steadfastly uninterested—and then the dream moved on. Beau was sitting in a car: it was Sheilah's car, and they were stopped on a gravel road somewhere in pastoral country with fields and streams and horses. In the distance there was an old, lovely nineteenth-century farmhouse. Sheilah was propped against the passenger door, her legs drawn up against her chest, and Beau was looking straight ahead. Oddly, he was wearing his combat fatigues, and he was asking Sheilah questions, slowly, deliberately. His impression was that they had not been together for a while, that she was seeing someone else—or had been. He didn't know, and was trying to find out and she was being evasive. Suddenly he shouted, "Look at me, dammit!" She did, for a moment; then with an expression of disgust, she drew herself up and got out of the car. She walked down the road twenty or thirty meters and climbed through a rail fence into the pasture with the horses.

The horses, four or five of them, raised their heads from grazing and slowly began to move toward her. Beau watched from the car. The radio hissed once or twice and was silent. A failed transmission. Sheilah walked straight toward the horses, awkward strides with her long legs and her backside jiggling ever so gently in her loose tan slacks. What in hell was she doing! Sheilah hated horses. She was terrified of them. And she was walking up to these horses.

Beau got out of the car and ran to the fence. He called to her but she paid no attention, acting just as his father had with the bodies. But *horses*—Sheilah was petrified of horses. Beau climbed through the fence and ran toward her but she had already reached the animals and was holding out her hand, allowing one of them to nuzzle it. They were surrounding her and she was stroking another down the long bridge of its nose.

When Beau reached her she turned her head to him and smiled. "Why are you out here?" he heard himself scream. "You're scared of horses!"

"Oh, I used to be," she said evenly. "It was so silly. They're beautiful, aren't they? Here, look at this one . . ."

Stunned, Beau backed away. He had ridden horses all his life, but suddenly these seemed malevolent. One of them began to amble toward him, tossing its head and snorting. Beau remained motionless, frozen, as if in a dream within a dream, as the huge animal came up. He reached out with one hand and touched it tentatively on its nose and the horse snorted again and Beau pulled back in fear. Cold, hard fear.

The plane lurched upward, then down again, and Beau opened his eyes, aware of a change in the engine's pitch. They had begun their descent and the nose of the plane was declined slightly, enough for him to see the Manhattan skyline. Sodom and Gomorrah.

Beau tried to analyze the dream. Sheilah was more present in the latest ones. What was his subconscious trying to tell him? That she had changed? That she could change? That she had the upper hand now? It was Beau who had actually broken their engagement, although it hadn't been a formal engagement in the first place.

It had happened after a particularly nasty argument. One night he'd made some offhand comment about a group of journalists who were circling like jackals around some poor under secretary of state who was caught up in an inconsistency that had been precipitated by his bosses. But Sheilah had taken it as a personal insult. She announced that Beau was deliberately belittling her chosen profession. He tried explaining that *he* had been a journalist long before she and that he'd only been commenting upon this particular case and these particular reporters, who seemed to him rude and badgering.

Sheilah would have none of it, and insisted that he had made his comment for her benefit alone. She then stormed off to bed and turned the opposite way when he pulled back the covers. The next morning, Beau concluded that a life with Sheilah would be a constant series of upheavals with her getting her feelings hurt or her hackles raised at any given time and lashing out even when there wasn't any reason.

He told her over breakfast. He didn't make a big fuss about the previous night's incident, but he nicely explained that he was afraid that if they married they would make each other's life a living hell. He didn't immediately call off the engagement, but suggested they talk about it. She actually agreed she might have been hasty in bringing him to task over the remark. He calmly reminded her that it wasn't the first time, and certainly wouldn't be the last. He took much of the blame on himself and suggested that they seriously rethink the marriage plans.

Sheilah was stunned at first, then angry, though not as much as Beau had anticipated. In the end she agreed, but suggested a cooling-off period. She had just been offered a chance to go to Europe to learn some of the ropes within the network and predicted they might feel differently when she got back. It made some sense and Beau agreed, deciding to get out of town for a while himself. He knew this wasn't the final scene. There would be a last act to be played, however it came out.

After the plane landed he stepped into a cab and the driver roared off onto the Grand Central Parkway heading for the city, racing between cars, hitting every pothole, braking hard. The cab was filthy inside and Beau's stomach muscles tensed, his hands holding on to the seat, his heart beating fast. It dawned on him that six weeks before, when he had taken a cab out to the airport on his way to Bienville, he'd had no such feelings of anxiety and odd remorse. A cab ride in New York is an everyday experience and one gets used to it, he reminded himself. But at what price? At what psychological price?

It took an hour for Beau to settle into his apartment. The housekeeper came once a week but he still had to unpack and get the feel of it again. He took a shower, then called his answering service for a long list of messages that had piled up while he was away.

Most were routine, but several weren't, including one from Toby Burr, Beau's producer for *In Fields Where They Lay*. Another call that piqued his interest was from Eric Pacer, who left no number, just a message that he'd call again. Beau hadn't seen Pacer in several years.

The third message of interest was from Katherine Whittle, Beau's old girlfriend from college—his first real love, in fact—but that was another story. She'd been Katherine Faulk back then, but later married Bienville's new congressman, Dan Whittle, the same Dan Whittle who had presided over Beau's "court-martial" at Singer Academy so many years before. He hadn't seen Katherine for nearly fifteen years. Yes, a long time and a whole other story. People were suddenly appearing out of the woodwork.

He decided to return the call from Toby Burr.

"Beau, ah yes," Toby said. "I was wondering when you'd turn up."

Toby Burr wasn't like most Broadway producers. He was a hustler all right, but he had class too, and a kind of laid-back attitude. He was an Oxford man, a Rhodes scholar, and he was honest, more or less. Furthermore, he cared about the plays he put on.

"There's some news," Toby said, "and I might as well prepare you for it now. There's been trouble with the play down at the Kennedy Center."

"What kind of trouble?" Beau felt his stomach drop.

"They're having second thoughts," Burr said matter-of-factly. "I don't know exactly what's going on, but I got a message the other day to get in touch with Widmire's office, and they said other people on the board have seen the play and it might not be strong enough."

"Strong enough?" Beau barked. "What kind of comment is that?"

"It's the kind of comment they make before the shit hits the fan," Burr said evenly.

"*What* isn't strong enough?" Beau asked. "Did they have any particular complaint? Hell, Toby, they agreed to this, you know . . ."

"I know, I know," Burr said. "Sometimes it happens, though. Could be they've got an offer for something they'd rather have. I won't be able to tell until I talk to Widmire himself. But I need those fixes. Are they all done?"

"All except for the interrogation scene. I've been doing a lot of thinking about it. It's crucial, but I haven't actually fixed it yet."

"That was the crucial one, you know," Burr said.

"Yes, I know. So what do we do now?"

"First, I've got to see the new draft and get together with Herb Warren. Maybe we'll go down and see Widmire himself. Try to put him on the spot. How soon can you get me the changes you've already done?"

"I have them here. I can messenger them over to you in the morning."

"How about getting them to me now," Burr said. "I'll send a messenger." He sounded ominous. Beau agreed.

"Good," Burr said. "Now how's everything else?"

"Compared to this, everything else is wonderful," Beau said.

After he put down the phone, Beau went to the liquor cabinet and got a bottle of scotch. He slumped in a chair, unscrewed the top and took an extra-large slug of whiskey. All the things he'd worked for seemed to be crumbling one by one. The first plays had been good—flawed, but good—he'd been learning. But *In Fields Where They Lay* was the difference between staying in the solar system and taking to the galaxies.

The idea of the play had been to identify the thin, almost imperceptible line between compassion and cruelty; Beau had merely used Vietnam as a vehicle. He had thought it worked. The setting was Christmas Eve, with a rifle company posted on a rainy hillside. It opened with the soldiers singing "Silent Night." One squad had fashioned a Christmas tree from C ration tin tops and shell casings and surgical field dressings, but the commanding officer ordered them to get rid of it on the grounds that outwardly celebrating Christmas might make the soldiers homesick, damage morale. This was how the play began.

Beau slipped a bound copy of the manuscript out of his satchel and flipped through it, taking another swig of the whiskey. He came to the interrogation scene. He studied it. The two interrogators were a sergeant and a private. The sergeant was the one holding the knife to the prisoner's navel. The private held an English-to-Vietnamese translation booklet. They were inside a tent with a lantern hanging overhead, above a folding wooden table. Offstage there was the sound of rain and thunder. The script said

ENTER LT. ROTH. Beau read on.

LT. ROTH	Who's he?
SGT. GRUEN	We found him with that bunch by the fake rice hootch. He had a pocketful of cartridges and a plastic bag full of fuses. And he was carrying this map.

> *(Nods to the table, where there is a tattered map, unfolded.* LT. ROTH *picks up the map and studies it.)*

LT. ROTH	Lord! It's us! Right down to the litter bags and the radio shack and latrine. You getting anything out of him?
SGT. GRUEN	Not much, sir. But I figured with the map and all, he must be . . .
LT. ROTH	Yes, I know.

> *(He puts the map back on the table and walks to the tent entrance and stares into the rain. Then turns to the others.)*

Do you know what's going on down there?

PVT. CRENNA	Sir?
LT. ROTH	Do you know what's going on down there?
PVT. CRENNA	No, sir.
LT. ROTH	Well, I'll tell you, Crenna. We're getting butchered. That's what's going on.
SGT. GRUEN	Sir, I think we can get it out of him.

> *(He touches the knife to the prisoner's navel and the prisoner flinches.)*

LT. ROTH They've got to be planning something. It's already started. We've had six contact reports since dark. They're moving all down in there. Setting up.

PVT. CRENNA He says VC come next week.

SGT. GRUEN He's full of shit.

(He jabs the knife a little harder into the prisoner's navel and with his other hand sweeps the cartridges and fuses off onto the floor.)

LT. ROTH *(Dejectedly running his fingers through his hair.)*

What about those others outside?

SGT. GRUEN They're just spear carriers, sir. I think this one's our man.

LT. ROTH Well, work on him. I'd say we haven't much time. We need to know their approaches. See if he'll point them out on the map he was carrying. I've got to get up to see the mortars. Holler at me if you get anything.

(LT. ROTH *leaves the tent.)*

(Lights out. A flash and a report from onstage. There is a commotion, footsteps. Lights up. LT. ROTH *enters the tent. The prisoner is lying on the floor, dead. A pistol is on the table, smoking.)*

LT. ROTH What happened?

PVT. CRENNA Sir, the . . .

SGT. GRUEN Sir, the prisoner, he shot himself.

LT. ROTH Shot himself? How could he?

SGT. GRUEN He just grabbed my pistol and shot himself with it. I had it laid out on the table—to frighten him.

LT. ROTH *(To Crenna.)*

He shot himself?

PVT. CRENNA *(Nervously.)*

Yes, sir.

LT. ROTH Why would he do that?

SGT. GRUEN Who knows why these bastards do anything?

PVT. CRENNA He says he wasn't VC.

SGT. GRUEN If he's dead, he's VC.

This scene had troubled Beau from the outset. He wasn't exactly sure why. It also troubled other people. The motivation of the prisoner was part of it. Why had he killed himself? Beau's mind drifted back to a similar incident the night they'd been overrun. It was all so hazy and surreal. He'd been hit himself that night, and all was confusion in the darkness, yet it came back in different ways in the dream. A play, though, was just a play. Characters could be made to do what the playwright wanted them to do—and *had* to, if the play was to be a success. But this play was different. It was such a part of Beau he sometimes didn't know where the play began and reality left off—or vice versa.

But already people didn't like it—important people. Perhaps the other plays had been flukes—a thought that had frequently worried him. He sipped again from the scotch, then dug out the fixes for the new draft and put them in an envelope, wondering as he did it if it was worth going through all the pain of rejection again.

There was always the *Courier-Democrat* job waiting for him, he thought sourly. Safe, secure, away from all this—back to the womb. But something else was pulling at him, something that had gotten him into this mess in the first place. He hated to quit, it was as simple as that.

Once Beau decided to do something, he found it almost impossible not to see it through. Perseverance had been drilled into him at home, at Singer Academy, at the University, in the Army and later as a reporter for the Washington *Times-Examiner*. No excuses. Get it done. Finish what you start. It was the same with Sheilah and their engagement—or whatever it was. He hated to give up.

The doorbell rang, and he answered without even looking through the peephole, thinking it was the messenger from Toby Burr. Instead, standing in front of him, preposterously dressed in an ice-cream-colored Miami Beach suit, collar open, hair neatly trimmed, was Eric Pacer.

"Hello, Cap'm." Pacer smiled.

"Good God Almighty!" Beau shouted.

Pacer had been living between Florida and the Caribbean islands for nearly six years and, until recently, making a fine living dealing in dope. His hair was shorter than the last time Beau had seen him, but the snaggle-toothed smile hadn't changed and the twinkle in Pacer's blue eyes was brighter than ever.

"Well, c'mon in, you old smuggler." Beau grinned.

"I'm retired from that now, Cap'm—even sold my yacht."

"What kind of a yacht?" Beau asked suspiciously.

"Forty-four-foot sloop. I called her the *Fake,* after that god-awful hill we didn't know was there till we ran into grief."

"No kidding," Beau said. "I was just thinking about all of that."

It had been a strange twist of luck and irony that Pacer had wound up with Beau's outfit in the first place. Beau was a newly commissioned lieutenant on his way to Vietnam when he got a letter from Pacer saying he was coming to Fort Benning to await orders. He had been drafted three months earlier and had finished his basic training. Beau was waiting for his plane when it landed and almost immediately took him off-post for a beer. He learned to his astonishment that Pacer had been trained as a radiotelephone operator. A thought occurred to Beau during their conversation.

"I know it sounds crazy," he said, "but how would you like to go over with my battalion, *if* I can get it arranged?"

Pacer thought about it for a moment, then said, "Well, old buddy, we've done crazier things in our day. Looks like we're all going anyway and it'd be a hell of a lot better to be there with you than with somebody I don't know."

And so Beau managed to have it arranged, after filling out endless forms and finally going to the colonel and pleading his case. The relationship between a line combat officer and his RTO was something between alter ego and master-and-slave. In addition to being Beau's voice and ears to his command and support units, the RTO served as bodyguard and general flunky, pitching and sharing Beau's tent, cooking and sharing his meals, seeing that his gear was in proper order and doing a dozen—or a hundred—other things to help and assist him. In Pacer's case, he was Beau's friend too, as he had been since the days of Singer Academy and the Five Funny Fellows.

Beau ushered Pacer into the apartment and offered him a drink.

"So what in the devil are you doing in New York?" Beau asked.

"Seeing the sights, mostly. Got myself a room at the Mayfair. Just wandering around. Tried to call you a few times but I guess you were out of town."

"I was down home—at the cabin at Still River. I've got a play I'm trying to finish. How long will you be here?"

"Just passing through, Cap'm. I'm actually on my way to Boston to talk to a guy about skippering his sixty-foot charter yacht that gets sailed down to the islands every winter. The pay's good, it's legal and all I've got to do is navigate and sit in the sun."

"And you've really given up the other, huh?"

"Yup. I made a little money. It's in a Swiss bank. Sort of a retirement fund. But that business has changed, believe me; it's different than it was when I got into it. Bunch of very rough people now. The law's breathing down your neck all the time these days and I didn't want to spend the rest of my life in the slammer. In the old days it was kind of fun. But I figured why not quit while you're ahead."

The fact that Pacer had become a dope smuggler didn't bother Beau nearly as much as Pacer's previous occupation just after the war, which, basically, was vagrancy. He had returned with Beau and had promptly gotten himself locked up in a loony bin somewhere out in Ohio, shortly after re-enrolling in graduate school at his college. It turned out that Lucy, his girl, hadn't returned to school that fall. She had gone off to participate in the anti-war movement. "Simply vanished," Pacer had written pathetically, "into thin air, without a word." During the first weeks of school, Pacer had tried to readjust to campus life. He had returned to his fraternity, with the beer swilling and raucous parties, and had tried dating a few girls, but nothing was the same. "Sometimes I feel like a hundred-year-old man," he once wrote. Beau knew precisely how he felt.

One day when Pacer was headed for class, walking across the campus quadrangle and thinking melancholy thoughts about Lucy, some young cadet officer from the ROTC who was drilling cadets had yelled at him to double-time it out of the area. Pacer, good-old-dutiful-meek-and-mild-pre-maturely-balding Pacer, awakened from his reverie, stalked over to the offending cadet officer, grabbed his rifle and nearly brained him to death. Furthermore, he then held an entire company of ROTC men at bay, scream-ing that they were fools, cannon fodder and several names fraught with sexual and scatological references. He was subdued finally by passing mem-bers of an athletic team and taken to the college psychiatric department for observation. Some weeks later, through the intervention of his father, a judge committed Pacer to a state-maintained insane asylum for an indeterminate period of time, so that he did not have to face trial for felonious assault, malicious mayhem, attempted murder and other less serious charges.

They were finishing their drinks when the doorbell rang again. This time it *was* Toby's messenger. Beau gave him the package and shut the door.

"How about some chow? There's a pretty good little French restaurant across the street. It's been a while since I've had any good frog food."

"Sure," Pacer said, and the two of them went out in the twilight.

"There's no way I'm ever going to believe that Tommy killed anybody deliberately," Pacer said. They had been discussing Tommy Brodie and the murder charge and my taking over the newspaper and offering Beau a job.

"I don't either," Beau said. "Even though neither one of us sees him very

73

regularly, I think we've both got a pretty good sense of him, and it's just out of character."

Pacer forked a sautéed mushroom and shook his head. "You think if we went down there we could do anything?"

"I don't know," Beau said. "It all seems pretty strange. I've been away from Bienville for a long time now and so have you. It's changed a hell of a lot, as you know. Used to be my old man knew every cop on the force; now nobody seems to know anybody. And Pappy tells me that old Fletcher Cross has become a big businessman and socialite. That ought to tell you something."

"Cross!" Pacer winced. "You're kidding. All that old bastard ever did was run the fruit stand where fourteen-year-old kids could get a pint of moonshine after hours."

"We were grateful for it at the time," Beau said, laughing.

"Yeah, but how in hell did he become legit?"

"Pappy didn't say he is; he just said he's gotten so important that he's a member of the country club and runs a couple of businesses—including some oil production company."

"Life is strange, ain't it?"

"That it is," Beau said, "that it is."

After dinner they went back to Beau's apartment for a nightcap. Beau poured two large brandies and they talked about old times: about Tommy Brodie and the Five Funny Fellows, about who was where in the Bienville hierarchy now, and then, inevitably, about Vietnam. Their discussion turned to a Christmas Eve fifteen years earlier when they were all dug in on a hillside.

"You remember when the Old Man came down and said we couldn't have the Christmas tree?" Pacer asked.

"I not only remember it, I'm writing about it," Beau said. "As a matter of fact, I'm glad you're here, because I'm having trouble working through a couple of scenes in my new play and I could use a technical adviser."

"Remember the 'CARE package' we all received from that anonymous donor in the States, the one that was a case of dog food with a note saying, 'You act like dogs, you might as well eat like them'?" Beau remembered. Suddenly the anger and the rage and hurt came flooding back, along with Private Reilly's going outside the wire after drinking half a bottle of bourbon and the 2nd Platoon listening post opening up on him. He also vividly remembered the gook they brought in, only a kid, and being in the interrogation tent in the rain, and then all hell breaking loose, the flares going up and the sight of many hundreds of people moving up out of the valley toward them. Beau remembered all of this only in strange fragmented flashes, so many pieces were missing.

"Whatever happened to the 1st Platoon?" Beau asked. "It seems to me they got overrun right away. They didn't stand and fight any time at all, did they?"

"Seemed a little like that to me," Pacer said, "but we were all running around like crazy people. I was living in my helmet then, trying to keep the net open to Battalion. I had a whole life in that helmet—air conditioning, color TV, stereo. Hell, I could have stayed in that helmet and never come out."

"I've tried to recall that night many times but I never can seem to get it straight. Every time it's different."

"Well, you were hit pretty early on. I remember trying to get you to move on back up the hill but you were hollering something that didn't make any sense. Lieutenant Sander was in charge and he said to let you be for a while 'cause he needed to use the radio. Hell, everybody was on the radio that night. Sounded like New Year's Eve in a crazy house. *You* were the craziest of them all. I never thought you were quite right after you shot the gook in the pagoda just after the shit hit the fan."

"Shot the gook?" Beau asked.

"Yeah. The little gook they got that morning, remember? Sergeant Homes and Wilson and that interpreter, Quay, or whatever his name, were all there, and you and I joined 'em—in that pagoda down by the river. You don't remember that?"

"Only a little. I remember something," Beau said anxiously, "but nothing clearly."

"And Sergeant Keith says he thinks the gook's from that Alpha Regiment that's been running around in the valley and he's got the gook standing there at attention in front of him trying to get him to point out their location on a map and he's got a K-bar knife and he's jabbing the gook in the belly with it—in the navel. You don't remember that?"

"Jesus," Beau said softly, feeling his palms turn damp. "Go on."

"Well, then you told Wilson to put a gun to the gook's head and Wilson took out his forty-five and the gook started smiling and nodding and begging and you said, 'Cock the fucking weapon,' and Wilson looked at you funny and you grabbed it and said something like 'This is what I mean,' and you cocked it and grabbed the gook and stuck his face in the map and then, well, I don't know exactly what happened but you shot the bastard in the head. Right in the ear. I knew you had lost it then. Everybody just stood there. And then you walked out of the pagoda and got in the jeep."

"I killed him?" Beau said distantly.

"Deader than a doornail. Wilson and Keith and I threw him in the river. We figured he'd just float downstream somewhere."

"Why?" Beau asked thickly.

" 'Cause we were worried about you. You'd have been in the deep *deep* dung if that news had got out."

"No, why . . . did I shoot him? Why did I kill him?"

Pacer looked at Beau quizzically. "Beats hell out of me, Cap'm. You don't remember?"

"Was it . . . an accident?"

Eric Pacer looked at Beau for a long moment. "I don't know, Cap'm. You just shot him, that's all I saw."

"Me?"

Pacer nodded.

"Just like that?"

"Just like that. Well, we were all feeling low. Sergeant Trewes got it that morning in the little village by the base of the hill. Then there was the mess with the Christmas tree and, well, I think you went a little crazy then."

"More than crazy," Beau mumbled.

"You were upset."

"Did I say anything?"

"When?"

"When I . . . shot him?"

"Not a word. You just walked out and told the driver to take us back to the position. When we got there, you went up to your tent. It was starting to rain pretty badly and we were getting reports from Battalion that there was a lot of activity starting. Lieutenant Wisner's patrol came in and said they observed a big party of gooks moving down the valley. I called into your tent and after a while you came out eating a can of C rats. That's when they started mortaring us and you got hit almost right away."

"Sonofabitch," Beau said. He got up without another word and went into the bathroom. He felt nauseated and sweaty. He ran some cold water and threw it on his face. He was breathing heavily.

When he came out he went into the kitchen, got some ice and made himself a very stiff scotch. He couldn't allow himself to think about this now. Morning would be soon enough. Pacer came in and leaned against a counter. Beau felt disoriented, confused. He had a vague recollection of being in the pagoda. He hazily remembered a young Vietnamese prisoner, but the events of the day were blurred—there had been commotion, shouting, Sergeant Trewes's body had been brought in—his legs blown off by a land mine. But shoot the prisoner? Beau shook his head in disbelief. Why would Pacer bring it up now—so casually? Why would Pacer lie? He thought he remembered the prisoner and the knife. He remembered somebody with a knife . . .

"You okay, Beau?" Pacer asked when he finally came back into the living room. Beau shook his head and sank heavily into a chair. His mind was reeling from drunkenness and from Pacer's awful revelation.

Pacer let himself out. At some point Beau staggered to bed, a fact he was sure of in the morning only because he woke up there.

During the next week, Beau put himself through a purgatory of recrimination and self-doubt. Most of it was about the shooting and his role in it, but inevitably those thoughts led to other things.

The next morning he phoned Pacer at his hotel and made him go over the events of that rainy night on the Fake one more time.

"I'm sorry," Pacer said straight off. "I thought you knew what happened. I didn't have any idea . . ."

"That why you didn't say anything before?"

"Well sure, I mean, it wasn't exactly cocktail party conversation. It happened. It's done. I never had any reason . . ."

"You don't know if it was an accident, then?"

"Could have been. Like I said, I thought you'd gone a little crazy after Sarge got killed. You just grabbed the gun. Maybe you didn't think you'd really squeeze the trigger. That's very possible. I don't know what you were thinking, though."

"And I didn't say anything."

"Not a thing, not then, not after."

"Good God," Beau sighed.

"Look, Cap'm," Pacer said, "that gook would have done the same to either of us and never thought twice about it."

"Maybe so," Beau said, "but to just shoot a man, an unarmed prisoner . . ."

"Listen," Pacer said, "there's no use getting all upset about it. One way or another, he'd probably be dead now anyway. We were ass deep in a war."

"It makes a difference to me."

After that, Beau came under the heel of a vicious depression, the likes of which he had never known before. He drank a lot, and the inevitable lethargy and paranoia caused him to rarely answer the phone or even go outside. He ordered in what he needed and began questioning his ability as a playwright and as a man. In the theater they say you're only as good as your last play—he wondered if that held true for your last woman.

Mornings were the worst.

He had believed that the good life he made for himself would all stay put. He thought he could keep the excitement, energy and high living going forever. He lived close to the edge during those halcyon days but managed to keep his balance. Now he wasn't sure. He saw himself in his forties, unmarried, childless, lonely and frightened in a city that had a reputation for swallowing up its stragglers.

Mornings were the worst.

The anxiety he felt was so encompassing that he didn't know how to treat it except with whiskey. The decisions came closer, receded, returned, faded again, bobbled out of reach, swirled and nettled him. Briefly he considered going to a psychiatrist, but he resisted. There was the apocryphal story of the once famous writer who began seeing a psychiatrist and never wrote again.

Mornings were the worst.

If they were sunny and bright he stayed in bed. He preferred gray, overcast skies. He fought his demons the best he could: he could shower and scan the newspaper over coffee. Soon he began reading everything in the paper, even the little items in the business section. After, there was nothing to do but start to feel the angst. He didn't eat much, and when he did, the food was tasteless and he had to force it down.

Three years earlier he had been on top, had made nearly a quarter of a million dollars, and it looked like it would keep on piling in. But taxes, profligate spending and the failure of his next plays had reduced his bank account and diminished his spirit. The money was gone and nobody was beating down his door to give him more. In fact, he was close to broke.

There were times during this week when he would talk to himself, like a crazy person. He was trying to get his bearings. Toby Burr hadn't called since receiving the revisions for the play and Beau was glad he hadn't. Now that he knew why he hadn't written that scene the way it should have been written in the first place, he wasn't eager to share his newfound knowledge. The sergeant hadn't shot the prisoner and he hadn't shot himself; the goddamn platoon leader was the killer and the goddamn platoon leader was Beau!

The more he turned it in his mind, the farther the play slipped from him. The whole premise was gone to hell now, and Beau knew it. Why in the world had he attempted to write it in the first place? He had always been too close to the story and the characters wouldn't do his bidding because they were too real. He actually dreaded the call from Burr, because he knew he was going to have to tell him he couldn't finish the play. He had to have time, which was already running out, and even time probably wouldn't do it. Mornings were the worst.

And then he came up for air. A person can brood for just so long before there comes a time when he's got to yank up on the stick or crash and burn.

Beau's recovery started with a phone call from Katherine Whittle.

Long before Dan Whittle entered the picture Beau and Katherine had meant something to each other. She had been his first love, and he had something they say you never really get over. Beau had known that Katherine was involved with Whittle, but not how seriously until he saw their wedding announcement in the paper. It made him feel a little peculiar to read that she was marrying, but by then he'd moved to New York. Still, despite his distance from her and Bienville, Dan Whittle kept creeping into his life at odd times. The ignominious "court-martial" incident made Beau feel uncomfortable, but there were other things too. Dan was a little too insincere, too goody-goody, too something—it was hard to get a handle on. As I said earlier, they were really a lot alike and that was possibly part of the problem. By some strange coincidence, Whittle had also known Sheilah some years before, but Beau never really understood what that relationship had been. She didn't talk about it, and Beau didn't ask. For all these reasons and more, Beau resented and disliked Dan Whittle, but until now he hadn't given him much thought. He hadn't set eyes on him in years. He had almost become history—until now. In any case, Whittle and Katherine were married and had children. So when she called, Beau was curious about what she wanted. It was a Saturday and he was finishing up the newspaper and bracing for another bleak day. Out of some impulse he answered the phone for a change.

"I'm so glad I caught you in," Katherine bubbled. "I'm here in New York to do some early Christmas shopping. I thought we might have lunch." Her voice was warm, rich with Southern undertones, but he thought he detected an edge. He became even more intrigued.

"I'd be delighted," Beau said.

"I'm staying at the Sherry Netherland."

"Perfect. It's only a couple of blocks from my apartment. I'll meet you there—at the bar in the restaurant."

"It'll be great to see you again, Beau," Katherine said. "I'm really looking forward to it."

"Me too," he said, wondering how she'd changed.

He had been standing at the bar at the Sherry Netherland for about ten minutes. He had arrived on time, and told the maître d' they'd need a table for two, preferably out of the mainstream.

As he recalled, Katherine could glitter without jewelry, but when she appeared in the door she was wearing a lot of it *and* an expensive fur. He looked at her for what seemed a long time but the only differences he could detect were some wrinkles around the eyes and a more womanly body. He wondered how she would think he'd weathered.

She stopped at the door, looked around theatrically, spotted him and rushed into his arms.

"Ooooooh! Beau!" she cried. He whiffed expensive perfume. She stepped back and looked him up and down. "Just as I thought, you're getting even better-looking. The years have done well by you!"

"And you," he said, a little embarrassed. Heads had turned— Something else that hadn't changed. Katherine inspired attention wherever she went.

The maître d', smiling officiously, led them to a good, private table and took an order for drinks.

Katherine, to Beau's surprise, ordered a martini.

"When did you start on those?" He smiled.

"Oh, just occasionally, to celebrate. I'm celebrating our reunion!" Her eyes glistened. She put her hand on his arm.

"I've followed your career, you know, all this time. We'd get our little gossip items in the paper down home—Suzy and whoever the other ones were. And the article in *Time* and the one in *People*. Everybody's so proud of you—especially Mother and Father. You're their only famous person."

"I am the least well-known famous person I've ever met," he declared modestly. "I don't even have an unlisted phone."

They talked, had lunch, talked more over coffee and Sambuca and then more coffee. At first it was just catching-up talk.

"I have two children. Did you know that?" she said. "Dan III and Tara. Three and five." There was a wistful look in her eyes.

"That's wonderful," he said.

It got late and the sun was setting over Central Park. Theirs was the lone inhabited table in the restaurant now and the last waiter on duty was shuffling impatiently by the kitchen door. Katherine was touching Beau on the arm, saying how much she had enjoyed a teleplay he'd done several years earlier, and she seemed to be getting a little high from the Sambuca, but she had always been a toucher. ("A toucher will touch anybody," a friend had once told Beau. "It doesn't mean anything.")

80

"The girl in your play *Pretending Paradise,*" she asked, "was she supposed to be me? I mean, oh, you know, wasn't she some of me . . . ?"

He smiled. "I wondered when I wrote it if you'd feel that way if you ever saw it. What made you ask?"

She ran her fingers down his arm and touched the top of his hand and held it in hers. "Because when I said . . . Oh, listen to me! I mean, when the *girl* says—what's her name?"

"Joyce."

"When *Joyce* says to him, 'I can't love you until I learn to love myself,' and he laughs and says, 'Ah—but you can never love yourself until you learn to love somebody else,' well, that's what I said to you, and what you said to me —remember, in college? About a month after we met?"

"Art *will* imitate life from time to time," Beau said, smiling.

A tear began to form at the corner of Katherine's eye. It ran slowly down her flawless cheek and she didn't wipe it away.

"Oh, Beau—"

"What's wrong?" He felt an obligation to ask, although he wasn't sure he wanted to know.

"The usual things, I guess. Mostly Dan and me. Some of the love's gone out of our relationship. A slow leak. Now he's fooling around. Sometimes I wonder if I'm really cut out to be a Capitol Hill wife."

"Maybe not," Beau said.

She squeezed his hand. "Do you want to come up to my room and have a drink?" There was that look in her eye. Beau felt like something between a heel and a martyr. He thought momentarily about Sheilah, but his emotions were mixed, as they had been during several dalliances in the past, and the fact that he felt almost no guilt told him something about his deteriorating relationship with her. Later, he would tell me there was something else, a slight but perceptible pleasure in knowing he'd slept with Dan Whittle's wife. It was a feeling he was not proud to have, but he felt it just the same.

"Sure," he said.

Katherine stayed in town for the rest of the weekend and the two of them spent much of it in bed, either at her hotel or in his apartment. He laughed for a change. They ordered smoked salmon and caviar and fresh, raw oysters. It made him forget the other things for a while. He told her all about Tommy Brodie, and that Eric Pacer was here in town, and at one point she asked if it was true he was going to run the Bienville *Courier-Democrat.*

"Now how in the world did that rumor follow me all the way up here?"

"The wife of a congressman has to know who the editor of the most powerful newspaper in his district is going to be," she said.

"Is this what you call 'getting to know'?" he asked curiously.

"In a manner of speaking."

"Suppose it isn't so," he said evasively.

"Is it?"

"I ain't made my mind up yet."

"But you might?"

"I might," he said. "But then, I might not."

"What would make your mind up?" she asked.

"Another whiff of the garbage on those streets out there."

"No, really," she said.

"I'm not kidding." He reached for a cheroot and lit it.

"But it must be exciting here," Katherine said. "All the people and the stores and the restaurants and the theater."

"It's exciting," Beau said, puffing on the cheroot. "But hell, I've done it all. The first few years were incredible, but now it's mostly the same. I've gotten to where I hate all that street noise—simply hate it. Starts at dawn with the garbage trucks and then the taxi horns all day and the fire engines and the police sirens all night. You have to keep your windows shut on the most beautiful days just to think straight. And with all the soot and pollution in the air, the windows get so dirty you can't see out of them. Darkness at noon."

"Well, yours are certainly clean. And you've got a lovely apartment."

"Thanks," he said, "but that one-bedroom flat costs me more than two thousand dollars a month."

"No," she said.

"Yes. And there's all the rest of it too—the hundred-and-fifty-dollar dinners for two, the most excessive taxes in the country and having to put up with surly waiters—all for the privilege of living in a city where nobody really gives a damn about anybody else."

"You sound bitter," Katherine said, sitting up in the bed and putting her head on his shoulder.

"Yeah, maybe I am a little. You know, in New York so much of it isn't who you are but *what* you are. If you've had a good play, everybody's your best friend. If you flop, they won't even look your way."

"Fame's fleeting."

"Don't I know it," Beau said, "and I'm tired of it—both having it and not having it when I should be having it. I'd just like to be unconcerned about it for a change."

"So you're going to go back home and run the *Courier-Democrat?*"

"I didn't say I was. I said I might."

Beau was truly sorry when she began to pack her suitcase on Sunday afternoon.

"I didn't even get to see one play," she said with a pout.

"That would have been reckless. People might have talked. There's an awfully active press corps up here," he said, smiling.

"That is, of course, divinely true."

"You've always had a nice ass," he said as she stood and began to put on her lingerie.

"And you still have that sexy little birthmark on yours."

"You remembered that?" he said. "All the way from college?"

"I remember everything."

"I was afraid of that."

"Of what?" she asked, adjusting her stockings.

"That you've got a long memory. That you'd never forgive me for what happened."

"For what? Oh, no, no, that wasn't what I meant at all. I'd forgotten all about that."

"But back then," he said, "you blamed me, didn't you?"

"Well, of course I did. I didn't know what to do. I was hurt, I was scared. It was . . . awful."

"I know," Beau said. "It's amazing how bad it seemed at the time."

"It was politics, I guess. I didn't really understand that then. It was all just college politics—and look what I've gotten my life into now—everything is politics. Why didn't I learn my lesson? One has to be so careful." She tossed her hair over her shoulder as she stepped into her skirt.

"Yes," Beau muttered, "careful."

"*We* have to be careful," she said.

"I wish you could stay another week."

"And that's all!"

"Any more than that, somebody might get suspicious."

"The somebody to whom you refer is much too busy with affairs of state or affairs of his own to even notice I'm gone."

"I'm going to notice."

"Then I'll just have to come back, won't I?" She smiled and touched his arm—Katherine had always been a toucher.

BOOK TWO

VICISSITUDES IV

Katherine

Winter 1965

College was a turning point in Beau's life. He rejected several small, elite Southern schools in favor of the state university. He'd spent most of his life in the confines of Singer Academy and he wanted his horizons to expand. Everyone, Beau included, expected that he would become a lawyer as his father and grandfather and uncles had done, but by the end of his first year, he knew law was not to be his path. Furthermore, he learned some things about people and power and about himself that radically reshaped the patterns of his future.

To his surprise, Beau found that he was truly a leader, not a follower. He also learned that he possessed an ability to control and even manipulate people; he could make things happen. He also began to grasp something of his own moral significance above and beyond the clashing of good and bad angels he'd encountered in church sermons as a boy.

He approached his first year of freedom with a sense of wonder and awe. The University was an old and hallowed institution in the state, a cluster of one-hundred-and-fifty-year-old brick buildings that evoked the ghosts of wisdom, power and destiny. His first year there was a jumble of contradictions best exemplified by two things: he made the Dean's List and every single date he made for every single football game was broken "for a very good reason."

This last indignity contributed to—or rather detracted from—his overall impression of the female sex and served as a cornerstone of resentment he built onto over the years. Since he started so young, this caused him some trouble in later life. In Bienville, and in the cloistered social set he ran with, such date breaking was unthinkable and any girl who practiced it would have found that "the Mouth" had been put on her. But up at the University, the freshman girls, especially the pretty ones, got such a rush from everyone (one once confided to Beau that she had received more than fifty invitations for dates in one week) that a great many of them began to conduct weird and disagreeable social triage, in which they would accept multiple dates to some social function and at the last minute make up their minds whom to go with. Usually these girls would select upperclassmen from the best fraternities or boys they thought could do them the most good. As Beau sat forlornly with his freshmen cohorts, drinking beer or bourbon in the dark corners of the off-campus bars, while the older fellows danced or necked with their girls, he began to drink from the well of bitterness and disillusion at the conniving nature of women. Naturally, there was a lot of conniving on the part of the men as well, but not being on the receiving end, he didn't see it that way.

Beau did not choose to become a member of a so-called social fraternity, though he was rushed hard by them. His choice to pledge Omicron was probably the first real and conscious decision he had ever made about something that would affect him permanently. It set a pattern that he followed the rest of his life. The fact was that Beau, coming from Bienville society, was *expected* to join a social fraternity—one composed of good-time boys, the sons of the wealthy; the layabouts and dilettantes whose main considerations were getting through the four years of schooling and at the same time seeing how much whiskey they could drink and how many women they could lay (or at least claim to have laid). I am embarrassed to say that I made this latter choice, and did everything in my power to get Beau to join me. I even ridiculed his waverings toward Omicron and snobbishly suggested that it would cause his social standing to suffer. I was a real horse's ass then and I have regretted it to this day, because I think he began to see me in a different light after that. He never said so, but I could feel it.

I think it must have been a difficult decision but in the end Beau chose Omicron, which, if not the "smartest" fraternity socially, was at least the smartest academically. It was composed mostly of a bunch of good solid country boys—the sons of farmers, feed-store operators, farm-implement dealers—who came to the University to get an education and move their lives forward or upward. Beau liked them because they were genuine and decent and different from him in little ways. At first they didn't know what to make of him but in the end everybody got along very well.

Omicron was active politically. In fact, it ran the political machine on campus. College politics might seem trivial until you consider that for many decades practically every congressman, senator, governor, bureau chief, agency head and a helluva lot of lawyers were graduates of the University and practically to a man had been involved in the politics of the Machine, which controlled all the important offices on campus and determined who would be student body president and who would be the editors of the newspaper, the literary magazine, the humor magazine and the yearbook. It was power and it was control and Beau found himself unwittingly embroiled in it during a tumultuous time in Southern history.

By his second year at the University, Beau was swept into the politics of the Machine, not because he particularly wished to be but because he was now assistant editor of the campus literary magazine and the older brothers of Omicron had taken him under their wing.

The Machine met in a small, inconspicuous, octagonal cupola located near the library, which was the shrine of the most coveted and prestigious honor society on campus, the Argyles.

The first time Beau was ushered in he thought it eerie. He almost expected to be confronted by chanting men in robes holding candles; instead he encountered perhaps a dozen of his fellows, squatting beneath a bare light bulb, drinking beer and shooting dice. Coincidentally, it was November 22, 1963, the day John Kennedy was assassinated in Dallas, Texas.

Beau had walked out of French class around noon when someone he didn't know came up and sounded the word: "Did you hear Kennedy's been shot? No one's sure if he'll live!" Back at Omicron they were gathered around the television set when it was announced that the President was dead. There was an air of electricity, uncertainty and even excitement surrounding the event. Kennedy had not been popular at the University because of his stand on segregation, but this was a great tragedy.

Beau needed to talk with someone, so he phoned Katherine Faulk, whom he'd known for years in Bienville but had only recently begun dating. She was weeping, distraught. "Hang on, I'll pick you up in ten minutes," he told her.

She was waiting for him on the steps of her sorority house, staring sadly at the sidewalk. When she got into the car, her eyes were red and her makeup smeared. He drove off with no destination in mind, just away from the school, into the countryside. Katherine alternated between sorrow and ire.

"They killed him! The bastards killed him!"

"Who is 'they'?" Beau asked. All anyone knew was that a lone suspect was being sought.

"They," she spat. "The ones . . . some kind of right-wing group or whatever! They just couldn't let him alone! Oh, I hate it! He was a good man, I just hate it!" She lapsed into tears again.

Beau gripped the wheel tightly and pressed on into the autumn countryside. It was just a few days before Thanksgiving and the cornfields had been cut to stubble and the afternoon was gray and cloudy. They drove to a large, quiet lake about ten miles from campus and got out. On weekends the area would have been crowded with students sitting on blankets, drinking beer and necking, but today it was silent and cold. They walked in a wooded area, not saying much. Beau felt troubled and confused by Katherine's reaction. Not because he didn't feel sadness and anger too, but because he wondered if he felt enough. That this pretty, bright woman could have such genuine, eloquent grief set him to thinking about his relative dispassion under the circumstances. Possibly it was all the things he was used to hearing: "Do you know what the bastard's done now? He's said they got to let 'em in the country club! He's letting the Supreme Court take over the country! They're gonna be going to class with your little sisters—big buck niggers!"—and all that billingsgate; it might have seeped in a little too far. It was late in the afternoon when he took her back to her sorority house. A terrible day for America, but ironically, for Beau it probably made him a better person. It made him sit up and think.

And so there he was at the Argyle shrine, staring at the dice game and listening to the smoking, beer-drinking inner sanctum of the Machine. After a while the members were called to order for their regularly scheduled monthly meeting.

Let's get started," said Roger Fairfax, a law student and an Omicron member; the others got to their feet and sat on the shuttered sills of the eight windows that encircled the little cupola.

"Well, at least we've got Lyndon Johnson in charge now," said a thick, neatly dressed boy who, twenty years later, would be running for governor of the state.

"Why don't you go screw yourself," said Harlan Hanson, another Omicron law student.

"It's the truth," the boy said, a little embarrassed. "I mean, goddamn Lyndon Johnson's not gonna ram any niggers down our . . ."

"For Chrissake, the President of the country's been murdered," Harlan said gruffly.

"And good riddance, I say," said a boy whose father owned a car dealership in a Black Belt town. Beau had an impulse to go over and smash the guy in the nose. He might have done it, too, had he not been a neophyte member.

"All right, all right," Roger Fairfax said. "Let's get this thing going and stop bickering."

Opposite Beau, on the far side of the room, sat Dan Whittle, now a law school senior, and the current president of the student body. He said nothing, but looked cool and casual and detached.

What ensued during the next two hours was an eye opener in Beau's young life. All the various jobs and positions which were available were divided up among the various representatives of the Machine. Sigma Chi, for instance, would get the post of student body president next year. Phi Gamma Delta would have the editor of the yearbook; Alpha Tau Omega would get the student president for the school of arts and sciences—and so on down the line. Beau would be chairman of the literary magazine, which paid a hundred dollars a month.

It was machine politics in its rawest form. These offices required an election, but the fraternities would vote as a block and get the sororities to do the same. Then, by cunning and bribery, they would be able to swing a certain percentage of the "independents"—non-fraternity and non-sorority people—by inviting a select few "leaders" to their fraternity parties and fixing them up with dates, good whiskey and suppers, so that they would go back to their dorms and rout out as many votes as possible for the Machine ticket.

The fraternities comprised only a fraction of the students at the University, but they totally dominated the politics. The independents were unorganized or lethargic or both. It was a classic example of how the many can be controlled by the few. Beau felt repelled by what he had just seen and heard, by the sheer cold smugness of it. But he accepted the system partly because he had no idea how to change it and partly because he was ambitious and wanted to be the editor of the literary magazine.

Nevertheless, the events of the day, the murder of the President, Katherine's sorrowful response to it, the ugly remarks by the young men that night, the calculating specter of machine politics, all had an effect on him. In a very real way, Beau was conducting his own seminar in ethics and even though he did not act then, the seed was planted and he would begin to slowly change in the months to come.

In the autumn of his last year at the University, Beau threw himself into the magazine and his studies and his relationship with Katherine Faulk, which developed the dimensions of a truly wondrous love affair. Katherine was a beauty in every sense, lustrous brown hair, hazel eyes, freckles, a wide, impish grin and long legs. She had spent her first year at Vassar, then family money got a little tight and she transferred to the University. She was not like most of the girls Beau knew. She liked to discuss literature and politics and art, yet she was also funny and lively, a partyer and a drinker. Many of Katherine's fellow students were wary of her because of this, threatened perhaps, but Beau thought she was magical.

He spent the summer before his senior year at the ROTC summer camp at Fort Bragg, North Carolina. He had signed up for the officer's course because he reasoned that if he was drafted to serve his two years, it might as well be as a lieutenant rather than a private. Also, there was no war then, and he'd received promises that he could be stationed in Germany or Paris or Hawaii or any number of exotic places.

While he was away that summer, an embarrassing and mean-spirited incident occurred on the campus. The governor of the state, having once lost an election to a raving racist opponent, publically vowed to place himself in the schoolhouse door to personally turn away any Negro the federal government might try to enroll. U.S. Attorney General Robert Kennedy decided to test this declaration. On a hot August morning, with television cameras rolling and reporters scribbling furiously in their notebooks, a confrontation took place as the governor, true to his word, stood in the doorway of the Admissions Building and refused to admit three black students. Moments after he had his say, the governor glared at the band of U.S. marshals prepared to arrest him and removed himself from the entrance. The blacks went inside and became the first ever to enroll at the University.

When school opened in the fall, there was still heated controversy and talk of riots by some of the students. The student body president, Dan Whittle, wasn't about to risk the political career he envisioned for himself by attempting to calm things down, and so the situation smoldered, and the wild talk continued, and people who had never been heard to use the word began saying "nigger." It looked like things might get out of hand.

Harlan Hanson had decided to get married over the summer and had not returned to law school for the fall semester, so Beau found, much to his surprise and dismay, that *he* was in charge of the Machine. He didn't like politics and he didn't like the Machine, but surely as the coronation of a prince upon the death of the king, he became its leader. Suddenly, he *could* make a difference.

Katherine and Beau discussed the racial situation at length. She was firmly in favor of integration, and while it ran contrary to everything Beau had grown up believing, he agreed that it was inevitable. It was his first encounter with a situation that had wide, long-term ramifications, and he realized that something could easily happen to cast a shadow over the University and, indeed, the whole state. With some misgivings, he became directly involved.

Beau ran an editorial in the magazine's first issue which called for calm, reason and acceptance of the situation. The day after its publication, Beau discovered that someone—or, from the look of it, more than one—had urinated under his door. He received some strange harassing phone calls at Omicron House—dirty names, hang-ups, but nothing more. It was worse for the editor of the student newspaper, who was also calling for restraint. One day he looked out his window to find a cross burning on his lawn.

Beau was hurt most by the reactions of some of his friends. It wasn't that they ribbed him; he could handle that—in fact, he wished they would. Instead, they actually shunned him. The way he saw it, he was simply a wave of reason in a chaotic sea. But the attitude he encountered was strictly "with us or against us," and at Omicron there were rumblings of a meeting to censure Beau, but nothing ever came of it.

It wasn't long after the first editorial that word reached Beau of the governor's unhappiness. He sat on the University's board of trustees and pressure was exerted to quiet Beau down.

"The governor's view," an assistant dean of men explained to Beau, "is that we must accept what has happened but not publicly. Furthermore, the governor feels that a literary magazine is not the proper place for political commentary."

"Well," Beau replied, "if you want my resignation, ask for it. And I'll fight it, and you'll have a real mess on your hands."

"Don't be a fool, Beau." The dean was a young man, not much older than Beau, and he had evidently been chosen to talk to him because there was a certain camaraderie there. "Your whole career is at stake. No matter what you decide to become in this state, people are going to remember what you did, and it'll cause you a lot of unnecessary trouble down the road."

"I don't think I plan to stay in this state," Beau replied, "but if I do, I'll remain proud of what I've done. And you can tell the damned governor that too!"

The "damned" governor was furious over Beau's response and completely unused to disobedience and insolence from some pup of a student—not to mention one from Bienville! He wasn't sure how he was going to do it, but he vowed to get Beau somehow, and he set one of his aides to working on it.

Katherine was Beau's great inspiration and support in all this. Had it not been for her, Beau would have been quietly publishing short stories and poems and nothing more, so it was doubly sad that she had to be the one to suffer because of Beau's actions.

A few weeks later, Beau was called into the office of the head dean, who presented him with a letter signed by the secretary of state, to which were attached several pages from Beau's literary magazine. Sentences, words and paragraphs had been underlined in red and the letter stated that it was the opinion of the legislative committee on Ways and Means that public money should not be spent to finance obscene, vulgar and socially unacceptable material in a magazine partly funded by state taxes. The clippings were mostly short stories Beau had printed, and while the language was not explicit, it did contain such words as "damn," "hell" and "sodomy," and there were one or two sex scenes that would have been permitted in *The Sewanee Review* or *The New Yorker*.

The letter suggested that a proceeding be held to determine whether or not Beau was "a fit person to carry the responsibility of presenting our young people with good literary material." It was also suggested that the legislature itself might conduct further inquiry into the matter.

Dean Hollis rubbed his forehead with his hands and looked distressed.

"Beau, we've got to deal with this somehow. They hold the purse strings, you know."

"These stories are good stories. You know that, if you've read them. I'm just trying to give the students . . ."

"Look, dammit," the dean cut him off, "we've got a tiger by the tail here. We cannot have the governor and the legislature up in arms against us. Don't you realize that! There's a lot at stake here—the whole University, not just your magazine."

Beau silently stared at the dean's tie. He had always stood on principle but this was something he hadn't counted on.

"What I want to do," said the dean, "is see copies of whatever you're going to publish *before* it goes to press. I think it's the only way to head off something that might turn nasty."

"To censor the magazine, you mean," Beau said in a tone of voice he didn't recognize.

"No, just to look at it—and then we can talk."

The dean looked harried and tired. He was a fair man, but Beau was causing him headaches he didn't need.

"I'd like some time to think this over."

The dean nodded. "We'll meet again next Tuesday."

As it turned out, a decision from Beau was not necessary, for something else intervened and set into motion a series of events that were hurtful and, as far as Beau was concerned, catastrophic.

He and Katherine had taken off for a football game in Nashville and Katherine had signed out for the weekend. The rules did not allow women students to enter a man's apartment, day or night, let alone stay there. She had to sign in and out whenever she was going to be away overnight, giving the name, address and phone number of her chaperone. The penalties for violating this were severe, including expulsion.

The affair between Beau and Katherine was both sweet and good. They were college students in love and it was such a pleasure to sneak off together to his apartment and make love for hours, then have supper and study before Katherine had to return to the sorority house. They both thought the rules were foolish, and they knew they were seldom enforced. Had they been, half of the student body would have been found in violation.

Beau's romance with Katherine Faulk gave him an emotional high. There had been other girlfriends, there had been sex, but this was something different. He was in love. Katherine's enjoyment of sex delighted Beau and he could make love to her more often than he would ever have imagined. In those days, before the sexual revolution, people did what they wanted but they were a good bit more discreet.

The day after the ball game, Beau and Katherine began the long drive back to campus. By the time they were near the University, Beau suggested that Katherine stay at his apartment with him since she was already signed out for the weekend.

"But I only signed out for Saturday," she said. "I'm supposed to be back at ten tonight."

"Well, you can call somebody and get them to sign you out for another day, can't you? Just say you're still in Nashville."

"I don't know."

"Oh, c'mon," he said. "I've got something I want to show you." They both began to laugh.

It was well past one in the morning when Beau heard a knock at his door. They had been asleep for hours and he untwisted himself from her to see who it was. Beau's apartment had a little hallway that led to a glass-paned door. As he sleepily wrapped a robe around himself, he saw, to his horror and dismay, that there were two state highway patrolmen on his front porch and that they'd seen him too.

He opened the door a crack, his adrenaline now flowing. "Yes?" he said.

"We're looking for Katherine Faulk," one of the men said. "We heard she might be here."

"Katherine . . . ah, she's, ah, I don't know where she is," Beau stammered.

"She's signed out to some people in Nashville, but someone called up there and they were told you two left early yesterday afternoon."

"Well, ah, we did," Beau said, "but well, we went down to, ah, we stopped off at . . ."

"Listen, son," one of the troopers said, "you mind if we come in and have a look around?"

"Well, ah, no, of course not," Beau said loudly, hoping Katherine would have heard the conversation and hidden. The troopers spotted Katherine's shoes on his living-room floor and her purse on the sofa as soon as they walked in.

"Where is she, son?" the trooper said evenly. "She in there? Why don't you just get her and tell her to come out. We'll wait here."

Beau nodded. He went into the bedroom and there was no Katherine to be found. He shut the door and looked around before he saw her frightened, pathetic face appear from beneath the bed.

"They know you're here," he whispered. "They saw your stuff."

She was trembling as she dressed and she was barely able to speak. Katherine was a strong girl but nobody had to tell her she was in serious trouble. He held her firmly in his arms.

"I'll call you later," she said as she kissed him. With great dignity she walked purposefully into the living room, where the troopers were waiting to escort her into the night.

The next morning Beau received a call at 8 A.M., before he left for class. He was wanted in the dean's office as soon as possible. He called Katherine and she was not in the sorority house. He was sure the dean of women had placed a similar call. Beau knew he was in over his head when he saw the dean's face.

"Well, you've gone a step too far this time. I don't know how much I can help you."

"What, may I ask, have I done wrong?" Beau said testily.

"Hell," said the dean, "couldn't you see that you were going to have to walk the straight and narrow after all the ruckus you've created? The governor and his people were just looking for something like this. Now they've got you!"

"Got me doing what?!" Beau cried. "I was with the girl I love. We were spending the night together. So goddamn what!"

"Don't curse in here!" the dean said sternly. "Let me remind you that you are a student at this school and that there are rules and you can't go around breaking them. This is serious, very serious business. You took that girl to your apartment for the night. She was fraudulently signed . . ."

"For Chrissakes," Beau said, "we're both twenty-one years old. That's the most archaic rule imaginable and everybody else thinks so too."

"You're in trouble, Beau, and I'm afraid your girlfriend is in worse trouble than you."

Katherine tried to call him three or four times before she finally reached him. She had spent the whole morning at the dean of women's office, mostly waiting outside while the dean talked to her parents on the phone and examined statements from the police and the sorority housemother. In the end she was suspended from school for the semester and she was in tears.

"I knew I shouldn't have done it, and you let me!" she cried. "Why, Beau? You knew what could happen!"

Beau could say nothing in his defense. He *had* talked her into it. Why hadn't he had the sense to suspect they might be watching him? He felt terrible.

"What are you going to do?" he asked.

"I've got to go home, I guess, and face Mother and Dad. I don't know what I'm going to do after that. The dean is writing them a letter."

"It'll be all right," he said optimistically. "Don't worry." He did not tell her that he had been put on disciplinary probation for the remainder of the semester and that the literary magazine had been taken from him.

Soon after, things began to fall apart for Beau. His classes held no interest and his methodical, hardworking schedule gave way to late nights of drinking and card playing. He visited Katherine on weekends, but everything was wrong there too. She concealed her feelings, or tried to, and her parents mentioned the incident which got her suspended only once, when Harry Faulk took Beau for a long walk to clear the air. He explained that he and his wife thought the rules and the punishment unfair. They knew how much in love Beau and Katherine were and they hoped all this would quickly lose importance in their lives.

But it wasn't easy for Katherine to forget. She didn't really blame Beau for what happened, not in the sense that she held him totally responsible for it. But she felt, despite herself, that he had somehow let her down; that he hadn't taken care of her. Katherine was big on being taken care of. Like many women then, she considered it her solemn, God-given right to have a man protect her, and it colored her feelings about their relationship.

Once or twice when Beau suggested coming to see her, she made excuses. She was working part-time in a clothing store and often had to work late or a relative was in town. Then one night, a Thursday in January just after final exams, Beau looked on the Omicron bulletin board and saw a message with his name on it: "Gunn, call Katherine after 7 P.M." Posted just beneath it was a note which said: "Willis—call the Cajun in New Orleans. He don't believe his grades."

Beau dialed her number and could tell straight off something was wrong.

"Beau, I don't think it's a good idea for you to come home this weekend," she said. She stopped there, leaving it to him to ask the question.

"All right, why?"

"Well, I just don't. I've been thinking about us, and it's just too much right now, me here, you there and all. I think we should see other people for a while."

"What other people?" he asked.

"Well, just 'other' people. I don't think we should be *going* together is what I'm trying to say." There was a long silence.

"Are you seeing somebody else?"

Another silence. Then she said, "Not exactly. But I've met somebody and I'd like to see him. He's a captain in the Army, stationed at Fort Benning."

"Well," Beau said, "that's outstanding. Go right ahead." And he hung up.

Tearing the phone out of the wall cost Beau forty-five dollars and merely added insult to injury when he finally pulled himself together after two days of hard drinking. Sometimes he'd sit alone in his room and play the guitar and once he spent an afternoon pounding away at the out-of-tune piano the fraternity kept in the house basement for rock-'n'-roll bands. But the music he played was hollow and the tunes sounded awkward and cheerless.

He moved through that last semester like a man floundering in a vat of lard. He financed his drinking and debauchery by fleecing sophomores at the around-the-clock poker games at Omicron House. He dated every good-looking girl he could lay his hands on and avoided the ones he knew he couldn't. He became a sort of one-man terror around school. He drove his car up onto the steps of a sorority house one night when his date didn't come out on time. He would have driven it right through the door if the steps hadn't torn out the muffler and caught the differential. One day, drunk, he ordered up a load of horse manure from a local farmer and had it dumped on the lawn of the office of the dean of men, a nostalgic prank that somehow reminded him of the days of the Five Funny Fellows. He quickly reacquainted himself with a fast-moving social set he hadn't seen in years.

All in all he was having a good time and Katherine was slipping from memory. He had become a guy the girls loved and he was enjoying it. Somewhere beneath this veneer he hurt, but he managed to push the hurt down. He knew that after graduation he would be going on active duty in the Army for two years, so he was determined to go through the motions of a carefree undergrad.

On one level, he knew he was screwing up, and he was well aware that his class cutting and indifference would exact a price later. At the time, however, he couldn't help himself. He didn't really care. In the end, Beau paid for his frivolity dearly. His precious A average was diluted seriously by two F's, two D's and a C in his last semester.

Once, during this period, Tommy Brodie, who was passing through on his way home from a small college in the Midwest, showed up at his apartment. Tommy had changed; he was still overweight, but he had aged and lost a lot of his hair. His eyes were watery and vacant. He and Beau got good and drunk and stayed out late. At one point, he told Tommy about what had happened to him—about getting caught with Katherine in his apartment and how it ruined their relationship.

"It was so *stupid*," Beau said. "I should have known the bastards were out to string me up."

Tommy sighed and looked into his beer. "It's the little mistakes that get you, you know. Like doing something and not thinking about it. A second can screw up your whole life."

Beau touched Tommy's shoulder. "That's way behind you. Won't be long, everybody'll forget about it."

"I don't think so," Tommy said. "But I know I ought to try. But it's hard, you know?"

Beau knew. He had been trying to be kind to Tommy, but even though nobody was going to bring it up to Tommy's face, everywhere he went in Bienville, for the rest of his life, there would be the whispers, the retelling of the story behind his back: *Killed a boy with a knife . . .*

"Yeah, put it behind," Beau said. "Hell, if I were you, Tommy, I'd think about going to Atlanta or someplace. Get the hell out of Bienville for a while. Atlanta's growing like kudzu. A man could do a lot worse than going to Atlanta."

Tommy gulped the last of his beer and motioned for another.

"Yeah—Atlanta's big all right. I don't know. I thought I'd try to get a job at the paper mill in Bienville. I was an accounting major and they're advertising for accounting people."

"Well, if that's what you want . . ." Beau said.

"God, I don't know what I want! I shouldn't go back to Bienville. I ought to go up to Atlanta or Nashville, but something . . . there's just . . ." Tommy began to sob.

"What's wrong, bub?" Beau asked. He patted Tommy's back as he cried into his hands.

"I can't help it. I want to go home. I just want to go *home!*"

Beau kept his hand on Tommy's shoulder for a while, until he composed himself.

"I'm sorry, Beau, you didn't need to hear that. It's something I've got to deal with."

"You will," Beau reassured him. "You've got some time. Just see how it goes."

Tommy wiped his eyes and looked at Beau gratefully. "So what about you? What're you going to do?"

"Me?" Beau said. "Going in the Army, bub. Going to sit on my ass in Garmisch, Germany, and take pretty fräuleins to the Oktoberfest. Might even learn how to snow-ski."

"Hey, that sounds great," Tommy said.

"Yep," Beau said. "Two years in Europe at government expense.

A few weeks later he was caught by surprise. It happened the night of the Military Ball, just a few days before graduation. All of the cadet officers were there and Beau's graduating class was expected to arrive early. As they came through the door, proudly wearing their sabers and braid and dress blue uniforms, expecting to be posted in exotic capitals like Berlin, Tokyo and Paris, a young Regular Army captain greeted them at the door and ushered them into an anteroom. When they were all assembled, the commandant, a full colonel, walked into the room and put them at ease.

"Gentlemen," he said, "I have some good news and some bad news. The good news is for all of you who plan to make a career of the Army. The bad news is for those of you who don't."

The commandant then read from a long telegram he had fished out of his pocket. "From the Department of the Army," he said.

"James, Harold D., reassigned Infantry School, Fort Benning, Georgia.

"Freeman, Roger S., reassigned Infantry School, Fort Benning, Georgia.

"Welkens, Thomas P., reassigned Infantry School, Fort Benning, Georgia."

And when he got to Beau's name, it was the same.

"Gunn, James P., reassigned Infantry School, Fort Benning, Georgia."

"Good Christ!" somebody whispered. "It's the whole damn class."

And so it was, for while these play soldiers had been going through their drills and instruction and dreaming of soft jobs at the Pentagon or cushy duty behind desks in Germany and France, Messrs. Johnson and McNamara and the Joint Chiefs of Staff had been cooking up plans to mobilize some 300,000 men for a little "brushfire" war in Southeast Asia and nothing was more sensible than to take graduating classes of straphangers and turn them into combat officers.

A nervous-looking boy on Beau's right glanced at him and whispered, "I guess this is for real, huh?"

"Yep," Beau said, "seems that way." But what the hell did he care? He'd been living pretty close to the edge anyway.

The City of Success

November 10, 1983

During the week after Katherine's visit with him in New York, Beau's orgy of self-doubt vaporized. There was something about Katherine that helped to ground him—something he'd never felt with Sheilah. Sheilah was more exciting, perhaps, but Katherine radiated goodness, rightness, made him feel anything was possible. He needed someone like that. He realized he hadn't known anyone like that for some time. Her visit brought back a flood of memories and, for a while, he was a prisoner of her charm.

Inevitably, a letter arrived from England and the old creeping infatuation with Sheilah began to infect him again. He realized that until he broke off with her for good—so that he could never go back—whatever relationships he had with other women would always be stained by Sheilah's presence in his mind. He had to deal with her, and soon. He simply wasn't ready yet.

He had spoken with Sheilah on the phone the night after Katherine left. He'd tried her until about six, London time, with no answer, then put through a last call well past midnight in England. By then he'd had four or five scotches.

Sheilah was home, in bed, and not very receptive. Late-night phone calls were one of her peeves.

"I went to Kew Gardens today," she said, "and then to Harrods. It was my day off." She yawned loudly. "Mike took me out to supper."

"Who's Mike?" Beau asked.

"The assistant bureau chief. He's been in Rome, and so I didn't get to meet him till Friday. You remember those guys I met on the Vineyard ferry a few years ago—the ones from Yale?"

"Yep," Beau said darkly. He remembered them. Sheilah had spent nearly the whole hour trip talking to them, leaving Beau sitting in a deck chair alone. It had bothered him then, and he wondered why she was bringing it up now, if not to antagonize him. And what the hell was she doing out to "supper" till nearly 2 A.M.? And why was this bureau chief or whatever he was taking her out on her day off?

"Well," Sheilah continued, "Mike is one of their brothers. It's a small world, huh?"

"Did Mike go to Yale?" Beau asked, trying not to sound sarcastic.

"Yeah," she chirped. "He was on the rowing team, but . . ."

"Did Mike row over to England?"

"Oh *God,*" Sheilah sighed. "You know, you really are childish sometimes."

There was silence between them for a moment. Only the warping and hissing of the transatlantic cable could be heard.

He decided to tell her about Bienville and the *Courier-Democrat.*

"You really aren't serious, are you?" she asked. He thought he might have detected a slight note of panic in her voice. He couldn't be sure.

"I'm serious enough," Beau said. "It's good steady money and it might be something I need right now. New York's getting to me. The play isn't going well. Maybe I need a change."

"But I thought you were going to fix the play."

"I still don't have it right. And we've got trouble with the Kennedy Center people. Looks like they might change their minds."

"What does Toby say?" she asked.

"He's worried."

There was another hissing silence.

"But what about me? What about us?" she demanded. "You know I can't just come down *there.* What about *my* job?"

"I thought about that, of course, Sheilah. And as I said, I really haven't made up my mind yet. But I don't think anything's changed between us since the last time we were together. I want to think it has but I don't."

"So I suppose you don't want to see me again," she said flatly.

Beau hesitated. Now was his chance. He could tear it right now if he wanted.

"It doesn't necessarily mean that, Sheilah. Not at all." He hated himself for saying it, but it *was* the truth. "When are you coming home?" he asked.

"In about a month. I was going to try to make it for Thanksgiving, but I've got a chance to go to Greece with some of the people here. They've rented a villa for the holidays. I just can't pass that up. You're not mad, are you?"

"Is Mike going to be in Greece too?"

"Oh, for God's sake," Sheilah sighed.

"Just asking," Beau said, trying to sound merry. "Well, I guess I'll see you when you get here."

"Yeah," she said. "Next month. Then we'll make some plans."

"Right," he said.

After they hung up, Beau poured another scotch. He tried picking up his guitar and playing it, but discovered his fingers were a little slow on the strings. He returned to the scotch with mixed troubled emotions. In a way, he felt smug over the Mike business. He had jabbed the needle in a few times and figured it had bothered her. He decided she was probably sleeping with Mike. Somehow he didn't mind too much. In a way, it was what made their relationship exciting. Suddenly his thoughts returned to Katherine and the weekend they'd spent together. Somehow he didn't consider that a betrayal, yet of course he knew it was. It troubled him.

He had spent Monday tidying up. He cleared his desk and paid past-due bills. He rearranged his files and answered old correspondence. Finally, Toby Burr phoned and they set up an appointment to discuss the play.

"Beau, I'm going to lay it on the line. There are real problems." They were sitting in Toby's office overlooking the Hudson River. Various theatrical awards were hung on the walls, including three Emmys and a Tony. Toby Burr was no lightweight, and if he said there were problems, he was most likely right.

"When I optioned this play I had high hopes. But I'm running into a lot of negative reaction. Hell, I've gone through Washington, Boston, Toronto, and yesterday I got turned down by the Ahmandson in L.A. What I'd been getting were minor objections, people saying, 'If this or that scene is beefed up, then maybe,' but what I'm feeling now is that they aren't willing to commit. Maybe it's the subject matter. Vietnam's tough. They'd rather have a musical comedy."

"Maybe I could turn it into one," Beau offered sourly.

"Things don't look good," Burr said.

"How about Philadelphia?" Beau was beginning to feel edgy.

"Haven't tried, but I don't think it's going to fly there either. If we want this play to go on, we might just have to go up through the soft underbelly."

104

"Off-Broadway?"

"*Or* even repertory."

"Repertory!" Beau shouted.

"I know, I know." Toby waved him off. "But I don't see any other way. It's not what we wanted, but it's a chance." He got up from behind the desk, walked to the window and turned around.

"Beau, it's a damned good play. It's got some problems, especially that interrogation scene, but I've got faith in it."

Beau nodded solemnly. He was appreciative, but apprehensive too. He'd thought long and hard about telling Toby about Pacer's revelations and about his fear that he'd never be able to get it right. But then, he thought, maybe there was still a chance. Maybe he could rewrite it—someday.

"Tell you what," Toby said. "I want to sleep on everything for a few days."

Beau sighed and stood up.

"By the way, have you done anything more with that scene?"

"No. I've been having new problems with it. I just can't work on it now."

Toby began to say something but Beau cut him off. "Listen, Toby, there's something I've got to tell you—I might be leaving New York."

"Leaving?"

"I've got a job offer. To run a newspaper in Bienville."

"Newspaper? In Bienville?" Toby was uncomprehending. "But what about . . ."

"If I go, everything will hit the back burner," Beau said. "Anyway, I only said I was *thinking* about this—I haven't made up my mind yet." He told Toby about the *Courier-Democrat* and how it might be good to get away for a while. He needed some time doing something different and he needed the money.

Toby listened, then sat down. "Well, I can't tell you what to do, Beau. Or what's best for you. I can only say that I've still got high hopes that somehow —even if we have to open in repertory or maybe Off-Off-Broadway—that this play is going to be big for you. And for what it's worth, I think you are a playwright now—not a newspaperman."

"And I appreciate that," Beau said. "Things have been strange lately. I can't seem to get a handle on where my life is going."

"You need a hit play to put things into the proper perspective."

"Maybe, but what if it's not a hit?"

"Well, it's always a risk; at least you can say you tried."

"I've already tried," Beau said. "You ought to know that. It's just that right now, I don't think I've got the whatever-it-is to fix that goddamn scene.

It might come later. But now, the more I think about it, the worse mess I make of it."

Toby shook his head and pushed his hair back. "Well, keep trying. Whatever you do, don't give it up. I've still got some tricks up my sleeve for this thing."

"Okay, I will," Beau said.

"That scene is what's really hurting us," Toby said. "It's all got to hang together or, in the words of the patriot, we will all hang separately."

"Right," Beau said.

Beau went out into the chilly November afternoon. The sun was depressingly hidden by tall buildings as he walked down Forty-fifth Street toward Broadway and the people along the sidewalks looked distant and hostile. He didn't like this part of town, but it was the hub of the world to which he had decided to belong—the theater.

To his surprise, the conversation with Toby Burr had not brought back his depression. In fact, he felt almost elated; as though a weight had been lifted. He began to realize that by all practical standards the play was now a failure unless some miracle happened, and he knew miracles couldn't be counted on. He was on the verge of a decision about his life and was in one of those nutty, lighthearted moods that bad news can sometimes bring on.

I phoned him early one evening a week later. He sounded tired, but quite cheerful.

"You were going to call me a week ago," I said. "Is this an indication that our friendship means nothing anymore?"

"Oh hell, Pappy, things have been sort of hectic. I know I said I'd give you a decision, but I'll need a little more time—not much, but this is a very big move for me. I have a lot of things to consider."

"How much time?" I asked.

"A week maybe. I don't know."

"Can you tell me which way you're leaning?"

"Yes, but I won't."

I changed the subject to quail shooting and thought I detected a wistful longing in his voice. He asked me about a hunt I'd been on a week before. He wanted to know about the dogs and who else was there and we reminisced about other shoots and the talk was more of shots missed than shots made. Something told me then that he was ready to come home, but I knew he was being pulled the other way too. I had done my own stretch in New York, six months when I was just out of college. I knew the temptations. I knew how glorious it could be: the beautiful women, the restaurants, the bars, the street sights and sounds, the arts. There were always a dozen important things going on, and I remember feeling that if I left for just a day I might miss something. I knew there were temptations in Bienville too, and that they were just as compelling as anything New York had to offer. You just had to be ready to give the other up.

"What's the deal on Tommy Brodie?" he finally asked. I was waiting for him to bring it up. I hadn't. Deliberately.

"We talked to your man Spinker," I said.

"He is not *my* man," Beau said. "I only put you onto him. What's his story?"

"Very cryptic, but interesting. I sent out a young reporter we have. She's only been at the paper a year, but she's probably better than most of the old-timers. I just thought a woman might have a better chance.

"She caught Spinker leaving his shift. He wouldn't talk to her at first, and when he did it was only for a few minutes on the way to his car. But if what he says is true, it might be a break for Tommy, and a hell of a good story too."

"Which is?"

"The dead girl may have been seeing a guy called Ben Grimshaw, the new operations manager of Universal Oil. They are the biggest supplier in these parts for barges, drilling rigs, pipe and so on."

"So?" Beau said.

"It seems that the night the girl was killed, she and Grimshaw were having a drink at a tavern near the docks—one of those Black Hole of Calcutta dives. An eyewitness to this is none other than our man Spinker."

"Oh, so now he's *our* man, is he?"

"Spinker tells my reporter that Grimshaw and the girl were having an argument. He has no idea what about, but they left together. A few hours later, her body is found in a vacant lot about four blocks away from the tavern, knifed in the heart."

"Why didn't Spinker go to the cops?"

"You know these people," I said. "They don't get involved. You told me that yourself."

"So how is Tommy Brodie connected?"

"I still don't know, and nobody's saying. But there are a few more interesting things."

"Such as?"

"Such as Grimshaw is—and was, long before he was made head of operations for Universal Oil—the right-hand man of none other than Fletcher Cross."

"Well," Beau said, "if there were such a thing as guilt by association, then I suppose he'd be guilty as sin."

"And there's something else. A rumor is going round that the district attorney is looking into the affairs of Universal Oil. I've put some people on it. They haven't been able to confirm anything, but something's sure going on. The D.A.'s burning the midnight candle over there; people coming and going at all hours, meetings at ten, eleven at night."

"Knowing those guys," Beau said, "they're probably just running a crooked poker game."

"Maybe so," I said, "but they have invited some interesting guests. My reporter watches them come and go nightly."

"Like who?"

"Like Gordon McWorth."

"No!"

"I thought that would surprise you. He's on the board of Universal Oil." Gordon McWorth had been a partner in Beau's father's law firm years before and I knew Beau had always looked up to him.

"What's he supposed to have done?"

"Nothing, maybe, but the D.A. sure is talking to him in the middle of the night."

"What more do you have?" he asked.

"I'll bet you'll never guess who else is coming and going at these sessions."

"Enlighten me."

"It's our own little representative to the U.S. Congress."

"Dan Whittle?"

"Himself."

From the way Beau sounded, I knew he was interested. I used one final gambit. I had been checking the wire services every day for the New York City weather report. This morning had called for rain, wind and cold. So before we hung up I told him it was seventy-five degrees and sunny.

Beau mulled things over for another week. Every afternoon he would take long walks through the bustling streets, bundled in an overcoat and scarf and an old hound's-tooth cap.

One afternoon he found himself in front of the Plaza. The entrance was teeming with the fur-clad wives of the very rich, shopping for the holidays. He studied the elegant old hotel, lit by the fading winter sun, and his mind harked back fifteen years, to the time when he'd first come to New York. What a neophyte he'd been then. A soldier without an army, a man without a job, without a woman, without a bank account and without the foggiest notion of what would lead him to this same spot a decade and a half later.

VICISSITUDES V

Soldier Brave

Summer 1967

For anyone who goes through a war, the experience becomes a benchmark. So it was for Beau, but only to a degree. His parents' generation marked their time as either before or after *the war;* his grandparents spoke of before or after *the war* too, except that it was World War I; and his great-grandfather, had Beau known him, surely would have divided the events of his life as occurring either before or after the Civil War. But Vietnam was not really that way.

It was never considered to be a real war; for most people it was a terrible curiosity on a nineteen-inch television screen. When Beau left for the fighting, there was virtually no opposition to the war. He was in the first big wave of troops President Johnson sent after expanding the conflict. These infantry divisions were comprised mostly of enlistees who had trained together for many months and there was among them an upbeat, "can do" attitude. The tour of duty was one year and they'd be sent home.

Beau was never a part of the later period of the war, which he figured must have been a nightmare. Oh, he had his problems, but his men became a team and tried to help each other get through a bad time.

Occasionally, in the field, Beau would read a story about people opposing the war or demonstrating against it. Being there himself, it was almost incomprehensible to him that people would do that. In his experience, when a country went to war everybody got behind the effort and supported the troops. Beau did not have time to concern himself with the anti-war move-

110

ment; there were too many other things to worry about at the time. But later, when he arrived back in the States and encountered demonstrators in the flesh, he began to realize that they were the vanguard of something far larger and more significant than he had imagined.

Beau was wounded and hospitalized in Japan for nearly two months. They patched him up pretty good, he thought, and he was actually walking a little after the first three weeks. By the time he was ready to leave he was walking fine with a cane and was sent home on a regular military flight to the big Army terminal at Oakland, California, where he was processed out of the service. On a cool and hazy June morning a few days later, he boarded the military shuttle bus that would take him to San Francisco's International Airport for the last leg of the journey back to Bienville. The bus was filled with ribald young men who, except for their rank, were the same as Beau; men who had seen death, who had suffered, who had endured things beyond their ages and were now certified free to pick up their lives where they'd left off. There was laughter and gaiety aboard the bus.

As they pulled into the access road near the airport, Beau saw a large group of people, several hundred or more, standing in the road. As the bus drew nearer, it slowed and Beau saw that these people were carrying anti-war signs. Some of the men had beards and long hair; many were dressed in odd, often colorful combinations of clothes. The women just looked good to him. Period. These were just about the first American civilians he had seen in a year.

"They've been at this all morning," the bus driver called back. "Nothing to worry about; just freaks and creeps jerking off."

The driver slowed even more, and the crowd parted to let the bus through. As they passed by, the demonstrators began to chant obscenities, shoot clenched fists into the air and bang on the side of the bus. The mood of gaiety the former soldiers had been enjoying subsided and they became quiet, because they were a little nervous, and then angry. Some of them shouted back and made their own obscene gestures through the windows.

Beau felt a panoply of emotions: confusion, anger and even embarrassment. He hadn't a notion as to what any of them might have done wrong to incite this kind of reaction.

When they reached the terminal all they experienced was indifference. No "welcome home," no "thank you"—they might as well have been invisible men. Times had changed.

The first few weeks at home were hard on Beau. He did not want to talk about the war, and after catching up on things that had happened while he was away, there wasn't much left to say. His parents looked a little older, a little more tired than he remembered, but they were sympathetic. They seemed to sense that he needed to be left alone and they didn't fall all over him. His father was especially proud of him, however, and came into his room one day after watching the news.

"You know, Beau, I don't know if we're doing the right thing over there, because it looks like a mess to me. Or maybe we're doing the right thing, but just doing it wrong. Whatever, just remember that *you* did the right thing. And don't let anybody try to take that away from you." His father clapped him on the back, gave him an awkward hug and left, shutting the door behind him.

For a long time, Beau felt awkward as a civilian. He'd lost more than forty pounds, so his clothes didn't fit him anymore. And he wasn't used to the little things, like the times meals were served. He was up at the crack of dawn, hungry, and he got hungry at five in the afternoon but dinner was served at eight. The sound of a backfiring car terrified him and he could not get used to the naked, vulnerable feeling he got from not having a weapon handy.

The war had reached its most pitiless intensity by now. Beau resigned himself to a nightly recitation of the fighting on the television news and accounts in the newspaper and so in this way it remained with him. There were certain lines in his face that had not been there two years before and a slight edge to his voice. His eyes looked darker to him, like someone else's eyes. It was not the eyes, it was their expression. But his spirit remained intact and he was looking toward the future.

Beau was simpler then, easier to know. He was energetic and convinced that he had some talent for writing or editing. He had returned from the Army with official commendations, and he entered the arena of the "real world," as they called it, like a man sailing into a fistfight.

The first thing he did was to write letters to the editors of dozens of magazines and to the editors-in-chief of book publishers in New York seeking a job. He believed his résumé looked impressive enough and thought he stood a good chance. But as the replies began to trickle in, Beau received a rude shock: triumphs made on a battlefield do not translate for people who pay hard cash for hard work. "Not enough experience." "All of our positions are currently filled." "We are not presently hiring." "We are only looking for a seasoned editor at the moment." A couple of the letters suggested that if Beau ever got to New York they would be happy to see him, but they did not offer encouragement beyond that. Thank you but no thank you.

And so the former captain in the United States Army and editor of his college literary magazine found himself assembling metal shelves for a dollar an hour in a factory in Bienville that manufactured tarpaulins and swimming-pool covers, in order to have enough money to put gas in his car and go out and drink beer at night with his friends.

When he came home in the afternoons he would anxiously go through the mail, hoping that the crumbs he had cast upon the waters might have stirred some interest. They had not. Soon he began to scour Bienville for serious work but even his hometown newspaper would not have him. Jobs were scarce. He went to advertising agencies and the few small public relations firms in town. They were nice, but positions were filled. He had managed to save some money from the Army, and he received a small pension because of his disability, but that wasn't going to stretch far.

It was late summer and scorching hot in Bienville when Beau found himself walking down a street after just being turned down by a public relations firm. Disliking himself for even applying for the job, he ducked into a sort of hole-in-the-wall bar to get a cool beer. He was sitting on a stool, sipping and adjusting his eyes to the light, when the door opened and a young woman was silhouetted against the bright sun outside. She stood there for a moment and he could see her figure through her thin cotton dress, but not her face. She called out his name and started toward him. It was Katherine Faulk.

She walked up and gave him an enormous hug. He could smell her, sweet and damp from perspiration. "My God," she cried, "it's you! It really is you! I was in a shop a block away when I saw you walk by, but I was in the middle of buying something and couldn't leave. I decided to walk in this direction and see if I could find you."

They went to a table and Beau ordered two beers and she wanted to know everything that had happened to him "over there." He told her a few things but he really didn't want to talk about it, because he suddenly realized that if he got started he might not stop. She wouldn't understand what the hell he was talking about anyway. How could she? You had to have been there. God help you.

"And you're living here now?" he asked.

"Living at home," she said. "I'm thinking about getting an apartment." That was rare in those days. Proper young women lived at home until they got married. They did not live in apartments.

She asked about his parents and his friends. He filled her in.

"What do you think about Pappy inheriting all that money from his grandmother?" she asked.

"I've been trying to talk him into giving it to me," he said. "I've been telling him how evil and corrupting money can be."

The conversation stayed on a simple, friendly course, but Beau felt strange. Katherine had receded into his past. He had thought about her hourly after they broke up, then daily when he was at Fort Benning and finally less and less. When he was "over there" he didn't have much time to think about anything. Since returning he occasionally had an impulse to call her, but he stifled it. He knew she hadn't married—he would have heard—but something between pride and fear kept him away. He decided now to play it cool, not to give her any hint that he might be interested in starting up again.

"Are you going with anybody now?" he asked. He hated himself.

"Well, actually I am," she said.

He wanted to crawl under the table.

"I'm seeing—well, you remember Dan Whittle, don't you? He's a lawyer now, working in the state legislature."

Beau grunted. He remembered him all right. He'd been "court-martialed" by him. "What happened to the Army captain?" he said sourly.

"He was killed." Katherine didn't flinch. She said it softly.

"I'm sorry," he said. Tough shit, was what he thought. He had seen so much killing and maiming and carnage that mere *news* of it didn't faze him at all.

"What are you doing now?" she asked.

"Trying to find a job."

"Doing what?"

"I really don't know," he said.

He brooded over that statement all evening long. It was true, he didn't know what was going to happen, and if he didn't make it happen, it wouldn't.

For a moment that afternoon Katherine had come back into his life and just as quickly taken herself out of it. Dan Whittle again. Goddamn Dan Whittle.

He went into his room and began assembling copies of his college literary magazine and some articles he'd written and a transcript of his college grades. The next morning at breakfast Beau announced to his parents that he was going to New York City to get himself a damned job!

Beau flew off to New York at the worst possible time, the end of August. Virtually no one was around; they were all up in Connecticut or Vermont or in Europe or in some place called the Hamptons. Only a handful of the people who might have been useful to Beau remained in the city. Those who saw him must have found him a peculiar sight indeed. His Army-cut hair had not grown back yet and his civilian suit was still three sizes too big for him. He must have looked like an extra from *The Grapes of Wrath*. Most assuredly he didn't fit the image of the typical editorial employee of *Time* magazine, because they didn't bother to grant him an audience with any editor but kept him in the personnel department. He was handed an application to fill out and given a brief interview by an Ivy League-looking man no older than himself. The man was smoking a pipe and squinted up at Beau as though he was some unbelievable freak.

"I've been glancing over these clippings of yours," the man said. "They're okay, but they read like college writing."

"They *are* college writing," Beau said testily. "That's where I wrote them."

"Right," the man said. He looked down at the papers again. "But you graduated when? Let's see . . . two years ago, right? So what have you been doing since?" He puffed on the pipe.

"I was in the Army."

"Really?" the man said, searching for Beau's résumé. "Not in Vietnam, I hope."

"Yes," Beau said.

The personnel man located the résumé and scanned it. "Ah, I see, an officer, huh?"

"That's right," Beau said. "It's all down there."

A cloud of smoke floated out of the pipe and the man got up and sat on the edge of his desk. "Look," he said, "your trouble is you don't have any experience. Do you know that we get hundreds of applications a month from people wanting to work for us? But we wouldn't hire the editor of the Harvard *Crimson* if he didn't have a few years' experience behind him on a daily paper. We'll keep your application on file, and if you can land a job and do well, send some clips and maybe we can talk again."

Beau thanked the man and went out into the steaming August afternoon. He had checked into the only hotel he knew in New York, a big place off Eighth Avenue where his mother had taken him when he was a small boy.

The intervening years had not been kind to the hotel; it had become run-down and seedy, but it wasn't expensive and that was what counted. He decided to go for a walk and soon arrived at Central Park South. There were people everywhere, and horse-drawn carriages and the smells and sounds of the city. He had never seen so many pretty girls. Beau sat on a step beneath the statue of a Yankee general and watched the girls. It had been a long time since he'd seen so many pretty American girls.

He sat there for nearly an hour, until the sun was low over the park. Walking back toward his hotel, he passed by the Plaza, with its polished brass railings and snappy doormen and a big picture window through which he could see a bar full of men drinking and laughing.

New York made a big impression on Beau and he made a lot of promises to himself. He told me all about them and about how I should move up there, what with all my money, but I never had the desire. He knew New York was a place he'd like to be. There was vibrance, excitement, energy; this was where it happened, whatever *it* was. Beautiful women, people in limousines, people who changed the world—not, as in Bienville, just people who controlled a town. Beau promised himself he'd live there someday. He also promised himself that he would wear nice clothes and order good wines and fine food and be far enough away from the stupid war to feel clean. He sensed there were great things coming to him in his life, if he could just help them happen. He knew he was the only one who could do it. This in itself was a revelation of sorts for Beau and it had occurred six months earlier during a bivouac in a rice field when, at the end of the day, old Sergeant Trewes had asked him, as they sat on a log eating their evening meal of C rations, just what it was that his parents taught him that was the most important lesson in his life.

Beau had tried to gather his thoughts and in the meantime he asked Trewes what *his* parents had taught him that was so important.

"Well, Lootenant," the crusty old sergeant had said, "I reckon it was that I have to be my own man, that I can't depend on anybody else."

Beau thought about this for a while, sitting on the log, just the two of them in the fading twilight, with the rest of the company bedding down for the night. Finally Beau said, somewhat to his surprise, "You know, Sarge, that's pretty interesting, because my folks—my old man at least—they were just the opposite. All my life I was told . . . well, that I had to be good, and do good, but in the end, it was always that, whatever I wanted, they knew the right people to pull the right strings to get it."

"Uhmp," Trewes said, tossing his coffee dregs on the ground.

"It's true," Beau said. "I never thought about it until now, but it's exactly the opposite of what your folks taught you, isn't it?"

"Yeah, Lootenant, I reckon it is." He spat and smiled his wolfish grin. "But I guess that's why you're an officer and I'm an enlisted man, huh?"

Beau had no answer, but the conversation stayed with him.

He had thought about it then too, but too soon there were other things to be dealt with, including Sergeant Trewes's death.

But now, standing here in the early evening in front of the fabulous Plaza Hotel, watching all the pretty women in office attire walking past on their way home, watching limos disgorge cargoes of beautiful ladies in sequined evening gowns and men in immaculate tuxedos, not just with properly polished black shoes but with shining black *patent-leather* shoes, Beau declared that when he *did* come to New York, it was going to be strictly on his own terms. As with many lives, there were a few surprises in store for Beau Gunn.

Beau stayed in New York a little more than two weeks and returned home seven hundred dollars poorer, which in those days was a tidy sum of money, especially for an unemployed, inexperienced gimp.

Beau's flight back to Bienville got in a little before ten in the morning and there was still a crystalline September dew on the ground as he drove through the town, past the pine-shaded park with its tennis courts and baseball diamonds and football fields. A tiny-mite football game was in progress, the referees looming like strange giants above the nine- and ten-year-olds. Ahead on the winding uphill street that led to his home was a station wagon bound for the countryside. Two bird dogs shivered nervously in the back. The sun was bright, and the sky was blue, a perfect autumn day. In a few hours the opening college football games would begin.

Beau bought a paper on the way home and made some coffee for himself and sat in the empty Saturday-morning living room. There was a story on the front page about a great anti-war demonstration in Washington. Two hundred thousand people had marched on the Pentagon, many of them college students not much younger than himself.

One of the photographs accompanying the story showed a very pretty girl placing a flower in the muzzle of a rifle belonging to a stone-faced soldier guarding the entrance to the building. For a moment Beau thought he recognized her as Lieutenant Whitley's girlfriend—Courtney—Courtney somebody-or-other. Whitley was Beau's executive officer until he was blown in half by a land mine. He had shown Beau some photographs of her once while they were bivouacked on a hillside a month before the company was overrun. She was giving Whitley some trouble and he'd talked about it now and then. Beau studied the picture from a different angle. It didn't really matter much, since Whitley hadn't made it back anyway. But Courtney—Courtney somebody . . ."

He got a cup of coffee and took the paper out onto the glassed-in sun porch. There was an article in the back pages that caught his attention: "Send Vets to Rehabilitation Camps—Congressman Urges." A representative from California who was up for re-election had delivered a speech stating that the Vietnam War was so savage and immoral that soldiers returning from it should be sent to special camps to be reindoctrinated in civilized ways. This

117

way, they would not unleash their brutish personalities on the American public.

He threw the paper across the room and went and packed a kit. He left his parents a note that he was going up to the hunting camp at Still River and he did not know exactly when he would be back. It was the first thing he'd really looked forward to since his return.

He was up at Still River nearly a month and might have stayed longer had he not promised to attend my wedding. He was rejuvenated and he told me he felt better than he had in a long while. He had fished the tangled delta swamps for fresh bass and bream and catfish and caught bait shrimp with a seine net. He shot a duck or two and an occasional rabbit even though they were out of season. He had managed to put on some weight and a number of us remarked on it. He had tried his hand at writing some stories about the war, but they had not gone too well. He decided he was still a little close to it all.

The wedding reception was held across the bay at the Oak Hall Hotel, of Five Funny Fellows fame. It was a large fancy affair with dancing and a buffet dinner and scores of people Beau hadn't seen in a long time. Over the evening he must have been asked a dozen times, "Beau, how are you? Where've you been? We haven't seen you in years." Somehow he thought they might have known. When he told them, they said things like "Oh, I didn't know." It was the indifference that got to him. Tiring of the din and laughter and drinking in the ballroom, Beau wandered outside, across the lush green lawn beneath the sagging live oak trees. He walked out onto a long pier, where he encountered another guest, a kindly-looking man in his sixties with graying hair and warm blue eyes.

"Quite a wedding, don't you think?" the man said, leaning against a rail, nursing a bourbon.

"Yes, it is."

"What do you do?" the man asked.

"I'm retired," Beau said grandly.

"Oh, so young?" The man looked at him curiously.

"Well, I'm recently retired from the Army," Beau replied. "Actually, I'm looking for a job but it's not going so well."

"What do you do?"

"I can write. I can edit. I want to be in that business . . . somewhere."

"Really? You got any experience?"

"Not since college," Beau said. "I keep hearing that I have to have experience, but nobody will give you any experience until you already have some." He told stories about his trip to New York.

"You sure you want to write?"

"Yes, sir," Beau said. "That's what I want to do."

"Well, it's important to know, because any decision you make now is probably going to affect you the rest of your life—things like where you'll live and who you'll marry and what style of life you'll lead. After a few years, things will be pretty much set for you. You probably won't change them. You're looking at the next forty years of your life. Every decision is crucial."

A beacon was flashing somewhere out in the bay and Beau gazed at it for a moment. He thought about his friends, most of whom were pairing off now. Wedding announcements were stacking up on his desk. Doctors, lawyers, employees of banks and brokerage houses. We were setting our courses as young men. In a few years, most of us would be successful, into our second houses and second children and country clubs and the rest of it. We hoarded security like thirsty sailors filling barrels with rain.

"I know," Beau said. "But I'm still going to give it a try."

"Well, I might be able to help you, then. I'm with the Washington *Times-Examiner*. We have a sort of training program to introduce young people to the newspaper business. It's tough, and you have to be good, but no experience is required."

"No kidding?" said Beau.

"Like I say, the pay's lousy, the hours are lousy and you have to fight it out with some pretty sharp competition. But I can tell you how to file an application if you want."

"God, I'd love that. By the way, I'm Beau Gunn." He held out his hand.

"I'm T. Y. Miller," the man said. "That's my niece who got married today."

"You don't say? Well, I'm a friend of . . . her husband's."

T. Y. Miller took out a pen and a slip of paper and wrote his name and address on it. "Drop me a line and I'll have them send you the papers to fill out."

"Thank you very much, Mr. Miller," Beau said gratefully. "I'll do it this week."

"The man you'll be dealing with is Gurk Henderson. He's the city editor. But I'll talk to him. I don't think you'll have any trouble."

"What do you do at the *Examiner?*"

"I'm the editor, son," T. Y. Miller said, downing his drink. "See you inside maybe." He walked away down the wharf.

Beau stood for a moment pondering this stroke of fortune. He must be telling the truth, Beau thought, because he remembered glancing down at T. Y. Miller's feet and noticing he was wearing brown shoes with his tuxedo. Only a newspaperman would do that.

VICISSITUDES VI

Washington:
The Newspaper Business

January 1968

To Beau, Washington was a dazzling, majestic city. He arrived on a winter's night, driving up Interstate 95. As he peaked a hill above the Potomac River, the city was suddenly spread out before him like an immense Oriental fan, its lighted white monuments and Capitol dome and twinkling bridges glowing in holiday style.

He spent the night in a hotel and drove to the *Times-Examiner* building the next morning at eight to report to his new boss, Gurk Henderson. It was the first time Beau had ever been inside a paper's newsroom and his first reaction was astonishment, followed by dismay.

All was chaos: the roar and the yelling and the clatter and the bustle. A hundred typewriters seemed to be going at once and clouds of tobacco smoke appeared to rise over each of them. The room itself was the size of a football field with low ceilings and a bank of windows at one end looking out over a freeway. It was a positively filthy place. Desks and floors were piled with trash: wadded-up copy paper, cigarette butts, plastic coffee cups. People would occasionally get up and walk to a long desk located near the center of the room and deliver sheets of paper. Telephones rang incessantly and a bank of teletype machines clanged away.

Suddenly, someone would desperately holler, "Copy!" and one of a dozen youths roaming the room would rush over and receive a sheet of paper and run it to the main desk. Beau noticed that a few of the people behind the desks were doing no work at all, but were staring blankly out of the window as if in a daze. At least one of them was leaning back in his chair with his hands folded behind his head, sound asleep. Nobody seemed to be in charge of any of this.

Beau took a few timid steps inside the room and saw that to his left was a long bank of perhaps half a dozen glassed-in booths where older and better-dressed men sat at their desks. They, he presumed, were the editors. All of them seemed busy reading something or talking on the phone, except for one rotund man in a bow tie and he seemed almost lonely, looking out through the glass at what was taking place.

A woman came walking down the aisle and Beau stopped her and asked where he might find Gurk Henderson. She sized him up for an instant, then pointed to a slender, balding man in a white shirt who was seated in a leather swivel chair on the opposite side of the main desk in the center of the room. All around him other men were madly ripping up copy paper and pasting it together again and shouting at each other or across the room. Gurk Henderson seemed absolutely detached from all this. Through half-rimmed spectacles he scanned each story as it was delivered and would occasionally nod or say a brief word to each of the other men. Beau walked down the center aisle and approached him tentatively.

He stood there for what seemed to be a long while before Gurk Henderson noticed him. When he did he simply looked up with steely eyes and an expressionless face.

"Mr. Henderson, I'm Beau Gunn. You asked me to arrive today."

Henderson's brow furrowed for a second, then a look of recognition came into his eyes. He motioned Beau toward a bank of chairs against a wall. "In a minute," he said. Already, Beau felt like he had done something wrong.

Nearly an hour later, a hideously loud bell rang and everyone stopped what they were doing. People began to get up and move around and the room quieted down, except for the telephones, which continued to ring. A lady came in with a coffee cart and a lot of people gathered around her. Gurk read a few more pages of something, then got up and went over to Beau.

"Sorry," he said, "we were on edition. It gets hectic. That bell means the presses have started. The edition has closed."

Beau nodded.

"Let's go upstairs and get some coffee."

Gurk was an ex-marine who had been in the Pacific during World War II. The two swapped stories for a while, then he explained Beau's job to him.

"We start you out on the dictation bank. There are five editions a day, and you'll be typing copy when reporters call in their stories to you. After that, or in between, you write obituaries, and maybe there'll be a night assignment every so often. After you've been here a few months, we'll evaluate your work, and if it's good, we'll put you into the individual training program and you'll get assignments like any other reporter. It's a snake pit there on the bank, though. Everybody is trying to knock off everybody else, so watch your step. When we go back down I'll introduce you to Margie. She's the head dictationist. You might as well get started today. By the way, don't call me Mr. Henderson. Call me Gurk."

"Right," Beau said.

Beau's first day on the dictation bank was a near disaster. Margie Wexler was a short, canny, ambitious girl who was responsible for handing out the dictation assignments as well as the obits and night work. She was next in line for the editorial program and did not welcome competition. She showed Beau how to put on the phone headset and where the copy paper was. He had scarcely loosened his tie when she looked at him with a wicked grin and said: "Dictation on Line Three."

The gruff voice on the other end of Line Three was Charlie Watts, one of the best reporters on the staff, and also one of the hardest on a young dictationist. He rattled off his stories at a frantic pace that was almost impossible unless you typed a hundred words a minute. Furthermore, anytime dictationists asked him to repeat a sentence he would yell and curse, which, of course, only served to get them rattled, so they'd make additional mistakes.

The story Charlie Watts was dictating was an important one. They were now on the third edition of the day and the deadline was fast approaching. The copy was a new lead for the banner story that day, involving statements that President Lyndon Johnson had made up in Boston about the resumption of bombing in North Vietnam. Beau's typing was okay; he could hold his own with the machine, but not with Watts. Several times Beau asked him to repeat a sentence and finally Charlie Watts exploded. "Just type it, you idiot, and let the goddamn desk figure it out," he snapped.

Beau, until recently a captain in the U.S. Army and commander of a hundred-and-fifty man combat company, was not accustomed to being spoken to that way. If he could have, he would have crawled into the phone and taken hold of Charlie Watts's neck and made him apologize. But he played the good soldier and closed his eyes and tried to keep up.

He had typed almost a full page when Charlie Watts said, "Okay, that's it —end it," but when Beau glanced down at the paper in the machine he was horrified.

Somehow, at some point, he had gotten his fingers on the wrong keys, just one digit off for touch typing, so that the whole last two-thirds of the story read something like this: Yjr ;sxu ntpem hpg uyhkped obe the hrint.

Beau winced. "Mr. Watts," he said, "I hate to tell you this, but I had my fingers on the wrong keys and I'm afraid you are going to have to give me the last part of that story again."

There was a brief silence, then Charlie Watts barked, "That's your problem, kid—I've got a plane to catch," and he hung up.

Beau was staring at the jargon he had created when he became aware of someone behind him. It was a kindly-looking older man, whom he later came to know as Mr. Colby, the national editor. The man took the copy out of the typewriter and examined it quizzically.

"What is all this?" he asked in disbelief.

"Well," Beau said, "it's Mr. Watts's story. You see, he was reading quickly and my fingers were on the wrong set of keys. Then he hung up and . . ."

"Yes, I can see that," Mr. Colby said. "But what are we going to do about it? This is the new lead!" He sounded almost as though he were about to burst into tears. "It's only four minutes to closing!"

"Well, I guess . . . I don't know," Beau said.

Colby was shaking his head in dismay and looking at the mess of copy paper when Gurk walked up.

"What's wrong here?" he asked.

Colby handed him the paper without comment.

"My God," Henderson said in astonishment. Then he looked down at Beau as though he wanted to strangle him.

"What are we going to do, Gurk?" Colby asked. "T.Y. knows this was coming."

Gurk shot the offending paper back to Beau. "Well, see if you can put your goddamn fingers on the right keys and sort this shit out." He walked away shaking his head in disgust. So Beau sat there with Mr. Colby looking over his shoulder, slowly trying to reconstruct the garbled story as the seconds to deadline ticked away. He knew it would be impossible, and he was right. Once, he glanced over at Margie Wexler and she slyly averted her eyes. The other dictationists smirked at each other. Beau had been initiated into the Big Time.

Beau was not to be outdone by small failures or large mistakes. He learned quickly and did his job well and after a few months Gurk called him in and informed him that he had been selected for the editorial program.

"You'll be working with Tom Bragg," Gurk said. "I wish you luck. You'll need it."

124

The work in the program was considerably less significant than anything an aspiring young journalist might imagine himself doing if he worked on a big-city newspaper. Beau's hours were obscenely unpredictable. Sometimes he had to be in at 6 A.M. and chase stories that had already appeared in the Washington *Post*, the *Times-Examiner*'s main competition. Other times he drew a particularly disagreeable duty called "night police" and was required to report to the pressroom at the police station at ten at night and stay there until six in the morning, listening to the calls on the police radio and ripping off up-to-the-minute teletype reports of crimes.

The feature assignments he got were painfully mundane: a story about a woman who grew a twenty-foot-high sunflower in her backyard, the semiannual centenarian story, the life of a murdered child. The salary, after deductions, was seventy-two dollars a week, and it was nowhere near the White House, or the State Department, or the Paris bureau, but it still beat hell out of taking dictation and writing obits. That's where they had you.

Tom Bragg turned out to be Beau's saving star. A kinder, wiser man could not be found on the paper. Tom had done everything from reporting to editing and he reviewed each of Beau's stories before and after they were handed in. Beau gave the copy for his first story to Tom late one afternoon after the paper had closed for the day. He had slaved over his lengthy report of a seven-hour community group meeting in which everything from transportation to trash was covered.

"Beau," Tom said, peering at him through thick eyeglasses, "I can only tell you this: if your story goes to the morning desk in its present form, they will be . . . distressed."

Two hours later Tom had helped him unravel the mess he had made and the copy was in presentable order. The story appeared the next day on A-1 and Beau took his bows from the other reporters and editors for having produced a page-one story his first day on the job.

With Tom guiding him, Beau's work began to improve and over the months he earned the reputation of a solid reporter. He had only a few weeks to go before the program was over but it was common knowledge that he would pass. A week later Beau was sent on an assignment which nearly cost him his job and soured a particular part of him toward what was then his chosen profession.

He had arrived at the office for the 6 A.M. shift and was having his coffee when one of the junior editors called him over.

"Cops found the body of a woman in a vacant lot near East Capitol Street and Third. Been dead since last night. Here's her home address, so get over there and see what her husband can tell you."

It was standard practice in those days. Someone was murdered and one of the young reporters was sent around to get a few quotes from the family or maybe a new angle for the story. Most of the time the family wouldn't talk, but you still had to try. It made Beau feel like a jerk.

He drove over to the address they had given him, a run-down middle-class neighborhood. He parked and knocked on the door repeatedly. He was about to leave when he saw a man in his mid-fifties coming up the walkway. The man seemed astonished at finding someone at his door that time of the morning.

"Hello, are you Mr. Ritter?" Beau asked respectfully.

"Yes, I'm Ritter." The man stopped for a moment at the bottom of the steps, then walked up.

"Well, I'm here about your wife," Beau said.

"Alma? What about her?" Suddenly, to Beau's dismay, he realized Ritter didn't know yet. He must have had an all-night job, coming in at this hour, and the police had not been able to find him.

"Well, Mr. Ritter, maybe if I could come inside for a minute . . ."

"What's this all about?" Ritter asked.

"If we could just go inside."

Ritter looked at him suspiciously, but he used his keys and unlocked the door. "Alma?" he called out. "Alma?" He disappeared into the back, but returned in less than a minute.

"What is going on?" he demanded.

Beau considered having him call the police. He considered leaving. But, finally, he decided against those alternatives. He took a deep breath.

"Mr. Ritter," he said, "I don't know how to tell you this, or even if I should, but I believe something has happened to your wife."

"What has happened?" Ritter asked, frozen in the doorway.

"I could have the facts wrong, but I believe she's dead."

Ritter said nothing.

"The police found the body of a woman in a lot near the Capitol and identified her as your wife. I guess they couldn't reach you, because they never release the names of victims unless they've notified the next of kin. I guess they fouled up somewhere, and I hate to be the one to bring you . . ."

Ritter's chest suddenly began to heave, as he gulped for air. Beau eased him onto a sofa. "I'll get you some water. Try to take deep, slow breaths." When he returned, Ritter was sitting motionless, staring ahead, tears welling in his eyes.

"I'm sorry," Beau said helplessly. "Is there someone I can call for you?"

"Not right now," he said. "I'll call them later." Beau sensed that Ritter was reluctant to confirm the news by making the call.

"I guess you want to be alone. I'll go now." Beau stood to leave but before he got to the door Ritter stopped him.

"Please don't go just now, stay for a few minutes. She is . . . she was really all I had. We've been married for thirty-six years."

He began to pour out the story of their lives together. They had come from a small town in Ohio during the Depression and lived in a tent for a while outside Arlington, Virginia. He'd gotten a job as a printer and when World War II came along things got a little better. They had no children but they'd bought this house and a car and made a life for themselves until suddenly it had all ended with a bullet from a mugger's pistol.

Beau called the police and stayed with the man for nearly an hour until someone from the police department finally arrived. He felt thoroughly shaken as he left. This was different from his experience with sudden, senseless death in the Army. These people had not expected death. He went into the bathroom as soon as he got back to the office. His face was pale in the mirror and for a moment he thought he was going to be sick. When he walked into the newsroom the editor who had sent him out looked up.

"Any luck?"

"No," Beau said. "The husband hadn't heard."

"What! So what did he say?"

"Well, what the hell do you think he said?" Beau snapped. "His wife had just been murdered. He was in grief."

"Right, did he say anything?" the editor pressed.

"Yeah, he said something. He said a lot of things. Told me their whole life story. I'll write you up some quotes." Beau started for his desk.

"Quotes, hell! This is front-page stuff. How many times do you get to see somebody who's just been told their wife is murdered? I'll get Gurk."

Beau turned on his heels. "It's not a feature story, dammit. Don't you see what's happened? The cops screwed up. I had to tell the man. What he told me is not for publication."

The editor glared at Beau. "I don't believe you, Gunn. You've just stumbled across an A-1 story and you don't even know it."

"I know it," Beau growled. "I'm just not going to write it."

"Well then, you'll damn well sit down and write out something and we'll get somebody else to write it. But this is your job, Gunn. I'm going to tell Gurk." And the editor disappeared inside one of the glass-booth offices.

A few minutes later Gurk stuck his head out of the door. "Beau," he called, and motioned for him to come inside. "What's this I hear? You had to tell the guy about his wife and he opened up to you and you don't want to write about it? Is this what I hear?"

"That's right. I don't think it's fair. The man was in total grief. He was . . ."

"I don't care. You get your ass out there and write a feature for the second edition, and just be thankful it was you and not the *Post* guy who got there first."

Beau looked at Gurk for a long moment. Their eyes locked in a kind of standoff. He could see Gurk's foot patting the floor in measured annoyance, as a downturned, icy smile pressed his lips.

Beau left without a word. He stormed to his desk, ripped out a sheet of copy paper, jammed it into the typewriter and began to write. An hour later he had finished the story. As the desk editor had predicted, it wound up on A-1 set off in a little black box with Beau's byline; Beau asked that the byline be removed for the remaining editions. He never spoke to Gurk about it again and he realized that he could have cost himself the program. He also realized that such tasks came with the territory. They were what Big-Time Journalism was about—get the story, no matter how unfair, mean-spirited or prying you had to be. In the end your superiors and your peers judged you by how many stories you managed to get on A-1, and how well written they were. That was all.

Washington in those days was like a city under siege, both from within and from without. It was months after Martin Luther King's death before the riots cooled down. The crime rate spiraled and there were ugly incidents of people being pulled from their cars and beaten. Demonstrators from every part of America descended on the capital with their plaints: Midwestern farmers who arrived on tractors, anti-war militants, pro-war groups, ecological zealots, women's organizations, union members with some ax to grind, blacks looking for a better deal in life. All staged demonstrations of some kind and each had to be covered. A lot of this work fell to Beau because he was the newest reporter on the staff. He ultimately became known as the "head-count man" because it was necessary somewhere in every story to estimate how many people were in a given crowd.

This chore was maddening. Springtime brought out the most demonstrators and some days he covered seven or eight different demonstrations, dutifully walking along behind the crowd, counting heads and jotting down what the demonstration was about. It was like counting parking-lot spaces. There was one afternoon in particular when he'd hoped to get off early because he had a date. He had covered three demonstrations in the morning

—two about the war, another about women's rights. He had two to cover in the afternoon. He went to one of them, a group of disgruntled Indians, and was scheduled to attend the last, a group of people from California who were protesting the plight of the sea otter.

Instead of going to that demonstration, however, Beau lingered at his desk and wrote a memo to Gurk in which he pleaded that it was a waste of good manpower to cover every demonstration being staged these days. He argued that nothing significant happened and that the police kept an estimate of the number of people involved. Beau could ascertain this information by simply calling the police department's public information office. He finished the memo just as Gurk had a chance to scan the dispatches on the teletype machine. Beau watched him rip a few of them off and return to his chair at the rim of the big front desk. Quickly he made his move. Gurk was staring at a teletype wire from the Associated Press marked URGENT when Beau walked up.

He leaned over his boss's shoulder and supported himself with one hand on the desk.

"Gurk, I want you to think about this," he said cheerfully, handing him the memo.

Gurk looked up and Beau thought he saw some little flash in Gurk's eyes that he didn't like, a kind of maniacal glint that foretold something far worse. Henderson glanced through Beau's memo, then, looking up at him in utter contempt and disgust, pointed to the AP brief, which read:

URGENT. POLICE REPORT A BAND OF DEMONSTRATORS PRO-TESTING TREATMENT OF THE CALIFORNIA SEA OTTER RAM-PAGED DOWN PENNSYLVANIA AVENUE TODAY, THROWING ROCKS AND OTHER DEBRIS AT THE WHITE HOUSE. EIGHT PEO-PLE WERE REPORTED INJURED. MORE TO FOLLOW.

They did not call Gurk Henderson the Smiling Cobra for nothing. As Beau read the wire copy he felt himself break out in a cold sweat; his knees got weak. Gurk did not chew him out. He didn't need to. He knew, and Beau knew, and Beau knew he knew, that Beau was on the shit list again.

"I'll check it out, Gurk," Beau said faintly, feeling Gurk's eyes burning a hole in his back all the way to the door.

The saga of Beau's unfortunate timing got around the newsroom and was told and retold for years to come, embellished by recollections from several reporters who had been standing nearby. They claimed that when Beau hurried away after leaning over Gurk, he had left behind a perfect imprint of his hand, etched in fearful sweat, on Gurk Henderson's desk.

For many weeks Beau labored under Gurk's cloud but he managed to re-establish himself through hard work and perseverance. He was a natural, gifted writer and many of his assignments that might have wound up in the back pages by the truss ads got front-page display because he had a talent for making things interesting.

During this period Beau was rediscovering, to his amazement, that he was quite attractive to women. He had not had much opportunity to really meet women since college. But the sexual revolution had begun and the Washington girls were far more forward than the girls back in Alabama, as well as more plentiful. The government employed thousands upon thousands of secretaries and office workers. And there were students from the various colleges nearby, and professional women, which was a group Beau was not experienced with at all. He had had his share of affairs; most did not last more than a few weeks.

These women were a distinctly different breed from the ones he was used to seeing. Many were smart and complex. Beau had been dating one girl for nearly a month, a feisty redhead named Robin who had come to Washington from Boston to work in a congressman's office. She had a wide variety of opinions about everything from economics to foreign affairs and kept Beau on his intellectual toes. He had begun to feel something for her beyond simple lust.

Their main disagreement was over the war. She was violently opposed to it and she sided with the more militant of the opposition. Whenever she began to sound off, Beau simply kept his mouth shut because he didn't see any common ground on which to discuss the issue.

He had, by this time, decided the war was simply stupid. He had seen so much horror on both sides. He wished they would simply win the war or pull out and get the damned thing over with. But normally he kept quiet, especially about his own role in the fighting. He just wanted to put it behind him and get on with his life.

Robin, however, would not let it rest. The quieter he got, the more adamant she was that they should discuss it. Then one rainy night they and some friends of his had gone out to a French restaurant in Georgetown and Robin had spent the evening talking about the immorality of the war, trying to draw Beau into the conversation. He didn't bite, and it obviously annoyed her.

Afterwards they walked out into the drizzle and were heading for the car, the four of them, when down the street from the opposite direction came a lone and lonely boot-camp Marine recruit. They used to dump them off back then, busloads of teenagers recently inducted and in training down at Quantico or the Marine Barracks. The buses would stop at the edge of Georgetown on Saturday nights and disgorge the bald-shaven recruits, who would try to have a good time until the bus returned to pick them up and take them back to their mean circumstances.

The boy was soaked and miserable-looking, shorn to the skin, walking alone in a strange town. Robin turned as he passed and said, "How many babies did you kill today?"

The boy turned to her, probably thinking she had said something nice; then, realizing what had actually been said to him, he turned and continued walking.

Beau wanted to go after him, but he didn't. It would only make it worse. He drove the other couple home and dropped Robin off at their apartment without a word. He never saw her again.

A week later there was a huge anti-war demonstration in the city— nearly fifty thousand people—and there was a lot of trouble. The police had become weary of being harassed, tired of being called pigs, and they were not particularly gentle with the protesters. Tear gas was thrown, nightsticks were used, rocks and bottles were hurled in response and the whole thing got out of hand. Beau, of course, was on the scene. They had sent him to the courthouse where those arrested were being arraigned. He waited outside while groups of half a dozen were brought in, handcuffed to each other.

In one of the groups Beau noticed a particularly beautiful girl. She was in her early twenties, tall and slender with long auburn hair and sad green eyes. She somehow looked familiar, but Beau couldn't place her. He decided to follow her group into the courtroom.

Before the arraignment judge, a marshal read off their names. When he got to the tall pretty girl he said, "Courtney Case, step forward."

Instantly he knew who she was! Whitley's girl. The girl from the newspaper photograph he'd seen in Bienville. She had stuck a flower down the muzzle of a gun during a demonstration.

"Because it's Saturday," the judge was saying, "I'm going to have to set bail at five hundred dollars apiece, or hold you all over until Monday morning, when you will reappear here and we can get your plea and get you some representation." He nodded to the marshal, who led them through the door to the cellblocks in the basement.

Can you beat that! Beau thought. It's her!

He walked out into the corridor and lit a cheroot, wondering what Whitley might have wanted him to do. He knew Whitley had been hurt by her. He still had the letter Whitley had written her just before he was killed. He had decided against mailing it. But he kept it in a little packet in his desk drawer.

Five hundred dollars, he thought. Where in hell could I come up with that at this time of day? Maybe a hundred. But five hundred? And the banks are closed.

Then he had an idea. He went around to the judge's chambers and knocked.

"Come in," the judge called.

"Sir, my name is Gunn. I'm with the *Times-Examiner.*"

"Yes?" The judge was busy taking off his robe, trying to reach the buttons in the back.

"Ah, can I help you with that, sir?" Beau asked solicitously.

The judge seemed grateful. "Yes, please. My bailiff isn't here today. I've got this duty till five and maybe longer. What can I do for you?"

"There's a girl who was just in your court. She was part of that group you just sent to the cellblock. I know her, and I'd be willing to vouch for her and put up her bail, but I'm afraid five hundred dollars is a little too much for me to scrape together on a Saturday afternoon. I was wondering if you might be willing to reduce her bail to, say, a hundred dollars. I'd take full responsibility . . ."

The judge looked at Beau. "Don't you think it would do her good to spend the weekend in the cooler? Maybe make her think a little more about throwing stuff at the police in this city?"

"Well, sir, it might," Beau said. "But this is kind of a special case." He explained to the judge about Whitley, who had been his executive officer and his close friend, and said that he thought Whitley would have wanted him to do this for her.

The judge weighed his argument. "All right, Gunn," he said finally. "Tell you what I'll do. I'll let her out on her own recognizance. But you'd better see she's here on time Monday."

The judge drew a form out of his desk and began writing on it. When he was finished he gave the paper to Beau and told him where to take it. Beau thanked him and went downstairs to the marshal's office and gave the paper to a man behind a wire cage.

The man studied it for a moment, then said, "All the women have been taken to the Detention Center. They can't keep 'em here overnight. You'll have to go over there."

Beau nodded. It took a while to get to the Detention Center because of police barricades and when he arrived he gave the judge's order to a dour, short-haired woman in uniform.

"Courtney Case, let's see," the woman said, checking a list. "Oh yeah, she was in that bunch they brought in about an hour ago. They're in processing now. You're going to have to wait till they're finished with her—be about half an hour or so."

Beau waited nearly an hour before one of the attendants opened a green metal door. Behind her was one of the saddest sights Beau had ever seen. Courtney's beautiful auburn hair had been shaved down to the scalp and she was dressed in a set of paper pajamalike clothing; her eyes were red from crying.

"You'll have to sign for her over there," the attendant said, indicating a window with another worker behind it. "Her clothes are in the bag she's carrying."

Beau tried to control his rage; he stormed over to the window and signed Courtney's release papers, glaring at the attendant as he led Courtney outside.

"I'm Beau Gunn," he said. "You don't know me, but I was a friend of Jim Whitley's. He was in my company. He told me about you."

Courtney was dazed, almost in shock. Beau got her to his car. "Where are you staying?" he asked.

She tried to say something, but burst into tears and put her hands over her bald head and cringed in the corner, sobbing. He drove them to his apartment, figuring she'd be better off there since she wouldn't have to see anyone.

When they got home he led her into his bedroom. "If you want to shower," he said, "go right in there." He looked in his drawer and found a blue balaclava cap. "You can put this on if you want," he said, shutting the door so she could be alone.

He heard the shower running, then after a while she came out.

"Thank you," Courtney said. She seemed more composed. "I'm sorry. I really didn't get who you are."

Beau explained it to her again and told her he worked for the newspaper. She looked like she was going to cry again when he told her about Whitley, but she was all cried out.

They had sent her to Processing, she said, where she was stripped and roughly searched. Then one of the matrons had said, "They all look like they got lice. We'd better send 'em to Sanitary," and a couple of the attendants had laughed and they had been taken to a room where their body hair was shaven. Next they were sent to a shower room and sprayed with some substance presumably intended to kill body lice. It astonished Beau that people could be so mean-spirited.

He told her how he'd managed to get her out but he didn't think the judge would do anything for the others.

"But you can bet I'm going to write a goddamn story about this and somebody's going to swing for it," he said.

That was the beginning for Courtney and Beau. Their relationship would open a new and troubled world to him; an embittered and disenchanted world, but also a world of sharing and of purpose. He also fell in love for the first time since Katherine.

Courtney was a strange girl. Girl, because she was not yet a woman, though she would reach her majority in a few months. She was passionate and belligerent but, unlike Robin, she did not have a facility for being cruel. She had dropped out of college her sophomore year to devote her time to the anti-war movement. The group she belonged to, the Allied Students Against the War (ASAW,) was headquartered in Washington and had begun principally as a lobbying organization, but as the bombings in North Vietnam continued the ASAW became more and more militant.

Courtney came from a solid middle-class family near Springfield, Massachusetts, where her father worked in an insurance broker's firm. Relations with her parents were deeply strained, because of her refusal to return to school and because she had drifted more and more to the left politically. It sounded to Beau like she used every opportunity to let them know it. Finally, there had been a terrible blowup over the Christmas holidays. After that, it was more or less understood that Courtney had chosen her own life and was no longer welcome to disrupt theirs.

Courtney's world was very different from Beau's. She lived in a kind of town-house commune in Washington—a "crash pad," she called it, with anywhere between half a dozen and a dozen of her associates, male and female, who seemed to sleep with each other freely. Courtney had managed to keep her romances confined to a single boyfriend at a time, although she changed them every so often, the way one airs a mattress. She did not want to go home that first night and Beau suspected it was because she did not want to see her current boyfriend the way she looked. As it turned out, he was wrong.

She wore one of his terry-cloth robes and the balaclava cap to cover her head and they sat and talked for a long time. She had been in love with Whitley before he went away to war and they talked about him at length and also about her. Later, she asked Beau about himself. At one point she opened her purse and carefully lifted out the bottom lining and produced a rolled joint of marijuana.

"Shit, am I glad they didn't find this. I'd be up the creek for sure." It was the first time Beau had seen her smile.

She lit the joint and offered it to him, but he declined in favor of a scotch and soda. He ordered them homemade soup and Reuben sandwiches from a nearby delicatessen. After dinner Courtney lay back on the couch and drifted to sleep. Beau sat finishing his scotch, looking at her face and her lithe body and athletic legs. He got a comforter and a pillow from his bedroom and tucked her in and turned off the lights and went to sleep himself.

The next day was Sunday. Courtney slept in while he put on fresh coffee and bacon and eggs and began to whip up a batter for French toast. She awakened and he heard her get up and go into the bathroom, where he figured she would get the aftershock of seeing her head shaved. It took her a while to come out, but when she did, she looked even more beautiful than she had the night before. She had found an old Navy commander's baseball-style cap that had been hanging in his room: blue wool with gold scrambled eggs on the bill, something he had acquired in a poker game the night before he left Japan. It fit her nicely. She had on her Levi's and had found a clean T-shirt of his to slip into. He admired her slender, long-legged figure, her nice breasts beneath the thin cotton of his shirt.

"Hi," she said in a throaty voice, leaning on the kitchen counter, looking up at him with big sad green eyes.

"Hi yourself, skipper," Beau said cheerily. "Hungry?"

"Getting that way," she said. She noticed that the coffee was perking and went over and turned it down. "Where are the cups?" she asked. Beau pointed to a cabinet and she got out two mugs. "Want some?" she asked. He loved the way she made herself at home. It was nice. Damned nice. Like she belonged.

At breakfast, Beau got his first taste of Courtney's political orientation. The front page of the *Times-Examiner* carried a photo of presidential candidate Richard Nixon.

"Don't you think Nixon's a monster?" Courtney asked.

Beau looked up from his plate, unsure of why he was being asked that question.

"What's he done now?" Beau asked.

"What's he done! What hasn't he done? And, of course, who knows what he's capable of doing," she said matter-of-factly.

"I hear he speaks very highly of you," Beau said casually.

"He's worse than Hitler. He's a shit."

Beau went back to his food, bothered by the outburst. Courtney sounded like so many of the others he had known—completely ideological. He didn't care much for Nixon himself, but he suspected Courtney of being a knee-jerk liberal, which went against his grain.

"Don't you think?"

"No, I don't," he said in between bites.

"Why not? Look at this country!" she persisted.

"Hitler," Beau said, "*was* a monster. He wanted to conquer the world. He annexed every country he could lay his hands on so that the Nazis could rule it. And he made a pretty good attempt at snuffing out an entire race of people, along with anyone else who opposed his policy."

"And what is Nixon going to do in Vietnam?" she demanded. "Kill everybody—right?"

"Nothing like that," Beau said. He hated these conversations, but this time, somehow, he felt he ought to put in his opinion. "How can you compare what Hitler did with Nixon? I don't believe you can seriously suggest there's any policy of genocide over there, can you? I mean, it's a war, and a certain number of people are going to get killed."

"What about Calley?"

"Calley went nuts," Beau said, "and they caught him and he was punished. Do you think Hitler would have punished his concentration camp commanders for killing Jews?"

"What about all the civilian casualties?" she persisted.

"It's a war," Beau said again. "I can tell you, in a war civilians get killed. Look at what we did to Dresden, or they did to London, or in Russia—wherever. Besides, I can't see how you blame Nixon for all of this anyway. He didn't start the damned thing. Kennedy did, then Johnson escalated it. Nixon seems to want to get us out of it!"

"I don't believe it!" she said. "You *like* that bastard."

"I didn't say I liked him. But I don't think you can accuse him of being another Hitler. There are better comparisons."

"Such as?"

"Well, ah, would you believe Mussolini?" he offered. She smiled for the second time. He had her.

Afterward they sat for hours, reading the paper and listening to music on the radio. Beau suggested they go see a movie. *The King of Hearts* was playing at a nearby theater and he figured he'd earn points by taking her to see something with an anti-war theme. She did love it, and when they left the theater she said, "I've got to go back to my place for a while."

He tried to hide his disappointment.

136

"Just for a little while," she said. "I don't have any of my things."

"Oh," Beau said. "Well, I'll take you up there, if you like."

"That's all right, I'll catch a bus. I'll call you later. Oh, I don't have your number."

He gave it to her and she walked down the block. When she reached the corner, she turned and waved. She was so very pretty. His heart felt warm. This had been the best Sunday he could remember. When he got home he began writing the story about the treatment of the demonstrators. He would have to wait until Monday to get official comment, but he knew he had a front-page story in his hands.

VICISSITUDES VII

Mesogenesis

October 1969

Spring in Washington melded into summer and then July and August wilted toward autumn and the beginning of a new decade. President Richard M. Nixon had, after winning a tumultuously close campaign marked by assassination and violence, presided over a nationwide emotional schism that threatened the sanctity of the country's most precious institutions. If ever there was a time for a young journalist to be in Washington, this was it, yet Beau continued to labor on the city staff under the thumb of Gurk Henderson. He became increasingly frustrated at what he felt was a half-assed deployment of his talent and energy. There were times he thought of giving it up and going to law school, or even into the Foreign Service. To assuage his boredom, he had begun writing short stories and one-act plays. He went to the theater and to the movies as often as he could and he kept a journal in which he would note innovative techniques and devices. Beau knew enough to learn. He was storing up for something, and, in the meantime, Courtney made life bearable.

They spent a lot of time together. It was not a sexual relationship at first because Courtney, with her head shaved, did not send out overtures and Beau didn't press the point. But both of them seemed to know it was coming.

In the evenings they went to plays, movies and concerts or just watched television at Beau's. On weekends they would take drives into the Virginia countryside or to the Annapolis waterfront, where they would sit on the seawall and watch the yachts sail through the harbor. Sometimes they would

138

visit the boatyards, where Beau would poke around old worn-down sloops. It was his dream to buy one of them when he got a little cash and put it right. He felt a sailboat would give him a sense of freedom. If everything else in his life went wrong, he could just pull up anchor and sail off into the sunset. It would be his safety valve, his security.

Courtney's spirit captured Beau's heart. It was solid and fair and true to the things she believed in, though she wasn't always sure what those things were. He was also attracted to an aloneness in her, a deep torment or frustration that Beau couldn't seem to lay his finger on. In that way she was perhaps like himself. For both of them it manifested itself at times in resentment and hostility for no apparent reason. Courtney was a rebel without a cause, but she occasionally shook the foundations of what he thought were truths, although she never really succeeded in cracking them. She had neatly divided the world into categories of "us" and "them," and although at first she had difficulty deciding in which category to include him, she eventually began to see Beau as a "them." Once she told him she had never met anyone like him before, which he took as a compliment until he realized that she did not necessarily mean it as one.

Beau was more or less apolitical, although he once described himself as a "Jeffersonian Democrat" just to get someone off his back at a party. He felt it was dangerous that both political parties seemed to believe in their dogma as religion and thus became inflexible, but, all in all, he really didn't give a damn.

Courtney, on the other hand, was quasi-radical, believing in change without having much of a practical solution upon which to base this desire. Opposition was oppressing everyone and had to be brought down. She tried to talk to Beau about it but finally gave up. It was his theory that Courtney would someday find something she wanted to *do* with her life and give up the crusade.

A wonderful bond developed between them anyway. They finally slept together one night after seeing *The Graduate* and having supper at a George-town restaurant known for good food, bad waiters and cheap prices. Over coffee their eyes locked and Beau said, "I'd like to sleep with you tonight." She smiled and said, "Yes, I'd like that too."

They walked to his apartment, arms twisted around each other's waist, excited by what lay ahead. They had a nightcap on the sofa and then found their way to the bed, where they made love.

Courtney was possibly one of the worst cooks Beau had ever encoun-tered, but every Saturday and Sunday morning she would make him breakfast. He did not attempt to involve himself in her efforts, though he dearly wanted to, for among his peeves were eggs with the yolks fried to rubbery firmness and toast burnt black and scaly. Her lone attempt at preparing pancakes left the kitchen looking as though a bomb-disposal squad had failed in its mission. Of course, it did not matter to him. His philosophy, highly refined through his participation in the war, was "don't sweat the small stuff." Courtney's auburn hair had grown back enough so that she no longer looked like a singed owl. Beau found her terrifically sexy and often found himself pinching her on the fanny or necking with her in dark theaters. She loved the attention and would frequently plant herself in his lap and entwine herself around him. Still, their relationship was not without problems.

Courtney began to have difficulty with the conflicting styles of their lives. She was not a hippie, but she did enjoy doing a few drugs with her friends—marijuana, Quaaludes, even some acid. She refrained from these recreational highs around Beau, but life with him was vastly different from what she had experienced over the past two years.

He did not have money, he was not financially comfortable, but he had access to some of the trappings, even in those days. He had friends with big houses in the hunt country and was somewhat plugged into the society set in Washington through old contacts from college and elsewhere. He got invitations to cocktail parties and steeplechase picnics given by preppy young men and women. These affairs were alien and discomforting to Courtney. Before falling in love with Beau, she had never been to a party where people just stood around and drank cocktails. In her group they sat on the floor and drank wine.

Beau figured that when she got used to these parties, she'd like them. Once he invited her to a black-tie dinner dance at a private Washington club. She waffled for nearly two weeks and finally begged off, saying she had to work late that night at the supermarket. It was only afterwards that it dawned on him she had nothing to wear to a party like that.

One Sunday in early fall they went for a walk in Rock Creek Park. The foliage was spectacular and they were following the creek bank near the bridle path toward a large meadow that was part of some private gardens operated with public funds.

"I'm worried about myself," Courtney said casually. "I mean, nothing's wrong in my life, I suppose. But it just doesn't seem to be going anywhere."

"You have plenty of time," he offered.

"It's not that I want a career or anything. It's just that *everything* seems to be wrong. The world is wrong. The country is wrong. I just seem to be living from day to day. Just existing, that's all."

"Well," Beau said from the height of previous experience, "one step at a time."

"I don't even have a home to go to anymore. I miss my parents. I know I brought it on myself, but it's kind of strange, you know?"

"You getting homesick, Courts?" he asked gently.

She bristled. "No, I'm not getting *homesick.* I just mean . . . Oh, skip it."

"Hey, I'm sorry." He put his arm around her shoulder. They were walking closer to the creek now, and the stream burbled gaily on its way to the Potomac River. She looked away for a while, then softened.

"Even you, Beau. I never really feel you know me. Who I am, what I'm doing, what I want. I think you believe I'm just a confused little girl."

"You're a very pretty little girl," he said. It was not the right moment to say it.

"See," she said, moving away from him. "That's what's wrong."

"Look," he said, "did it ever occur to you that maybe *you* don't know what you're all about? What you stand for?"

She turned. "Yes, it has, but I'm working on it. Things have to change, for me and for this country."

"And you're going to do it, right?"

"I'm going to try."

"How? By getting yourself arrested and thrown in jail?"

"If it's necessary."

"How about voting? That's the way to change things, you know. Or don't you believe in democracy?"

"I haven't had the vote until a few months ago, and besides, I don't believe it works."

"Well, why are we here, then? Walking in this park? We're under the Constitution."

"*Some* people have rights. But what about the blacks? What about . . ."

"The blacks have the same rights as we do," he snapped.

"Where? In Alabama? In Georgia? In Tennessee?"

"That's changing," he said sullenly. He knew she had him there.

"How much would they have changed if it hadn't been for Martin Luther King? He didn't mind getting thrown in jail."

There she had him too, but Beau wasn't about to concede, because he thought that if he gave her the point, she would leap for the kill. For a split second his mind tried to imagine what she would say next if he were to agree with her. He couldn't be sure. It was too gray an area. He decided not to chance it. He didn't want to have to defend issues he wasn't sure he believed in. He didn't want to be having this discussion.

"Courts," he said, "we could spend days arguing about this. It's not worth it. We each have our views. Why don't we let it go at that?"

"Because it's important to me." She lit a cigarette. "Sometimes I think you actually believe in the war. Maybe because you fought in it, I don't know. You never talk about it."

"What good does it do to talk about it?" he asked. "It isn't going to stop it. It isn't going to win it or lose it. I was there, for Chrissakes. Don't you think I have an opinion?"

"You've never given me one if you have."

"It's complicated."

"How is it complicated? Either you're for it or you're against it. You can't just *not care!*"

Beau sat down on a large rock beside a little creek pool. He lay down his cane, picked up a pebble and tossed it in. He sat quietly watching the ripples. In the distance a siren wailed. Courtney had taken off her shoes and was cooling her feet in the water about ten feet away. He sighed audibly. He didn't want to get into this. For a moment his mind saw the battle in a place they had called "Happy Valley." He pictured the aftermath: the dormant greenish lumps scattered in the tall brown grass with the pitiless sun baking down on them and the mud-covered survivors of the Crazy Horse Patrol, bloodstained, horror-eyed. The hand of death had swept heavily across the valley that afternoon. They had walked right into it. And had it not been for Carruthers, the giant Negro from Savannah, they might all . . .

"Do you think it's wrong, or don't you? I'd really like to know."

"I *don't* know," he replied quietly.

"Well, what about Whit? He was your friend—my friend. He's dead. Dead!" She spat out the words. "For what!"

"His father asked me the same question," Beau said. "I couldn't answer then and I can't now. I don't know. Whit had a rifle company to look after and he did it the best he could."

"That's not enough!" she cried. "Maybe you can't say what you think about it. Maybe you feel guilty."

"Listen," he snapped, "I don't feel guilty about anything. You don't know what it's like over there. Killing is a part of the day. It's a part of your life. Whether it's you who's doing the killing or somebody you know who's being killed or some gook. Kill and move on, kill and move on, be killed and the company moves on. When you're in it, you don't have time to worry about whether it's right or wrong, you just worry about your ass and the asses of the people you're responsible for. How can you understand that? You've never been in that position."

"But now. What about now? You're here, you're safe!"

"All right. I think it's wrong. I think it's stupid. We should not have become involved. Now we have to find a way to get out of it."

"Stupid. You say it's stupid, but what I'm asking is whether it's morally wrong."

"You cannot argue the morality and the practicality at the same time," he said.

"I'm not asking you to." She paused. "Do you think it's immoral what we're doing over there?"

"Yes, but I've seen what the VC and the North Vietnamese are doing and that's immoral too. I have walked into villages and seen a dozen human heads perched on stakes because the VC decided to teach somebody a lesson. I do not consider that exemplary from a moral standpoint."

"I agree, but what about the women and children we kill when we bomb indiscriminately? Is that moral?"

He was suddenly reminded of Colonel Patch's shrieking statement into a field telephone one day when they were supposed to be calling in an air strike on a small hamlet. "Burn 'em out," the colonel had shouted. And then: "I don't care who's in there! Women and children burn like anybody else."

"Women and children," Beau muttered. Why is it always women and children? In the end he had seen so much killing that it made no difference to him. Women, children, men, dogs, water buffalo. As long as it wasn't you or somebody you knew. He knew he had become hardened somehow. There never seemed to be anybody he could talk to about it. And even if he had had someone, what would he have said?

"You're right," he sighed. "It's immoral. It's all immoral. And now, if you don't mind, I'd like to talk about something else."

This was the turning point in Beau's relationship with Courtney, although neither of them knew it then. He could not answer, with any satisfaction, questions that were turning her life upside down. In ordinary times, perhaps, Courtney would have been in college, looking forward to a career and marriage and children. But here she was, devoting her energies to radical causes at the expense of prosperous security and, to his mind, digging herself further into a mire of ideology. They were different, Courtney and Beau, but he refused to see it. Beau had always believed that if two people loved each other, then nothing as mundane as politics could stand in their way. It was only later, much later, that he would find out he was wrong.

"I want to talk about this now. You *know* it's immoral, so why the hell aren't you doing something about it?" she persisted.

"Because there's nothing I *can* do about it," he replied somberly.

"Yes, there is. You can speak up! You can write about it in the paper. You can show the world you aren't going to stand for something that's immoral."

Beau was looking across the creekbed and into the deep blue sky, as if he could see forever. The conversation saddened and annoyed him. He wanted it to end.

"Well," she said, "what about it?"

"What about what?"

"Are you going to do anything?"

He shook his head. "It ain't my style."

The following month, at Thanksgiving, the Pacer arrived in Washington. Beau found him sitting on his doorstep when he returned from work one afternoon and was astonished by his appearance.

Eric Pacer had never been a good-looking man; he was short and plump and his hair had begun falling out when he was in his late teens. His face was pockmarked and one of his eyes wandered to the left.

But now he had a mop of tangled shoulder-length hair extending mostly from the sides and back of his head. He was wearing some kind of caftan or robe and a pair of worn sandals and a wild string of beads around his neck. When he smiled at Beau his teeth looked gray.

"Good heavens," Beau said, "what happened to you?"

"Guess I wouldn't pass inspection now, would I, Cap'm?"

"I'm no longer in that business," Beau said, embracing him. "Come on in and have a drink."

After the incident on the ROTC field in Ohio, Eric had remained under psychiatric observation for more than a year before being released. He immediately set out to find Lucy, who had vanished thoroughly into what was then known as the "counterculture"; even her parents had no idea where she was. Pacer began hanging around with the freaks and hippies, hoping for some clue, and gradually he began to enjoy their lifestyle. He wasn't particularly anti-war, but he was turned on by the drugs and the laissez-faire attitude which governed their lives. He bought an old van and drove it across the country and back looking for Lucy. He was now on his way up to New York, because he'd heard there was a girl named Lucy working in one of the protest group offices there.

When Courtney arrived at Beau's they all went to the grocery store and bought some spareribs and two large bottles of wine. They barbecued the ribs on a little charcoal grill on the steps of Beau's apartment and Pacer found a kindred spirit in Courtney.

She was warmly comfortable with Pacer, more so, Beau thought, than with himself. They talked a strange language that excluded Beau and was punctuated with phrases like "far out." He understood the words, but not the fullness of their meaning. Eric had met some people Courtney knew in California and the two of them had a hell of a good time telling stories and drinking the wine and hashing over things. After a while they lit up a joint. Beau abstained, switching to scotch, but, whatever the method, they were all blown away by the end of the evening. The dark Georgetown streets resounded with their laughter.

The next night they went to see a movie, a mildly anti-war film made in Sweden called *Elvira Madigan*. With all its slow-motion shots of blond girls running across open fields, it seemed to Beau, as he remarked later, "more like a two-hour Clairol commercial." But Pacer was so caught up in the photography that he spent the entire next day inside the theater, hiding in the balcony between shows, smoking grass and taking pictures of scenes from the movie with his camera.

Pacer stayed for nearly two weeks. For the first few nights he slept at Beau's on the couch; then Courtney suggested he could use her room in the commune house. It was good having Pacer around; he provided a sort of Puckish relief and eased the tension between Courtney and Beau. She seemed to feel more relaxed with the Pacer around. When he left, things really began to go sour.

During the winter and early spring, Courtney grew more and more distant from Beau. She spent days with her own friends and only stayed with him on weekends. He was at fault, to some degree, he decided later, for he was intolerant of her views and insensitive to her feelings. She began to feel somehow inferior around him and the gap between them seemed greater, suddenly, than he had realized.

Courtney had a very open and, to Beau, disturbing attitude about sex. Sometimes she talked blatantly about wanting to make love to somebody she knew or had met. It hurt his feelings. Once, at a party, she even asked Beau if he didn't think that a certain girl there would be good in bed. It was unsettling.

Whatever the reasons, he began to realize that Courtney was drifting away from him. He wondered what she did on the nights when she stayed at the commune. He didn't feel he had any right to ask and that was part of the problem too. They had arguments and Beau sometimes responded unfairly.

Having grown up with a father who could not bear to lose an argument, Beau found himself occasionally slipping into the same pattern.

Courtney began to spend a lot of her spare time working at the office of the ASAW. She seemed to be getting angrier about the politics of the war, and since Beau could not share this anger, they found themselves with less and less to talk about. One day in April she announced she was going to Boston for a large demonstration at Harvard. When Beau came home the next evening, he found that she had removed all of her belongings from his apartment: sneakers that had been left in his closet for months, birth-control pills from the medicine chest, a hairbrush, a cotton bathrobe. On his desk was a large gift-wrapped package in which, when he opened it, he found a new shirt in his size, a pack of the cheroots he smoked, a photograph of them that Pacer had taken and a Zippo cigarette lighter upon which was inscribed: "To Beau, from Courtney—always."

Beau was heartsick, although it took him several days to discover it. At first, and characteristically, his reaction was one of anger. When the weekend came, he realized how much he truly missed her. He even missed the fights. Perhaps, if he had tried harder, had been more patient . . . He considered going to Boston to find her and persuade her to come back. But he knew better. Courtney had a mind of her own. She had been planning this for a while. The engraving on the lighter must have taken several weeks. Besides, his pride was involved. It was *she* who had left *him* and Beau Gunn did not beg. His emotions vacillated between anger and longing, but as weeks passed he grew accustomed to her absence.

Then one day about two months later, Beau was reading the wire clips and came across a small story in a United Press wire out of Boston. THREE KILLED IN HIT-AND-RUN, the headline said.

> Three anti-war protesters died this morning when
> the driver of a hit-and-run car veered into a group
> of demonstrators near Harvard Yard.

The story went on to say that several of the other demonstrators were injured and that the driver of the car had apparently swerved into them intentionally. At the bottom of the story the names of the dead were listed. Last on the list was "Courtney Case, 21, of Springfield, Mass."

Beau stared at the wire copy, his eyes riveted on Courtney's name. He felt angry and sad: he could not believe she was dead and, finally, he felt very empty—all the old feelings from the war. Tears welled in his eyes, but he didn't cry. Gurk was sitting at his desk when Beau handed him the wire copy.

"I'd like to do an obit on this girl. I knew her. Very well."

Gurk looked at the wire copy again and furrowed his brow.

"Yeah, okay," he said, going back to his editing.

Beau went to his desk and put a piece of copy paper in his typewriter. He wrote: "Courtney Case, 21, of Springfield, Mass., died yesterday after being struck by a hit-and-run vehicle in Boston."

He stared at the page, his hands still trembling on the keys. Half an hour later he was still sitting there, but no more words had come. He ripped the page from the machine and threw it in the trash and stormed out of the office to find the nearest bar. He knew they'd never print the obit anyway. They didn't run obits on people out of the area unless they were very well known.

During the next year Beau threw himself into a carnival of work and hard play. In those days drinking was something of a ritual at the *Times-Examiner,* as it probably was at most newspapers. Once someone posted on the bulletin board an actuarial table from an insurance company showing the mortality rate for various professions. To the surprise of none of them, journalists were at the top of the list. Probably half the desks contained a bottle of whiskey. A particular group of mischief-makers known as the "Wallwalkers" occupied the left side of the room in the back, and Beau's seat was on the fringe: close enough to be friendly but not close enough to actually belong. There was Billy Dash and Charlie Swanson and Tim Hendricks and Tommy Strong, to name a few. For years they held a daily luncheon at a seedy little restaurant not far from the office and would occasionally get so plastered that they could barely return to the office to finish their work for the day. When this happened, they would have to support themselves by walking the length of the newsroom with a shoulder rubbing the hospital-green wall that ran along the main aisle. Their heads often lolled against the wall at these times, leaving a kind of arty series of hair-stain streaks that became the trademark of the Wallwalkers.

In no other business would this degree of drunkenness have been tolerated, but somehow the Wallwalkers were among the finest writers of journalism in the world. Beau fell in with them. He did not become a Wallwalker— though one or two afternoons he came perilously close—but he enjoyed their company. These were old and serious alcoholics who would down six to ten martinis over lunch. All were bright and charming and animated and amusing when the lunch began, and Beau was fascinated by their stories. As the afternoon wore on, of course, the various disappointing personalities began to appear. Around 3 P.M., after several hours of drinking, they would weave back to the office and begin to write stories for the next day. Beau, at twenty-eight, would usually drink a few beers with them and was in far better shape than they, but occasionally, on Fridays, he would lapse into the martini syndrome and wind up useless for the rest of the day.

Once, after a particularly long lunch, the Wallwalkers went to a local wine-and-cheese shop and purchased the smelliest brand of Limburger sold. They secretly taped a large piece of it to the top of Gurk Henderson's desk drawer. On another occasion, after some hard boozing, they all decided to drive up to Baltimore to see a strip show. On the interstate they passed a huge apartment building in flames, a column of black smoke billowing into the air above it. Nobody in the car said anything until Billy Dash nudged Tim Hendricks. "Tim, did you see anything?" "Nope," Hendricks replied. "I didn't see anything either," Swanson said. "You see anything, Beau?"

"Not a thing."

They all smiled knowingly and continued on their way.

During this period, Beau began to move up rapidly at the *Times-Examiner*. His first "beat" was the local courthouse, then the federal courts, then the Justice Department for a while. There was seldom a day he did not have a front-page byline. He had begun writing a weekly column which appeared on Saturdays. His social life was erratic but it didn't matter. For a while he went out with a gorgeous but dull woman named Sandy who had been a *Playboy* centerfold two years earlier. He dated a socialite named Carol and a lawyer named Jill. On fall weekends he would go fishing in the Virginia mountains or hunting. He sailed whenever he could with friends who kept boats. He attended lots of cocktail parties and played golf at the Chevy Chase Club. Life did not seem particularly satisfying, but for some reason Beau didn't believe he was really living it; instead, he saw himself avoiding it by a variety of tactics—including the activities he engaged in. He had begun work on another short play, a one-act, which he had titled *Such a Pretty Girl*. It was loosely based on Courtney. He tore up the first draft and began rewriting it as a full-fledged multi-act play, but he had no idea of what he was going to do with it.

Then, in the summer of 1972, an event occurred which would have a considerable influence on his life. On a Saturday morning, the paper received word that the Democratic National Committee offices at the Watergate complex had been burglarized and half a dozen men apprehended.

It seem like a trivial thing at first. They didn't even bother to call Beau in for the arraignment of the suspects, but on Monday the Washington *Post* reported that an address book found on the person of one of the men contained a telephone number for a White House office. Beau got onto the story and there was a brief flurry of revelations as it became known that one of the burglars was a former CIA officer and another was employed by the office of an adviser to President Nixon. Still, everything died down for a month or so until a couple of enterprising reporters for the *Post* broke the news that linked the burglary with higher and higher officials and attempted to tie the affair together with a whole series of dirty tricks played by the Republicans upon the Democrats. The sources for these stories went unnamed, but at least some of what was reported was verifiable. Suddenly, the stories began coming at an alarming rate, at least to the editors of the *Times-Examiner*. The Watergate affair, as it had been branded, was becoming a major scandal and they were being scooped.

A decision was made to assemble a team of *Times-Examiner* reporters to compete with the *Post*. Beau was among those selected. He knew his way around the courts and the prosecutor's office, but he was skeptical about the validity of the *Post*'s stories.

The team met every afternoon in a glass-enclosed office belonging to one of the managing editors assigned to the story. There each would report what he had found out and they would attempt to make sense of it. At one meeting, the discussion centered on a report by the *Post* that the U.S. Attorney General had been implicated in the incident.

"Look," Beau said, "I've been chasing these stories for over a month now and all I run into are dead ends. Who are we dealing with over there? Carl Bernstein and Bob Woodward. I have known them since I was covering stories about the women who sell poppies on Veterans Day. They are hype artists. Their *source* is probably a disreputable, disgruntled Democrat."

Gurk Henderson puffed on his pipe. "Well, there is a certain amount of that kind of sentiment here. But we do know that at least some of what they're saying is confirmed."

"And a lot isn't. I think they're being irresponsible," Beau offered. "I mean, look at the Haldeman business. I think we're chasing wind. It's embarrassing. I've spoken with the Attorney General myself, and he's assured me this is a load of horseshit."

"Do you believe him?" Gurk asked.

"Over Bernstein and Woodward? Absolutely."

To say that Beau was wrong about the *Post*'s Watergate revelations would be, of course, a gross understatement. Partially because of his assurances, the *Times-Examiner* team was reduced in size and budget. The rest is history. The *Post* won a Pulitzer Prize and the *Times-Examiner* had egg on its face. Had he been working for the *Post*, Beau would have been fired or sent to cover ladies' auxiliary tea parties in the suburbs, but the *Times-Examiner* was a family-owned newspaper and family was family, so instead of demoting him, they gave him a better job. At least that was how he saw it.

T. Y. Miller himself asked to see Beau, who fully expected at least a dressing-down. Instead, he received the following speech:

"Beau, I know from talking with Gurk that you were opposed to the idea that there was anything to Watergate. Now, I hired you, and I've watched you with pride over the years. You have good style, you tell an interesting story, but somehow you just . . . simply . . . blew . . . it." He let those last words drag out.

"I don't like the 'heads must roll' approach. If your head rolls, other heads must also. I don't blame you for our missing—or misapprehending—the story. But I do think that you could be put to better use elsewhere at the paper."

This is it, Beau thought. Here's where he tells me I'm going to be covering the County Sewer Commission in Upper Marlboro.

"I've observed that you're very good on feature stories. You can combine human tales with a sort of homespun philosophy and it works," T. Y. continued.

Christ, he's going to put me back on the watermelon beat. Beau began to quietly panic. I will be covering the hundred-year-old-man stories.

"So I've decided you'll be given your own column, three days a week. You may write about anything of interest. You'll be given a travel budget and the salary puts you at the top of the pay scale under the union contract. I think you'll be more comfortable with this job, and better situated to do what you do best. Good luck."

Beau was stunned. He could not have wished for a better assignment.

The column was perfect for him. In time he became a minor personality in Washington. Invitations poured in. He discovered that he had gained a certain amount of power and that his *opinion* was now worth something. He wrote about poor local people done in by federal red tape. He wrote about presidential dinners at the White House. He went to Northern Ireland and reported on the troubles there. He wrote about a hog farmer in Southern Virginia who was squeezed by the recession. This experience gave him insight into his private writing too. He began to be able to employ adjectives, adverbs, similes and metaphors in his reporting; he began to marshal his thoughts philosophically—all while writing for a *newspaper*.

One evening he was attending a cocktail party at the home of a lobbyist who was known for assembling politicians and beautiful women in the same room. Beau noticed a tall, voluptuous blonde, wearing white slacks and a blue sweater, talking with Bienville's congressman, Dan Whittle. Beau was instantly reminded of the "unpleasant incident" back at Singer Academy, and wondered what had become of the affair Katherine and he were having way back when. This evening, it was neither the Honor Council episode nor Katherine Faulk that concerned Beau; he was interested in meeting the tall, good-looking blonde.

For half an hour Beau kept glancing in her direction, trying to figure out how to get over there to meet her without looking too obvious. A couple of times she seemed to be returning his glances. He had gone back to the bar and was waiting in line for a drink when he felt someone beside him. When he turned, he came face to face with his future.

"Hi," she chirped, extending her hand, "you're J. P. Gunn, aren't you? Don't you do the column for the *Times-Examiner?*"

"That's me," he said, "but they call me Beau."

"I'm Sheilah Price. I like your writing."

Beau warmed to this advance.

Revelations

The last of autumn's leaves cluttered the brick-walled garden beneath Beau's window and a chilling northeast wind swirled them around in dervishlike circles. In the distance he could see the bare branches of trees in Central Park. Winter was coming to New York City.

Sheilah had been on his mind most of the morning; perplexing him, gnawing at the backside of his thoughts—at what he called his "lizard brain" —that part of us that does not reason, but simply reacts. Beau was reacting to a vision of Sheilah naked in bed, and memories of her naughty, unabashed lovemaking—the absolute abandon she released in the game of sex.

But in the light of even this dismal day, Beau's rational powers battled these feelings, and he resolved again that he must break it off completely with her, fix it so there'd be no going back and then get on with the rest of his life. It had been nearly five years since they'd met—hard to believe. He wondered how he could have gotten so involved with a person like Sheilah, who he *knew* would make his life miserable. He couldn't get her out of his mind. How in hell did it come to this? It was New York, he suddenly decided —goddamn New York! With all of its phoniness and loneliness and day-to-day dog-eat-dog attitudes. People, normal people were forced to live their lives as though it was D-Day and they were about to face annihilation. "Fuck New York," he said aloud. He fixed another cup of coffee and took a sip.

Maybe it's not New York, he thought. Maybe it's me and the people I run with. The fast lane. But then, what other lane is there in New York? New York *is* the fast lane. I have got to get out of the fast lane.

He was at his desk, outlining the next-to-last scene for a television play, when the phone rang. It was Katherine.

"Beau, I'm in New York again. Can we have a drink?"

"Where are you?" he asked, surprised. "I thought you were going to call." It had been almost a month since she'd reappeared in his life and he had finally decided their affair was just one of those flings that middle-aged married people sometimes treat themselves to. But as the days passed, he had begun to hope he was wrong.

"I just came up for some shopping—on the spur of the moment. I'm at the Sherry Netherland. Shall we meet in the bar?"

"Give me an hour," he said, a little annoyed at the short notice, but delighted she was back in town. It was Saturday and his plans were easy to cancel. It would be nice to be with Katherine.

It was three o'clock when he arrived at the hotel. The afternoon had become sublimely depressing. Multitudes of early Christmas shoppers scurried past the elegant hostelries around the park and down Fifth Avenue, on their way to and from Saks, Bendel's, Tiffany's, Steuben's and the other fashionable stores.

"I thought you'd be unable to come because of a busy social calendar," Katherine said, greeting him. She was wearing black slacks and a black sweater beneath her fur coat, and her hair was tied back. At her feet was a shopping bag filled with wrapped presents.

"That's for the leisure class. I have to work for a living—even on Saturdays."

"But surely some gorgeous woman has pressed you to have lunch. I understand it's a ritual up here."

"I don't go out with gorgeous women anymore—they're too much trouble."

"Are you telling me you're washed up at age thirty-eight?"

"Forty," he said.

"Thirty-eight," she commanded. "If I stopped at thirty-eight, you must too. Anyway, you've had all the best girls for nearly twenty years. Now what do you want?"

"I think I want a scotch." He didn't like women talking about other women in his life, even when they were joking.

"Why all this interest about me and other women?" he asked.

"Oh, I don't know," she said. "I met one of your pretty women down in Washington last summer."

"Really? Who?"

"Sheilah Price—a television reporter. I think she said she was off to London for a while."

Beau raised his eyebrows. "Now there's a coincidence," he said wryly.

"We were at a party at the Barrows' on Labor Day. She came up and introduced herself to me. We were talking about Bienville and she asked if I knew you."

Good old Sheilah, Beau thought ruefully. Time was running short. She'd be back in three weeks. "Well," he said, "she used to go out with your husband, you know. Long before I met her. Did he tell you?"

"He didn't need to," Katherine said. "She made that plain."

"What did you think of her?"

"Very nice-looking—and *very* well put together."

"Yes."

"And aggressive."

"Yes."

"I didn't much like her."

Beau changed the subject. He really didn't want to talk about Sheilah. Obviously Sheilah hadn't mentioned the extent of Beau's involvement with her. He and Katherine talked for a while about silly things, then she glanced beyond him to the window.

"Oh, look," she cried, "it's snowing!"

He turned and noticed the darkness of approaching winter.

"What time is it?" she asked.

"Five after four."

"I've got to go pack. My plane leaves at seven-fifteen and I'm not half ready. I have to get back tonight. There's a dinner party at some ambassador's. Dan is picking me up at the airport."

"Well, that's a . . . I mean, I was rather looking forward to seeing you—to having dinner or something."

Katherine looked away, then began to smooth her skirt under the table. She took a sip of her drink, sighed and reached over and touched Beau's hand.

"I guess I'm not really cut out for this," she said evenly. "I tried to get up the nerve to call you from the minute I got here. You're the reason I came, of course, but every time I picked up the phone I put it down again." She began to cry and he pressed her hand harder. Good Lord, he thought, three weeks ago we were lying in bed together, and now it's already "honest hour."

154

"Whatever else I am, Beau, I try to be loyal. And whatever else Dan is, he's a member of Congress. Oh, I've wanted you, thought so much about you over the years, but I'm . . . stuck. I have two lovely children, I'm a congressional wife and I do love my husband, even if . . ." She stopped and looked away.

"What?"

"Even if he's been fooling around with your friend Sheilah."

Katherine dabbed her eyes and drew a deep breath. Beau was staring at her.

"You didn't know?" she said. "No, I guess maybe you wouldn't. Well, they've been seeing one another for a while. I don't know how long, a few years maybe—I only found out a couple of months ago."

Beau was flabbergasted; he felt himself flush. "How do you know?"

"I know. People talk. They might not come right out and say it, but they drop enough hints. He's been seen having lunch with her, out of town with her. I knew it was true the first time I saw them together at that party. There are other things I won't mention."

"Jesus." Beau ran his fingers through his hair and swallowed his drink.

"Maybe it's the reason I looked you up," Katherine said. "I told myself I just wanted to see you, but maybe I wanted to show him."

"A grudge fuck," he said, instantly regretting it.

"I didn't think of it that way, but maybe. I guess in a way I did want revenge of some kind. If she could go to bed with my husband, I could go to bed with her boyfriend. It was childish and stupid, I know, but it turned out to be more than just that. I've always felt very close to you. I missed you—in college—even after I started dating other men."

"Why didn't you call me? Why did you just let it go?" he said. "God, Katherine, I loved you."

"I don't really know. We've been over that. I was confused and hurt then. I've always thought about you, always loved you, even after Dan and I were married. I used to wonder what it would have been like, you and me."

"Have you asked him about Sheilah?"

"No. Lord knows, I've started to a hundred times. But what good would it do? I mean, maybe I don't *want* to know. I hope it's just an *affair*, nothing serious. But then I think, what if he's really in love with her? Then what do I do? How do I handle it?"

"I'm sorry," Beau said.

Katherine stared vacantly across the room. Her makeup had smudged her cheeks. Beau moistened the edge of a napkin and dabbed her face. It was all too complicated to comprehend. How long had the affair been going on?

he wondered. He suddenly realized that it must have been going on for a while. Sheilah had once casually mentioned to him that she needed sex at least once a week. Beau was often in New York or elsewhere, and who better or safer to do *it* with than a married man?

Katherine drew a ragged breath and dried her eyes. "Well, I guess I've made a fool of myself."

"In no sense of the word," he replied. He tried to seem composed for her sake. He looked for the waiter and ordered two brandies.

"I suppose I wanted you to tell me something about her," Katherine said, looking Beau in the eye with fierce determination.

He fumbled for a cheroot. "Sheilah and I have been more or less engaged for a while," he said.

"You're what!" she cried. Now it was her turn to be astonished.

"Not anymore," Beau said. "We broke it off, I suppose, just before you met her in Washington. And then she took that stint in London. It was never a formal engagement—it was just sort of an agreement. It lasted about a year."

"This has been going on for more than a year," Katherine said.

"It doesn't surprise me. Very little surprises me anymore." He knocked an ash off into his saucer. "No—I take that back; what you've just told me surprises me."

"What's she like?" Katherine asked, crying again.

"I think you put your finger on it when you said 'aggressive.' She's hard to deal with sometimes. In theatrical terms you might say Sheilah's got a good first act, but the rest of the play needs work."

"I wonder how she latched on to Dan."

"I don't know. She met him a long time ago, when she was young—just out of boarding school. That was before I came to Washington. They went out, something happened. She never talked about it, and I never asked."

"That would have been pretty soon after he got elected and came up to Washington," Katherine said. "That would make sense. There was a period when I was still in Bienville and we didn't see each other very often. I suspected he was seeing somebody else but I never knew for sure."

"That's probably it," Beau said.

"Do you think she's in love with him?" Katherine said, more composed now.

"I don't know. Sometimes I wonder if Sheilah is capable of really loving anybody. I wonder the same thing about me. Sometimes."

They talked for a while longer but Beau was reluctant to get too deeply into the subject. He felt violated by this revelation, even though he and

Katherine had done a tango. Sheilah's betrayal didn't bother him as much as it should have if he truly loved her. He felt a kind of relief in finding this out. It was certainly going to make his decisions a lot easier.

Katherine was looking at him across the table. Beau wondered if she knew about her husband's dealings with the district attorney in Bienville. He was tempted to ask her, but he didn't. At the moment, he didn't give a damn.

"So now," Katherine said, straightening herself, looking through her purse, "what will you be doing tonight?"

"Oh, I imagine I will go home and read a good book, as they say."

"Really?" she asked. "I hope I didn't upset any of your plans."

"I didn't have any that were of importance—honestly."

"But I saw in the paper this morning that Johnny Taylor, that big literary agent, is having a bash at Tavern on the Green. That's your crowd, isn't it?"

"Wasn't invited," he said.

"Well, you're his friend, aren't you? He probably didn't know you're in town. Why don't you just call him up."

"I am well versed in getting myself invited to parties. Besides, I don't have my tux. It's in the cleaners'. They're closed."

"Don't be silly. You can rent one."

"I don't wear other people's clothes," he replied.

She sighed. "Well, I suppose I ought to leave. I have to make that plane." She reached for her shopping bag and stood up. She kissed him on the forehead. "Bye," she said, and he smiled and squeezed her hand.

"Have a good flight." As an afterthought, he called out to her, "I'm sorry."

Then she was gone and Beau was alone. He went to the bar and ordered a scotch. He relit the cheroot and looked at the swirling snow outside. It had formed a thin coat on the sidewalk and the parked cars. Dear Katherine, sweet Katherine. He downed his drink and motioned the bartender to bring him another. A good feeling came over him, bolstered by the whiskey perhaps, and it was not unlike what he'd experienced coming out of Toby Burr's office the day he learned his play was down the drain. It was a crazy kind of elation, a lapse in the psyche that allows you to be intensely gay when everything is falling down around you. He remembered feeling it once or twice during the war—temporary insanity perhaps . . .

But he knew the decision he'd just made was perhaps the sanest thing he'd done in years. He was going home. Home to Bienville and the *Courier-Democrat* and away from New York and Sheilah and all the phoniness that he'd encountered in the theatrical scene. I have had a pretty long run, Beau thought, and now it's time to close the show. Start out fresh and new at age forty, and put out the best damned newspaper in the South. Stop drinking and carousing till all hours of the night. Get myself back in shape. Get rid of Sheilah's ghost and get my life straightened out. He was very excited. Yet he desperately wanted to be with someone tonight. It was too late to call a date and he simply couldn't face Johnny Taylor's rat-fuck party alone—even if all the right rats were going to be there.

As he was staring out the window, mulling this over, a vision passed. A tall girl with amazing blond hair whisked by in a mink coat. He got only a bare glimpse of her face, but his impression was of soft, pale skin and a good nose, full lips. A compulsion overwhelmed him; he grabbed the check, glanced at it and flipped down a ten-dollar bill and hurried out into the street.

The girl was waiting at the corner for the traffic light, snow gently falling on her head and shoulders. She shook her blond mane, watching the light, waiting for the green to cross. Beau took long strides and caught up with her just as the light changed. She was about to step off the curb when he fell in beside her. He threw his scarf over his shoulder and said, "Excuse me."

Slightly startled, as New Yorkers are apt to be when accosted on the street, she turned toward Beau, her eyes wide with surprise, and then Beau's heart sank. She was in her mid-fifties. Face-lifts, cosmetics and dyed hair had made her a fair target at ten paces, but no closer.

"I beg your pardon?" she said.

"No, I'm sorry," Beau fumbled. "I thought you were someone else. I'm very sorry."

She tossed her head and strode across the street, leaving him at the curb. Beau stood there for a while watching the other pedestrians cross. He rubbed his hands together for warmth and looked down Fifth Avenue with the Christmas decorations newly strung across it—bright lights and snow.

Across the street the woman in the fur coat had hailed a cab and was stepping into it. He watched as she shut the door and the cab drove away. All at once Beau felt that weird rush of release again and it suddenly dawned on him that he was actually grateful that the woman was not someone he wanted to try to get involved with.

At least, he thought, I didn't have to try.

BOOK THREE

BOOK

THREE

The *Courier-Democrat*

Two days later, Beau landed at the Bienville Municipal Airport. The evening before, a Sunday, he had called me. I was about to take my wife to dinner when the phone rang. He said, "Pappy, if you still want yourself an editor, you've got one." I hooted with joy.

He further surprised me by saying he'd be here the next day—on Monday. When I sensed he was ready to leave New York, I didn't know he was *that* ready. We'd never even discussed his salary, but I guess he figured I'd do right by him.

I picked up one of his suitcases from the luggage ramp at the airport. "Have you decided where you're going to stay?" I asked.

"Not really," he said. "I'll find something while I'm here."

"Listen," I said, "we've got that guest cottage out back. It was done over last year and it's really super. Why not stay there until you find something. Stay as long as you want. I can have a phone put in tomorrow."

He looked at me and nodded and didn't say anything until we reached the car. "Okay, Pappy," he said, "you've got yourself a freeloader." I was delighted.

On the way home he asked about possible corruption on the staff of the paper, something I'd mentioned to him a month earlier.

"I made you a sort of welcome present this morning," I replied. "I fired four people—two editors and a reporter and a sports columnist. I believe that

161

leaves you with a pretty clean slate. If you find anybody else doing anything unsavory, let me know and I'll fire them too."

"I appreciate that, Pappy." He leaned back in the seat and closed his eyes, a satisfied smile on his face.

"I didn't want you to come down here and have to start firing people. It's easier for me to do it. This way you don't get instant resentment."

"Thanks," Beau said.

I got him home and put his bags in the guest cottage and told the housekeeper to make it ready for him. We went into my house and I ushered Beau into the library, where there was a bar.

"I don't think so, Pappy," he said when I offered him a cocktail.

I was again surprised. Beau Gunn rarely turned down a drink, no matter what time of day or night.

"I thought we'd have a toast to the *Courier-Democrat* and its new editor-in-chief," I said.

"Fine, Pappy, but if you don't think it's too much of a sacrilege, I'll just have soda water. As of today, I'm off the sauce—at least while I'm in this town. Newspaper reporters are drunk enough as a group without their editor setting a bad example."

"Well, there's something else to celebrate." Happily astonished, I poured Beau a glass of soda water over ice. "Drunk or sober," I said, hoisting my glass, "I have no doubt you're the best man for this job."

"Sober," he said.

That night Beau had dinner with his father and the next morning he and I drove to the *Courier-Democrat* building. It had been in the same location for a hundred and seventy years, but the name of the paper had changed once and the present plant was built in 1927. Some of the people working for us looked like they had been around then.

A hush fell over the newsroom as Beau and I walked in; people stopped what they were doing—however little it was—and stared. Some had vacant, fearful eyes. The *Courier-Democrat* was not a unionized paper.

I led Beau into my office and beckoned for Horace Moulton to come in. He knew what I wanted. Horace had been the managing editor of the paper for fifteen years. He was the operations guy, the one who moved and shook and got things done, most of the time. Horace was an old-time newspaperman; he'd been with three or four other papers in the South before signing on with us in the 1950s—the days when reporters wore hats with press cards in them and said things like "Hold the presses!" and "Rip out page one!"

Horace's big interest was fires. He loved to cover them. Even deskbound, as he was now, people said he would perk up like a Dalmatian at the firehouse and chug over to the window to see what was going on whenever he heard a fire engine's siren. This morning he was wearing a green editor's visor and a white shirt; he brought a copy of the first edition front page when he came in.

I introduced him to Beau and he handed me the paper, which I inspected briefly—as though I knew what was going on. Then I gave it to Beau. Centered above the fold was Beau's photograph and a headline that read: "J. P. Gunn II to Head *Courier-Democrat.*" Beneath it was a subhead that said: "Decorated War Hero and Noted Playwright Comes Home." Beau inspected the story and attempted to look embarrassed, but I knew he was pleased. Horace Moulton was beaming.

"Who wrote this story?" he asked casually. There was no byline.

"I did," I replied. He looked at me for a moment, then back to the story, then laid the paper on my desk. "Didn't anybody teach you how to spell 'cataclysmic'?" he said, referring to a line I had lifted from a review of his first play. I looked at Horace Moulton and saw his eyes roll up a little and then he glowered in the direction of the copy desk out front where two antiquated proofreaders hovered over their work. Beau looked at us both with a merry twinkle in his eyes as we shuffled our feet.

"This will be your office," I said grouchily. "I'm moving to the publisher's quarters, one floor up, and glad of it. You can have anything you want in here; just give a list to my secretary." The office had a big wooden desk and a long table in front of a big window that looked over Prince Street.

"It's fine the way it is," he said. "The only thing I'll want is another small desk out there in the newsroom. I want it right in front of the rim. A desk, a chair and a typewriter—nothing else. No visitors' chairs. People can stand— they won't be here that long anyway."

"Done," I said. "You want to get some lunch?"

"Thanks, Pappy, but I'm going to poke around here for a while, then maybe take a walk. Alone." He went out with me to the corridor that ran alongside the rows of reporters' desks. There were about twenty desks, ten in a row, leading up to the rim, where the editors sat. Only two or three of the desks were occupied. A telephone at one of the empty desks began to ring. It continued ringing as Beau surveyed the room.

"Isn't there a switchboard to pick up calls?" he asked.

"No. We don't have one. People call back if they don't get an answer."

"Will somebody answer that damned phone!" Beau said loudly.

Two people, an editor at the end of the rim and one of the other reporters, leaped up, wild-eyed, and dashed for the ringing phone.

Beau nodded and we walked out together. "We wouldn't want folks thinking nobody's home at eleven in the morning, would we, Pappy?"

"Maybe I ought to see about installing a switchboard," I said.

Beau walked out of the *Courier-Democrat* building onto Prince Street. The sky was gray and a bank of sullen clouds hung over the northeastern end of town, out over Bienville Bay. It was chilly, the wind blew and Beau shoved his hands into his pockets and began to walk. It had been nearly twenty years since he'd lived here, and he found that progress had arrived.

The center of town wasn't really there anymore. It had become a shambles of cheap clothing stores, furniture outlets and accessory stores. Dingy movie theaters and record shops cluttered the blocks. This evolution had begun with the development of large suburban centers in the 1960s. In Bienville, the white population, bounded to the east by the bay and the south by the river and the north by the Negroes, pushed westward, and with them went new schools, roads, parks and, of course, the inevitable shopping malls. The old story.

But for two hundred years, the core of the town had been here where Beau was standing. It had revolved around an oak-lined square with a fountain and a round bandstand that was called the Parade. In Beau's time, there had been wonderful drugstores with soda fountains and delicious Creole restaurants and variety stores like J. Kress and F. W. Woolworth, with whole sections devoted to pets and toys, and sporting-goods shops and grand old hotels with marble lobbies and stained glass and fountains inside and a lot of people you knew on the streets. At the main wharf on the riverfront, longshoremen unloaded bunches of green bananas by hand from the huge white fruit company ships and you could sit on iron benches there and watch them for hours. The Gothic railroad station bustled with hissing passenger trains headed for New York, Washington, Atlanta, New Orleans, St. Louis and other exotic destinations.

Now all was changed.

The Parade had become a haven for vagrants. After dark, the area became a weird sort of Sherwood Forest where the Merry Men were dope dealers, muggers and homosexuals. The lone variety store that remained had become shabby and dilapidated, as had the three once grand movie houses which now offered a fare of sex films and martial-arts pictures. The hotels had long since closed and some were torn down, succumbing, like the movie houses and the variety stores, to the lure of the shopping malls. The drugstore had closed its soda fountain and most of the seafood restaurants had moved. Only the shells of those institutions around which Beau's early life had evolved remained.

Yet with the newfound affluence of oil and shipping, there was a move afoot to restore the old section and save the historic old homes and buildings. Some progress had been made in this direction, but there was a long way yet to go.

Meandering toward the old commercial wharf, Beau felt a few drops of rain and ducked into a seedy luncheonette for a cup of coffee. Across the street was the boarded-up shell of the once proud Raphael House hotel. Its ballrooms had hosted some great bands in Beau's time—Artie Shaw, Stan Kenton, Count Basie. A sour remembrance nettled Beau when he thought of Artie Shaw. One critic of his second play had sarcastically written: "As a playwright, Gunn genuinely merits comparison with Shaw—Artie Shaw." He finished his coffee and left two quarters on the counter. As he walked into the street, he sent up a prayer that the IRS would get the critic.

Past Howell Street, the river came into sight, brown from upstate rain silt. Several ships lay against a pier with little activity around them. Ahead was the old slave market, a white stucco building now used for police offices, and above it, a newer building, the county detention center, with rows of iron-barred windows. Behind one of them, Tommy Brodie sat chain-smoking, probably suffering from the d.t.'s. Beau crossed the street and walked beneath moss-draped oaks on soft St. Augustine grass, savoring the lush spongy carpet of its thick green blades. A gust of cool air from the direction of the storm lapped around him as he went up the steps to the detention center.

"I would like to see Thomas Brodie," he said to a uniformed man behind a counter.

"Are you his lawyer?" the official asked. He was fumbling with a visitors' register.

"No."

"Family?"

"No, just a friend."

"Visiting hours for friends is on Sunday," the officer said. "Noon to three-thirty." He turned his back and began doing something else.

"I am the editor of the Bienville *Courier-Democrat,*" Beau said evenly. "I would like permission to see Mr. Brodie."

The officer turned and looked harder at Beau. There was a newspaper on his desk and he glanced at it and looked back.

"All I know, sir, is that if you ain't the lawyer, or family, visiting hours is Sunday. Maybe I'd better go ask somebody. Wait here." He left through a rear door and was gone for five minutes by the clock on the wall.

When he returned, there was an older, white-haired officer with him, a large man with steel-gray eyes and a lieutenant's bar on his collar.

"Can I help you?" he asked.

"My name's Gunn. I'm a friend of Thomas Brodie and I'd like to see him if possible," Beau said. "We grew up together."

"Well . . . Mr. Gunn," the lieutenant said. "Brodie isn't here anymore. He's been moved for security purposes to another location."

"Really?" Beau said. "Where?"

"That is privileged information," the lieutenant said. "You'd have to talk to the captain about that."

"Can you direct me to the captain, then?"

"Captain's out to lunch. Prob'ly gone for the day. He's got some stuff to do this afternoon. Be back in the mornin'."

"Thank you." Beau nodded and walked out. It had begun to rain hard. By the time he got back to the *Courier-Democrat* he was soaked. Things had picked up a little in the newsroom. Most of the reporters who'd been out on morning assignments were back typing their stories for the afternoon edition. There was a little bit of that electricity he remembered from the Washington *Times-Examiner*. He went into his office and sat behind the desk, reading a copy of the morning edition. Nervous and curious eyes glanced at him through the glass partition.

He was plagued by a nagging doubt that he wasn't up to taking charge of a newspaper circulating to two hundred thousand readers, serving a city of nearly half a million and growing. All of it, from the hard news to the society pages to the food section, sports, business—even the comic strips—would be his responsibility now. He had never been an editor. He had always hated editors, in fact, and now he was not only *an* editor, he was *the* editor. The thought of it suddenly made him want a drink. A nice tall amber scotch with soda and ice that would calm his nerves. He decided to get a cup of coffee instead.

"Is there a place to get some coffee here?" Beau asked a bald-headed man bending over some copy on the rim.

The man looked up, startled, then got to his feet. "Yes, sir. There's a coffee machine down the hall to the right." Other men on the rim had stopped their work and were looking up too.

"Thank you," Beau said, and nodded.

"Yes, sir," said the man.

"My name's Beau. I'll get to know all your names pretty soon. Let's keep it informal."

The man nodded, but remained standing as Beau walked out of the room and down the hall. He put his money in the machine and was waiting for the coffee cup to fill when a young woman walked up. She had gotten off the elevator and headed straight for the coffee machine. She was attractive, in her early twenties, with soft brown hair and brown eyes and good skin. She was wearing a wet cotton raincoat and held a dripping rain hat in her hand.

"Typical December weather," Beau said. The girl was fumbling in her purse for change. Beau reached in his pocket and found a quarter and put it in the slot. "Black?" he asked. He took his cup away.

"Oh no, I've got it somewhere here," the girl said.

"Black?" Beau said again, smiling.

"Yes, black," the girl said, still rummaging around in the purse. Beau punched the button for black and a cup dropped down and began filling. The girl had fished out a handful of coins and she counted out two dimes and a nickel and thrust them at Beau. He took her coffee from the machine and handed it to her.

"No reason the editor of a newspaper can't buy one of the staff a cup of coffee."

The girl took the coffee and was still holding out her palm with the change in it when Beau's comment sunk in.

"You—you're, oh, *you're* Mr. Gunn?" she managed to say.

"Beau—please. We're going to keep it informal here."

"Yes, well, I'm Eleanor Campbell."

"Oh, you're the one who went to talk to Spinker about the Brodie case?"

"Yes," she said, surprised that Beau would know.

"Good. After you have your coffee and get settled in, come see me in my office." He left her standing by the machine and went back to the newsroom, where he found Horace Moulton.

"Horace, I want you to get somebody to bring me each of the editions for the past week, then one edition for each week for the past six months, just at random."

"Yes, sir."

"Beau, Horace. That's the way it is from now on."

Eleanor Campbell appeared at Beau's door carrying a file and wearing a black dress with small green polka dots on it. He motioned her to a chair.

"I gave a copy of this to Mr. Moulton; he asked me to type up my notes," she said. "He didn't want a story."

Beau took the file and read through it. There wasn't much there he hadn't already heard. He pushed back in his chair and relit his cheroot.

"What was your impression of Spinker? Did he seem like he was credible?"

"Well, yes, I suppose . . . I can't see why he'd lie. He didn't even want to talk to me."

"Have you checked any of this out?"

"Well"—she hesitated—"not too much. Mr. Moulton didn't tell me to check it out. He just said to type up the notes."

Beau turned his chair toward the rain-spattered window, glancing down at the notes in the file.

"Sometimes a good reporter will check things out without having to be told," he said gently. Then he handed back the file. "Make me a copy of this, please."

She stood up. "Yes, sir."

"Beau," he called after her as she walked out.

Horace Moulton arrived with a stack of the newspapers Beau had requested.

"Horace, I want you to call a meeting of all the staff for tomorrow afternoon. What would be a good time?"

Horace scratched his chin. "About five. Most of them will be here then."

"Good, but I'd like *everyone* to be here. Send out word, okay? Get them together in the newsroom. It won't take long. And can you get someone to drive me to a place where I can rent a car?"

"I can take you myself."

"All right, we can talk about a few things on the way. He put on his jacket and picked up the stack of newspapers and the file on Tommy Brodie.

Beau arrived the next morning before the six-thirty shift got in and began going through the back editions of the *Courier-Democrat* he hadn't got to the night before. He made an occasional note or two on a legal pad.

Just before noon Eleanor Campbell knocked at his door. "Mr. Gunn," she said timidly.

Beau rolled his eyes.

"I've made a few calls about the Brodie case."

"Come in," he said.

"I got the dead girl's mother on the phone last night. She hadn't seen much of her daughter over the last months she was alive, but she knew she was going out with some guy. She couldn't remember his name, but she said he worked for Universal Oil. So that could be this guy Ben Grimshaw. At least it fits."

Beau nodded. Eleanor seemed pleased with herself. She studied some notes.

"I also called this man Cappy, who's the owner of the Port of Call, the bar where the dead girl and whoever she was with were supposed to have been having their argument. He said all he knew was that a man and a woman were in the place the night of the murder; the man left and the girl stayed for about half an hour. She left by herself."

"What do you make of it?" Beau asked.

"I don't know, really. It doesn't quite fit Spinker's story, but in some ways it does."

"Thank you," Beau said.

When she had gone he picked up the phone and dialed the number of the lawyer assigned to Tommy's case. He wasn't in, so Beau left a message on his answering machine. Then he dialed his father's office and spoke to the old man.

"I need to know something," Beau said. "How can I get in to see Tommy Brodie?"

"In the jail?" his father asked.

"In the jail—some jail, I don't even know which. I went over to the Bienville municipal lockup and they said he'd been moved. Wouldn't even tell me where. They also said that unless I was his lawyer or family, I couldn't see him except on visiting days."

"Well, I don't really . . ." the old man said.

"Isn't there somebody you know on the force? The chief, perhaps? Somebody who could bend the rules a little?"

"No, not really," his father said. "I've been out of that kind of law practice for years. I know who the chief is, but I don't know him personally. Have you tried the D.A.?"

"Not yet. Do you have any pull with him?"

"I'm afraid not," the old man said. "Like I told you, I don't practice that kind of law anymore. The D.A. would be your contemporary, not mine."

Beau thanked him and hung up. Ordinarily, his father would have bent over backwards to help. It almost seemed like he didn't want to try this time. Beau tried to make sense of it. Maybe he's just getting old. Maybe he's tired. He found the number of the district attorney and called him.

"Congratulations," Evan Roche said when he got on the phone. "I read about you in the papers yesterday. It's good to have you home."

"Thanks. It's quite a change for me."

"Big change from when we were at Singer," Roche said.

"It is that," Beau replied. He vaguely remembered Roche from those days, an unruly and undisciplined boy four or five years younger than himself. He couldn't imagine how he got to be D.A.

"Listen, Evan, I need a favor. I need to see Tommy Brodie and the cops are being pissy about it. They won't even tell me where he is."

"Well," Roche said, "ah, that's a little bit of a problem. We're still interrogating him and we're trying to keep, ah, undue influences away from him."

"I'm not an undue influence," Beau said. "I'm his friend and have been for twenty-five years. I just want to see if there's anything I can do for him. Can you tell me at least where he is?"

"Well," Roche drawled, "I'm afraid that's sort of privileged information right now."

"What do I have to do," Beau retorted, "get a writ of habeas corpus drawn up?"

"No, no—now don't go flying off in all directions, Beau. I can probably arrange something."

"When?" Beau asked.

"What's convenient?"

"How about thirty minutes?"

"Thirty minutes!" Roche cried. "Why, we couldn't even . . ."

"How about after lunch—about two o'clock?" Beau said. "That gives you about four hours."

He heard Roche sigh on the other end of the phone. "All right. I'll see what I can do. You call the lockup this afternoon. Ask for Captain Saltzman. I'll tell him to expect your call."

Iron bars slammed shut behind Beau as he and a guard walked down a dimly lit hallway on the third floor of the jailhouse. They came to a cell at the end that had a door with a glass window in it. The jailer opened a lock and swung the door. Sitting on a bare bunk, surrounded by padded walls, was Tommy Brodie. He was wearing jail-issue clothes and looked as if he hadn't had a night's sleep in weeks. When Beau walked in he stood up and looked as if he was going to cry, but he didn't. He stuck out his hand. The jailer shut the door and left them alone.

"Hello, Beau," Tommy said weakly. His grip was strained, his lips thin. "I couldn't believe it when they said you wanted to see me. I mean, did you come all the way from New York?"

"No, no. I just got into town a few days ago, but I'm here for a while now, Tommy. Maybe for good—Pappy and I are running the *Courier-Democrat.*"

Tommy hadn't seen the papers, so Beau filled him in. When he'd finished, Tommy smiled and said, "You know, I think I always knew you'd come back home someday. It's kind of strange that it'd be when I'm in trouble again. Seems like you're always here when I'm in trouble."

"Well, the important thing is to try to get you out of it. Pappy tells me you said you didn't have anything to do with the girl's murder. Is that so?"

"I swear it," Tommy said. "I never even knew her. I mean, I knew who she was, but I never spoke a word to her."

"Pappy said you told him they found a knife—the murder weapon—in your apartment."

"It wasn't my knife. I never had a knife like that anyway. It was one of those hunting knives."

"But what was it doing in your apartment?"

"I don't know," Tommy said dejectedly. "Somebody put it there, I guess. What's the difference? What with everything else that's gone on with me, who's going to believe what I say?"

"I will, for one, if you shoot straight. Now, Pappy also tells me you have an alibi but you won't say who it is."

"I will if I have to. If it comes to that."

"It's already come to that. Look, you're charged with murder, Tommy. It can't *get* any more serious."

"Nothing's happened yet," Tommy said, "except that I'm in jail."

"But why do they keep moving you around?" Beau asked. "They said you were somewhere else yesterday, and now you're back . . ."

"Oh, they've been doing a lot of that," Tommy said. "They moved me to Clifton, and then over to Wrighttown, and then back here, and then . . ."

There was a jangle of keys in the door to the cell and then it opened. The jailer was there, motioning to Beau.

"I need a few more minutes," Beau said.

"Time's up. They said to give you fifteen minutes."

"Nobody told *me* that."

"Look, time's up," the jailer repeated.

Beau was frustrated, but he knew he had to keep his temper. "Okay, okay." He turned to Tommy. "There are some things we need to talk about— some things I know about, all right? I'll be back in a day or so. What about this lawyer they got you? He any good?"

"Oh," Tommy said, "he's . . . I don't know, he's okay, I guess."

"Has he been to see you more than once?"

"Time's up," the jailer said again. "That's all for today."

"Okay!" Beau said. He turned as he was leaving. "Hang on, you hear? We've got to talk again in a day or so. I'll try to set it up." As the jailer locked the door, Beau saw Tommy sag onto the bunk and bury his head in his hands.

Back at the office, Beau spent the rest of the afternoon going through the back editions. When five o'clock came around he was glad to see the newsroom filled with milling reporters and editors. There was a low steady hum of conversation. Horace Moulton appeared in the doorway. "They're all here," he said.

"Horace, I am going to stand on top of that desk they put out there for me yesterday. Will you check to see if the chair is sturdy enough for me to climb on, and if it isn't, get one that is?"

"Certainly," Horace said.

Beau was in his shirt sleeves, tie loosened. He tore two pages out of the legal tablet he'd been writing on and stuck them in his back pocket and looked out at the sea of anxious faces in front of him. He was a little nervous himself. It reminded him for an instant of being back in the Army. He put a foot on the chair seat and stood with his hand holding the chair back. He prayed the gimpy leg wouldn't give out on him now. He hoisted himself up and stood on the desk.

"For those who haven't heard, my name is Beau Gunn, but please call me Beau." A chuckle ran through the assembly.

"I don't know how things were done around here before, and I don't care. It doesn't matter anymore. As of right now, this paper is going to start changing and keep changing until it's a real newspaper and not a daily forum for flummery wrapped up with advertisements. There are stories out there, good, solid, important stories—just as important to the people of this city as the stories in New York or Washington.

"This," he said, bending down and picking up a copy of the afternoon edition, "is not one of them." He pointed to a story prominently displayed on the front page. The headline said: "Pan of Grease Burns Three."

"What we want to print on page one is news. This is *not* page-one news. It ought to have been put back by the grocery ads.

"I am told there is political corruption in this city. I hear there is racial unfairness. I understand there is unwise spending of the taxpayers' money. We are in the business of uncovering and reporting these things. We must bring them to the attention of the population.

"We are going to be less concerned from now on with somebody's grease fire. All of you will have to work hard. Those who don't will hear from me.

"Now," Beau said, "there is one further matter. As I'm sure you're all aware by now, several of your colleagues are no longer with us. They were fired before I got here. The reasons are probably known to you.

"I am well versed in the pitfalls associated with working for a newspaper —especially one that doesn't pay high salaries. It's very tempting when a department store offers you a discount for mentioning their name in a story, or when somebody offers to pay you for inside information. There are a hundred ways to be corrupted in this profession and a thousand people out there who would like to corrupt you."

Beau paused and looked around. Several of his employees were studying their shoes. "All I have to say is this: If I catch you, your ass will ride on my shoe all the way out into the street. Do I make myself clear?"

Some people answered, others nodded, but they all got the message.

"One way or another," Beau said, "we are going to publish one of the finest newspapers in the nation and those of you who are left will be proud to be working here. Thank you."

He carefully stepped down from the desktop and walked back to his office. In the newsroom the staff drifted into little groups to discuss what they had just heard. After a while people went about their business. They had expected more from Beau, but he didn't work that way.

The next morning Beau summoned the plant manager to his office and told him to remove the glass partitions around the teletype machines. "I want this place to sound like a newspaper. A newspaper has teletype machines clicking away."

He also asked for and got the approval to hire two copy boys.

"We need to instill a sense of urgency here," he said. "I want people shouting, 'Copy!' I want to see copy boys rushing around, moving stories up to the desk."

He got the okay for a switchboard hookup for the phones in the newsroom so they'd always be answered. He got rid of the coffee machine in the hallway, replacing it with a coffee cart with fresh-brewed coffee and good doughnuts pushed along between the rows of desks by a jovial woman who had been a member of the cleaning staff. He'd heard that a lot of typewriters were broken and reporters had to move from desk to desk to type their stories. He got a man from a local repair service put on permanent retainer to keep the machines working. He asked the business office to do a study of the feasibility of converting to word-processing computers. He even had a suggestion box installed outside his office.

He read every edition of the paper with hawklike perseverance, every word of every story, no matter how small. He began sending notes when something pleased him *and* when it didn't. By the end of the week, he was beginning to have a feel for who the best and worst reporters and editors were.

On Thursday afternoon he sent Eleanor Campbell a note to come see him when she returned from her assignment. "Eleanor," Beau said, "I want to review what is known about the Brodie murder case." She smoothed her dress, flipped open a pad and sat with her legs crossed, ready to write.

"So far," he said, "here's the picture as I see it: A secretary at Universal Oil is stabbed to death. Three days later Tommy Brodie is arrested, arraigned in the middle of the night and charged with murder. The police and the D.A. aren't talking, and Brodie says he didn't do it.

"Now, from Mr. Spinker we hear the dead girl was seeing Ben Grimshaw, manager of Universal Oil's operations and a former assistant to Fletcher Cross. Spinker claims he saw Grimshaw and the girl at the Port of Call, where they were having an argument. They leave together and several hours later her body is discovered.

"The mother of the girl confirms her daughter was seeing a man who might fit the description of Grimshaw. The guy who owns the Port of Call confirms that the girl and some man were in the bar that night, and says that the man left alone and the girl left half an hour later, also alone. Is that right so far?"

Eleanor looked up and nodded.

"Now, according to the cops, Brodie's being moved from place to place for security reasons and the cops are reluctant to say where he is at any given time. Meanwhile the D.A. has been conducting some kind of business at all hours of the night involving, among other people, Gordon McWorth, a member of Universal Oil's board of directors, and Dan Whittle, the congressman from this district. A cloak of secrecy has been spread all over this. Do we know anything else?"

"Well, a little something," Eleanor said. "A couple of days ago I decided to go to the courthouse and check the arrest records for Grimshaw, Brodie and the dead girl."

"Nice move. And?"

"Grimshaw is clean. A traffic violation three years ago, that's all."

"And Brodie?"

"Arrested for public drunkenness six times in the past ten years. And once, about three years ago, for disorderly conduct and possession of a deadly weapon."

"What was the weapon?" Beau asked.

"A knife," she said.

Beau spun his chair around and looked out the window as he ran his fingers through his hair. So she hadn't turned up anything about the Five Funny Fellows incident. It wasn't surprising. Tommy had been a juvenile then, and his name wouldn't have been in the records released to the public.

But this thing a couple of years ago with the *knife!* He turned back around again.

"Eleanor, I want us to make a full and thorough investigation of all this, and I want *you* to do it. I want you to spend all your time on it, unless there is a real emergency here.

"I want to know why Tommy Brodie is being moved around. I want you to talk to this lawyer, Melcher, and see what he knows. I want to know for a fact that Ben Grimshaw and the girl were seeing each other. I want to know who was with her in that bar the night she was killed. Did they or did they not have an argument? Did they or did they not leave together? And I want to know if there's any connection between the murder and whatever the D.A.'s doing up there at night. Universal Oil seems to be cropping up in all sorts of places lately. And find out what the hell Congressman Dan Whittle has to do with any of this. I want you to report directly to me and no one else. I smell something."

After Eleanor left the office, Beau got up and paced around for a while. He indeed smelled something. He also had a funny feeling about it all. These were people he had known for years. He was beginning to wonder how well he had really known them.

Tommy Brodie

December 7, 1983

At 11:05 A.M. the following Monday, a fire broke out aboard a Universal Oil freighter named *Cassandra,* which was moored at the docks. At 11:20, the ship exploded. It rattled the windows of the *Courier-Democrat.* Horace Moulton appeared at Beau's door a few minutes later.

It looks like we've got a big one," he said. "Some ship just blew to hell and back at the terminal. I have Peter Watkins on the phone. He went down following a report of a fire. He says there are dead and badly burned people all over the place. I'm going to send Stewart down there, and Coats, as soon as he gets back. He's got a photographer with him."

Beau looked out his window. A huge column of black smoke was rising over the waterfront.

"Horace," he said evenly, "what I think you should do is send every goddamn reporter we've got down there, and every photographer too. When a ship blows up in the harbor, that's big news."

Horace looked around the newsroom. "Well, there's old Jim Malbis," he said, "the boat and automobile editor. I guess we could send him, but I'm not sure what he'd do except get in the way."

"What about those two over there?" Beau pointed to a pair of women sitting at adjacent desks, talking to each other.

Horace looked around. "Oh," he said sourly, "that's the Sob Sisters—Nadine and Doreen. I don't think they'd be of much use."

"Are they reporters?" Beau asked quizzically.

176

"Well, yeah, but they just do feature stories. Interview the ninety-year-old woman who didn't get her welfare check, or the little boy who got lost at the shopping mall—that kind of thing."

"What did you call them?" Beau asked in astonishment.

"The Sob Sisters is what we call them around here. We don't use them to report real news."

"You bring them in here to me," Beau said. Horace disappeared and returned a few moments later with the two fidgeting women.

"Ladies," Beau said. "There has been a big explosion down at the terminal. A ship blew up. People are dead, more maybe are dying. I want you both to get down there and find Peter Watkins. Check in with him and then start giving us as much as you can about what's going on. Try to get some firsthand accounts of the explosion. See if you can find out anything about the people who were killed and hurt—their families—anything."

The two women looked at each other in dismay. "This isn't what we do, Mr. Gunn," one of them said weakly.

"You're reporters, aren't you?" Beau stared at them coolly.

"Well, yes, but . . ."

"Then if you value your jobs you'll get down there and do what I say. There's a good human-interest angle in this and you're going to find it."

The two women exchanged glances and left the office. Beau could see them talking animatedly to each other as they gathered their things together.

He drummed his fingers on the desk. "Sob Sisters, my ass," he muttered. "Horace, look over in sports and business and see if you can round up anybody else. And who's the best rewrite man you've got?"

"Rewrite?" Horace said.

"Yes, you know," Beau said impatiently. "You've got a breaking story, a lot of reporters in the field, they're phoning in—*somebody* back here has got to put the story together."

"We really don't have anybody special," Horace said. "We just use whoever's around."

"Good God," Beau groaned. "All right, I'll do it myself. Put all the calls through to my desk by the rim. And make sure there's enough copy paper by my typewriter. How much time till the next edition?"

Horace looked at his watch. "Twenty-five minutes."

"I want your man down there to be ready to dictate in fifteen." Beau began rolling up his shirt sleeves. "The first thing I want him to tell me is what started the fire and what exploded. If he can't find out for sure, tell him to get somebody official to make a guess. Send one of the copy boys down to get the first roll of film from the photographer and get it the hell back here on the double."

"Right," said Horace.

"Oh, and one more thing."

Horace poked his head back in the door.

"I don't want to ever be told that one of our reporters can't cover something—Sob Sister or not."

"Right," Horace said.

Beau spent the next nine hours at his desk in the newsroom writing stories from the reporters' accounts and issuing instructions on what they should do next. The *Courier-Democrat* carried the story with banner headlines across its next three editions and with several photographs of the burning vessel. For the overnight, Beau assigned the Sob Sisters to locate and interview relatives of the twelve dead men. He ordered one reporter to stick to the fire marshal like glue and see if the cause could be determined. He ordered another to the hospital to report on the condition of the injured. The teletype machines clattered away in the corner, as the copy boys scurried around getting new pieces of the story to his desk. There was a lot of hollering and shouting. When Beau stopped for a few minutes to have a fresh cup of coffee, he thought the place was beginning to look a little bit like a newspaper.

At seven-thirty that night, Eleanor Campbell came in and walked up to Beau's desk. He was on the phone with Peter Watkins, who had been down at the terminal since just after the explosion. One of the Sob Sisters was on hold on the other phone. Eleanor stood there until Beau hung up. Before he could pick up the other line, she said, "I need to talk to you."

"Talk," he said.

"Thomas Brodie is dead. He hanged himself in his cell at the Caballa County jail this afternoon."

Beau's jaw dropped. "What! What the hell was he doing way up in Caballa County?"

"Well, that's what the sheriff told me. I'd been checking out some things and I went over to see if I could find out where he was. They gave me the runaround. I was waiting in the sheriff's office when he came in and said Brodie was found hanging from a piece of cord at five-thirty."

"Jesus," Beau said. He rubbed his forehead. "Go write a story about it. Keep it simple. Then go back to our morgue and see what you can find to do a proper obituary. Actually you can do that tomorrow. I want to see it before it goes in." He picked up the phone and began taking notes from a Sob Sister.

At 10 P.M., on his way out, Beau saw Eleanor Campbell in a far corner of the room. He walked over and sat down on the edge of her desk.

"I guess it goes without saying that I'd like you to find out everything you can about this. Where was he before Caballa? Why was he back in the county jail? See if you can talk to the person who found him. Find out how it happened."

"I'm sorry, Mr. Gunn. I know he was a friend of yours."

"Beau," he said, and went out into the night.

Beau got home, put a pot of tea on the stove and took a shower. Later, sipping the tea, wearing a large terry-cloth robe, he opened his address book and got a number where Eric Pacer had said he could receive messages. The number, in Miami, was answered by one of those precut answering-machine tapes with a lot of music in the background and a theatrical voice. Beau waited until the beep sounded and said, "Eric, this is Beau. I'm in Bienville and will be at the office tomorrow. Tommy's dead. I thought you might want to come home."

He poured another cup of tea and was staring blankly at a wall when the phone rang. It was Eleanor Campbell.

"Beau?" she said softly. "It's Eleanor." It was the first time she'd called him Beau.

"What's up?" he asked. It was almost midnight.

"I think I found out why they were moving Tommy Brodie around," she said.

"Really? Why?"

"Well, I stopped over at the jail on my way home. There's a deputy sheriff who works there who's a friend of mine. I just thought he might know something. So I went in, and sure enough, he was there. We had a cup of coffee and I got him talking about Tommy Brodie and it turned out he was the one who had driven him up to Caballa County a few days ago."

"No kidding," Beau said.

"Seems he had asked the same question when they told him to take Brodie up there. He was told the chief of police had ordered it and he asked why. His boss said he didn't know but that he understood the order came all the way from Judge Grumman."

"Grumman?" Beau said. "Hell, I know Grumman. He used to be . . . Goddamn! Wait a second. Grumman used to be Gordon McWorth's law partner after McWorth and my old man parted ways."

"I didn't know that," Eleanor said.

"Yeah," Beau said, "before he got elected judge."

"That's interesting, isn't it?" Eleanor said. "Anyway, it looks like Grumman is the one ordering all that moving around."

"Well, good work. We'll look into this tomorrow."

"Yes," Eleanor said. There was a silence and then she said, "There was something else I called about."

"Yes?" Beau began to stack several boxes of matches, one on top of the other.

"Well, I . . . I just wanted to know if you were all right. I mean, I know he was your friend and, oh, I don't know, I was just worried about you, I suppose."

"No, I'm all right," he said. "I'm a little tired and sad, but I'm okay."

"I was just wondering."

"Thank you, Eleanor. It was nice of you to think of me. I'll see you in the office tomorrow, okay?"

"Okay," she said. "Bye."

Beau put down the phone and sipped at the remaining cold tea in his cup. He decided Eleanor was a very nice girl. Nice and smart and pretty. Then he checked himself. Better watch it, boy. Bad policy to fool around in the office. Still, he wondered about her as he sat there, a good, warm feeling in his body. It was really sweet of her to call. Maybe taking her to dinner sometime wouldn't hurt anything. They could talk business . . .

I felt a great sadness on the morning of Tommy Brodie's funeral. The day was extraordinary for mid-December, even in Bienville. The air was clear and still; the sun shone warm through the big oaks in the cemetery and made little dancing patterns on the green grass around the gravesite. Beau and Eric Pacer and I—all that was left of the original Five Funny Fellows—stood together outside the tent that held Tommy's coffin. Eric had flown in that morning and Beau seemed particularly happy to see him. There weren't many other people there, which I suppose we had expected, considering the cloud over Tommy's life and death. After the services the three of us went up to Tommy's father to introduce ourselves. He was an old, sad-looking man with reddened eyes, which he kept dabbing at with a handkerchief. Tommy's mother died years before.

"You boys always stood by him and I'll remember that. I figured we might as well bury him in Bienville," the old man said weakly. "His mother and me moved to Tallahassee a long time ago—after the other happened. I guess you know that, but this was always his home."

Beau asked Mr. Brodie where he was staying and he named a motel near the interstate. He said he was leaving for Tallahassee that afternoon. Beau asked if he might send a reporter by to talk to him. He didn't say what for, but left the impression it might be for some kind of obituary. The old man agreed. On the way back to our cars, Beau told us what was on his mind.

"Pappy," he said, "how'd you like to have the Pacer working for you?"

"Me?" Pacer said. "What's all this?"

"Well," Beau said, smiling, "it has occurred to me that I need a special assistant. A spark plug, if you will; somebody fresh and not already on the staff who is going to be *my* man. Somebody who can get things done in the day-to-day operations of the paper. When I need more desks in the newsroom, or typewriters, or computers, or whatever, I'll just tell him, and he'll see that it's done. He'll be my right hand and sometimes my left too. He'll keep his ear to the ground and let me know what's happening in the newsroom."

"Sounds all right to me," I said.

"Sounds like what I did sixteen years ago humping your damn radio around the boonies," Pacer said.

"It's more than that," Beau said. "Look, Pacer, you need a job, right? And I need you. You're loyal and you're thorough and you're smart."

"And I was headed for the islands to lie in the sun and skipper yachts around."

"That can wait. This is important. I'm calling you back on active duty."

"I'm retired. I'm exhausted. I've been on airplanes all night just trying to get down here."

"You're not retired anymore," Beau told him firmly.

"What's it pay?"

Beau and I looked at each other and smiled. "I'll make it worth your while," I said.

We stood around for a minute or two longer, hands in pockets, shuffling our feet. Pacer shook his head and changed the subject.

"Poor old Tommy, I still don't believe it."

"Neither do I. He wasn't the sort," I said.

Pacer made excuses and left for his parents' house to get some sleep. I asked Beau if he'd like to have lunch before going back to the office. I wanted to find out what he knew about the Brodie case.

"I don't think so, Pappy. I thought as long as I was down this way I might take a drive to my grandparents' old place on the river. I haven't been there in years—not since the big house burned down. I thought I'd wander around there a little, and come into the office later."

"Maybe supper tonight, then?"

"I don't think so," he said. "I think I might have a date."

Beau drove to the interstate and then got off at an exit about ten miles from the center of town. At a dingy service station he phoned Eleanor Campbell and told her to go see Tommy Brodie's father and find out anything he might know. He also told her to have dinner with him that evening. Then he turned down a county road and headed toward the old Gunn place on Blackwater River.

The rusting iron gates at the entrance hung askew on their brick columns. Beau drove about fifty yards up the narrow lane paved with oyster shells until a fallen tree blocked his way. He got out, took off his jacket and started walking. It was a half mile through creeping vines and rotting deadfall before he reached what was once the lawn.

Buck Hollow had been built by Beau's great-grandfather in the 1850s. In those days there had been much more land, and it was fertile bottomland. It wasn't fertile enough for cotton growing—the fabled Black Belt stopped a hundred miles north of Bienville—but Beau's people weren't farmers anyway. Buck Hollow was a summer place. By the standards of the day, the house was modest, a large two-story cottage raised twelve feet off the ground for protection against storms and hurricanes, with a wide porch all the way around it. The lawn had once consisted of nearly three acres of cultivated roses, azaleas, hydrangeas and thick St. Augustine grass. He had played here as a boy and it was a magical place. He made his way through a path of tall weeds until it began to open up a little. The roses had vanished and the azaleas had gone wild without pruning. Some had grown to be monstrous—ten, fifteen feet tall—and were slowly being choked out by honeysuckle vines that covered them like cloaks.

He shoved through until he saw the river in the distance and the charred ruins of the old house among a patch of oaks. It was not as he'd remembered it; the house should have been closer to the river and the trees should have been thicker. Of course, many of them had fallen, as though in sorrow at the waste. All that remained of the house were the chimneys and tall supporting columns that had been set into the ground a hundred and thirty years before. Beau stood among the ruins facing the clear river that flowed gently to the south.

When he was young this place was "the country." His grandparents had made it their year-round home in the 1930s when the main road was paved, but it had still been an hour's drive from downtown Bienville. Now it was almost within the city limits and only ten minutes or so from the interstate.

As he walked around he remembered the weekends spent hiding among the shrubbery of this lawn. When he was older he roamed the acres of forest, shooting quail and ducks along the river. Always he remembered lying on the big porch on hot summer nights, watching the shooting stars while his grandfather listened to the baseball games on his FM radio, one of the first in the city.

After his grandparents died, they used the house for weekends, but stopped after vandals looted, then torched the house some ten years ago. He hadn't been back since. Neither, in fact, had his father, who couldn't bear to see it anymore. They had gone there, the two of them, a month after the fire and his father had wept and never returned. As with the cabin up at Still River, much of Beau's past was here in the debris.

He left his jacket on a limb and wandered around for a while, investigating the little places he remembered, a tree he'd climbed, a pocket of grass he'd lain upon gazing up at the sky, a bramble of bushes that had produced the sweetest blackberries imaginable.

Finally, he decided to walk down to the hollow itself. It was about a quarter mile from the main house. His grandmother had told him that her father had named the place Buck Hollow after killing a deer beside the pond there in the 1840s. Beau was surprised to find that the traces of the old path from the lawn to the hollow were still visible, leading beneath tall pine trees and a tangle of swampy growth. Suddenly he found himself on top of a rise of high ground, looking down. For a moment it seemed the hollow hadn't changed at all. At the far end was a pond, upon which several mallards floated lazily. The shallow parts were abundant in cattails and reeds.

The bottom of the hollow and the slope leading to it were surprisingly green for this time of the year. Weeds had not taken hold, just overgrown grass. At one end was a ramshackle barn and stable and a fenced-in paddock where Beau had learned to ride.

Set up against the sloping hillside, Hollow House was a weathered brick cottage that had begun as an icehouse for the main place. Slaves had built the round cornucopian icehouse with a slate roof that looked more like a turret than anything else. Around the turn of the century Beau's great-grandfather built onto the structure, using the icehouse as a base, adding beautiful French windows and two small wings. He loved the little house, Beau's grandmother said, and he would sit by the fire and carve animals from driftwood and reminisce about the War Between the States, in which he had served as a Confederate cavalry officer. She would have to send someone to fetch him for meals.

Beau made his way down the slope toward the house. Pear and peach trees, most of them in poor shape, surrounded Hollow House and a little brook burbled just outside the front door on its way to the pond. A tiny bridge that had been built over it remained, leading down to a sort of garden—not a formal garden, but an attempt at one—with rotting wooden benches and a miniature pond fashioned out of stones built up around a dammed-in section of the brook.

Ivy covered the steps to the house, ran brazenly through the front door, and covered part of the living room too. Most of the panes were broken out and the sills were rotting. The brick was in need of refacing, but the slate roof was as solid as the day it had been finished.

Beau put his foot tentatively on the ivy-covered steps and reached for the weathered front door, which stood ajar. The mallards on the pond suddenly took off in a rush of wingbeats.

The insides were a shambles. But the ceilings were in reasonably good shape. The floor was tightly constructed of wide oak planks, in need of refinishing, but solid. There was no indoor plumbing, no kitchen and no heating except for fireplaces. Beau explored further. It was damp and cold inside the house.

The living room had a large bay window with small French panes that looked out over the pond and the marsh beyond it. The turret room—the old icehouse—was in the middle and had a Dutch door that opened to a view of the pond too. In the other wing was a large room that had been used to put up guests during holidays and family reunions. As a boy, Beau had slept down here on summer nights, on a cot set out by the windows. He would get up at daybreak and go to the pond with a rod and fish for green trout.

He stepped back into the sunshine and the whole bottomland spread out gladelike before him. In the little brook he saw a newt and a few tiny minnows on the sandy bottom; a good sign. There wasn't a sound; it was almost as removed from civilization as the hunting cabin up at Still River. He stood back, looked at the house and made some rough calculations.

It was a wild idea, but possible. It would take a lot of work. Maybe it wouldn't be worth it. He needed a place to live. He was certain his old man would be pleased. He might even chip in to help restore the place. It was only twenty minutes from the *Courier-Democrat*. Not a bad investment.

Beau walked down to the pond and picked up a piece of a branch and threw it in, watching the ripples spread. He looked back at the house and ran his fingers through his hair, and knew somehow that he had made the right decision to leave New York. He already felt healthier from his enforced sobriety. He didn't intend to give up alcohol forever, just a few months maybe, and then perhaps he'd have a little wine with dinner. With the pressures of the job, this was a place he could come home to. The thought occurred to him that it would be nice to have a woman to come home to as well. Eleanor came suddenly to his mind but just as suddenly he began thinking about Sheilah. He knew she got back from Europe Saturday night. At some point he was going to have to deal with her. Actually it was himself he would have to deal with, but he did not understand this then.

"Two things," Eleanor Campbell said. She was sitting in Beau's office late that afternoon after spending nearly five hours with Tommy Brodie's father.

"First, he was a homosexual."

"What! How do you know that?"

"His father told me." She had taken the old man for drinks in the bar of the Holiday Inn where he was staying. After a while he opened up to her.

"The father said Tommy was apparently embarrassed about it. He didn't find out about it until recently," she said.

Beau shook his head and blew out a deep breath. "What's the other thing?"

"That business over at the D.A.'s office is definitely some kind of criminal investigation, because they are reading people their rights."

"Who is?"

"The D.A. is."

"How do you know?"

"Because I know a secretary who knows the D.A.'s secretary and she told me."

"How did she know?"

"The D.A.'s secretary told her."

"Are they placing charges?"

"I don't know. That's all my source knew."

"Keep after it. Anything else?"

"That's it."

"Good," he said. "Now, what would you like for supper tonight? We can talk more about it then."

Beau took Eleanor to a small, expensive and somewhat pretentious French restaurant that advertised French-Creole cooking. Actually, he didn't take her there, he met her there—a suggestion she made. He was seated in the small, but plush and dimly lit bar drinking a club soda and lime when she came in. She looked lovely in a black pantsuit, her long dark hair flowing over her shoulders.

"Hi," she said. "Am I on time?"

"To the second." Beau motioned to the maître d' and he ushered them into the candlelit dining room to an out-of-the-way table for two.

"What'll you have?" he asked as the maître d' hovered over them.

"I think I'll have a martini," she said. Beau looked at the maître d' and nodded.

"Straight or rocks?" the maître d' asked.

Eleanor looked at Beau and then burst into a giggle. "I've never *had* a martini. I just ordered it because it sounded suitably sophisticated."

"It is." Beau turned to the maître d'. "Make it with Bombay gin, very dry, straight up."

The maître d' nodded. "Olive?"

"Olive," Beau said. And then they were left alone.

"What are you drinking?" Eleanor asked. Her eyes were curious, genuinely wanting to know, unlike so much of the obligatory society chat he'd been used to.

"Club soda," he said. "Healthy."

"No alcohol?"

"Nope. I left that in New York City."

"I suppose it's a difficult place to live."

"It's an impossible place to live—and a lot of impossible people live there."

"It must be exciting. I'd love to go there one day."

"Exciting, yes," Beau said dryly, "but that wears off." He noticed her furrowed brow and realized that he might have sounded jaded—for that matter, he *was* jaded.

"It's not bad, actually," he offered. "It's a wonderful city in so many ways. Full of life—all kinds of it."

"So why did you decide to move back here?"

"Well, a lot of reasons. Pappy—ah, Mr. Turner—said he wanted me and then I was sort of spinning my wheels with a play I'm writing and . . . ." He paused; it suddenly occurred to him that Eleanor was a very good reporter indeed. In the short space of a couple of minutes she had him telling her all sorts of things about himself.

"Why don't you let *me* play reporter for a while?" he said.

"Oh, I'm sorry. I didn't mean . . ."

"No, it's okay." He waved her off. "I'd just like to know more about, ah, the people who work for me."

"Shoot."

"All right, how old are you?"

"Twenty-three."

"School?"

"Sophie Newcomb."

"Ah, New Orleans."

"The city of sin." She laughed.

"Born?"

"Upstate. On a farm in Greer County. My father raises cattle and corn and pigs and sometimes cotton."

"A good ole corn-fed farm girl, then."

"Does it show?"

"Only in pleasant ways."

A waiter arrived with the martini and put it before Eleanor. Beau reached over and took the stem between his fingers and lifted the glass to his lips and took a deep whiff.

"Ah," he said, "a very dry martini."

"Taste it, if you like," she said.

"No, no, thank you. Just a sniff is all I need. It brings back a great deal of pleasure."

"Were you ever married?" Eleanor asked.

"Nope."

"Never wanted to?"

"Sometimes," he said. Sheilah came pestering back into his thoughts like a mosquito. He wished he could drive her away with a brush of his hand. Before this line of questioning could continue the waiter mercifully reappeared at the table and began reciting the specials for the evening.

Beau ordered shrimp étoffé and Eleanor got sautéed speckled trout. They felt each other out some more before the first course was served. During the meal they became wrapped up in business talk—the paper, the staff, the editors, Beau's high hopes and Eleanor's keen observations.

"I've only been with the paper a little over a year," she said, "but since you came, it all seems so different—more real."

"Have you ever been in a big-city newspaper's newsroom?"

"No. I've never been in *any* newsroom except the *Courier-Democrat*'s."

"Someday I'd like to show you one. It's like nothing else I can think of, especially when a big story's breaking."

"I'll bet you've seen some good stories in your days," she said.

"A few."

"Did you cover Watergate when you were a reporter?"

Beau suddenly burst out laughing and Eleanor looked pleasantly puzzled.

"Yes, indeed I did!" He told her the story, all of it, about how he almost single-handedly blew the biggest political story to hit the front pages in twenty-five years. She listened, fascinated, and laughed with him and made consoling remarks when he began to deprecate his investigative reporting abilities.

"You just trusted the wrong people, that's all," she said at one point.

"Well, I'll tell you this," he said, "it's not often that a fellow gets a second chance, and from what all my instincts are telling me, the Brodie affair and the Universal Oil investigation are going to be a Watergate in microcosm."

"Do you really think so?" she asked wonderingly.

"Yes, and I don't intend to blow this one."

Bienville

Beau Gunn had an uncanny way of persuading people. It was just the right combination of authority, guile and some undefinable element of his personality that instinctively made people want to follow him. I have seen this in very few people, but Beau had it, all right. Ever since I could remember.

He worked his magic on Eric Pacer, our former drug enthusiast, who wanted nothing more than to skipper yachts in the Caribbean. Beau took him to lunch and persuaded him in an hour to join the staff of the *Courier-Democrat* as "special assistant to the editor." Pacer had few if any affairs to clean up, since most of what he owned he carried in a suitcase—except for a fat bank account in Switzerland. He agreed he'd be ready to start the next day or so. In the meantime, Beau began cracking heads at the office.

"What more do you know about this?" Beau was saying to Peter Watkins, the reporter who had been the first on the scene at the ship explosion. He was standing beside Watkins's desk and in his hand was a copy of the follow-up story Watkins had turned in for the next day.

"Nothing, really," Peter said innocently. "It's just a follow-up on the explosion story. Horace told me to find out whatever I could and do a piece."

"According to this," Beau said, "the manifest for that ship called for her to be carrying a load of cement. Bound for Honduras."

"That's right."

"Then what the hell blew up?" Beau asked.

189

"Well, I, er, guess the boilers or something."

"It wasn't a steamship, Peter. They don't have steamships anymore."

"Well, it may have been the fuel tanks, then. I don't really know."

"It was oil, Peter. Oil—we said that in the *first* story."

"Right," Watkins said sheepishly.

"Have you seen the fire marshal's report?"

"No, I went over, but it hadn't been finished yet."

"And that was when? Several days after it happened?"

"About that," Peter said.

"What is the regulation on fire marshal's reports?" Beau pressed. "Isn't there something that says they have to be filed by such and such a time after the fire?"

"I really don't know. I don't cover the fire department. I cover . . ."

"Maybe you ought to find out, Peter," Beau said icily. "Doesn't it strike you as odd to have an explosion of that magnitude—an oil explosion—on a ship that's supposed to be carrying a cargo of cement?"

"I guess I never thought about it."

"Think about it for a while and let me know." Beau went back in his office.

He lit a cheroot and swiveled his chair to the window, drumming his fingers on one of its arms. I have inherited, he thought, a sorry lot of reporters here. No initiative. No instinct. No curiosity. He wondered if they had ever been taught reporter's skills, or if the knowledge had been wrung out of them after they got here. Whatever it was, he was going to have to build a fire under them until they got the picture.

"Here's to my new administrative assistant and my finest investigative reporter," Beau said, lifting a glass of iced tea. He, Eleanor and Pacer were sitting around a restaurant table after a long Sunday brunch.

"Listen, you two, how about a little drive around town?" Beau said. "I haven't had much time to look around since I've been here. It might be fun. You know, Eleanor, Pacer and I can show you all the places where we used to get in trouble."

"Great," she said.

"There ain't enough time to show you all of them," said Pacer.

Soon they were driving on the outskirts of the black part of town, past dumps and fenced-in junkyards. Beau turned down a little dirt street lined with a few sycamore trees. Black children were playing with a miniature football in the street.

They had been in the car for nearly two hours, Beau and Pacer regaling

Eleanor with stories of the past, of the Five Funny Fellows and Singer Academy and all the rest of it. Beau even drove them by the old house on the hill where his Halloween had ended forever. Eleanor was sitting beside him, and when he told his story of that humiliating night, she had instinctively put her hand on his arm and given it a squeeze. Beau had felt a warm tingle run up his spine.

"Where we going now, Cap'm?" Pacer asked.

"To the office. I think it's time you got a look at it."

"The partition is going to be set up here," Beau continued as he walked Eleanor and Pacer around the office. He pointed to a space with filing cabinets and a stack of bound newspapers. "I'll put a door here leading into my office, and one here to this corridor, and a desk."

They were standing by the rim, in the center of the newsroom, which was deserted and quiet except for the occasional tick of the teletype machines.

"I'm still not exactly clear on what you want me to do, Cap'm," Pacer said.

"Neither am I, but it will evolve in time. When I say 'troubleshooter,' I know that's a loaded word. I need a right-hand man here—somebody with an instinct to know what's going on and where the problems are. The first thing you'll have to do is familiarize yourself with the staff. I'll introduce you around tomorrow, but you'll have a lot to do on your own. Talk to people, ask questions; if certain people need help, give it to them. Insulate me from the unnecessary crap, but make sure I'm aware of it anyway.

"You should get a big stack of back issues of the paper and go through them meticulously. The best way to learn about a paper is to read it. See who's doing what. Is it concerned with certain issues? If so, what are they? Who's important in this town? Ask questions. Ask a lot of questions."

"You're really taking this pretty seriously, aren't you, Cap'm?" Pacer had said the same thing to Beau in Vietnam when Beau was running around frantically trying to get the company organized for something or other. Back then the activity had seemed to actually relax him a bit.

"You're damned right I am. I've got to, if I want other people to take us seriously."

"Oh, c'mon, Cap'm," Pacer said. "It ain't as serious as the war, is it?"

Beau turned to Pacer. "You're damned right it is. A newspaper is as serious as it gets." Eleanor was sitting on a desk smiling, enjoying the tête-à-tête.

"It ain't as serious as World War II, is it, Cap'm?" Pacer persisted.

"It can be," Beau declared. "Let me tell you something. Let me tell you both something.

"A newspaper can be a voice for a whole city. If the newspaper is bad, and if its judgment is bad, if it only represents some of the people, only covers society affairs and business events and fires and crime and disasters, and doesn't get at the root problems, if it doesn't include everybody in its coverage, or slants the news, then it doesn't do any real good, and maybe it does more harm than good.

"But if a newspaper is good, and if the stories it prints are accurate, true, fair and unbiased, then it assumes a role of leadership in the community and people respect the stories and opinions that it prints and it gets them to thinking and talking. They don't have to *like* the stories and opinions, but they've got to respect them, and people—at least the majority of them, and I believe this—don't respect arrogance or stupidity or incompetence and, furthermore, they know it when they see it."

"It ain't as serious as the Civil War, is it, Cap'm?" Pacer asked innocently. Eleanor burst out laughing.

"All right, all right," Beau said grouchily. "I can see that neither of you people have any dedication to a higher purpose." He put one arm around Pacer's shoulder and the other around Eleanor's and pointed them toward the door.

"Let's get the hell out of here," he said, "before somebody catches us and puts us to work."

The next morning broke clear and pleasant, with the temperature in the high sixties, a hint of spring in January. Beau got into the office and, much to his surprise, found Pacer sitting in his cubicle poring over stacks of old *Courier-Democrats.*

"Thought I'd get an early start," Pacer said. In another corner of the newsroom, Eleanor sat at her desk wearing a pair of tan slacks and a pink sweater, looking fresh and radiant.

They had kissed last night after they left the newsroom. Beau had dropped Pacer off at his parents' house and then taken Eleanor back to her car at the restaurant. She lived in a small apartment, and while she hadn't said it outright, he suspected that she was a little embarrassed to let him see it and felt more comfortable meeting him places.

He had pulled up next to her car, a battered compact, and when he got out to open the door she had been waiting for him on the other side. It had been nearly dark and in the chilly winter twilight they had faced each other, nearly twenty years apart in age, she the exuberant, beautiful young reporter, he the aging but still handsome embodiment of all she hoped she might become. Neither of them had spoken, but as he stood there, she had stepped closer to him and so he had taken her by the shoulders and bent slightly to kiss her on the lips. He had felt her warmth as she drew to him and the sweet taste of her mouth on his. It had not been a long kiss, or a particularly passionate one. But both of them knew that would come later. When they drew away, he saw the dying sunlight sparkle in her eyes and, for the moment, there was nothing else but her.

"Okay," Beau said to Pacer, "let's get down to work. I'm having the morning news conference in my office in about ten minutes. I'd like you to be there, to listen in and to meet some people."

Ten minutes later he introduced Pacer around and went over the items on the news calendar. The main topic on the agenda was a bill up for vote in the state legislature that would extend a badly needed aid package to the city's public schools.

"What do you have as background?" Beau asked Clarence Massy, the state editor.

"I don't quite understand what you mean," Massy said. He was a thin, gaunt-looking man in his late fifties.

"I mean, has your reporter up at the capital filed background material yet—the B matter?"

Massy looked at Horace, and Horace took up the slack.

"No, he hasn't," Horace said. "He usually just files the whole story when he gets it."

"What if it breaks on deadline?" Beau asked.

"He's pretty good at filing," Horace said. "He can dictate a . . ."

"Look," Beau said, "get on the horn and tell him to file all the background now, so we don't have to scramble if the thing breaks late."

Massy left the room and Beau looked at Horace. "It just occurred to me that nobody around here cares if an edition goes by and we miss it." Beau seemed to be chewing his words. "Just because we're the only paper in this town doesn't mean we can sit on our ass and let things slide by. As of now, we have a policy of getting any new news into the next goddamn edition we send out. Understood?"

Horace and the others nodded. A few additional matters were discussed and everybody got up to leave.

Before the end of the day, Eleanor Campbell came into Beau's office. He had just ended a conversation with a local architect about restoring the house at Buck Hollow.

"I got a lead on what the D.A.'s up to," she said, taking a seat.

"Tell me about it." He got up and closed the door.

"It has something to do with oil and gas. The reason I say that is because somebody I know down at City Hall overheard a guy in the Raphael House bar talking about Washington. It turns out he's been here for more than a month, staying at the hotel. My guy picked up from the conversation that this fellow's from the Department of Energy. And he also said he's seen him go up to the D.A.'s office a number of times. Once or twice late in the evening, when they were holding those meetings."

"What else?" Beau asked.

"Not much now. He goes to the Raphael House bar every afternoon. I thought I'd try to get to him and see what he's doing here."

"Good," Beau said. "Keep on it."

"There's one more thing—something that's been bothering me about the Brodie case."

Beau leaned back in his chair and reached for a cheroot. "Shoot."

"The knife the girl was killed with—how did they know to look in Brodie's apartment for it?"

"Find out," Beau said. He took a puff of the cheroot and went back to some papers on his desk. She moved to the door and was about to leave when Beau stopped her. "By the way, you want to have dinner tonight?"

Eleanor broke into a smile.

"Sure, chief."

After she left, Beau sat puffing on the cigar, trying to sort out the puzzle. Why weren't the cops talking, or, more to the point, why had they clamped the lid shut? What was the connection between Tommy Brodie, the dead girl and the meetings at the D.A.'s office? Why did Tommy Brodie kill himself— and did he? Poor Tommy, Beau thought. Poor old Tommy Brodie. Whatever he became started long ago, in a time of enchanted summers.

Vox Populi

The next morning, a Friday, Beau sent for Eleanor Campbell.

"I think it's about time we started a brushfire."

She looked at him puzzled, and he motioned her to sit down.

They had had dinner the night before at Danatreux's: fresh pompano and crabmeat salad and oysters Bienville. After dinner Beau had taken her to a small nightclub to listen to some very good jazz musicians. Beau had dared the fates that night by having his first alcohol—a single glass of a rather good white wine. To his surprise, he didn't really want any more and this pleased him. Afterward, they walked down a quiet brick alleyway to the street where Beau's car was parked. Eleanor held tightly to his arm, her head resting against his shoulder. When they reached her apartment building, they kissed and said good night. Beau drove away knowing that this was all going to have to lead somewhere. He still wasn't sure he was ready for it.

"The more I think about this Brodie affair, and about Universal Oil and whatever's going on over at the D.A.'s office, the more I think there's a very direct connection," he told her, squinting into the sunshine pouring through his office window. "I don't know exactly what it is, but sometimes if you run a story and sound like you know things you aren't reporting yet, it gets things heated up with whoever *is* in the know and somebody starts talking."

Eleanor sat with her hands folded in her lap, listening. Beau saw a sparkle in her gray eyes. She seemed very pleased that he was entrusting *her* with this story.

"In cases like this," he continued, "it's been my experience that a lot more people than you think know something. Maybe they don't know all of it, but you set the brushfire, and get them stirred up, and sooner or later one or two will run out of the woods thinking his ass is on fire and start hollerin'."

"Now, let's review what we know." He looked at a legal pad on his desk. "We have three events—first, the death of the girl, Brodie's implication, his death. Second, the investigation, or whatever it is, of Universal Oil, and the fact that Congressman Whittle is somehow involved. Third, the highly suspicious fire on the Universal Oil ship a few weeks back. The question is: how, if at all, are these connected?"

Eleanor was taking notes, but Beau stopped her. "For the time being," he said, "I think we can just talk about it." He went back to his legal pad.

"Now, we know Brodie was a homosexual. So if he killed the girl it wasn't over sex. We've also learned that the murder weapon was found in his apartment. This fellow Spinker says Brodie didn't do it. The girl was seen with Ben Grimshaw the very night of the murder and they had an argument shortly before her body was found, right?"

"Right," Eleanor said.

"Okay. Now, Ben Grimshaw runs Universal Oil, and Universal Oil is involved in some kind of super-secret investigation by the D.A.'s office. A number of bigwigs in this town, including our own congressional representative, have been seen going in and out of the investigator's office. And furthermore, a ship belonging to Universal Oil, which was supposed to be carrying cement but was in fact carrying oil, mysteriously catches fire in the harbor and the fire marshal's report is 'lost.' "

"But what's our connection?"

"Ben Grimshaw," Beau said, "who used to be in league with Fletcher Cross, who has been involved in practically every scam and chicanery around here from real estate to the dog track."

"But *how* is he connected?"

"We're not in a courtroom and we don't have to be hampered by a bunch of legal proof. Look," he said, "it's all this damned official secrecy that's got me intrigued. In all my experience, it's been a general rule that when the authorities start hiding things, they've got a reason, and usually that reason involves something they don't want the public to know. Why don't they want us to know it? Usually because the information will create a scandal. Why, for instance, was Brodie moved from here up to the Caballa County jail? Did he say anything to anybody before he died? Did he leave a note?"

"And why would he kill himself?" Eleanor asked.

"Did he?"

"Well, yes—I mean, that's what they said."

"Have you looked at the coroner's report?"

"Well, I—not yet. I didn't think . . ."

"Do it."

"And what about Spinker?" she asked. "I mean, we promised not to use his name. He's the only witness who's come forward to place the dead girl and Ben Grimshaw together that night."

"There were other people in the bar. They have to know something. What about the owner, the bartender, a waitress?"

"I've already talked to them. They say they don't remember anything."

"Talk to them again," he said. "Here's what I want for Sunday: do a takeout on this whole business, assemble everything we know, down to the last shred, and put it in a story. I'll run it on the front page. Don't try anything fancy, don't make any unfounded claims, just get in all the facts and outline the questions that are still unanswered. The television stations will pick it up and maybe create some kind of clamor for truth. After that, every new fact we get we'll run. We'll hound these people until they start talking straight."

Eleanor nodded. She was a little perplexed by the assignment. Policy on the *Courier-Democrat* had generally been to report whatever the authorities told them—they did not make waves, and they certainly did not suggest in print that the authorities were lying or holding back. *That* was the reason the paper's reporters had always gotten along with everyone down at City Hall. This was going to make things difficult.

"I want to see the story by eleven Saturday morning. We'll work over it that afternoon."

"Yes, Mr. Gunn," she said, smiling impishly as she stood and straightened her skirt.

"Beau," he said crankily, returning to the papers on his desk.

He had spent much of the week writing memos to the staff. In one afternoon he sent out nearly two dozen, either complimentary or critical, though there was little he found to compliment. He edited most of the major stories himself, but continued to be disappointed by the quality of the pieces, particularly in the metropolitan-news section. Some stories didn't make sense and others would have missed the point entirely. Some didn't press hard enough for information or didn't include enough background in the article for the reader to be properly informed.

"Look here," he said to one middle-aged reporter named Terry Smith. "You have a story on a plan to raise property taxes on second homes. What

197

have you done with it? You wrote six paragraphs and not one of them describes the impact of such a bill if it passes. Do you have any idea how that bill will affect all those condominiums they're building along the coast? What do the builders say? What do the real estate people say? Aren't you aware that things done in the legislature have an impact on the public at large?"

Smith sat quietly as Beau chewed him out, then left apologetically. When he was gone, Beau sent for the editor who approved the story. "If this kind of thing continues to happen I'm going to assign you to writing obituaries," he said curtly.

Beau ordered a larger bulletin board installed in the newsroom and tacked up numerous general memorandums. He had quickly become aware of the slackers and the incompetents and he reassigned them to areas where they could do the least harm. He had decided against firing anybody, because he believed everyone should be given a chance to shape up. He called in the people who wrote the headlines and read them the riot act.

"I want you to make damn sure that whatever headline you put on a story is referred to in the first three paragraphs. A first-year journalism student would know that!"

He began making subtle changes in the layout of the newspaper. There would be no more than six stories on the lead page of a section. He simplified jump heads, straightened out column alignments and introduced subheads. He worked his ass off.

One day Beau summoned the editors of the various news departments. It was time, he felt, to express his ongoing dissatisfaction with some of their judgments. His annoyance had been building for weeks.

He addressed himself first to Mrs. Marks, the "Living Style" section editor:

"Please," he said wearily, "don't let me ever see a silly horoscope leading this section. Horoscopes are for superstitious idiots. If we have to run one, we will not run it as news or as a news feature. It belongs in the back of your section.

"And the same goes for 'Dear Abby' and that other one—what's her name? Put 'em in the back pages. People who want to find them will. I want to see stories. *Stories* about *people.*"

Beau stood up and paced around.

"What in hell are you people *thinking?* There are over half a million people in this area, and every one of them has a story. We're assuming that the most important thing in their lives is a damned *horoscope* or some dimestore psychology from a Chicago woman? This section should lead with a feature on culture—art, architecture, literature, films, music, food—it's supposed to be about lifestyle. Okay?"

Mrs. Marks, quite unaccustomed to being spoken to in this manner, sat quietly and nodded her head. Before she could speak, Beau directed his attention to the society-page editor.

"This," he said, holding up a copy of the morning edition, "is *not* society news." The lead story informed readers that members of a certain family in the north of the county were planning a covered dish and pound cake picnic the following weekend.

"Society news is news about extraordinary people. Bienville has operas, balls, symphony concerts, extravagant private parties attended by interesting and sometimes powerful people who are often horse's asses but nonetheless comprise 'society.' The job of the society editor is to establish just who constitutes this group and write about them—not about pound cake parties."

The society editor was a thin woman in her forties with a 1960s beehive hairdo. She seemed as taken aback by Beau's lack of appreciation of her work as Mrs. Marks, but again he moved on before she could react. He turned on Philip Pope, editor of the editorial page.

"Phil, why is it that we offer the people of this community five different right-wing columnists every week? Isn't there any diversity of opinion? Can't we find a wire feature service with some different points of view?"

"Well," Pope said in his meek drawl, "we've got the black guy. He's a liberal."

"Yes, and what do you expect him to be, a white supremacist? Good Lord. We run one black columnist once a week and call that a diversity of opinion. Goddammit, what we're trying for here is some kind of *balance.* We don't want to *tell* people what to think. We want to provide them with a variety of opinions so that they can think for themselves. For heaven's sake, I grew up on this diet myself. It wasn't until I left here that I discovered there was a whole world of viewpoints out there. I want you to find me some alternative columnists and have a list on my desk in the morning."

Next in line was the state editor.

"We have an election coming up," Beau said testily, "and a man from this city has a chance to become a United States senator. Can you explain to me why we are using *wire service* copy to report his campaign? Why aren't we covering this campaign ourselves?"

"It costs money," the state editor said. "We don't cover state politics unless it happens here."

"We do now," Beau said. "You get somebody on that campaign and I want a fresh story every day and you let *me* worry about the money."

Beau continued kicking ass straight down the line: foreign news, agricultural news, sports—even obituaries. When he was finished, he didn't ask for questions. He figured he'd let them think about what he'd said and then give them a chance to voice their opinions in a week or so. After they left, Beau turned his chair to the window and leaned back, reflecting on his own thoughts about what a newspaper should be. He had grown up with the *Courier-Democrat,* delivered to his home every morning and afternoon. It was no wonder so many Bienvillians were poorly informed and backward-thinking. Their most prominent publication was a badly written, opinionated, amateurish daily wipe. He had resolved to change that, and now he was facing the reality of doing it. He knew they needed some new blood, but it would have to come from the ranks of the bright young college graduates who could be enticed to work for low pay for a chance to learn the business. Perhaps he could establish a scholarship or a recruiting program. He resolved to take the matter upstairs.

Eric Pacer, on the other hand, was working out even better than he'd expected. Beau had sent him on a variety of missions—dealing with the truck drivers and the route men, the telephone company and the parking-lot people. Pacer helped iron out kinks in the new central switchboard, set up systems and made sure requisition forms were dealt with promptly. He went around to meet city officials and establish relationships that would help improve coverage in case of emergencies. He got new water fountains in the hallways and oversaw the working conditions in the news departments by dealing directly with the maintenance supervisor. One day Beau turned Pacer loose on a news assignment, albeit an important one, which, as it turned out, would shatter some illusions—Beau's included—but also shed light on some other matters.

The story Eleanor Campbell prepared on the Tommy Brodie–Universal Oil affair ran as scheduled in the Sunday editions. As Beau suspected, it didn't just raise eyebrows, it caused hell to be raised.

First thing Monday morning the public safety commissioner was on the phone to Beau.

"I can't understand how you can make all these damned accusations against the police department," he growled.

"We made no accusations," Beau said calmly.

"Then what do you call this? 'The police have steadfastly refused to reveal even the slightest details of Brodie's involvement in the murder'!"

"That isn't an accusation," Beau replied, "it's a simple statement of fact."

"It *sounds* like an accusation to me. It sounds like we're covering up something."

"It sounds that way to me too. I'm glad we're in agreement."

"Good Lord, man," the commissioner sighed, "this is a murder investigation."

"And your suspect is dead, so what reason have you got to keep denying the public its right to know why he was arrested and then moved around from jail to jail? If you're so damn sure Brodie did it, you can't indict a dead man, can you?"

The commissioner groaned in exasperation. "You don't understand, it's more complicated than that. There are other things . . ."

"Like the connection between the murder and Universal Oil?"

"You don't know what you're talking about," the commissioner said angrily.

"Are you denying it, then?" Beau asked.

"I'm not commenting."

"Good," Beau said. "Then we'll say that."

After he hung up, he summoned Eleanor.

"I want you to do a page-one story, next edition. I've just had a conversation with the public safety commissioner."

"Commissioner Refuses to Deny Link Between Murder and Oil Company," the headline read. The rest of the story retold what had been in the Sunday editions. As Beau had promised, they would continue to repeat the facts in future stories until the paper's readers would demand to know the answers. In Washington, this ploy had been known as "Putting on the Big Heat."

That afternoon Beau sent for Eleanor Campbell and two other reporters: young Tim Harte, a Yale graduate he'd just hired, and Bill Spaulding, a competent middle-aged reporter who covered county politics.

"I want to set up a team," Beau said. "Something about this whole Universal Oil–Brodie business smells rotten to the core and it's getting worse by the day. Eleanor will be in charge, but here's what I want you to do.

"Eleanor, you give me a piece on Tommy Brodie. I want you to find out everything humanly possible about him. What was his life like for the past ten years, who were his friends, which places did he frequent, where had he lived, how did he spend his days and nights? I want you to talk to anybody who knew him or knew who he was. I want a total picture of him—a finely honed profile.

"Tim," Beau continued, "you do the same for Gordon McWorth and

Trevor Blount, the bank president. See what you can find out about their personal finances. What connection do they have with Universal Oil? Have their lifestyles changed recently? That sort of thing.

"And, Bill, your job is to profile Fletcher Cross and Ben Grimshaw. I want to know everything about them, as though I've lived their lives day by day. I want to know *everything* about Grimshaw's relationship with the dead girl."

Bill Spaulding nodded as Beau looked at the three of them.

"There's another party in all this, and it's Dan Whittle. There's a ton of stuff in the clips on him, but I want you to keep your eyes open for more. Is there a connection between Dan and any of these others. Any questions?"

"When do you want this, Beau?" Tim Harte asked.

"Soon as possible. Make it your first priority. I'll tell the desk you're working on this exclusively except in the event of an emergency. Let's see what you come up with by the end of the week."

After the three left, Beau tapped on the glass of Pacer's cubicle, motioning for him to come in.

"I've got something I want you to do," he said.

"Name it, Cap'm," Pacer said merrily.

"I've put three reporters on the Universal Oil story. But I want you to do a little poking around too. Find out just what Universal Oil does for its living. It's a private company, so there aren't any public financial reports, but I'm sure there are people who have access to them. Let's see what they own, what they rent, what they build, dig, pump, buy or sell. You might have to go to the tax assessor's office and pull deeds. Ask around, but be discreet. Find out what the destroyed ship was doing at Universal's terminal claiming a cargo of cement. Also, see if you can get hold of the fire marshal's 'lost' report. The idiot reporter who was supposed to ask tough questions and not take lies for an answer can't find his ass with both hands."

"Anything else, Cap'm?"

"Yeah. Did the Army do that to you?"

"Do what, Cap'm?" Pacer stared down at himself.

"Make you afraid of barbers?" Beau smiled wickedly as Pacer turned to leave.

Whatever his general dissatisfactions were with the *Courier-Democrat*, Beau had seen noticeable improvements at the paper since he came. It looked better, both graphically and in content. Moreover, the staff's attitude had improved dramatically. After an initial period of fear and confusion, they had become members of a team. Beau was becoming proud of them. There was a perceptible change in the atmosphere of the newsroom; it had started to hum, especially around deadline, just like the old newsroom in Washington. Even Nadine and Doreen, the Sob Sisters, had shaped up and were doing lively, often funny features, and what was more, they had both changed their hairstyles and begun to wear nicer clothes.

The desk editors and copy editors had started to improve too. Beau found that he was sending them fewer memos and that some of the old practices—like putting beauty pageant stories on the front page—were quickly fading away. Beau began to think that the *Courier-Democrat* just might get its Pulitzer Prize, after all.

One day Beau caught Eleanor alone in the hall.

"Listen," he said. "Remember that hunting camp I told you about up on Still River? Well, I'm thinking about going up this weekend. It's the end of the duck season, and I thought I'd do a little hunting. It's awfully pretty up there in the delta, even in the winter, so I thought maybe you'd like to come along."

"I'd love to," she said. "When do we leave?"

"I was thinking about going up early Saturday and coming back Sunday."

"Oh, I'm scheduled to work the early shift Saturday morning."

"Well . . ."

"Unless . . ."

"No," he said. "Go ahead and work it. What time are you off?"

"About one-thirty."

"Okay. Why don't you bring your gear with you and we can leave from here. I need to be in the office for a while myself. If we get off by two, we should be there in plenty of time for the evening shoot.

Eleanor was sitting in the front of the boat and Beau was at the tiller of the outboard. It was chilly in the late-afternoon sun as the little wooden boat skimmed over the still waters of Frenchman's River and then up into the lower marshes of the big delta. Conversation was made impossible by the drone of the motor, but Eleanor would turn around once in a while and smile at him, her hair blowing in the wind. Several times she pointed to something —a big heron, a flight of ducks. Once they saw two deer plunge into the water from the marsh and begin swimming across.

It was nearly four when they reached the camp. Beau pulled the skiff to the wharf and tied it up. In the two and a half months since he'd been there, winter had taken its toll. One piling had been dislocated and the deciduous trees were now stark and bare. Beau climbed out and put their gear on the wharf with Eleanor's help, then he pulled her up to him.

"Let's go in and build a fire," he said.

It was cold in the cabin, damp cold, and musty too. They opened a couple of windows and got several big pieces of firewood from the pile on the porch. Beau laid some sticks of fatwood on the grate and crumpled papers under them. He carefully arranged the logs on top, opened the flu and took the lighter down from the mantel. There was an old spark of recollection as he held the lighter in his hand. It was a chrome Zippo and bore the inscription: "To Beau, from Courtney—always." He'd left the lighter up here some years ago. It was a permanent feature of the mantel, a gesture of some sort, so that her memory would be preserved in the light of cozy fires on a wooded lake in deep woods a thousand miles from where she died. Beau struck the lighter and touched it to the papers. In moments, they had a blazing fire.

"It's beautiful up here," Eleanor said. "It's so quiet."

"I know. I love it here. No roads, and this time of year at least, not many people willing to ride almost two hours in a boat to spoil the solitude."

Beau stored the rest of their gear inside and put a pot of coffee on the butane stove. He piled several more logs on the fire and found some hip boots in a closet and gave them to Eleanor.

"We'd best get a move on. The ducks won't start flying till twilight, but we want to be set up by then.

"You told me you'd shot before," he said, "but I never asked what kind of gun. I brought you one, but it's a double."

"What's that?" she asked.

Beau grunted. He went to the hard leather gun case he had brought and flicked the bronze catches open. Eleanor stood beside him as he raised the lid to reveal a matched pair of beautifully engraved double-barrel shotguns resting on a pad of green velvet. He lifted the smaller of the two and handed it to her.

"This is a twenty-gauge," he said. "It doesn't have nearly the kick that this other one does. Do you know how it works?"

"Oh sure," she said. "This is the kind my daddy let me shoot. I think it belonged to my grandfather."

"Good," he said. "We'll go over it again when we get set up."

They were back in the boat again, motoring slowly along a marshy bank above which tall cypress and cedar trees loomed like stark sentries. Abruptly, Beau turned the boat almost directly into the marsh. Eleanor must have thought they were going to collide with it, for she turned back to look at Beau in alarm, but suddenly the marsh parted and they were in a tight little slough, no wider than the boat. Beau cut the engine and there was only the sound of the marsh reeds brushing against the gunwales. He stood and used an oar to pole a little further until they came to a rickety and half-rotten landing that went up into the marsh. He pushed the boat up to it, took his gun and got out, helping Eleanor along behind him. From the landing, equally rickety and slippery duckboards made a path in the marsh back toward the stream. Beau led the way until they came to a small, uneven wooden structure which looked as if it might have been nailed together before Beau was born by a one-armed drunk during a hurricane. In front was about five feet of marsh grass, hiding it from sight of the stream. This was the shooting platform.

"My God, it's lovely up here," she said, brushing her fingers against the wood as she gazed about her. The stillness was almost overwhelming; nothing, not a faint breeze, not a ripple on the water, not a bird. Beau interrupted the quiet by breaking open his shotgun and inserting two shells in the chambers. Eleanor did the same. Beau showed her the safety and reacquainted her with other features.

"When they come," he said, "they'll come from downstream. The wind's blowing from the north, and they'll land into the wind, just like airplanes do." It was quiet again for a while.

"What was it like being a famous playwright?" Eleanor asked suddenly.

Beau smiled, his eyes still scanning the low horizon. "You say 'was,' I think I still am."

"Oh no," she said, "that wasn't what I meant."

"Well, it's probably more accurate than you think, but it's a fair question. What was it like? It was interesting. I got to know a lot of famous people. After a while you begin to realize they put on their pants one leg at a time just like everybody else. The actors and actresses could be a pain in the butt at times, because they've all got egos as big as the moon."

"Which was your favorite play? That you wrote."

"Oh, I guess it was my first, *Such a Pretty Girl.* I think your first really good creation is usually your favorite. Maybe it's just sentimental." Beau suddenly ducked his head.

"Look there!" he whispered. Before Eleanor could get a glimpse of anything there was the heavy sound of wingbeats. Beau stood up straight and there were two enormous blasts from his gun. She saw the first duck tumble through the air and pitch dead into the water and then a second, just behind it. Half a dozen others in the flight rose swiftly into the sky and headed over the trees. The quiet returned.

"I'm going to get those," he said, stepping into the marsh in his thigh-high boots. If any more come, just lead 'em a foot or so and blast away—but don't shoot low or you'll ventilate my britches."

"Guess what I saw out there," he said after he'd put the two ducks in a safe place behind them.

"What?"

"Bear tracks."

"Bear!"

"Don't worry. I think I know who they belong to. You see, there's an old fellow that lives up here. Last time I came, I thought he was done for." Beau told Eleanor about the old bear, about how he'd been going to shoot it and about its miraculous capacity to survive.

"That's wonderful," she said. "And do you think it's him?"

"From the size of the tracks I'd say it has to be."

"I hope we see him before we go."

"Yeah, so do I."

They were quiet again in the stillness of the swamp. Twice they saw flights of ducks but they were high above the trees.

"Didn't you ever think about getting married during all that time?" Eleanor asked. There was something straightforward in her questions. Somehow she didn't seem to be prying.

"Once, I guess," he said.

"So why didn't you?"

"Jesus, Eleanor," he said, laughing, "you're an even better reporter than I realized."

"Do you mind?" she asked innocently. "I'm interested. I mean, how could a good-looking, famous playwright in New York not have every beautiful girl in the world throwing herself at his feet?"

"I didn't like people throwing themselves at my feet. If I want a doormat, I go out and buy one. It's not a characteristic I would look for in a wife."

"Well, I don't mean it exactly like that. But surely you've met plenty of eligible women."

"I'm not gay, if that's what you're driving at," he said.

"No, silly, I mean . . ."

"There," he hissed, "coming in!"

Diving low and flying straight down the little stream was another group of ducks.

"Black mallards," he said. "You take the first one."

The ducks were about twenty-five yards from the platform when Eleanor pulled the trigger. It was a clean miss and she shot again but too late.

"You were shooting behind them. You've got to lead them more—like letting them fly into your shot pattern."

"I'm sorry. You should have shot."

"Nah, it was a good try. Look, it's getting pretty dark and we've got a couple of nice ducks for supper. Why don't we call it a day."

"You're the boss," she said.

The cabin was toasty warm by the time they got back and Beau heated some more coffee, offering Eleanor a shot of brandy for hers. The fire crackled loudly as they went about preparing dinner. Beau cleaned the ducks and stuffed them with apples and celery and onions and wrapped them in tinfoil, into which he poured a cup of sherry. Then he placed them in a Dutch oven above the fire.

Eleanor made a salad and cooked wild rice they'd brought and Beau prepared a gravy out of several dozen herbs, spices, powders, sauces and vegetables.

"I still want to know about the one who got away," Eleanor said.

"Damn, you are persistent," he said. "Well, all right, I suppose I ought to tell you. Until just recently, I was engaged."

She stopped peeling a tomato and looked at him.

"Is she famous?"

"No, she's not famous," he said.

"Rich?"

"No."

"Good." She laughed and put her arm around his waist. "Then I don't have competition I can't handle."

The dinner was delicious; the duck turned out just right, steamed in the sherry and flavored with the celery and onions and apples. Beau's gravy was a masterpiece and her salad was better than the Four Seasons'. Beau had tucked a bottle of fine Bordeaux into his bag and they had a glass of it with the meal.

"So tell me," Eleanor said as they washed the dishes, "are you still in love with her?"

"If you don't want to know, don't ask," he said.

"I'm asking."

"I don't know," Beau said.

"Oh?" She didn't look up from the dishes.

"You asked for the truth. I'm telling you. I don't know how I feel about her. I don't know if I'd call it love; I still care about her. It's just that, well, I might as well be honest with you, I've had trouble with other relationships because of her."

"What kind of trouble?"

"Not *trouble*," he said. "And there haven't been that many other relationships. It's just that sometimes I can't shake her from my mind."

"Want to tell me about her?" Eleanor said.

"No, I really don't want to get into it."

Afterward, they sat in the darkened room, in front of the fire. Beau had taken a mattress from one of the beds and pulled it close to the hearth. They stared into the fire and talked until it was late. Beau told her about his days in Washington and in New York and, finally, about Vietnam.

Eleanor had only been a child during the war and she, like many of her generation, didn't really understand it. All she'd heard or read was that it was bad and that we'd lost.

"We didn't lose," Beau told her, "we quit. There's a difference. We were winning in the field—slowly maybe, and painfully—but we were winning, and the politicians cut us off. They made a treaty with the North Vietnamese that they knew was a sham but they made it anyway to mollify the people at home. Just get that straight—we didn't lose the war, we quit."

The fire needed another log. When Beau came back, Eleanor had stretched out on the mattress, and he lay down beside her.

"So it sounds like you're still hung up on this girl, huh?"

"Yeah, in a way I am, but it's getting better by the minute."

"I'm sorry I'm asking all these questions," she said, snuggling close to him. "I guess I'm just curious about the kind of woman you would love."

"Sheilah wouldn't be a good example. I think she was probably an aberration. Now, let's put that subject to bed."

"I've got a better idea about who we should put to bed." She raised up on an elbow and kissed Beau gently on the mouth and then passionately and he kissed her back and once again there was, for the moment, nobody else in the world but her and this time he didn't pull back.

Beau awoke at two or three in the morning. Eleanor was sound asleep, her head resting on his shoulder. The fire had gone out and it was getting chilly, so he decided to rebuild it so they wouldn't have to get up in the cold. Using a flashlight, he gathered kindling and logs and lit the stack with the Zippo that Courtney had given him. As the fire blazed he studied the inscription and it suddenly hit him.

Katts—Kitty Katts!

That was Gordon McWorth's wife's name, or her nickname anyway. Courtney Case. Kitty Katts. The names were enough alike so that he was suddenly reminded of Mrs. McWorth's maiden name. And Katts was the name of the girl Tommy Brodie supposedly stabbed. Laura Katts.

It was an unusual name in a town the size of Bienville and most of the Kattses were related somehow. So was the dead girl related to Gordon McWorth by marriage? And if she was, how well did he know her? She could have been a niece, or his wife's cousin.

Beau was quietly pacing around, excited. He thought about waking Eleanor, but she seemed to be sleeping deeply. It wasn't much but it was something; a connection, a possible connection. He lit an oil lamp and set the flame low. He picked up a notebook and wrote down the name Katts, then sat in the big overstuffed chair and began doodling around the names of the parties involved: Katts, McWorth, Universal Oil, Grimshaw. Grimshaw, the man said to have been dating Laura Katts, worked for Universal Oil. McWorth was on its board of directors.

In the ashtray beside the chair was a half-smoked cheroot. Beau relit the cigar, turning the lighter in his fingers before laying it down. "To Beau, from Courtney—always." "Thank you, Courtney," he muttered quietly.

He stayed up until daybreak. That's when Eleanor opened her eyes and found he wasn't there. She looked around the dimly lit room until she saw him sitting in the chair.

"Beau?"

"I've found something!" he said. "Something that might explain a lot."

"What is it?" she said, sitting up.

"A spark from an old flame," he said, handing her the lighter.

Beginning of the End

"Laura Katts was Gordon McWorth's cousin by marriage—his wife's first cousin."

Eleanor and Beau were sitting in his office making notes. Through the glass partition of the small adjoining office, Beau could see Pacer sorting through some files he had asked him to read.

"Her mother married McWorth's sister's son. She told me her daughter was not close to McWorth but then she told me something else," Eleanor continued. "About a month before Laura was killed, McWorth phoned the house and asked to speak to her. She wasn't there, but her mother gave her the message. She didn't know whether her daughter had called him back or not."

Beau rubbed his chin. "You think that's off?"

"Yes, I do. I mean, if the two weren't close, if there hadn't been any contact for years, then it seems odd McWorth would be calling her, doesn't it?"

"Curious," Beau said. "So what's your next move?"

"I'll call Gordon McWorth, I suppose, and see if I can get him to answer a few questions."

Beau nodded silently as Eleanor's eyes searched his.

"I think I've got a better idea; I'll call Gordon myself," he said. "I've probably got a better shot at it, because I've known him since I was knee high. Anyway, I want you to stay on top of Mrs. Katts. What you just told me is

210

an interesting piece of information. People like Mrs. Katts know a lot more than they say. They know a lot more than they think they know, too. I want you to prod her memory about her daughter's every connection with McWorth, Universal Oil, Ben Grimshaw. Visit Laura's friends too. Find out who they were and if she told them anything. Find out absolutely everything you can about her."

"Okay. Anything else?" Eleanor asked.

"Get some results," Beau said, smiling. Eleanor stood and smoothed her dress and produced a small brown bag from her purse.

"I've got something for you," she said, handing the bag to Beau. He took out a small jar and examined its contents quizzically.

"It's pickled okra," Eleanor said. "I made a whole batch last fall. I've got some pickled squash too, if you want some."

"Why, thank you," Beau said, genuinely touched.

Beau asked Eleanor to ride with him down to the Buck Hollow property during lunch. They picked up some barbecue sandwiches and root beer, but on the drive down Eleanor seemed distant and a little fidgety. When she saw the pond and the house, she loosened up some.

"Oh, Beau, it's beautiful. Look at all these trees."

"Magnolias *and* bay trees. You can't do any better."

They poked through the old house in the fading winter sun as Beau described his renovation plan: the library was going here, the living room there, a new fireplace, vaulted ceilings. He and the architect had done a lot of talking.

"I hope you'll be spending some time here when it's finished," he said.

"When do you start?" Eleanor asked. It was not lost on Beau that she didn't respond to his suggestion.

"In two days. I've got the finished plans back from the architect. They're running power in here tomorrow. How about supper this week?"

"Well, which day?" she asked.

"How about day after tomorrow?"

"Do you mind if we make it early? I don't know if I've told you, but I've been jogging every morning. I get up at the crack of dawn."

"Early it is," Beau said.

As she turned to face the pond, he walked behind her and put his arms around her.

"What's wrong?" he asked.

"I don't know. It's silly, I guess, but I've been thinking about us. I'm a little scared."

"I think I'm a little scared too."

"I wish I hadn't asked you about Sheilah. If I hadn't, then I wouldn't be scared."

"Hey, what happened the other night wasn't casual. And I'm glad it happened. I've been feeling good about it ever since."

"You have?"

"Damn straight."

He turned around and kissed her. She began laughing and put her head on his chest.

"You're right. I know you're right. I'm sorry, Beau, I really am."

"One day at a time," he said. "We should take it one day at a time."

When they got back, Beau picked up a phone book and found Gordon McWorth's number.

"I want you to know how proud we are of you, Beau," his old man's former law partner said. "Kitty and I and all our friends followed you in the paper for years. You've really done well for yourself."

Beau thanked him and got around to the business at hand.

"I didn't realize until just recently that Laura Katts was related to you."

"Yes, she was. A tragedy, a horrible tragedy. Of course, I don't see that side of Kitty's family too often, but I remember her from when she was just a little girl."

"You know, Gordon," Beau said smoothly, "I'm calling because we found out from Laura's mother that you called her a few weeks before she died. I was wondering if you could tell us about her and about that call. Why did you call her, by the way?"

"Call her? Me? Umm, I don't remember making any calls to her, Beau. Of course, that was a long time ago. I'd have to refresh my memory."

"What about Universal Oil, Gordon? Why this strange nighttime investigation? What's the story?"

McWorth laughed. "Ah, so this is a professional call?"

"Did you ever doubt it was?" Beau said. "Listen, we've got two highly suspicious deaths and an investigation into your company. I may be crazy, but they all seem somehow related."

"Related? How are they related?" McWorth said, an irritated edge in his voice.

"Well, we know the girl was seeing Ben Grimshaw, your operations manager, at the time she was murdered."

"Well, for Chrissakes, Beau," McWorth boomed, "that's not *related* to us. Grimshaw is an employee. We don't make rules about the women our employees can see. Besides, the police say Brodie did it. Probably a robbery or an attempted sexual assault."

"It wasn't a robbery and it wasn't sexual assault," Beau said. "Brodie was a homosexual and her purse was found near the body."

The line was silent for a few very long moments.

"Oh, hell, Beau, who knows what it was, then. But everybody in town knows Brodie killed that boy. He wasn't right, Beau. He never was. What does any of this have to do with Universal Oil?"

"I don't know—yet," Beau said. "What about the D.A.? What's going on?"

"You know I can't talk about that, but it's purely technical anyway. It'll all be over in a few weeks."

"But it does involve Universal Oil?"

"Beau, I can't talk about it."

"What about Dan Whittle? How's he involved?"

"Beau," McWorth said impatiently. "I am under instructions to let this matter rest between the parties involved and I am not going to violate that recommendation."

"Can you tell me the names of the corporate officers of Universal Oil? I know Fletcher Cross is chairman. Who else?"

"That's public record," McWorth retorted. "I'd like to know why you're asking me a bunch of cockamamie questions."

"Just curious," Beau said pleasantly.

"Well, tell me how your father is. I haven't seen him in a while."

"He's fine. He says he hasn't seen you either."

"I guess it's because our offices aren't downtown anymore. Give him my best, will you? Tell him I'll be in touch."

"I certainly will," Beau said. He put down the phone and stared out the window. He didn't believe Gordon McWorth. He didn't believe a word he'd said.

"And so what I really can't figure out," Pacer announced, "is why they don't just sell directly to the majors—to Texaco, Getty, any of them. They don't seem to do much business except in the import division."

Beau nodded his head and stared into space. They were having dinner at Danatreux's.

"Maybe they have a contract with some small refinery," Beau offered.

"Maybe," Pacer said, "but if they do, nobody in the oil business seems to know anything about it."

Over a supper of gumbo, red beans and rice and fried crab claws, Pacer told Beau the curious story of his investigation of Universal Oil.

The papers of incorporation showed that in addition to Fletcher Cross and Gordon McWorth, Trevor Blount, president of Bienville's largest bank, and several other prominent businessmen were on the company's board of directors. There were twenty-five thousand shares of stock out, with a listed value of ten dollars a share, but the owners of this stock were unknown. Ditto the assets, income and liabilities. In truth, not very much of Universal's affairs were known, because a private company is not required to file public statements.

Pacer had found that in addition to selling and leasing drilling and piping equipment, Universal Oil had an import operation that brought foreign oil into the country. They also owned mineral rights to an estimated twenty thousand acres of oil-rich land in upper Bienville County. This property produced an estimated one thousand barrels of oil per day, according to the people Pacer questioned.

But no one could, or would, say what the company was doing with it.

"Maybe they're storing it somewhere," Beau said, baiting Pacer.

"Maybe," Pacer said, "but why? What would they have to gain?"

"I don't know."

"Most of the people I talked with told me Universal would probably have a hookup to a pipeline owned by one of the major oil companies. That way they'd sell their product directly. But they don't have one. They've got storage tanks and a pipeline of their own, but that area is off-limits and you can't get in there unless you travel by river. They've got all the roads blocked off and posted."

"You mean guarded?" Beau asked.

"Not exactly. There's just one guy at the gates, and unless you've got some kind of pass, he won't let you in."

"Sounds sort of odd, doesn't it?" Beau asked.

"I suppose," Pacer said, "although there's nothing illegal about posting no trespassing signs. Boy, what I wouldn't give to get a look at what they're doing. I might run a night patrol up there one of these days. Go in by river and have a look around."

"I don't know about that," Beau said. "I don't want you arrested for trespassing. We'd better talk about this tomorrow in the office."

"Right, Cap'm," Pacer said. "Look, it's getting late. We should go." They finished off their coffee and stood up.

"If anyone can get to the bottom of this, it's you."

"Thanks, Cap'm."

When Beau got back to the guest cottage the phone rang. It was Toby Burr calling from New York.

"I've got some good news. The Kennedy Center has given us a reading, after all."

"Yeah?"

"They like it. They say if we can show them something satisfactory, there's a good chance they'll put it on this spring. I don't have to tell you that could lead to Broadway in the fall."

"I wonder why," Beau said absently. He hadn't thought much about the play for weeks. It almost seemed unreal.

"Who knows why, but it's damn good news. You're going to have to be there, however. I need you to work on that interrogation scene. Bring it up to Washington and let's see how far you've gotten. They'll have some questions for you too."

"I don't know if I can come, Toby. I'm running a newspaper down here and we've got a pretty big story on our hands."

"Jesus God, Beau, you've got a chance to have a hit Broadway show here and you're worried about a newspaper! God, man, you've spent three damn years on this play! All you have to do is rewrite one scene to satisfy these bozos at the Kennedy Center. They'll get their money's worth and this could make you a pile. Don't let yourself down, Beau—and don't let *me* down. Remember, I've got an interest in this too, you know?"

"Yes, I know," Beau said. "When is it?"

"The seventh or eighth. On a Tuesday at eleven A.M."

"Okay, I'll be there. I have some personal business in Washington and I might as well get that over with too."

"Fine, that's fine, Beau. We're back in business."

"Right."

The next week was a mélange of dissatisfactions and frustrations for Beau. He'd been running the *Courier-Democrat* for about six weeks and the progress was slow in certain areas—too much deadwood, too many bad habits formed over the years. Little things, but Beau thought they were unprofessional. He decided to send long memos to the copy and editorial desks. He was in the process of writing one when his phone rang. Loyd Spinker was downstairs and wanted to see him.

"Sit down," Beau said, offering Spinker a cup of coffee as the *Courier-Democrat*'s editor settled back in his chair to hear what his visitor had to say.

"You still looking into that thing with Brodie?" Spinker asked.

"We certainly are," Beau said. "Did you see the stories we've been running?"

"I seen some of them. They ain't none says he didn't do it."

"Well, we don't have any proof that he didn't do it. All we can do is speculate. We know he had no apparent motive to kill her and you say you saw her with Ben Grimshaw the night of the murder. The police, on the other hand, say they found the murder weapon, a knife, in Brodie's apartment."

"I don't care what they say," Spinker grumbled. "Tommy Brodie weren't guilty."

"Well, you must have some reason for saying that." Beau waited for a response. Spinker was twisting his fingers and looking at the floor. Beau cleared his throat. "Do you?"

"I got to know you ain't gonna write about this," Spinker said, looking up. "I want your promise."

Beau reached for a cheroot and clipped off the end. "I can't make any promises. This is a newspaper. If we have news, we have to decide ourselves whether to print it or not."

"Then I come to the wrong place," Spinker said. He got up and started for the door.

"Wait," Beau called, unprepared for Spinker's departure. "Look, sit down for a minute and maybe we can work something out." Spinker walked back to Beau's desk and stared at him fiercely.

"The problem is that I don't know what you know. Suppose you tell me that *you* killed her—would you expect me to just sit on that?"

"I ain't killed nobody, and Tommy Brodie ain't neither."

"How can you be so sure?"

" 'Cause we was together that night."

"You and Brodie?"

"Me and Brodie."

"Where?"

"Couple of places."

"In that bar, or whatever it is?"

"Yep."

"Where else?"

Spinker hesitated for a moment as he looked out the window. It was a gray, wintry day, unseasonably cold for Bienville.

"Where else?" Beau repeated.

"His place."

"His apartment?"

"Yeah."

"When?"

"After we left the bar."

"So you and he were in the bar and then you left and went to his apartment?"

"No. Not directly. I mean, I seen him in the bar, and then I left and then he left a while later and we met up at his apartment."

"And how long were you there?" Beau asked.

"All night," Spinker said, looking out the window again. Spinker and Tommy had spent the night together.

"Well," Beau said, "if I remember right, the time of death was put at around eleven o'clock. Where were you then?"

"With Brodie, at his place. I left for work about six. Nothin' unusual, then three days later the police come and arrested him."

"Did you see the knife the cops said they found?"

"There weren't no such knife at Brodie's," Spinker said.

"But the cops found one in his apartment."

"Maybe they put it there."

"Why would they do that?"

"Hell if I know. Maybe somebody else put it there."

"Had you been to his apartment before?"

"Yeah, we was friends."

"Have you told the police any of this?"

"What do you think? Would *you* tell the police? Would you want them to know? Would you want it all over town that you was . . . that you and Brodie was . . . ?"

"Yeah, I know," Beau said quietly.

"Tellin' would get me involved. How do I know they wouldn't try to blame it on me too?"

"So why are you telling me this?" Beau asked finally.

" 'Cause Brodie ain't done it. He's dead, and somebody else killed that girl, and he's getting the blame."

"Well, what do you think I can do?" Beau asked. "This is obviously an important piece of information, but you don't want me to quote you."

"I don't wanna get in trouble, but I want you to write the truth in your newspaper."

"How can I? You won't talk for the record. I need *you* to say these things."

"Me!" Spinker cried. "I don't want you writing about *me!* I just want you to tell the truth about Tommy. He didn't kill that girl."

"Well, how am I supposed to claim to know that without a source?" Beau asked incredulously.

"Just say it is confidential. That's what they do on TV."

"That's TV," Beau replied. "I'm not sure we can do that."

"You got to—you hear? I told you I didn't want to be involved in this thing," Spinker said, his brows pinched and his lips sucked in tight against his teeth.

"But you *are* involved. You're a material witness."

Spinker was shaking his head. "I done the wrong thing comin' here. I should've kept my mouth shut."

Beau got up and walked to the other side of the desk next to Spinker. "No. You did the right thing," Beau said. "You just don't understand how a newspaper operates. If I run a story that says an unnamed source claims to be an alibi witness for Tommy Brodie, the various parties can subpoena me and make me tell them who the source is."

"I should have kept my mouth shut," Spinker repeated.

"No. Look, give me your phone number and I'll be back in touch, okay? I won't do anything till I talk to you."

Spinker wrote his number on a piece of paper and left the office without saying another word. His fists were balled and he moved with hard, anxious steps, not looking at anyone.

The night before he left for Washington, Eleanor cooked Beau dinner at her apartment, which was above a garage in an older section of town. The place had few amenities but she'd fixed it up nicely and it was comfortable and cheery.

The supper was wonderful: pot roast, creamy mashed potatoes and fresh green peas. She served a nice red wine with the meal and afterward they had coffee and homemade cookies in the living room.

"So you'll see Sheilah when you're in Washington?" Eleanor said.

"Yes," Beau said. "I've got some things at her apartment that I need to bring back."

"Will you tell her about me?"

"If she asks, but she probably won't. Sheilah's so egomaniacal she probably wouldn't imagine me seeing anybody else as long as I had her."

"Are you going to stay with her?" Eleanor asked.

"Look," Beau said, a little annoyed, despite Eleanor's disarmingly innocent and honest way of asking questions. He felt crowded into a corner. "Frankly, I don't know. I haven't even called her yet. But I have no intention of resuming anything with her. Other than knowing that, you're going to have to cut me some slack. After all, Sheilah and I saw each other for over five years. I owe her a call to say I'm coming into town. At the least."

"I'm sorry," Eleanor said. "I just want to know what's going on."

"So do I. When I find out, I'll tell you," he said.

He got up to leave but Eleanor put her cool hand in his and kissed each of his fingers and the backs of his hands.

"I love kissing you," she said, kissing his chin and then his lips, her mouth pressing softly against his.

"What a nice surprise," he said holding her tightly. "I feel exactly the same way."

The day of his flight, Beau and his father lunched at the same expensive and somewhat pretentious French restaurant where he had taken Eleanor. The old man didn't care for the food and only picked at his plate. Under different circumstances, Beau might have agreed with his father, but instead he made an effort to enjoy the food since it had been his idea to come and it was the only French restaurant in town.

"When are you coming back?"

"The end of the week, maybe sooner," Beau said, pulling off another piece of crusty bread.

"What about the girl?" his father asked suddenly.

Beau sighed and shook his head. "Nothing's changed."

"The marriage is definitely off?"

"It was off the minute I took this job. There isn't any way Sheilah would quit her job and move to Bienville."

The old man looked puzzled; it was outside his sphere of comprehension that a wife would not join her husband wherever he worked, but he said nothing.

"There are other reasons too, of course. I told you some of them."

His father nodded and poked at his food.

"There's something I've been meaning to ask you," Beau said, spearing his baby carrots. "Do you know anything about these investigations the D.A.'s been holding in the middle of the night? I hear they have something to do with Universal Oil."

The old man stiffened a little but continued to pick at his food. He was moving a piece of sauce-slathered beef around with his fork. "No. I don't know anything about that," he said.

"Did you know Gordon McWorth has been there three or four times? Our people have seen him coming and going."

The elder Gunn shook his head. "No. I didn't know. No idea," he said firmly.

"Have any ideas?" Beau asked.

"No. I don't." The old man's voice sounded sharp, agitated. Beau didn't know what to make of it, but he knew his father wasn't happy about being asked these questions. He wanted to find out why.

"What's Gordon doing now? Isn't he on the board of directors for Universal Oil?"

"As far as I know," the old man said.

"When did he leave your firm? It was while I was in Washington, wasn't it?"

"Yes, I believe so. We dissolved the partnership some ten years ago."

"Has he got anything to do with this investigation?"

"I've *told* you, I don't know anything about it. I don't see Gordon much anymore."

"But he must have something to do with it. Fletcher Cross too. Are they connected? Gordon and Fletcher Cross?"

"Why are you asking me all this? What does it have to do with me?" There was something overly anxious in the old man's eyes and voice. He was tapping his fingers nervously on the table. He was obviously disturbed by the grilling.

"You know Gordon. I have to know what's going on with Universal Oil and this probe the D.A.'s conducting." Beau was beginning to feel annoyed himself. The old man was either holding back or trying not to help. Usually when Beau asked a question, he got either a dissertation or a sermon.

"I don't know why you want to get involved with those people," his father said. "There must be better things to occupy your time."

"Not necessarily. You have to admit this is all pretty unusual. The district attorney holding meetings in the middle of the night and not telling anybody why. He *must* be up to something."

"I expect the district attorney will tell you when he's ready." The old man drained his glass of Beaujolais.

"Yes. He'll let us know what he wants us to when he wants us to know it." The old man forked another piece of meat and suggested dessert. Beau could tell the conversation was clearly at an end. He poured them more wine and his father changed the subject.

"The cottage at Deer Pond is coming along."

"I'm glad," the old man said with obvious relief," I always liked that spot myself. Used to spend hours there when I was young. It's a nice, peaceful little place."

"I've just got to hold the builder's cost down," Beau said.

"You better watch those people. They'll take your last dime." The old man ordered strawberry shortcake and coffee. As soon as the conversation had shifted, his father's mood had lightened. The change was not lost on Beau.

BOOK FOUR

BOOK
FOUR

VICISSITUDES VIII
Sheilah

Spring 1971

If, as the philosopher John Locke would have us believe, every person is born with a blank mind and human personalities are formed solely by what we learn, then Sheilah might have been easier to explain—and I think it's necessary to try to explain her because of the hold she had over men like Beau and the hold she didn't have over men like Dan Whittle.

I'm not sure I subscribe to this Lockeian theory of Tabula Rasa, because some people seem to be born with a mean streak. Strange mutations of genes gone sour. I've known some of these people and there isn't any really explainable reason for their behavior; nothing in their upbringing, education or experience. If one didn't know better, one would think that from the time they were little tots the meanness simply seeped out of them. It was developed and refined over the years, until eventually they became the bullies, liars, backstabbers, spoilers, manipulators, cheats, professional heartbreakers and other cruel creatures of the earth that they are.

Some people, of course, are made cruel by circumstances. Abuse any animal and sooner or later it's going to be trouble. With humans the results are probably worse, since half the time you're not looking out for the subtle kinds of meanness they can inflict. Given the right set of circumstances, life can turn almost anybody mean.

Sheilah Price wasn't truly mean, but she did have a callous streak that could be as cruel and cutting as the meanest of mean.

She could also be irresistibly sweet for long periods. She was able to cry

225

tears of empathy at the hurt of others: the truly mean cry only in self-despair. Looking back, I think a lot of Sheilah's meanness stemmed from the degree to which she had been hurt and from fear. She might, for example, stub her toe and a person wishing to comfort her would be assailed with a barrage of insults, many of them deliberately intended to wound. But there was also a deeper kind of hurt she suffered, a void or barrenness someplace in her soul, a kind of terrible loneliness.

My perception of Sheilah is formed from bits and pieces I picked up from here and there; conversations clouded in time and speculation to fit the pieces together. I never really knew Sheilah well, though I came to dislike the things she did, whether I had witnessed them or simply been told about them. There *was* something extraordinary about her, I know that; I guess Beau recognized it too. There was a kind of aura surrounding her, as though she were close to breaking through some barrier that would propel her into great happiness. She seemed frightened by it, however, and fear does some funny things to people. If Sheilah had not been quite attractive and very smart, the meanness might have done her in. But, as it was, the boys became tantalized by it and Sheilah began to use this to her advantage as she grew into womanhood. Later, it would become a magnet for the men too.

Sheilah was raised near Philadelphia, out in a part of the country where horses and divorces are two of the principal topics of conversation.

Her family was on the cusp of main-line society, and her father was well liked by a lot of influential people but divorce came early. After a hasty second marriage, Sheilah and her sisters and brothers found themselves living with their mother and stepfather in a historic stone manor house overlooking part of the Schuylkill River. As a child she was chubby and terrified of horses, though they were as commonplace as trees. Horses and divorces. One of her most unpleasant memories originated in her stepfather's insistence that she clean out the stalls in the barn on Saturdays once she turned eleven. She opened one stall and a big roan hunter bit her on the shoulder. She ran crying down to a spot by the river that was her own special place and sobbed away the afternoon.

At supper her stepfather asked if she had completed her chores and, furious to learn that she hadn't, refused to allow her to attend a friend's birthday party that night. He supervised the stall cleaning for nearly two hours while she stood up to her knees in hay and horse manure. Horses and divorces.

At fifteen she was sent away to a fashionable boarding school in Connecticut and she did poorly in her studies. Her social life wasn't anything special either, mainly because she had sprouted to a height of five feet ten and was skinny as a rail. The girls called her Olive Oyl. She was knock-kneed and pigeon-toed and had a large bump on her nose and lips far too full for her long, thin face. She was always awkwardly tagging along with a much more popular girl and, in her spare time, reading romantic novels and dreaming of the day when she might become beautiful. She hadn't liked being fat, but this new body was worse.

Two years later, she simply blossomed. Her figure became lush, and her lips sensuous, and the nose accommodated her long face and pointed chin and gave her the profile of a Renaissance Madonna. She wore her blond hair below her shoulders, as was fashionable in those days of hippies and protest (though she never joined any movements or demonstrations). Her blue eyes set off her peaches-and-cream complexion and her surprisingly large, prominent teeth enhanced her further.

But even so, there was something a little "off" about the way Sheilah looked—almost as if nature had played one of those strange optic tricks with her features. Beau had once joked that she and Picasso would have made a fine pair. Sheilah had just missed being beautiful, and she had just missed being ugly. Handsome would be the best way to describe her.

But the boys, and soon afterward the girls, sought her out. Of course, many teenagers go through this transformation, but in Sheilah's case the effect on her personality was profound. She became an assertive ringleader. She developed an aggressive walk that other girls tried to imitate; long-legged strides with a full arm swing, but somewhat clumsy too—like a child wearing her mother's high heels for the first time. Mostly, Sheilah became the opposite of the things she'd been before.

A year before this transformation occurred, Sheilah was asked on a blind date by a football player from a neighboring prep school. He was an oafish, handsome boy who, even at his early age, aspired to be a stockbroker.

The date went badly. The football player lugged Sheilah around in a cursory way, failed to introduce her to his friends, danced with other girls and got rid of her as quickly as he could. She responded to these humiliations by curling up in her dorm for the rest of the weekend, too miserable to do anything but read a pulp "bodice-ripper" novel.

The following year she encountered the boy again at an interschool function and he failed to recognize her. The whole night he stared at her from various places in the room and, having obtained her name from a friend, phoned her two days later to ask her out.

She accepted, and at the end of the evening she kissed him good night.

Theirs was a long, wet, passionate kiss. She stopped him from feeling her breasts only after he had rubbed his hands over them for a few solid minutes.

The next night, when he picked her up for a party, she was distant and aloof and flirted openly with other boys. When she saw that he was becoming positively livid, she took his hand and smiled. When he took her back to the guesthouse where she was staying, there was more kissing and even a bare-breasted feel this time. When she saw that he was frantic to go further, she leaped out of the car, blew him a kiss and went inside.

The next week when he called for a date, Sheilah refused. In fact, she stayed in alone that weekend with other plans. But a week later, when he called again, she accepted. This time she was even more distant and aloof, and when he sought to pick up where they had left off in front of the guesthouse two weeks before, she cut him off at first base. The next night he took her to a lovers' lane, but she played coy and silly and only let him kiss her cheek, deftly turning her head at the instant his lips came close to hers. The boy was in a lather and finally began to beg and plead. At this point she set upon him like a dervish, informing him what a dumb jackass he was and saying that she despised him and his adolescent groping. The ballplayer was crestfallen and drove her to the guesthouse in silence.

When he stopped the car, they sat there quietly for a few moments, both looking straight ahead. Then she reached over and took his hand in hers, purring that she was sorry if she hurt his feelings, and then allowed him a long, arousing kiss and a lengthy feel of her breasts before she was off into the night. She never saw him again, refusing his many calls. Sheilah could be that way.

During her last year in boarding school Sheilah was raped—more or less —at least that's the way she saw it. She remains ambivalent on the question to this day, and once told Beau about the incident, confiding that it might have been *she* who was to blame for it. She had been walking through town near school when she came across an older boy, heavy and not very attractive, but with a certain rough magnetism about him. He had asked her to walk with him in some woods and Sheilah complied and after they stopped by a stream-side they began to neck. After a while the boy began to grope and feel and Sheilah's mind began to race with nervous wonder over what the "big deal" was that all the girls were talking about back at the dorm. She let him go a little too far—she knew that—but by the time she realized it, he was forcing himself on her, then in her, and despite her sudden frightened protests, the boy climaxed.

At the time, Sheilah wasn't particularly indignant about it, though she came to feel that way later. She was mostly disgusted and mostly with herself and the matter might have rested there had it not been for a detestable episode that followed later that evening, something that would have a profound effect on Sheilah for many years to come.

It had been dark when she finally got back to her dormitory. She sneaked up the back stairs to her room, only to find her roommate, Roxanne, lying across her bed, studying.

"Well, where've *you* been?" Roxanne asked inquisitively.

"Out for a walk." Sheilah started toward her closet but the other girl rose up in delightedly feigned shock.

"Looks more like you went for a *crawl!*"

"What do you mean?" Sheilah asked, staring in the mirror at her disheveled self.

"Look at your back!" the other girl cried.

"Well, I . . . ." Her blouse was grass-stained and a button was missing.

"And *look* at your *skirt!*" Roxanne squealed. To her horror, Sheilah looked down at several whitish blotches on the front of her blue skirt.

"It's not . . . I . . . ." she stammered.

"You what!" the girl cried in delight, examining the skirt herself. "*I* know what *those* are! Little Sheilah's been out *doing* something naughty, hasn't she?"

"You're cruel," Sheilah replied defensively. "I haven't . . . ."

"Come on!" Roxanne said. "Who was he?"

"You don't know what you're talking about." Sheilah hastily removed the blouse and skirt and tossed them into her closet. She pulled on fresh clothes and left for the library. Behind her, Roxanne rushed down the hall to tell the other girls.

When Sheilah returned later that night there was no one in her room. She undressed and prepared for bed, but just as she was about to turn out the light, the door burst open and a dozen of her classmates flocked in. One was dressed in a black, preacherlike outfit and carried a Bible. Another girl wielded a broomstick, which she carried like a shotgun. The group formed a double row and began to hum the wedding march. Down the aisle marched Roxanne with Sheilah's skirt draped royally over her arm.

The "minister" began to intone the opening lines of the wedding ceremony: "Dearly beloved, we are gathered here tonight to bear witness to the holy matrimony of Sheilah Price and her unknown lover, whom we shall call John Skirt." The other girls tittered.

Sheilah thought she might faint. Her head reeled.

"Do you, John Skirt, take Sheilah as your lawful wedded wife?" Roxanne moved the skirt up and down in a nodding motion.

Suddenly Sheilah knew she was going to be sick. She tried to rise from the bed, but the other girls pushed her down. She screamed but one of them pushed a handful of the bedclothes into her face. Terror-stricken, Sheilah began to vomit. She threw up on herself and on the bed, and as the girls stepped back, uncertain and nervous, she leaned over the bedside and retched again onto the floor. She finally stopped, but continued to hang over the bed, her long blond hair dangling in the pool of vomit.

The wedding party slowly backed out of the room in embarrassment, leaving Sheilah's roommate to deal with her. Roxanne tried to comfort Sheilah, putting her hand on her back and trying to get her to lie back. But Sheilah stared at her in such a silent, penetrating fashion that Roxanne became flustered and mumbled something about the lateness of the hour and crawled into her own bed.

The long racking sobs started when the lights went out. Sheilah hid herself beneath the soiled bedclothes and stayed that way long into the night, crying until the tears simply stopped because there were no more.

VICISSITUDES IX
Dan Whittle

Autumn 1972

How Sheilah got involved with Dan Whittle is a curious bit of irony, but had she not, she probably never would have become involved with Beau, or for that matter, made as much of herself as she eventually did.

After graduation, Sheilah decided against college. She had had enough of school for a while. During her last semester she traveled to Washington half a dozen times and stayed with an older girlfriend from Philadelphia. She found herself going out on dates with several exciting, bright young men who worked on Capitol Hill or in the Nixon administration. These were not boys, and after that, college did not seem interesting enough. Sheilah's goal in life at eighteen was to marry someone charming, handsome and rich. Washington seemed just the place to find him.

So the summer after her graduation, Sheilah got a job as a secretary in the office of a Pennsylvania congressman and began to enjoy a world free of the restrictions and regimen of boarding school. She shared an apartment with three other girls and looked forward to attending a glittering array of festive events: embassy parties, formal dinners in gracious Georgetown homes and so on.

Unfortunately, she did not get along very well with her roommates. They were gossipy girls, a little older than she, and Sheilah despised the way they pried into her affairs. She had developed an intense desire for privacy that stemmed in large part from that awful incident at boarding school. In fact, Sheilah developed an almost paranoiac concern for her privacy, and whenever one of her Washington roommates would giggle or make any remark or observation about anything to do with Sheilah's whereabouts or dates, her nerves would become frazzled and she'd get testy.

Also, the frantic social life and political scene she had envisioned herself in never really materialized.

There was, to be sure, a little of that, but most of the men Sheilah found herself with were lower-level aides or young lawyers, who would take her not to the Sans Souci or the Sulgrave Club ball but to the pubs on Capitol Hill, where they would attempt to get her to agree to go to bed with them.

This continued for several years, and Sheilah was becoming disenchanted with Washington, with her job and with men.

She had learned early on that men were easy to manipulate, and she refined the technique with each new beau. Her basic approach was to keep the man completely off balance. If he wanted to do A, she would opt for B. If he said he liked X, she would like Y instead. Sex was an omnipresent force to be used either separately or in conjunction with other procedures to get a man on the verge of an all-consuming frothing insanity; then she would suddenly become irresistibly nice and agreeable and loving and usually get whatever it was she wanted. Sometimes, of course, she went too far and the man would vanish from her life, but she had become pretty good at judging when this would happen and these mistakes became few and far between.

Sheilah observed the reactions of the men in her life the way a scientist might study laboratory rats. She had come to the conclusion that men were fools. Not dumb or ignorant, for the ones she dated were college graduates, witty, sharp and advancing in their professions. But Sheilah thought men were *supposed* to be that way, and it really didn't count for much when she could control them like marionettes. She could do it! Little Sheilah, who'd been fat and weird as a child and so skinny and ugly as a teenager, who'd gotten bad marks in boarding school, who was always getting bawled out for something at home. She could do this!

And then she met Dan Whittle.

Dan Whittle presented a new challenge for Sheilah. He was to be taken seriously.

Sheilah had been invited to a big garden party in Georgetown at a house shared by six young men who worked on the Hill. She and her date arrived late and the party was in full swing. She decided it was going to be a boring evening because she recognized so many of the faces around her. Beer was being served from kegs and a loud, raucous din surrounded the place and could be heard a block away. After a couple of years, Sheilah had tired of such affairs.

She had been there less than twenty minutes and was about to suggest to her escort that they leave when she spotted Dan Whittle. He was standing in a corner of the garden beside a torchlight, talking with a pretty girl.

Sheilah didn't know who he was, but she felt immediately attracted to him. He wasn't a particularly handsome man, but he had an understanding sort of look on his face while he talked with the girl. She could tell from his dress and manner that he was out of place here; as out of place as she herself felt. He wore well-fitting brown slacks and a shirt that looked tailor-made, open at the collar with the tie undone. A good-looking madras sports jacket was slung over his shoulder and he was leaning slightly against a garden wall.

Sheilah excused herself, leaving her date to get lost in the crowd. She climbed the stairs to the porch and concealed herself in a group of people, so that she could observe Dan Whittle undetected. She watched him nod vigorously, then the girl bussed him lightly on the cheek and walked away. Sheilah decided to make her move. She was in luck; he was still standing there when she walked up to him. She had maneuvered up from behind, so that he wouldn't see her, and she began to fan herself with her hand to suggest that she had come from the crowd because of the heat.

"A little warm in there, huh?" he said charmingly.

"Yeah, really," she replied. But it sounded to her like he'd spotted her ruse. This excited her, but made her more wary.

"Have you been here long?" he asked, shifting position to talk to her.

"Just a few minutes, but it's really too hot. I hate these parties."

"Then why do you come to them?" he asked casually.

Sheilah kept her feet planted and leaned forward. "I'm sorry, I didn't hear you," she said. She'd heard him all right; she needed time for an answer.

"I asked why you're here if you hate these parties," he repeated. Her heels began sinking into the grass. She knew when she was licked, and walked nearer to him.

"Oh, I don't know. My date was invited. Sometimes they can be fun, but I don't like things this big."

"How come? You don't get to really meet enough people?"

"Oh, I don't come for that," she said. Now he had really put her off balance. Her interest increased.

"Well, I do," Dan Whittle said. "I mean, nobody wants to admit it, but what do most of these people come for? The conversation or the beer? Certainly not for the fresh air."

"Yeah." She smiled. "I guess you're right." She stuck out her hand. "I'm Sheilah Price."

"Nice to meet you, Sheilah Price. I'm Dan Whittle," he said, shaking her hand firmly but gently. She thought he held it a fraction of a second longer than necessary and her knees became faintly weak. He had great eyes—big brown penetrating eyes—and a nice, honest smile.

"Nice to meet you too," she said.

"You work on the Hill?" he asked, taking a sip of his beer.

"Uh-huh—for Congressman Roberts."

"Sam Roberts?"

"He's the one." She repositioned herself slightly so that one of her hips was cocked out. She put a hand on the hip and managed to tug down her dress just enough to make the neckline a little more revealing. She watched Dan's eyes and was pleased when he took passing notice.

"How about you?" she asked.

"I'm on the Hill too."

"Really? Whose office?"

"Congressman Whittle's," he replied casually.

"What state's he from . . . oh! . . . Whit . . ." she stammered. "Oh, I'm sorry. I . . ."

"Don't worry about it," he chuckled. "There are over five hundred and fifty of us—and besides, I've only been here since the first of the year."

"Well, what state *are* you from?" she said casually.

"The South," he said. "The Deep South. It's probably why you didn't recognize me. It's a long way from here."

She smiled broadly. Over Dan's shoulder she could see her date at the edge of the crowd. He was talking with a couple of people but several times he had cast a glance in her direction. He wasn't the kind of fellow she wanted Dan Whittle to think she dated, so she decided to end the conversation quickly before he decided to join them.

"Well, I've got to go now," she said. "It was nice meeting you. I hope I'll see you again." It was a ploy that sometimes worked: walk away abruptly, before they'd had the chance to lay out their best line. Sheilah knew that if he was interested in her, he'd figure out a way to find her.

"Bye," he said, lifting the beer glass, but not moving.

By late Monday morning, Sheilah had obtained most of the vital information she needed about Congressman Dan Whittle. He was thirty-four-years old, single, a Republican from Bienville. His father had been a judge and his grandfather a justice of the state Supreme Court. He had attended a military school in Bienville and the state university, where he had also taken his law degree.

Other information gleaned from library clippings told her he was considered one of the most eligible men about town. He kept a fairly low social profile, but had been reported in the company of fashionable women by the local press. He skied, played golf and had once been hosted by the President aboard the executive yacht, *Sequoia*. Why hadn't she heard of him before? Well, she didn't read the newspapers often, and his offices were on the other side of the Capitol from hers. Sheilah mulled over all this during lunch and well into the afternoon, trying to figure some way of bumping into him. Then, just before five, amid the normal pandemonium of a congressional office, someone shouted across the room, "Sheilah, line four." She picked up the phone. It was Dan Whittle.

She could not go to bed with him the first night—she couldn't appear to be an easy lay; this much she knew. But she would have, if she could have gotten away with it.

He took her not to the Sans Souci but to an intimate French bistro called Dominique's. She felt they got on well, and she tried to be alluring without being gushy. At the end of the evening he drove her home and kissed her lightly at the door. By that time, she would have balled him on the spot, but he didn't ask.

He called again two days later and invited her to a party at the home of Mrs. Marjory Merriweather Post. It was an elegant affair, with the guest list as impressive as the food. Sheilah was seated across the table from Dan, sandwiched between an Assistant Secretary of State and a senator. They were discussing the complexities of the Vietnam peace negotiations and Sheilah was as lost in that conversation as a giraffe might be walking down Pennsylvania Avenue. Occasionally, one of the men would turn to her for an opinion. She was excellent at responses that meant nothing and shielded her ignorance. She felt Dan Whittle's eyes upon her from across the table. She knew he knew she was bullshitting.

When the evening was over, he suggested they go to his apartment for a nightcap. Dan lived in a nice, comfortable apartment in Foggy Bottom, not far from the State Department. He was on the tenth floor and his windows looked out over the Potomac River. It was one of the most beautiful views she had ever seen; the river bridges arching across the water to Virginia, the Lincoln and Jefferson Memorials and the Washington Monument illuminated against the star-splattered sky.

Sheilah settled into a leather armchair while Dan excused himself. On a rosewood table were current copies of *The New Yorker, Foreign Service* magazine, *The Times* of London, and *The Saturday Review*. There were two large built-in bookshelves, each filled with hardcover volumes. Dan returned, his tie loosened and collar undone. He put on a record, a concerto by Haydn.

"What can I get you?" he asked.

"Oh, wine, I suppose."

"Red?"

"Fine."

He disappeared into another room and Sheilah sat captivated by the sight of the city and by the evening. She felt wonderful. She was falling in love.

"Here," he said, handing her a glass. "Cheers."

"Oh, the evening was so nice," she said. "Did you have fun?"

"That's supposed to be *my* question," he said, laughing.

"I really did."

"What did you and the senator talk about?"

"The war," she replied, suddenly nervous. "The peace talks. He and that other guy really know what's going on."

"What'd they say?" Dan asked.

"Oh, I'm not sure, really." She was beginning to squirm a little. "I think it was whether or not we ought to stop bombing North Vietnam. The senator was saying we shouldn't and the other man—what's his name . . . ?"

"Curry."

"Mr. Curry was giving a different opinion."

"Which side did you favor?"

"Well, neither one, really." She suddenly realized she was being tested. She was out of her league and she got defensive. "I didn't follow most of it. It was just a bunch of *talk* anyway."

Dan got up and fetched the wine bottle and poured a little more into their glasses. Before he could sit back down she stood too, and excused herself to go to the bathroom, bumping into him lightly as she rounded the corner of the sofa.

"I'm sorry," she said, reconsidering. "I must have had too much wine to drink at dinner." She touched his arm. Dan turned, took her into his arms and pulled her tightly against him. They were about the same height, and his eyes looked directly into hers. She gazed at him as intently as she could, trying to communicate: you're beautiful, I love you, I want you. He kissed her, first gently, then passionately, until she could feel her own desire rise in her body with tingling, anxious sensations. When they finally came up for air she rested her chin on his shoulder and looked again at the beautiful view. Her maneuver had worked like a charm.

They necked on the couch for the next half hour. Dan Whittle was a pretty clever lover, and he explored her body every way she could imagine. He had her blouse open and her skirt up and she was lying on top of him with

236

her large breasts touching his chest, massaging his head with one hand and his organ with the other. She unzipped his fly and stroked him, and when she had his erection out and in her hand she sat up and slipped him into her. She gently moved up and down, whispering his name over and over.

"I've got to tell you something about me and dinner parties," she said afterward. They were lying in the dark and she was smoking a cigarette. "I don't feel comfortable at them."

"Oh, why not?" he asked.

"I'm not really sure. It might go back to when I was a little girl—eight or nine—and my parents let me stay up for a dinner party at our house."

"Got into it too young, eh?" Dan asked, laughing and rubbing her thigh.

"No—now I'm serious. I'm telling you something." She sounded cross. He was smart enough to know that she was trouble and probably always would be, but there was enough that he liked about her to keep him interested. She was an immensely attractive and sensual young woman, despite her paradoxical and ever-changing moods. He liked the fact that she'd stand up to him—even though most of the time she did it under the wrong circumstances.

"My parents were having this big party for about twenty people and they let me eat at the table. I was feeling very grown-up and everybody at my end kept asking me questions. I was just talking on and on and the meal was over, except for dessert, and then, all of a sudden, I noticed that everyone at the table was watching me."

She stopped for a moment. "Go on," Dan said.

"And then my stepfather said, 'All right, Sheilah, you've talked enough for tonight, it's time for bed.' He got up and took me away from the table before dessert was served. I was so humiliated, so hurt and mad. I was wearing this new dress Mother had bought me and when I got to my room I began cutting it up with a pair of scissors while I cried and cried."

"Poor kiddo," Dan said, rubbing her head affectionately. "I can see the kind of effect that might have on an impressionable child." He made a mental note that she actually cut up her new dress.

The affair between Sheilah and Dan Whittle lasted not quite four months, but it had a very profound effect on Sheilah's life. For the first few weeks it was heaven. Sheilah had never been so happy in her life, but after the bliss wore off she found herself trying to become more assertive, and this involved manipulation. Sex, of course, was the key. She was careful in her employment of her technique, because she recognized that Dan was no-body's fool, and she didn't want to risk losing him.

The trouble was that she could pull all the strings, but the marionette wouldn't dance. He always seemed a jump ahead of her. If he'd suggest X and she'd suggest Y, then he would simply compromise with Z—or worse still, accept her Y with pleasure and equanimity. She began to wonder if he hadn't figured out her game. It was maddening.

Part of the trouble was that she couldn't find any vulnerability in the man. No soft spot where she could get her hooks in. Once, she tried cutting off sex for a while, but when he didn't phone after four days she caved in and called him, hating herself for doing it.

The relationship coasted into rocky waters. Sheilah began to get the impression that something was dramatically wrong. At the parties and din-ners they attended, Dan sometimes spent the whole evening talking with other people and when they got home at night there would be little conver-sation between them. The sex was wonderful: energetic and creative and totally satisfying. But after a while Sheilah began to detect a slight waning of interest on his part. She conjured up ways to please him, becoming a virtuoso of oral sex, buying the barest, laciest lingerie she could find, but still it seemed to degenerate.

Finally, one morning just before Christmas, the whole tenuous relation-ship broke apart in a shocking, humiliating episode that would change Shei-lah's life forever.

It was a rainy Sunday morning. Sheilah had stayed over with Dan after a dinner party honoring the governor of his state and two constituents. Much of the talk the night before had involved a dam project the constituents were trying to push through and they were trying to persuade Dan and the gover-nor to assist them in procuring federal aid. The conversation had been thor-oughly boring to Sheilah and she was anxious to leave; Dan had promised to take her to the Cellar Door in Georgetown, where one of her favorite musical groups was playing. But the talk grew more intense and Dan pressed with questions that seemed to require longer and longer answers. The later it got, the more uncomfortable Sheilah became. She began to show her displeasure by playing with her hair and shooting Dan darting, jerky glances. Finally, he ended the discussion smoothly and they left, but it was obvious things were strained.

He had said very little to her on the way home, and when they got to his place, they went straight to sleep. He was up early the next morning and fixed them breakfast. He sat in his robe after breakfast reading the Washing-

238

ton *Post* and having another cup of coffee. Sheilah felt restless. She wanted to turn on the television, but she knew Dan wouldn't approve, so she went to the window and stared out at the cloudy, rainy day. She began to fiddle with the radio dial, changing the easy-listening station to something a little harder. She liked the Simon and Garfunkel song they were playing, so she turned up the volume and went into the kitchen to get a Coke. On her way back to the living room, the song ended and suddenly the Rolling Stones came blasting into the room. She was halfway across the room, anxious to turn down the sound, when Dan yelled, "For Chrissakes, turn that damn stuff down right now!"

Sheilah had one trait that she was completely unable to control. She could not abide criticism. Her stepfather had left her that legacy. Whenever someone would criticize her, she would slam a ring of defenses around herself and go on the offensive as quickly and lethally as possible. At those moments, Sheilah existed only to hurt.

She had been on her way to turn down the music, but even if she hadn't been, what was wrong with it? Why wasn't she allowed to express herself in his apartment?

"Just because you don't like that kind of music," she snapped, "doesn't mean I don't."

"Listen," Dan said, "it's Sunday morning, and that might be Sunday-morning music for you, but it isn't for me. It's just noise for me, and I think I've mentioned it enough times for you to have the consideration not to put it on."

"Oh, for Pete's sake. Is the big man upset?" she said sarcastically. She was *going* to turn it down! He was wrong, and she was being blamed for something she didn't do.

Dan dropped the section of the paper he was reading and looked directly at her with an expression she couldn't remember seeing before. His words came out even and measured.

"You know the problem with you, Sheilah? You're dumb. You're just plain ignorant. And that's sad."

"And what are you?" she snapped, stinging from his attack. "Smart? Hah! I saw you sitting there with those guys last night, letting them talk you into that project—whatever it was."

"You don't even *know* what it was," he said. "Did you ever stop to consider how much you don't know? You never read anything. You don't even read the damned newspaper! You flip through *Vogue* and read the labels on clothing. You don't really *care* about anything either, other than yourself."

"That's not true!" she screeched. "I read all the time! I read magazines and I care about a lot of things!"

"Oh, you'll look at *Time* and *Newsweek* when I press you to and then you go straight for the fashion or entertainment section. I've watched you 'read' them. You put them down after three or four minutes." Dan stood up and confronted her. "What *do* you care about, Sheilah? What do you *want* out of life? What do you want from *me?*"

Sheilah was dumbfounded. She could think of no reply. She wanted to say something like "You can't even get it *up* half the time!" but something stopped her. The danger signal canceled out the impulse to rage. Her only recourse was to cry, which she did, breaking into sobs, facing the chill sheets of rain slanting across the gray Potomac River below. She expected him to come up and put his arms around her. When he didn't, she turned to find him staring at her in a cool, detached way.

"Look," he said, "it's not working out between us. There's too much age difference or something. I've been thinking about this for a while now— you've got your own life to live."

"What do you *mean?*" she gasped.

"Just what I said. I don't think it's a good idea for us to see each other anymore. I mean, I'd like to see you occasionally as a friend, but I . . ."

"As a friend! We're not friends!"

"Well, you're probably correct there. We're not friends. Sheilah, I'm going to tell you something. Your priorities are all screwed up. When I say you're dumb, I don't mean it literally. I mean you're young, you're uncultivated. You're *ignorant* and you aren't doing anything about it. I've tried to get you interested in things. I've given you books—you haven't read one of them. I've . . ."

"I have! That's not fair!" she protested. "I've started two of them!"

"Let me finish," he said. "You really aren't interested in anything. In a relationship, I need an *exchange* of ideas. I don't want to be the teacher all the time, or just hand out advice." He sighed. "Look, if you're going to operate in this town you're going to need to know something about politics, more than you pick up around the coffee maker at the office. You have to *understand* politics. How many times have you actually sat through a session of the House or the Senate?"

She began to say something, but he cut her off.

"You have to know something about history, about literature and sociology and political science. I can't understand . . . with your background. . . . Food, wine, theater, art and architecture; these are things that make you an interesting person."

240

"So now I'm not interesting," she said viciously. Her temper was boiling.

"No, dammit, you aren't!" he said loudly, shocking her back into silence. "You've got nothing to say, and you can't get by in this town with just a big pair of tits and long legs. Jesus Christ, go to college. And stop being such a slob. Learn to pick up after yourself. Do something! You could go to school at night at George Washington or American University. Right now you're just treading water. Learn to swim, Sheilah, learn to swim."

"What are you *doing!*" she suddenly cried. "Why are you saying this to me? You're only trying to hurt me!"

She was losing. She was losing him. It could have been so right, so perfect!

"Look," he said, "I've got some things to do today. I'd better take you home."

Sheilah was beside herself for weeks. She couldn't believe a radio tune had caused her this pain. So trivial. So unfair. She did not eat much and she didn't accept dates. She sat home at night and read books. She read the four or five that Dan had given her, then she bought more. She liked fiction best, preferring eighteenth-century novels with their episodic plots of love and death and relationships. It kept her mind off Dan Whittle, for whenever she thought of him, and it was often, she pined away in her heart. It also proved him wrong; she *was* reading. There were times when she convinced herself that he would call her, but he never did. She wished she had left something important in his apartment so she'd have an excuse to see him, but she hadn't. She arranged to go to his office building often, in hopes of bumping into him, but she never did. The closest she came was to sneak into the viewing gallery when Congress was in session. She'd stand high above the assembly and watch the back of his head far below. It hurt more to see him and not be with him, so she stopped going.

Fortunately, Sheilah was a pragmatic person. Otherwise, there's no telling what might have become of her. Eventually she saw the logic in Dan's parting speech. If she was going to have a meaningful relationship with anybody she'd want to be with, she was going to have to change. So she investigated the possibilities of college.

Her stepfather had once offered to finance her education after she graduated from boarding school, but when she declined, he cautioned that the offer would not be repeated. He was true to his word. Her real father had fallen on hard times financially and was not able to help.

She opted for American University. It was a small school but it offered a degree in media journalism. She had always thought it might be fun to be a television reporter. The first year was difficult, not only because of her studies but because she had to get a job in a clothing store to finance the tuition. Her schedule put a dramatic crimp in her social agenda, but she plunged into her studies with a vengeance.

To her consummate surprise, Sheilah found that she was a good student. Her first grades were all A's and B's. Her second year she made the Dean's List. Apparently the years she had spent working since boarding school had been good for her. She graduated with honors and a degree in media science.

Just two weeks later, she got a job with an around-the-clock radio station as a part-time local reporter and part-time office girl. Her social life remained basically uneventful, but it didn't matter so much during this period. She worked ferociously and kept a sharp lookout for any opportunity to advance. The men she dated were unremarkable, for Sheilah had, after her experience with Dan Whittle, made a conscious decision not to become involved with men who were either interesting enough to fall in love with or smarter than she. The women's liberation movement was starting to take hold then, and she embraced those elements that served her purpose. A smart man was dangerous to Sheilah, hard to control, and while there was a side of her that was fascinated by the challenge of smart, aggressive men, she resolutely avoided them. And then she met Beau Gunn.

VICISSITUDES X
Triangulations

Spring 1978

After their first meeting, Sheilah was as taken with Beau as he was with her. They had stayed at the cocktail party until it started to break up, talking quietly in a corner. Beau thought about suggesting they have dinner together but decided against it, tactically; nor did he ask for Sheilah's phone number, since he already knew where she worked. He would wait three days before calling her.

When he did, she was a little cool, because she'd been on pins and needles thinking he might not call. She had recently begun to dream up ways to call him without looking like she was on the make. He did not ask her for a "date" as such; he asked for a "weekend." This was a bold move for the first time out but Beau was feeling bold. There was a small house party going on across the Chesapeake Bay, over in Oxford, Maryland, at a quaint little inn on the Choptank River where Beau and some friends had rented a big old house owned by the inn. Some people were sailing over in their boats and others were driving. Sheilah hesitated for a moment when Beau made his proposition, so he discreetly added that he "didn't chase girls around couches," and that seemed to make it okay.

When they arrived, Sheilah was duly impressed by Beau's circle of friends; there was a correspondent for the New York *Times,* two or three Ivy League-looking lawyers, a brace of Virginia "horse country" couples and the first secretary at the British Embassy and his charming wife. Sheilah felt much at home, and thought Beau couldn't be more polite or attractive. They went to a nice little restaurant for fresh oysters and crabs and walked back to the inn with a cool spring breeze rustling in the elms along the roadside. Later they drank brandy in front of a roaring fire while the Englishman entertained them with amusing stories of his uncle, a duke, and the late Winston Churchill. When the evening finally ended, Beau sent Sheilah off to her room with a kiss on the cheek and a question in her mind as to whether or not she was really attractive to him, or just a date he needed for the weekend.

Beau had told her the next day was for sailing, so she put on her sexiest bikini, figuring that ought to stir something up. It did: every man except Beau did a double take when she walked down into the big living room. He was playing it cool.

The sailing was glorious in the warm May sunshine. Beau and Sheilah had gone on a small boat, a day sailer, with one of the Ivy League-looking lawyers and his date, and around lunchtime they put in to a small cove and took a lunch basket to the beach. Sheilah decided on a different strategy after lunch. She slipped on a bulky sweater and a pair of oversized shorts and without saying anything to anyone she got up and wandered down the beach. Beau found her there half an hour later, lying in the sand with her head on a large rock, face turned up toward the sun. He lay down beside her and without saying anything leaned over and kissed her and she responded, slowly at first, then passionately, and when they broke it off he rested on his elbows looking down at her for a moment and said, very simply, "I want to make love to you tonight." And they did.

That was that, so far as either of them was concerned. They became a pair. Sheilah was on her best behavior so far as it was possible. They went to movies and plays and out to Wolftrap to the theater and to concerts and parties. Lots of parties. She told Beau about herself, usually when they were lying in bed after making love. She told him a little about the affair she had with Dan Whittle several years before. She did not mention how it ended or that her memory was long when it came to being hurt. By now she was an up-and-coming newscaster for a major-market radio station, just one step away from moving up to television, and she was happy with her new man. Beau felt the same way, but with a few reservations.

At first, he decided that what Sheilah really lacked was tact. She was a product of the 1960s and early 1970s when young women first began coming out of their emotional hives and expressing themselves freely but hadn't quite learned to temper free expression with a certain amount of restraint. Sheilah's favorite word seemed to be "bullshit," and "asshole" ran a close second. She greatly overused the word "boring," but she herself was *not* boring. Beau was certain of that.

But if she felt like being cuddly, no one could be cuddlier. If she wanted to cook for him, it was a joy to see her at work in the kitchen. And she had some surprisingly astute intellectual instincts. Mostly, though, it was the sex that was too good to be true. It was as if they were taking out their aggressions and frustrations on each other, so that in the end both felt strangely cleansed.

During this period, Beau's column for the *Times-Examiner* was extremely popular and syndicated in more than two dozen papers. He was making a good deal more money than he ever thought he would in the newspaper business and he had moved to a charming floor-through apartment in Georgetown overlooking the river. Within a year he would ask Sheilah to move in with him and she would accept. He had bought a pretty little sloop and they used it on weekends sailing the Chesapeake near Annapolis. Everyone thought they were a handsome couple. And they were.

Sheilah got her first break in television when Beau prodded the producer of a local station to give her an audition. Within a month she was a reporter covering local stories. From time to time Beau would feed her tips that the reporters on the *Times-Examiner* had given him. She was able to make an impressive difference in her news coverage because of this and because she was simply hardworking.

Beau had also begun to labor diligently on his first play, *Such a Pretty Girl*, and to his surprise and delight, when he sent it off to a theatrical agent in New York who was recommended by a director at the Kennedy Center, he received an enthusiastic reply. The agent said he would be pleased to show it around and even suggested some changes which Beau found useful.

Less than a month later the play was bought by Toby Burr and Beau received a check for $1,500 as an advance against royalties. It opened the following spring to good notices, moved on to Broadway, and Beau was off and running. He quit the paper and devoted himself to playwriting. He made a sizable income from *Such a Pretty Girl*, nearly $280,000 before it closed, and he used part of it for a down payment on a small but elegant apartment in a fashionable part of New York City, where he was now spending about half his time.

It was then that Beau began having the dream again. He had the dream for a year or so just after he got back from the war, but it had gradually gone away. He was surprised one night to find himself being shaken awake by a terrified Sheilah, who was startled by his screams. He lay there for long minutes, sweating, his chest heaving and his heart beating rapidly. He told her it was simply a nightmare, nothing more, but he had been afraid that night to go back to sleep for fear it would return and the next day he had been unable to work; his hands were shaky and he was unsure of himself. Afterward the dream returned with a certain but unpredictable regularity—and he was never totally free of it.

Sheilah, in the meantime, was growing and maturing in a way that both pleased and disturbed Beau. He could see that she was cut from good journalistic cloth. She worried over her stories and was meticulous about doing them just so. She worked late and often received midnight phone calls at the apartment from a variety of sources she had cultivated. She had her eye on the networks and they had their eyes on her. Several times her local stories made the national news. She was relatively happy during those days and even enjoyed commuting back and forth between New York and Washington.

To some extent, Beau kept her off balance just as Dan Whittle had done. Although she was more sophisticated now and more settled in her life. The small, idiosyncratic insecurities were less noticeable and less troublesome to her. The fact that Beau was away so much actually helped things. Sheilah wasn't the jealous sort in the first place and Beau had given her no cause for alarm. While he was in New York she occasionally went out to dinner with men, some of whom were her sources or potential sources, and some of whom she just found interesting. She told Beau these were business meetings and she expected no less out of him, even going so far as to speculate that if he had a fling every once in a while it would do no harm as long as she didn't find out about it. Pursuing that logic, she had a fling or two of her own, just to let off some steam.

Things began to come to a head between her and Beau when she was hired by one of the networks to do national news at a time when Beau needed to move to New York more or less full-time.

Sheilah could sense that Beau was drifting away from her. He was spending less time in Washington and they tended to argue more often when they were together, despite, or perhaps because of, these separations. Both of them were headstrong and the arguments were a way of communicating when there was little else to say. In another way, they were probably the result of frustration on the part of one or both of them, but in any case there was a lot more bickering.

Each time Beau returned to Manhattan from a visit he seemed to take a few more of his things with him. At first it was articles of clothing, then books, then odds and ends such as a painting or a lamp. He moved the sloop up there at the beginning of one summer and kept it on Long Island Sound. Finally, he told her he was being forced to spend too much time in the city and it might be a good idea if she took over the Washington apartment lock, stock and barrel. He stored a few of his things there, and left her with about half the furniture and a promise that nothing had changed between them, although both of them knew he was not being honest.

Love, for Sheilah, was a perplexing emotion. She was not given to "dating around" for any length of time. Most of her life she had gone with one guy at a time, for however long it lasted. Once they broke up, either there was a brief slack period until she found the next fellow or she had already picked him out while dating the last one. Most of these affairs had not been particularly satisfying for her, but they were adequate and convenient; providing her a sexual outlet, a buffer from loneliness and a secure platform from which to observe the rest of the world. Dan Whittle had been her first experience with love; Beau had been the second.

She couldn't explain why, but she truly cared for Beau. She was fascinated by him, by the way his mind turned, by his work. She read his plays and offered heartfelt suggestions. It wasn't until later that the plays came to represent a threat more trying than if there had been another woman. It got to the point that she sometimes wished there *was* another woman. She could deal with that problem.

When she got the call from the network, everything she had done—all the hours, the wearying frustrations and the herculean effort—finally paid off. She began as a reporter, which would ultimately lead to a correspondent's job if she was good enough. She intended to make it. Sheilah threw herself into the job with the determination of a mountain climber. She was careful not to be the prima donna Beau had warned her against. She played the good soldier, took her orders and waited for her chance. She knew it might take a year or two or three, but sooner or later, if she was patient, it would come. What neither Beau nor Sheilah could foresee was the sudden and ironic way Sheilah's career would be made and how it would affect them both.

Two weeks after she got the job Sheilah was assigned to cover a hearing at the Capitol. It was not an on-camera job—those were left for the correspondents—but she was told to attend a hearing of the Natural Resources Committee of the House of Representatives and relay the events of the proceedings to the newswriters who would turn it into copy for the anchormen. Dan Whittle was a member of the Natural Resources Committee and he noticed her from behind the podium as she entered the room. He smiled and nodded as she sat down. He stopped her in the corridor after the meeting was adjourned and caught up on what she'd been doing. He told her briefly what he'd been up to and mentioned that he was married to a certain Katherine Faulk of Bienville. Sheilah was surprised at the intensity of the pain she felt, but when he asked her to join him for lunch, she went along, because it seemed impossible that Dan was now out of reach. She had mixed feelings about his marital status; in a way it relieved her of any decision about whether or not to get involved with him again. But in another way it stimulated her. Upon their arrival at the Capitol Hill Club, Sheilah excused herself to go into the ladies' room and primp. She applied fresh lipstick and undid the top two buttons on her blouse. She was about to leave when she decided to slip out of her bra. She had beautiful, firm breasts that swayed softly against her silk blouse. She also let her hair down so that it fell around her shoulders, but she spent most of the lunch brushing it back from her forehead and trying not to play with it or put it in her mouth the way she usually did.

Dan nibbled but he didn't bite. By the time lunch was over he had, by her own count, glanced at her tits at least a dozen times, so she knew he was still interested in *something*. And she could tell he was impressed by the fact that she was now wielding power of her own with one of the largest media corporations in the world. She told him about her own engagement to Beau, and Dan seemed surprised and impressed, because Beau's reputation was pretty well known in Washington, and of course, he had grown up with him in Bienville too.

Up in New York, Beau was discovering what overnight success was all about. He became convinced that whenever a new talent came on the Manhattan scene, he, she or it was immediately and thoroughly swept up in what society columnists describe as the fast lane. Beau, of course, was no exception. It damned near wrecked his career.

One of the first places to which he was introduced was Elaine's, one of the hottest night spots in the city. He had heard a lot about it before he "arrived." An acquaintance familiar with the place introduced him to Elaine herself. She seemed very nice but his reaction to her restaurant was not unlike his astonishment the first time he entered the newsroom at the *Times-Examiner*. From all he had heard, he expected some kind of subdued, elegant bistro, but instead he found himself in a bedlam. The noise was like feeding time in a chicken coop. Waiters speaking little or no English jostled patrons in the narrow aisles; the bar area was a mob of sullen faces who would never get a table and knew it. A few tiny lamps set along a wall of medieval-looking murals gave the place its only light, and the customers were jammed like sardines at small checkered-cloth tables, eating in the dark. Later he discovered that the effect of this lighting was far superior to anything on a stage or movie set—it took a minimum of ten years off the age of anyone entering the place. But the whole of it, the noise, the light, the people, seemed to bulge at the seams, like a fat person squeezing into a pair of old trousers.

That first night a waiter handed Beau a note that had been sent by a famous movie actress who had seen him come in. In polite terms it mentioned that she wanted to fuck him. He thought it was somebody playing a joke until his eyes adjusted to the dark and he recognized the actress sitting at a table in the corner with a man who looked like one of the Three Stooges and, in fact, might have been one. The actress gave him a little wave and a smile.

Pretty soon the society people got hold of Beau. All the society people did was throw parties. Sometimes there were five parties a night, followed by a dinner and a dance. Beau became the "extra man" for practically every calendar event in town that season. The society women dragged him from party to opening to screening, showing him off like a trophy. The society women all seemed to be divorced, some three and four times, and lived in extravagant floor-through apartments on the Upper East Side. To Beau's astonishment, each had more telephone lines than a bookie operation.

In the summers everybody went out to the Hamptons, a collection of little ocean villages at the tip of Long Island. The artsy people went to East Hampton and the society people went to Southampton; the critics and journalists were relegated to Sag Harbor on the opposite side of the peninsula. Everybody gave luncheons at which mysterious food was served. Beau could eat for hours at these affairs without recognizing anything he ate except maybe a piece of celery or a roll.

Sheilah came up to see him as much as possible that first year, but the network job kept her tied to Washington most of the time. Besides, she didn't care for all the parties. She could tell something was happening to Beau and tried to warn him against it, but he was oblivious. He was enjoying himself and time alone would be his instructor. It took him nearly two more years, but he learned the lesson in an ironic and unpredictable way. Like so many young writers who move to New York, Beau tried to capture what he saw there in his next play, only to discover that while he had been largely successful in capturing it, all it mostly depicted was a bunch of shit. The critics were waiting for him, as they did for everyone else.

Down in Washington, a curious relationship had developed between Sheilah and Dan Whittle. About six months after she last saw him, Sheilah had bumped into Dan again at the Capitol. He took her for another lunch and then, a few weeks later, for another. She discovered that these meetings had a cathartic effect; it was like facing the old bogeyman, only to discover it wasn't really a bogeyman at all. All the time Beau was up in New York assing around, Sheilah and Dan were having lunches or cocktails in secluded places. He began talking to her about his life, and she opened up to him too. They never even held hands. After Katherine and Dan had a baby, a boy, Dan liked to talk about him. Somehow even this made Sheilah feel good. She began to see a side of Dan she never knew existed—the long-anticipated vulnerability was finally apparent.

But somewhere between her frustration at the way things were going with Beau and the old nerve that Dan had struck way back when, Sheilah couldn't let well enough alone. She began to desire Dan again and started to make her move. The buttons on the blouse came undone again and she'd reach over and touch his hand while they were talking; she'd bring up conversations with sexual intonations and wore skirts that showed a lot of leg. Once in the parking lot of the Capitol Hill Club, after they had a couple of cocktails, she took his arm as he walked her to her car. He leaned against her and she responded. One thing led to another and they drove to a nearby motel and screwed like teenagers. Naturally, from then on, the relationship took a different course.

Spring, summer, autumn, winter; they met when they could—when he could, actually—sometimes once a week, sometimes less. Sheilah found herself falling in love with Dan again, but she fought it, for she was smart enough to be wary of the consequences. They were lunching at her apartment one day when he let it slip that Katherine was expecting another baby.

Sheilah was hurt, despite herself. Dan had pretty much stopped talking about Katherine and his marriage after they had started up their affair. He was either being discreet or kind, she never knew which, but she appreciated it. Now, the new baby seemed almost an affront. It brought the whole predicament home. She asked him about his intentions. She couldn't help herself and Dan was more honest than she expected. He told her straight off that he couldn't afford a divorce because of his political career. The voters of Bienville would *not* understand. He did not tell her whether he was still in love with Katherine and she didn't ask. But what he said was not enough for Sheilah. She suddenly felt used and betrayed by him for the second time. It didn't occur to her that the movie playing in her head was different from the one playing in his, and as she was prone to do in such situations, Sheilah lashed out.

"So," she said, "you're a *very* married man cheating on his wife? Is that it?"

"If you want to put it that way, I guess so," he said evenly.

"And what about *me?*" she cried. "What am I supposed to do? Just lie back and get screwed and thank you for the privilege?" She was beginning to get worked up and Dan knew it. He wanted nothing to do with Sheilah when she was like this.

"Look," he said, "I thought you enjoyed me as much as I enjoyed you. You certainly seemed to. Why did you think it was going to be something more?"

"Because!" she said. "Because all this time you've . . ."

"Never. I've never told you I loved you, Sheilah," Dan cut her off. "I've never told you that I had any intention of breaking up my marriage. I've never lied to you."

"But you *implied* these things!" she spat. "You know you did! You told me you and your wife weren't sleeping together. You told me . . ."

"Yes, I did—and for a while we weren't—but now we are, as you well know by my announcement that a baby is on the way."

"Yeah!" Sheilah shouted. "I wonder! I wonder if it's yours. I don't think you can even get it up with anybody but me—that's what I think!"

Dan's patience finally cracked. He grabbed her shoulders and looked at her coldly.

"You know, Sheilah, I'm wondering why on earth you would ever think that I would actually divorce my wife and marry *you*. Divorce isn't inconceivable in *any* marriage—mine included—but marry *you?* Good God, Sheilah, I would have to have my head examined if I even entertained the thought of putting up with this sort of neurotic crap for the rest of my life."

"You bastard!" she hissed. "You dirty, impotent bastard. Are you gay? And here I was thinking you were somebody I could love. You're slime."

Dan suddenly burst out laughing and his laughter drowned out the rest of her accusations. She stormed out of the room, shouting, "Get out! Get out of my house! Get out of my life, you jerk! You bastard!" She called him every name she could think of as he put on his coat. She was still doing it after he shut the door and walked down the quaint streets of Georgetown.

After that, Sheilah became almost obsessed with getting revenge on Dan Whittle. She didn't know exactly how or when, but her memory was long and she felt she'd been wronged and wronged mightily. She wasn't going to let him walk away unscathed, no matter how long it took.

Once Dan was gone, she had to do something about her own life and she knew it. After all of Dan's talk about children, she began to want one of her own. It might be some small measure of revenge—show him she could fall in love and have somebody else's children—so she'd kill two birds with one stone. Sheilah was in her late twenties by now, and she knew she didn't have infinite time. The clock was running, both for having children and for finding a husband. Beau, of course, was the logical candidate, but their relationship was on rockier ground than ever. He was, in fact, making something of a fool of himself up in New York, jacking around with the society people and jet-setters. Earlier in the year, his picture had appeared in one of the tabloids with a movie actress hanging on to him. He had called Sheilah immediately because he figured she'd see or hear about the photo. He told her the actress was just a drunk who had latched on to him coming out of a party and there was nothing more to it than that. He had lied. The actress was tipsy, but he had taken her home with him and she had not left his apartment for two days.

It took a heavy blow for Beau to pull out of his reverie of glamour, glitter and the nightlife. When *Tennis, Everyone?* opened at the Helen Hayes it was received with something less than enthusiasm. It closed two days later, and Toby Burr and some other people were out a lot of money. Beau's popularity was in a tailspin.

Because of her schedule, Sheilah hadn't been able to come up for opening night, so she had arranged to see the play over the weekend. By then it was too late, but she came up anyway to commiserate with Beau. It was early spring and they went for a long walk in Central Park. The trees were just beginning to bud and tulips and violets sprouted among the new shoots of grass. It was late afternoon. A Sunday.

"I guess I have no one to blame but myself."

She snuggled close to him. Sympathy always brought out the best in her. "You can't worry about that now."

"I know, but it's really put a dent in things. I've got to start pulling myself together."

"How far along are you on the new one?" she asked.

"With the Vietnam play? I've almost finished the first draft. It's got problems too, but I think I can solve them."

They sat down on a park bench and basked in the strong spring sun.

"I think I'd better get the hell out of here," he said.

"Back to Washington?"

"I don't think so. Someplace else."

"Where?"

"Home, maybe. You remember I told you about that little cabin we've got up in the delta. I could go there. It's so far up in the swamp no one even knows what a distraction is. I have to get some serious work done or I'm done."

Sheilah leaned back and stretched. "Oh God," she said yawning, "I know what you mean. I really do."

"Why? You having problems too?"

"Not really." The sun glowed over her face and sparkled in her eyes.

"What, then?"

"I don't know," she said distantly. "I'm wondering if it's all worth it. What I'm doing. I mean, here I am with a job thousands of people would die for, and sometimes I say to myself, so what? I get so involved in all these stories I'm working on. I go home at night and I find myself really worrying about what's going on in Afghanistan, or getting angry about the budget. You know, you can get so close to what's going on that you actually feel like you're a part of it, and then you suddenly realize you aren't—you're just covering it —presenting it for some damned television show. You realize you're not really an integral part of anything. Instead, you're just looking for angles to make the people you're covering seem stupid or incompetent or deceitful. I actually find myself feeling *good* when we catch a politician screwing up. It's sick."

"That's the way you're supposed to feel, I'm afraid." Beau was wearing a scarf and he tossed one end of it around the back of her neck and used it to pull her head against his shoulder.

"Sometimes," she said, "I think, why am I doing all this? What I'd really like is to get married and have babies and a nice little house in the suburbs— all the things a woman's supposed to want. What have I got now? Pressure. Every day of my life; pressure, competition, tension."

"You've got me, I guess." Sheilah turned and kissed him gently on the mouth, then eagerly and passionately. They walked back to Beau's apartment, arms entwined, and went to bed.

The following weekend Beau went to Washington and he and Sheilah drove to an inn in the Virginia countryside. It was an exceptionally relaxing time and they spent hours sitting on the porch, reading in the warm April breeze. Beau took Sheilah canoeing on a creek and they picked wildflowers. At night they lay together in a big bed upstairs in front of a smoldering fire that kept out the chill.

"Sometimes I think I'd like to have a baby right now," she said softly.

"Hummmm," he murmured, "that might not be such a good idea. You'd better think it over. Besides, I think you ought to give me some warning if you start making plans that include a baby."

"Don't worry," she said, biting his ear. "I will."

Beau and Sheilah's romance was renewed after that. He vowed he was through with life in the fast lane, and to a certain extent he didn't have much to say about it anyway. Nobody wants a loser hanging around and the invitations that used to pile up in his mail began to dwindle noticeably. Beau threw himself into his work and conspired with Toby Burr to make his big comeback with *In Fields Where They Lay.* Toby was supportive and helpful, and when Beau told him he was going South to hole up for a while, he couldn't have been more pleased.

One weekend Sheilah came to New York and they drove to an old country hotel in Connecticut to spend the night. Beau was feeling a little down because a scene in the play wasn't going well and he was having trouble fixing it. He had been true to his word about giving up the social life, but he was feeling a kind of withdrawal. He missed the fun. As a result, Beau had been somewhat lonely and he'd been wondering what his life was going to be like for the next twenty years. Without the glitter he had become accustomed to, he needed to fill the void. The idea of a home and babies and a loving wife suddenly began to appeal to him. Sheilah had gone for a walk early that morning and he sat on the terrace of the inn and watched her return. She walked across a field of daisies, stopping every so often to pick a few. She was wearing jeans and a pink sweater that made her cheeks glow and her hair seem even more golden. She looked as happy and innocent as a child. He decided he loved her and the things that disturbed him before seemed to recede. He actually began to believe that if she were a mother and had her little house and her security, her difficulties and anxieties would disappear. On that late-spring afternoon, when she reached the terrace with her flowers, he stood up and asked her to marry him.

Valediction

February 7, 1984

Sex. Sex or loneliness, Beau didn't know which one—they were very connected at times. With Sheilah, the sex seemed everything while it was happening. He knew that very soon he was probably going to cut himself off from her forever. He would miss it, there was no doubt about that. The jetliner was descending and banking in a turn to the right toward Washington. From his window seat, Beau got a glimpse of the Chesapeake Bay glimmering to the east, and the flat, geometric farmland around it.

A lot of the women Beau had slept with enjoyed sex but weren't very good at it for some reason. They didn't seem to think they needed to become actively involved or they acted like they were trying to remember steps from an instruction manual. Sheilah wasn't the only woman he had thoroughly enjoyed going to bed with, but she *was* in a class by herself.

The winding Potomac was beneath them now, the landing gear lowered, the air brakes whined. In the fading twilight, the white-columned home of some long-forgotten planter would appear now and then through the winter haze of gray and brown as they glided toward the runway.

Perhaps he was still in love with Sheilah—at least in some peculiar way. He felt almost paternal toward her. She admired his stature as a writer. She had always looked up to him, and he guessed that she also felt inferior around him. Perhaps that was the reason he often felt intense when he was around her. There was a part of her that was always withdrawn, blunted by her own desires. He wondered if she was lonely. He wondered how she viewed sex, if it was some separate thing, a treasure that nourished her and allowed her to become all of the things she normally was not. Somehow he wasn't really upset that she had been seeing Dan Whittle on the sly. If he wanted to use it, he had a perfect excuse for calling off the engagement with no further ado. But he'd had his own indiscretions too. He was trying to be fair, but he was sorry Sheilah had chosen Dan Whittle, of all people. Suddenly, he really didn't know what he was going to say when he saw her. All he knew was that, somehow, he had to get out from under her spell.

Beau took a taxi from the airport, and as they turned onto the George Washington Parkway, then took the Key Bridge exit into Georgetown, a feeling of nostalgia overtook him. He liked Washington. He liked who he was when he lived here. When he got to the apartment he had once shared with Sheilah, he felt more at home than he liked to admit, even to himself.

It was a floor-through in an old Federal town house on a cobblestoned street near Georgetown University. Beau had rented it several years before he made the move to New York and even in those days it was a steal with its parquet floors, high ceilings and big windows overlooking a courtyard garden in the back. There was even a view of the river in autumn and winter when the leaves were gone.

The key was where she'd told him it would be and he put his suitcase down in the hall, deciding to leave it there until she got home. She'd said she'd be at the bureau until after the 7 P.M. broadcast. There was time and distance between them now, and he didn't want to presume to place the suitcase in her bedroom. Besides, he didn't know if he'd be staying or going.

Beau paced through the silent rooms. She had made more changes. In her spare time Sheilah had taken up sewing and needlepoint, and it seemed like every piece of furniture was adorned with one of her projects: needlepoint pillows of flowers and vegetables graced the chairs and sofas; tables covered in macramé cloths looked a little fussy for his taste.

After a while a key turned in the lock and Sheilah appeared in the door. "Hi," she said, drawing out the *i* in her kind of breathless affectation. Beau stood up and they greeted one another with a friendly hug. He felt the soft crush of her big breasts against his chest as she wrapped her arms around him. He noticed she offered her cheek, not her lips, to be kissed and she was wearing her blond hair pulled back on her head; two ominous signs, he knew. When she wanted to feel open or sexy she would almost always leave it down. She did not smell at all—no perfume, no distinct body aroma of any sort—and she wore little or no makeup. She had once declared that she preferred to remain "refreshing," rather than scented and painted.

"You look great," she said, stepping back. "Must be a lot of sun down there, huh?"

"Most of the time," Beau said, smiling.

"God, I miss the sun," she said, putting her briefcase on the floor. "So tell me, how's the play going? Did you finish it?"

"Most of it," he said. "I've got one scene left that needs some work." The truth was that he'd worked on the scene on the plane and gotten nowhere.

"And your father—how's he?"

"Spry as ever," Beau said.

"Well, I've got some exciting news. I think I'm going to have a story on tomorrow. How about that!"

"Great," he said, genuinely pleased for her. "What is it?"

"Oh, it's dull, dull—another inflation story—but there's a release tomorrow afternoon at three from the OMB, and Moorseby can't cover it because he's got something at the White House, so they told me to take a crew and work something up."

"That's terrific," Beau said. "You're moving up fast."

"Not as fast as I want, but it's something. I've got to do some research tonight so I'll know what I'm talking about."

Sheilah seemed distracted as she puttered around for a few minutes; she told Beau about London and about how she'd bought some china. She suggested an early dinner, so they went to a small restaurant on Wisconsin Avenue known for good, inexpensive food and surly Irish waiters. Sheilah wolfed down her meal and seemed in a hurry to get back to start her reading. Beau insisted that they order coffee and a dessert. She hadn't even noticed that he wasn't drinking.

"Well," she said, sipping her coffee, "You certainly have put yourself out of reach down South, haven't you?"

"A little, I suppose," he said. He'd been wondering when she'd get around to bringing it up. She was smiling across the table at him. He knew Sheilah pretty well; she was keeping her options open. Evidently she'd sorted out their situation and realized there wasn't anything she could do about it for the time being. Of course, they were in a public restaurant and Sheilah hated scenes. He knew this would be a good time to tell her it was all over. He felt his hands begin to tremble on the handle of the coffee cup.

"You put *us* pretty well out of reach yourself," he said finally.

"*I* did?" she said. "Why do you say that?"

"By carrying on an affair with Dan Whittle for the last three years," he said.

"Dan . . ." Sheilah gasped. "How . . . what makes you say something like that?"

"Oh, come on, Sheilah. Don't try to pretend you haven't been."

"Who told you that!" she said. She was flustered and her cheeks were red.

"His wife," Beau said calmly. "She's an old friend of mine."

"Wife!" Sheilah cried. "How would she know? He must have told her . . ."

"He didn't need to," Beau said. "Apparently you two weren't very discreet. It seems like everybody in town knew about it—except for me, of course."

"Well, we saw each other occasionally—but I don't see why you're bringing it up now. It's over—and besides, don't try to tell me that *you've* been squeaky clean living up there in New York all this time. What about you and that actress? You didn't fool me with that phone call. She was hanging all over you in that photo—in the damned *newspaper!*"

"I didn't have an *affair* with anybody. I might have played around a little —a few one-night stands—but there's a difference."

Sheilah squirmed in her chair. "I don't want to talk about this in here. There're too many people around."

"That's why I brought it up now," Beau said serenely. "I knew you wouldn't throw a screaming meemie."

"You bastard!" she hissed. "You just brought this up to hurt me and make yourself feel better."

"Maybe the latter," Beau replied. "But if anyone's hurt here, it ought to be me."

"Why? Because I saw somebody else for a while when you were up there screwing every good-looking woman you could lay your hands on and getting drunk every night! You make me sick, getting pious and holier-than-thou over this. What did you expect me to do?"

"I didn't expect you to fall in love with an old enemy of my youth."

"Well, I needed someone. I wasn't getting it from *you*, not with any regularity, that's for sure. And when I did, you were too damn drunk to do anything half the time."

"I'm not drinking anymore—did you notice?" he said.

"Yeah? It's about time. Too bad you didn't quit a couple of years ago. Then maybe I wouldn't have had to go to somebody like Dan Whittle. At least I make him hard."

"Oh, so that's it now, is it, Sheilah?" Beau said. "Tell me what a lousy lover I am?"

"I'll bet I'm the only one who can really turn you on, and if you want to know, it was damn hard work most of the time."

"I'm sure it wasn't too difficult for you. You've had a lot of experience."

"Enough."

"I bet."

"You know, I can't believe you're doing this! You're manipulating me deliberately, aren't you? You know exactly what you're doing to me."

"To you?"

"To me, yes—and to us. You're trying to make me feel so bad that I'll start an argument with you so . . . so . . ."

"So what, Sheilah? What am I trying to do?"

"You're trying to weasel out of our engagement. You want to break it off and make me look responsible. To break us off so *I'll* look bad."

"The engagement *was* broken off already, or didn't you remember?"

"Then why are you here? You don't mean to tell me you called to say you were coming and wanted to see me for old times' sake. You don't expect me to believe *that.*"

"I don't expect you to believe anything."

"I need to go," she said. "I need to get out of here and get home."

Beau motioned to one of the surly Irish waiters, who brought him their check. He paid it quickly and they went outside. Wisconsin Avenue was bustling with evening shoppers and bar hoppers; there was an air of holiday gaiety in the streets. Sheilah walked slightly ahead of him as they returned to the apartment. When she unlocked the door, she left it open for him. He came inside a few minutes later and found her standing in the middle of the room. She had unpinned her hair and tossed it back around her shoulders. Beau picked up the suitcase that was still standing in the hallway and started to leave.

"Where are you going?" She still sounded angry, but she didn't seem to want the conversation to end.

"I'm going to find a hotel room and get some sleep. I've got a big day here tomorrow."

"Where?" she said.

"At the Kennedy Center—have you forgotten? They're doing a reading of my play. That's why I came to town."

"No. Where are you going to get a hotel?"

"I don't know," Beau said. "But I'll find one."

"Well, you'd better call first—try the Georgetown Inn—here's the phone." Sheilah's fingers had begun working the buttons of her blouse as they talked. Her silk blouse dangled open and she shrugged it off, revealing her magnificent breasts in a lacy black bra. The clerk at the hotel said there were no vacancies and Beau hung up. Sheilah kicked off her shoes. "Try the Madison," she said. Beau got the number from information and dialed. As it rang, Sheilah sat on the couch, pulled up her skirt and began taking off her panty hose. The operator gave Beau room reservations, and as he was waiting, Sheilah stood and unclasped her bra.

"I'm going in the other room to get undressed," she said casually. He knew what she was up to.

"Yes," Beau said to the clerk. "Do you have a single room tonight? Fine. Yes, the name's Gunn—J. P. Gunn. One night—maybe two." Out of the corner of his eye he could see her in the bedroom; she slipped out of her skirt and was standing in front of the mirror massaging her breasts and tossing her long blond mane. "Wait a minute," Beau said into the phone. "Listen, let me call you back, all right?" He hung up the receiver and went to the bedroom door.

"Is this for my benefit?" he asked.

"Of course not," she said, watching him in the mirror. Her fingers played over her nipples, pulling them erotically.

"Like hell." He needed to call the Madison back. He needed to leave. She turned and slipped out of her panties and opened the closet door for a nightgown. "I've got to go to sleep." She yawned. "I've got a big day tomorrow too."

"You really know me," Beau said. "I'll give you that." He took a step into the room.

"I don't know what you mean," she said. "I'm getting ready for bed. You've already said your piece about us. I'm sorry you feel that way; I really am, but I don't suppose there's anything I can do about it."

"I don't know whether you can do anything about it either, but if you're trying to arouse me, you're doing a pretty good job of that."

"Yeah, well I always did . . . do a pretty good job." She smirked.

"No doubt about that. Come here." He was surprised at how husky his voice had become. He wanted her, desperately. He needed to lose himself in her passion, against her sweet, beautiful skin.

She turned and walked within inches of his reach. He ran his eyes over her body and moved one arm so that a finger could trace a line down her belly. She shivered.

He kicked off his shoes and unbuttoned his shirt. His chest hairs had been bleached by the sun and his dark skin shone against his open white shirt.

She did come to him then. "Are you this tan all over?" she asked, biting his nipple and running her hands over his buttocks. She lay down on the bed.

"The place up in the swamp is really secluded," he said as he pinned her shoulders to the mattress with his hands. She writhed seductively under him.

"When are you going to do me?" she murmured. "When? I need you. I need you."

"I'm going to give you the fuck of your life," he said, sliding his lips over her breasts, rubbing his body against hers.

"Uhhh-huh," she whispered, "that's what I want. I want you to fuck me."

He knew she really meant it and he knew if he stayed tonight he'd never leave. He also knew the best way to tell Sheilah it was really over was to leave —now.

"I want you, but I'm not staying. I guess I don't want you *that* badly. Sorry, baby." He was lying through his teeth. He wanted her so badly he could barely get into his loafers and out of the room.

"You bastard! You fucking asshole!" she screamed. "You'll regret this. If you leave, I'll tell you this . . ."

"You don't have to, I already know," he said, turning at the doorway.

The next morning Beau lay in bed for a while, staring at the Madison's colonial decor. During the night, the dream had returned to Beau with renewed fury, and this time the dream had a beginning, a middle and an end. He had dreamed it the way it happened. The *real* story, the real dream—on the hillside, at night, he had seen himself with the .45 pointed at the head of the Vietnamese and felt himself pull the trigger and saw the man's head simply explode before his eyes. He awakened in a sweat and sat up in bed for a while. He wanted Sheilah next to him, someone, anyone to hold and have hold him. Instead he counted the gilded fruit baskets that marched across his wallpaper and tried not to think—at any cost.

This morning it was the play that bothered Beau. In a little while he would have to face Toby Burr and the directors of the Kennedy Center for a reading and examination of a scene that he couldn't write. To have the lieutenant actually shoot the prisoner in the play would destroy the whole premise of what he'd been trying to do; and yet *he* couldn't write it any other way—that was how it happened. He was a prisoner to the facts. Beau was in a hell of a fix and he knew it, and right now all he wanted was to get back to Bienville and the paper and Eleanor. The one thing that *had* gone well had been last night. He didn't know how he had managed to get out of that room, but he had. She'd been right; he had deliberately crushed the last life from their relationship. He didn't know he was going to do it that way, but when he looked back on it, there was no better way to prove to Sheilah that he considered it over.

Beau ordered some coffee from room service, showered quickly and dressed. He got the number for the Hay-Adams from the operator and called Toby Burr.

"When'd you get in?" Toby asked cheerfully.

"Last night. Listen, can I come by? I need to talk to you."

"How about breakfast?" Toby said. "Why don't you meet me here in the dining room."

"Okay. Thirty minutes?"

"You got it."

"Toby, I don't know how to tell you this, except straight out." Beau was nervous and fidgety and would rather have been any other place in the world except here, walking in Lafayette Park in front of the White House with Toby Burr, who had just spent the last half hour at breakfast trying to raise Beau's spirits for the meeting with the Kennedy Center people. Beau had listened dutifully without saying much. When their check came he got Toby to go for a walk in the sun.

"So maybe that explains some of my problems with this play. I'm just too close to all this. I haven't had a chance to sort it out yet. Maybe I can, but not right now."

"Jesus," Toby said again, rubbing his chin, "what in hell am I gonna do with the Kennedy Center people?"

"Just go to the reading yourself and make up some excuse about why I'm not there. See what they say. Maybe they'll have some suggestions I can use." He felt queasy and ill at ease and he knew he needed to be back on a plane headed south. Toby stood up and brushed off his coat.

"And you don't think you can even come over and just answer their questions for a little while? They might not even ask any questions."

"I'm sorry, Toby, I really am. But right now I've got to save myself. I'm going through a rough time and I've got to get some things straight with myself."

"Yeah," Toby said. "I guess I can understand that. I've been in hard spots before. Beau, if your not being there ruins this deal, I won't be able to work with you any longer. I have people to answer to, people who will lose money because of *In Fields Where They Lay.* Responsibilities are unbreachable contracts. I have mine and you, unfortunately, have yours."

"Sure, Toby. Do as you see fit."

Beau turned and walked toward Pennsylvania Avenue. He had to check out and get to the airport.

Universal Oil

February 25, 1984

I'd observed Beau Gunn from various angles through the years and sometimes his patterns could be followed as simply as the way a man on a hill with
a spyglass can follow a horseback rider traversing a valley below. The rider
may become hidden behind folds in the ground, or disappear into copses of
trees, but if the man with the spyglass leads in the direction the rider is
headed, the rider reappears. Usually the rider will follow the known road,
but on occasion, to make faster time in his journey, he tears off into the brush,
risking the horse that's under him and his own neck in the process. If the man
on the hill were to turn his instrument around and look through the other
end, he would of course see a different picture: that of a tiny horseman
galloping relentlessly toward someplace, without the surrounding scenery to
lend the picture perspective. Or you can twist the spyglass out of focus and
the rider will become a blur; motion without concurrence, without resolve.
There were times when Beau's life appeared that way to me.

How do you take the measure of a man? Do you concentrate on his
virtues and vices or do you try to explore the particles of these: the warmth,
the loneliness, the passion, the love and the potential for hatred? How do you
truly sound the depths of his obsessions and depressions or mark the heights
of his glories? What of his fears? How do you measure those? How easily can
you record a man's successes and failures, his generosity or greed?

During the next week, the connection between the dead girl, Universal Oil and the D.A.'s investigation began to crystallize.

Beau arrived at the Bienville airport from Washington about 8 P.M. and went straight home. He thought about calling Eleanor but decided against it; he was tired and his mind was filled with too many things that he didn't want to discuss with anyone. In the morning Eleanor and the others were surprised to see him back in his office; he hadn't been expected for at least two more days. Despite his unexpected arrival, his day was filled with back-to-back meetings and he wanted to get through them so that he could meet with the architect who was working on his house at the site that afternoon. Once or twice he noticed Eleanor looking at him through the glass partition and he thought about calling her in, but before he could make up his mind the phone would ring or somebody would appear at the door. By lunchtime, when he went looking for her, she had vanished.

He left her a note telling her he was sorry he hadn't had a chance to speak with her alone yet and told Horace he was going to work until two and head out.

The architect had told Beau he would be working at Buck Hollow while Beau was in Washington, so he got in his car and headed out of town.

Beau was more than satisfied with the work's progress and strolled down to the duck pond after their discussions ended. It was placid and still except for a few burbling fish swirls. He heard a car pull up and turned to see Eleanor Campbell stepping out of her car.

"I hope I'm not disturbing you," she said when she was within earshot of Beau, "but I just found out something that I thought you'd like to know right away." She was standing with the sun behind her, a slender figure with dark hair that fell in curls around her shoulders. She was wearing one of those below-the-knee dresses and Beau thought she looked quite smart.

He made his way slowly up the slope toward her, because his leg had been bothering him again, but he wasn't using the cane and didn't want to. When he got close, he could see a smile cross Eleanor's lips. She wasn't beautiful, but she was certainly very pretty in an unusual and beguiling way.

"I'm all ears," Beau said.

"I love this place," she said, looking around.

"It holds a lot of memories for me," he said.

"I've just come from a long talk with Laura Katts's mother. You were right, she knew things."

"Oh?"

"For one thing, Ben Grimshaw—at least Mrs. Katts and I believe it was Ben Grimshaw—used to get a little rough with Laura. She came home at least twice with bruises on her face and arms. Her mother asked about them but she wouldn't say where she got them. The mother is almost certain it was from the guy she was dating—and we think that was Grimshaw."

"Go on." Beau began to pace up and down, his hands jammed in his pockets.

"But the most important thing I got from Mrs. Katts is a real humdinger: about two weeks before Laura died, she apparently wrote some kind of letter or memo about Universal Oil. The reason Mrs. Katts knows this is that one night Laura came home very late—two, maybe three in the morning—and she was upset. Mrs. Katts could hear her sobbing in her room, but she decided against going in.

"The next morning," Eleanor continued, "the mother went in to straighten up the room and found some notes that Laura had written. From the sound of it, it was just a draft, a partially written letter that she probably finished the next day. It wasn't addressed to anybody, according to Mrs. Katts, but it said something to the effect that someone 'should look into the dealings of Universal Oil,' and went on for a page or so, but Mrs. Katts said she really didn't read it closely because it didn't mean anything to her then."

The man working on the windows had stopped and was putting his things in his truck. Beau suggested they go over to the house and sit down on the steps.

"Is there a copy of this letter?" Beau asked.

"Mrs. Katts doesn't know. After the funeral, she put a lot of Laura's things in boxes and stored them in a closet. There is a desk that Laura used and other places where something like that might be. She's going to start looking through them tonight."

"Well," Beau said, "that *is* interesting, because it definitely ties Laura Katts to Universal Oil, which is strange, because she didn't work for them, she worked for the title company."

"But she dated Ben Grimshaw," Eleanor said.

"Yes, if it can be proved, but somehow I feel there's another connection —that phone call from Gordon McWorth that he can't remember. Grimshaw is one thing, McWorth another. That's two important links."

"I'd like to see what she wrote in that letter," Eleanor said.

"So would I. Go over to Mrs. Katts's house. Get her to start looking through those boxes *now*. We need to know what's in that letter."

There was a lengthy pause, and then Eleanor slipped her hand into his.

"How was Washington?"

"Interesting," he said.

"Did the play business go well?"

"I don't know," Beau said. "I didn't go. I chickened out at the last minute."

"What do you mean?"

"I choked. I didn't go to the reading. I suppose I let everybody down."

"But why?" she asked. "I don't understand."

"I don't either, really. It's complicated, and I'll explain it to you sometime. But I'd rather not now. You don't mind, do you?"

"No, of course not," she said. "But are you okay?"

"I'm fine."

"And what about the other?" she asked.

"Sheilah? Well, that was interesting too."

"How so?"

"It's amazing," he said, "how the mind works. Sometimes you can dwell on a thing, torture it until your perspective gets so twisted you literally can't see the forest for the trees. Emotions get turned inside out so that they don't make any real sense. They just keep feeding on themselves and I believe that's what I let happen with Sheilah and me. I saw her, yes. And all of a sudden I realized—truly realized for the first time—what a disaster it would have been to stay involved with her. Rationally, I knew it all along, but my emotions wouldn't let me accept it. There was this constant battle between two sectors of my mind." He stopped for a moment to collect his thoughts.

"So what happened?" she asked. He burst out laughing. Leave it to Eleanor to cut through the bullshit and ask the appropriate question.

"Okay, you want to know? I'll tell you. I told her to kiss off and for the first time I actually meant it. It is a great relief."

Beau looked out across the little pond. A pair of mallards had emerged from some bullrushes and were paddling along the marsh in the late afternoon sun. He put his arm around Eleanor and pulled her to him.

"Welcome home," she said.

"Yes. I really am home. Thank you." He kissed her and he really meant it.

Two days later, Beau was having lunch alone at Danatreux's when Trevor Blount, president of the Consolidated Bienville Bank, approached his table.

"Afternoon, Beau," Blount said, "mind if I join you for a minute?"

"Not at all, Trevor, have a seat," Beau said. He had just finished a platter of boiled shrimp and was sipping the rest of his iced tea.

The waitress came by and asked if Trevor wanted anything and he ordered a martini.

"Didn't know y'all drank those down here," Beau said genially.

Blount chuckled. "I just eat the olives." He leaned toward Beau conspiratorially—it reminded Beau of his days at Singer Academy, from which, in fact, Blount had graduated a decade before Beau—and said, "We ought to talk about the Universal Oil thing."

Beau set his glass down. "Oh? That's interesting. I've been meaning to talk to you about the same subject."

"Really?" Blount said. Now it was his turn to be surprised.

"Well, we found in the papers of incorporation that you're a board member, Trevor. And as you probably know, the *Courier-Democrat* is interested in finding out what's going on with this investigation the D.A.'s running."

"Yes, ah, well—that was what I wanted to talk about too, Beau." Blount's patrician face, normally a little pink from overindulgence, seemed to grow pinker.

"Go ahead, it's your dime," Beau said casually.

"Well, I, er, I'm not sure how to say this, but you may not realize what's at stake here, Beau. I mean, I know the goddamn district attorney's trying to mess with Universal's business, but it's really a bunch of technical crap. He's just wasting everybody's time. The bank has a stake in all this—Universal is our client—and we'd like to see the thing end."

"What's this all about, Trevor?" Beau asked. "After all, you are on the board of directors of Universal."

"Well, yes—I am, I am, but that's just because of the bank, of my position. After we agreed to finance them, Universal asked me to join the board. I think it was just sort of a goodwill move."

"So then you can tell me what this investigation's all about, can't you?"

"I, ah, well, no, I can't. I mean, I'm really not sure myself. All I know is that it's a procedural thing . . ."

"C'mon, Trevor—the D.A.'s been calling in everybody from Gordon to Dan Whittle and holding meetings in the middle of the night. Are you going to tell me that as a member of the board of directors you don't know what it is they're trying to find out?"

"Ah, no, I'm not going to tell you that, Beau. Because I do know some of it, but I'm under instructions not to say anything about it."

"Instructions from whom?" Beau asked.

"The D.A. Why don't you ask him?"

"We already have. I imagine you already know that he won't tell us anything."

"And for good reason, Beau. There's nothing to tell. It's just a simple little matter that's about to be cleared up and we really would appreciate it if you guys at the paper would let it rest. Let the D.A. handle it."

"Who would appreciate it?"

"I would, for one," Blount said.

"What about the bank, Trevor, would the bank appreciate it?"

"Well, yes, they would too. That's one of the things I wanted to tell you. The bank would appreciate it very much."

"How would they appreciate it, Trevor?"

"How—well, they just would, that's all. I don't have to say anymore."

"And if we don't let it drop, if we keep on with our investigation, then would it be safe to say that the bank wouldn't appreciate it?"

"Ah, yeah, I believe it would be safe to say that."

"And how would the bank show its displeasure?" Beau asked evenly.

"Oh, hell, let's not get into all that. I didn't come here to threaten anyone. I want to discuss *positive* things."

"And I want to discuss the *truth*, Trevor. I mean, it isn't lost on me that the bank is one of our biggest advertisers. Should I assume that might change in the future if we persist in looking for the truth?"

"Now, I didn't say that, Beau. I am trying to look at this in a positive light."

"But you're suggesting it, aren't you?"

"It is a possibility," Blount said. "But that's not . . ."

"That's all I wanted to know, Trevor. Now, why don't you pick up your goddamn martini and drink it somewhere else."

In the meantime, Eric Pacer had been doing some investigating that had uncovered startling information—the more so to Beau.

Beau had been up in the state capital for a few days, trying to reorganize the *Courier-Democrat*'s confused and inefficient news bureau there. When his plane landed back in Bienville, on a Sunday morning, he decided to stop by the office, hoping to spend some time catching up on paperwork and other odds and ends.

He found his mail stacked neatly on his desk and began sorting through it absently until he came to a white *Courier-Democrat* envelope with his name on it. Inside, he found a lengthy and detailed memorandum from Pacer, summing up what he had discovered over the past week while looking into the affairs of Universal Oil.

"As I see it," Pacer wrote, "they have got the scam of the century going."

Pacer had managed to infiltrate Universal's operations area some twenty-four miles north of the city by renting a small boat and rowing in the dark to a deserted riverbank, then walking through a wooded area to a place where metal sheds were kept. Inside the unlocked metal sheds he found hundreds of fifty-five-gallon drums, filled with oil. There was an operations room of sorts, filled with file cabinets and charts, but it was locked and Pacer didn't want to risk being accused of breaking and entering.

The next morning, a Wednesday, he had parked his car near the main gate and waited to see what kind of activity he could observe. About seven o'clock workers began arriving and at eight-thirty a large truck left the compound. In the back he could see the oil drums stacked high. He followed the truck down back roads to a Universal Oil landing that was posted as a "Fueling Point."

He backed his car into the woods and watched as workers loaded the drums aboard a small nondescript freighter. More trucks arrived throughout the day, until Pacer estimated that approximately five hundred barrels had been loaded. That night, as Pacer watched, the freighter headed downriver toward Bienville Bay. Using bayside roads, Pacer managed to follow it as it made its way into the ship channel and headed for the Gulf of Mexico.

Beau read on with interest.

Pacer went into the Bienville Port Authority the next morning and acted like he knew what he was doing. He checked the roster of departing vessels and learned that the freighter was bound for the Caribbean island of Haiti with a cargo of seven hundred and fifty barrels of oil.

Pacer then returned to the "Fueling Point" site and found that another freighter had tied up there and was also being loaded with oil drums. A second check of lading records showed that this ship too was headed for Haiti. It made Pacer curious. What would Haiti need with crude oil? Gasoline, yes. Motor oil, yes. But crude oil?

On Friday night he drank at several of the waterfront dives that local seamen patronize. He struck up some conversations and always managed to mention Haiti. At one point a semi-drunken sailor two stools down leaned over and informed him that he had just returned from there.

Pacer bought the guy a drink and learned that he had been a member of the crew that delivered some oil drums to Haiti from Universal's "Fueling Point." The oil was off-loaded and the freighter was then reloaded with more oil drums, which were eventually removed from the ship by trucks from Exxon and Texaco and Shell and other big oil companies, and either returned directly to Bienville or sent to other ports along the coast. The sailor said he had made dozens of such trips during the past year or so.

A ship leaves Bienville with crude oil and returns with more oil, so what's the point? The sailor solved that problem for him too by telling him about a little refinery on Haiti where Universal was trucking all its oil.

Pacer began to wonder why somebody would bother to ship freighter after freighter of crude oil all the way to Haiti to be refined just so they could bring it back and sell it to the majors, when the majors already had cheaper and better refineries here.

He was asking this question aloud as he turned to leave, when the sailor announced that he bet he knew. He told Pacer that Universal was probably trying to "hoodwink" somebody into thinking it was "foreign" oil to get around the controls.

Pacer prodded him about this comment, trying to get more information, but the sailor became suspicious of him suddenly and seemed to decide that he had said too much. He refused Pacer's next offer of a drink and moved to a table with some decidedly rough-looking companions, all of whom began glancing Pacer's way. Never one to stand on ceremony, Pacer left. Quickly.

For the next day or so he did more research into the oil business and turned up some interesting information.

Universal Oil was bulk-packaging crude oil from their own wells—oil which, because of a price ceiling set by the U.S. government, cannot legally be sold in the States for more than $10 a barrel—shipping it to a small refinery in Haiti and then redirecting it back to the United States, where it is sold as "foreign" oil at prices of up to $35 a barrel.

"A shipload of a thousand barrels of domestic crude is worth approximately $10,000 if sold legally in the States, but refined and sold as 'foreign' oil, it could command as much as $35,000 on the foreign spot market. Each shipload Universal routed through Haiti and brought back into the country grossed them about $25,000, less expenses. It was a thoroughly illegal scam."

"Hot damn!" Beau said aloud, smacking the top of his desk. He thought about Pacer's estimates on Universal's drilling operations. If they were actually carting as much as a thousand barrels a day down to Haiti, they were taking in nearly ten million dollars a year in mostly illegal profits. Ten million!

He put down the memo and lit up a cigar. Things were beginning to fall into place. No wonder the pressure was on for him to stay out of Universal's business. This was obviously what the D.A. was looking into. Was he investigating because of Laura Katts's letter? Was she killed because she knew too much? This was really something! He wanted to talk to Pacer right away and phoned him at home.

Within hours Beau had his team in his office for a meeting.

"I want a complete investigation of all this," he said, perching on his desk. Sitting in chairs around the office were Pacer, Eleanor, the young Yalie, Tim Harte, and Bill Spaulding.

"Tim," Beau said, "I want you to get on the first plane down to Haiti and find out everything you can about Universal Oil's presence there, the refinery or whatever it is, everything. Haiti's a tricky country, so I want you to stay at the Olafson in Port-au-Prince. It's expensive, and I wouldn't normally put you up there, but I want you to look flush. Take a thousand dollars from the cashier and get a receipt. If you've got to pay somebody off, do it. Just keep careful records.

"Pacer, continue to keep your nose in everything that's going on here but don't get caught doing anything illegal.

"Bill, I want you to comb through all the records at the Port Authority, see who's been shipping what according to the bills of lading. And then I want you to pump the D.A.'s office for information about this investigation. Somebody's bound to break.

"Eleanor, stay with the Laura Katts story and the Brodie case. We're close to cracking this whole thing wide open and we can't stop now. You and Mrs. Katts may still find Laura's letter. Any questions?"

Nobody had any, so Beau sent them on their way, except for Eleanor, whom he asked to dinner. She went to her desk to get something and Beau sat looking out the window at the deserted Sunday streets of Bienville. It was a strange town, his town. It was a pleasant place to live, to grow up in, and to return to, but it was still a city ruled by a corrupt aristocracy. Old money had perpetuated itself in Bienville for nearly three hundred years. He was going to have real trouble from here on out, he knew. The old money was very shrewd and knew all the rules, because they themselves had invented the game. Beau knew more than most, because, in some ways, he was a part of the old money and it bothered him. It was one thing to nail a mobster extorting dockworkers, quite another to expose someone who had once been a good friend. These were the things he contemplated as he looked out the window that Sunday afternoon, but there were other things descending on Beau too, just as swiftly as a desert whirlwind. One of them, though he would never have dreamed it then, was that Sheilah Price was coming to town.

Family Ties

There was one significant piece of information that Pacer left out of his report on Universal Oil—but only because he didn't know about it. It was the list of stockholders, which, as it turned out, comprised a startling if not shocking roster of Bienville's leading citizens. In fact, it read like a Who's Who of the town's finest families—doctors, stockbrokers, lawyers, wealthy widows, corporate executives, real estate brokers, shopping center developers, some twenty-three investors in all, including, to Beau's embarrassment and dismay, his own father, James Payton Gunn, Sr.

Beau did not have this list when he gave the signal to run the story on Universal Oil the Tuesday after he received Pacer's memo. In fact, there were a lot of things he didn't know or couldn't prove, but he decided to "run up the flag" and see who saluted.

He called me into the meeting that he held the night before the story ran, since it was a fairly sensitive matter. Eleanor was there, and Bill Spaulding and Horace Moulton. Tim Harte was in Haiti.

"We're learning as we go along on this one," Beau began. "We know that Universal is shipping domestic oil down to Haiti, refining it there and then reselling it here as 'foreign' oil, which, as far as we can establish, is a violation of the law and an extremely profitable enterprise.

"There are elements of this story I am satisfied with, and some I'm not," Beau said.

"For instance, we cannot actually *prove* that Universal Oil is doing these

272

things. All the allegations are hearsay, but I think that we can now attempt to link the supposed allegations in the dead girl's missing letter and the import scam at Universal Oil. Bill called the D.A. this morning. All we got was the same old 'no comment,' but of course he's going to pursue it further."

"What do you think, Eleanor," I asked.

She was about to answer when there was a knock on the glass partition outside Beau's office. It was Lulu, the switchboard operator.

"I've got a lady on the line who says she has to speak with you, Eleanor," Lulu said. "She says it's very important."

"You can take it in here," Beau said to Eleanor, pointing toward his phone. Eleanor picked up the receiver and we continued our discussion in fierce whispers. I was very concerned that Trevor Blount had threatened Beau—and the paper—with advertising reprisals if we kept writing about Universal. As a businessman, I knew Bienville Consolidated did over a quarter of a million a year in advertising with us. But I felt equally concerned as a citizen and a publisher. This was exactly the kind of thing that had eaten away at the city for who knew how many decades—bribery, payoffs, threats, corruption, favors—it was exactly the kind of thing that needed to be rooted out. The "old boy" network had grown too fat and done too much damage for me to sit back and let it get away with this too. I had pledged myself to run a good, decent newspaper, and no damned bank president was going to scare me out of it.

"Go with it," I said as Eleanor hung up the receiver. Beau smiled at me and then looked questioningly at Eleanor.

"I've just had some news," she announced. "That was Mrs. Katts. Last night she found her daughter's letter—or at least a draft or notes or whatever it is. From what she said on the phone, I think it supports everything we've got."

We all listened on the edge of our seats as Eleanor, reading from her notepad, recited the dead girl's sketchy but damning allegations.

"According to Laura Katts," Eleanor said, "she was hired by Gordon McWorth, her cousin-in-law, to work part-time at night in the bookkeeping department of Universal Oil. The date she was hired shows she had worked there for about six months before she was killed.

"She worked one and sometimes two nights a week, mostly with Ben Grimshaw, Universal's operations manager, keeping a set of books as he directed. He gave her invoices and sales statements and certain bills to pay and checks to write. It was her understanding at the time that she was being hired simply to supplement the regular bookkeeper in the office, but she became suspicious after a while that she was actually keeping a separate set of books.

"One night she located the regular bookkeeper's files and learned that her suspicions were correct. By this time, she was seeing Ben Grimshaw, and one night she asked him about it. He denied that separate books were being kept, and she didn't press it anymore until, during an argument, Grimshaw hit her more than once. She was terrified of his abuse, and threatened to go to the authorities with what she knew. He beat her again.

"Among other indiscretions, Laura found that she was writing a monthly check for a thousand dollars to the assistant head inspector of the Bienville Port Authority, whose name she recognized. She didn't know why he was getting this money, but she could guess. Other checks, ranging from two hundred to a thousand dollars a month, were written to people whose business with Universal seemed very cloudy, to say the least. *And,*" Eleanor said, trying to keep the excitement out of her voice, "you'd better hold on to your hats. The highest-paid recipient on this list—two thousand dollars a month— was somebody named A. O. Whittle. She checked the address in the phone book and did not find an A. O. Whittle but she did find at the same address where the check was being sent an Arthur Daniel Whittle, our congressman."

"Goddamn!" I said as Beau whistled through his teeth.

"Where's the letter now?" Beau asked.

"The mother's bringing it over in a few minutes."

"Good. When she gets here, call upstairs to the legal department and get a notary down here and get her to attest that the handwriting is her daughter's."

"How are you going to handle this?" I asked him.

"Like calcium-deficient chicken eggs, and you know what you're likely to get on your tie if you're carrying those around. On the surface, it's a very big story. Very big. I'll need to take some chances, but I can't be foolish or we'll be raising chickens and the paper won't exist. Meantime, I'm going to go with the Universal story we've already got—link the company to the investigation, at least mention that Whittle's been seen in attendance at these sessions, or whatever they're called, and see what that gets us."

"It seems strange," I said, "that they would have just mailed out those checks to these people. I mean, after all, they were bribes to officials and a damn congressman. And letting a girl keep separate books and write the checks and everything, when she wasn't in on the deal. It just seems odd."

"It was stupid," Beau said. "Plain stupid. But I'll tell you my theory, Pappy. I think that this sort of thing has been going on for so long in this town that they just got careless. If my guess is right, I'll bet they don't even consider that they've done anything wrong, with the exception of Laura's death. It was just another instance of breaking the rules to screw somebody out of money. And then when the girl decided to talk, everybody panicked and it all got out of hand."

"Yeah," I said, "I think that makes perfect sense."

I went back to my office, leaving Beau to handle the machinery that would turn this information into news. I must admit that I was both excited and apprehensive. It was, I realized, a hell of a story, as Beau had said, but a dangerous one too. We didn't need libel suits against us. Or, for that matter, advertising boycotts, but I had bought a paper that I wanted to report the truth and create controversy. I was getting my wish. I was reminded of that old saying about being careful what you wish for, because you just might get it. I trusted that Beau would do the right thing.

The story that ran across the top of page one the next morning discussed the cloudy circumstances surrounding the investigation of Universal Oil and hinted at a link between the investigation and Laura Katts's murder. The story contained holes that Beau was unable to fill by press time. Beau did not disclose that Universal had been illegally selling its own locally produced oil as "foreign" oil, because the only information we had on that was the word of a drunken sailor. Nor did it disclose Loyd Spinker's claim that Tommy Brodie could not have been involved in the Katts murder because he and Spinker had been having a homosexual liaison that night. Beau had tried to reach Spinker at work and at home to try to persuade him to allow us to print a watered-down statement from him, but Beau was told he had not reported in that day.

The story did reveal much of what was in Laura Katts's letter, including her suspicions that separate books were being maintained by Universal and that the company was paying money to various public officials, including Congressman Dan Whittle. We did not explain why.

All of us expected the "shit to hit the fan" after the story ran, but it did not—at least not in the way we expected. In fact, one of the few phone calls we received about the piece came into Beau from Gordon McWorth, and that was two days later. Gordon asked to meet Beau at an out-of-the-way bar that afternoon. McWorth, who later testified for the government in exchange for a lighter sentence, gave this version of his conversation with Beau on the witness stand months later:

"And so I said to him, 'Look, Beau, there are things about this mess that you don't know, and you'd better the hell know them.'

"When he asked what that might be, I told him. In a way, I guess I was appealing to his sense of public spirit when I told him that the investors in Universal Oil were among his lifelong friends—and even closer. I told him that if he continued stirring things up, it was going to get a lot of people in trouble over nothing.

"He asked if these people deserved to be in trouble, and I said I didn't think so. I told him we just about had the situation under control with the district attorney, but that if he kept on publishing unsubstantiated information and rumors, it was going to stir up a bunch of hornets, and a lot of folks were going to get stung—including, maybe, himself.

"He asked me what I was talking about and I told him that his own father had put up fifty thousand dollars to join Universal Oil's Haitian project and had been receiving dividends of approximately thirteen thousand dollars a month.

"And then he asked if his father and the others knew exactly what their investment had gone for, and I told him, 'Yes, of course they did. Why the hell do you think they'd put up that kind of money in the first place?'

"He seemed dismayed by this, and he asked if the district attorney was going to indict the investors. And I said I didn't think so, because we'd worked out a deal where we simply paid the money back and that it was really a technical matter—at least that's the way the D.A. was planning to look at it now—that we had only technically violated any laws. I said that we had worked very hard to keep the situation under control, and that if he kept publishing all this stuff, it was going to get out of hand.

"And then he asked about the girl and I told him I didn't know anything about that. And he accused me of lying to him when I said I didn't call her, or couldn't remember calling her, and I admitted that I had called her, because we needed some bookkeeping done, but that I knew absolutely nothing about her murder, which, of course, wasn't exactly true.

"And I also told him that I had been in touch several times with his father, to try to get him to call Beau and put a lid on this, but that he refused, and so that's why I decided to do it myself. I kept trying to emphasize to him that all we did was *technically* violate some laws and regulations maybe, but that we weren't criminals and that it wasn't going to do the city any good to have this kind of exposure."

At this point the prosecutor asked McWorth what Beau's response to all this was.

"He told me to 'go to hell.'"

"Go to hell" may have been Beau's sentiments to Gordon McWorth, but the fact of the matter was that Beau had a tiger by the tail and he knew it. His first move was to call his father and arrange to meet him at his home that night, but before he could do that, just as he was cleaning off his desk and preparing to leave the office, Sheilah Price walked in, pretty as a picture.

"Well, I never thought I'd see the day when I'd be standing here," Sheilah said sweetly. Beau froze in his tracks, staring like he was seeing a ghost. In many ways he was.

Sheilah had taken the afternoon flight from Washington to Bienville after the wire service teletype in her bureau clattered out an encapsulated version of the *Courier-Democrat's* lead story that morning. She convinced her boss that Whittle was probably in big trouble and a U.S. congressman being accused of taking money from a private corporation was national news. Sheilah had also told the bureau chief that she knew Whittle from their early days in D.C. and that she was the perfect person to be assigned to the story.

"I can get to the bottom of all of this in ten seconds flat," she told him.

Sheilah's motive later became crystal clear to me, but no one—neither her editors at the network nor Beau or I—understood it then. Perhaps Dan Whittle did, but as Katherine told me later, Dan thought he could "handle" Sheilah. It was, in Sheilah's mind, her "finest hour." As I said earlier, she had a long memory and the humiliations Dan had put her through twice were still heavy on her mind. Also, I think she had some idea of putting Beau back on her string. Even though he'd signed off on her too, Sheilah liked to keep her options open when she could.

"This is like old home week"—Sheilah smiled—"but I was kind of hoping you would tell me what you know about all this."

"I'm afraid I can't do that," Beau said, still stunned to find her in Bienville. He asked her to sit down and got her a cup of coffee. "Why don't you ask the district attorney," he said again after the umpteenth question from Sheilah.

"That's where I'm headed after I leave here, but just for old times' sake, can't you give me *something* more to go on. Let me see that letter from the girl that was in the story."

"Nope," Beau said. "I can't see any reason to give the television networks a scoop after we've slaved our asses off to get it. I never thought we'd be in competition, but it looks like we are."

"We always were," Sheilah said. "I suppose you suspect the money Whittle received was a bribe?"

"Why don't you ask him. You've certainly been close enough—or is that a private matter?"

Sheilah didn't even flinch. "A story is a story, Beau," she said piously. "I've called Dan. He won't talk about it. But I'm here on assignment, and you and I have certainly been close enough too. I wouldn't have thought, after all we've meant to one another, that you'd have me dangling in the breeze."

"Really? Is that what you thought? Just give you the story?"

"That's about it."

"You're amazing, Sheilah, fucking amazing. The fact that you've been having an affair with the man for years carries no weight? For you or for him?"

She squirmed a little. "My affairs are none of your business anymore—you made that clear."

"Well, I'm certainly glad to hear that I made something clear, because you aren't listening to me now. You're not getting this story handed to you on a silver platter—not by me. You can do the same work we've done and have your story. By the way, what does Congressman Whittle think about your covering the story?" Beau asked.

"Look, he knows I'm a professional. He knows I have an obligation to the network. He tried to talk me out of it, of course, but it's you he's upset with. He thinks *you're* the one who's trying to do him in."

"Me?"

"He's very agitated—nervous. I spoke with him on the phone yesterday. It was late and I think he'd been drinking. Word around Washington is that he's been drinking a lot lately. But he was mad as hell at you—and scared."

"Why me?" Beau asked. "I'm just reporting the facts."

"He doesn't see it that way. He knows you blame him for our breakup and he also knows you had a sweet little affair with his wife."

Beau's face lost some of its color. "Dan Whittle did not break up our relationship. There was nothing to break up. He must have gotten his misinformation from you. And as for his wife, that's none of your business."

"Touchy, aren't we?" she asked, removing a small mirror and a tube of lipstick from her purse.

"Sheilah, I could have done without having you around right now. You are self-centered and self-righteous and selfish. You think only of yourself."

"I knew there was some reason we almost married; it was because we're so much alike. Don't you think?" she asked as she smoothed coral lipstick over her lips.

"No, I don't. I think you're an asshole."

Beau excused himself and left, sending Horace to escort her to the front door. He was rattled and disturbed by her presence. Mostly because just the sight of her made him want her, and everything in his psyche told him to stay away.

"You might have told me about it," Beau said quietly. He was sitting in the living room of his father's home—his old home—drinking a lemonade. The old man was sitting opposite him, looking out the window, drumming his fingers nervously on the chair arm. Beau could see that his jaw was working and that he was terribly upset.

"If you'd mentioned it before—I—I don't know what I would have done, but there might have been some way to help you."

"I don't know why *you* had to get involved in all this," the old man said angrily. "A newspaper is not supposed to ruin the lives of the people it is there to serve. Not to mention ruining the town's reputation."

"As a matter of fact," Beau said, "the newspaper is very concerned about the community and its residents. And besides, there is apparently a murder involved—maybe two."

"There isn't any murder involved as far as I'm concerned," his father said. "All I did was put some money into a company that promised to return my investment two or three times over. And that's what it did."

"And you knew from the start it was illegal?"

"I knew it might be borderline—but that's all! But so what? What was wrong with it all? All the law said was that the price of domestic oil is controlled at such and such a barrel—and what we did was to ship the domestic oil to a foreign country, where, to my mind, it then became 'foreign' oil. It was processed and then shipped back here. What in hell is wrong with that?"

"Apparently the district attorney thinks there's something wrong with it, because he's holding some kind of investigation . . ."

"He's not holding a damn investigation, Beau! He's trying to work it out with us. The only reason he gave a hoot in the first place was because of that letter the girl sent. And she didn't know what she was talking about."

"No? Then it's not true? The phony books, the money paid out to all these authorities—including this district's representative in Congress!"

"I don't know anything about all that," the elder Gunn spat. "All I know is that I entered into what I thought was a good investment that involved—if anything—a borderline legal question, and now, thanks to you and your paper, I may wind up losing my money *and* my reputation. Why, I could go to jail."

"Oh, Dad," Beau said sadly. "Don't you see it's more than that? A girl's been murdered, Tommy Brodie's dead, and who's to say he wasn't murdered too. Don't the facts speak for themselves? Here was this girl who was keeping illegal books. She gets mad and threatens to expose everyone to the authorities. Suddenly she turns up dead and . . ."

"And I say Brodie did it," his father said flatly.

"Well, he didn't," Beau replied. He told the old man about his conversations with Spinker and Spinker's alibi for Brodie, but his father wasn't convinced.

"Even if it's true, all it says is that Brodie didn't do it. God, son, what you're asking me to believe is that Gordon McWorth—a lifelong friend of mine—had something to do with murder!"

"What makes you think he didn't?" Beau asked. "I think that under the law . . ."

"Dammit, don't you quote the law to me! I've practiced the law for fifty years—and I know it a lot better than you do. And I can tell you this: whatever they want to do, they've got to *prove* it in court—in front of a judge and jury. And I'll fight it tooth and nail, because my reputation in this town is on the line."

"So is mine, Dad." Beau stared at a picture of his mother and his father and himself that was hanging next to him on the wall. He was nine or ten and his parents looked so young.

The old man turned and stared out the window again. The silence lasted a full five minutes before Beau rose to leave.

"I'm sorry if I've let you down, son," his father said, without looking up.

Beau turned from the door. "No, no, you didn't let me down."

"I have and I've disappointed you."

Beau went over and put his hand on the old man's shoulder. "Look, don't worry. I'm going to try to look out for you. I don't know what's going to happen, but I want you to know that I love you."

Beau heard a sob catch in his father's throat. "Just do your job, son. I'm too old to get in your way."

"You get some rest," Beau said.

"It was just a smart investment. I didn't think it would come to this," the old man said.

"Nothing's happened yet. We'll talk tomorrow."

That night Beau and Eleanor were having supper at Danatreux's when Sheilah walked in with a young assistant D.A. who looked fresh out of law school. She was dressed for the occasion, Beau noticed, in a tight white sweater and form-fitting black slacks. Her hair brushed seductively against her shoulders as she walked. It was unavoidable that they pass by Beau and

Eleanor's table, inevitable that they stop and say hello, but ironic that it was the young assistant D.A. who initiated the conversation.

"Hi, Eleanor," he said, "how are you?"

"I'm fine, Bob," Eleanor said. "Beau, this is Bob Carlson with the district attorney's office. Bob, this is Beau Gunn."

"Pleased to meet you," Beau said, and before the D.A. could make his own introduction, Beau shocked Eleanor by introducing Sheilah Price.

"Well, it's nice to meet you," Eleanor said when she had recovered. "I've heard a lot about you."

"All good, I suppose," Sheilah said, taking Bob's arm and smiling at Beau.

"Of course," Eleanor said, casually placing her hand over Beau's. The move was not lost on Sheilah.

Young Bob Carlson was looking around for a waitress to seat them, but Sheilah couldn't resist the temptation to ask what was on her mind.

"Are you two, ah . . . *seeing* each other?"

"I suppose you could say that," Eleanor said serenely. "I see quite a lot of Beau and he certainly sees me."

"Well," Sheilah said, frowning slightly, "it's nice for Beau that he's found somebody close to his own age."

"Yes"—Eleanor smiled—"we're both thirty."

Beau burst out laughing. Sheilah seemed to be forming a reply when Bob Carlson gestured that the hostess was waiting to seat them. He nodded to Eleanor and Beau and they left.

"Well, she's certainly a hot one, I'll give you that," Eleanor said when they were out of earshot. "What's she doing here? Why didn't you tell me?"

"I didn't have a chance. She walked into the office this afternoon while you were out. She says she's covering the Whittle side of the story for the network—congressman in trouble, that sort of thing. I was absolutely shocked when she walked in. The thing is, and I guess I haven't told you this part, she's been having an on-again, off-again affair with Whittle for years."

"No!"

"Yes. I found out about it from Whittle's wife."

"His wife?"

"That is another story," Beau said. "What about this kid she's with—the assistant D.A.? Does he know anything?"

"He doesn't know his ass from third base." Eleanor giggled. "I've known him for about a year. All they ever let him do is traffic cases. He's a sweet guy and he even tried to help me on this, but when he asked one of his bosses what was going on, they told him to mind his own business or they'd put him down in truant court."

"Well," Beau said, "I'm relieved, because I'd say that young man is in for a surprise tonight."

The Vision
of Distance

March 3, 1984

Ironically, it was Sheilah who turned up the most damning evidence against Dan Whittle, but in the end, Beau got the blame for it.

The *Courier-Democrat*'s editor worried for more than a week about his father and the other people whose lives he was preparing to turn upside down. During that time he sat on the story, though other vital pieces of information were beginning to fall into place. Sheilah had aired a story on the nightly news which reported that Whittle was being accused of accepting money, though she did not go so far as to suggest that he was accepting bribes.

At this point, Eleanor was devoting her time to the question of who killed Laura Katts. Beau and Eleanor tried to narrow it down one night during supper.

Eleanor had definitely established that Laura Katts was dating Ben Grimshaw at the time of her death. People with whom she worked, as well as her friends, knew of no one else she might have been seeing. She figured that left the Universal Oil people with a damned good motive for needing her out of the way, since they knew she was planning to blow their extremely profitable and illegal operation.

"And the next question," she said to Beau at their daily briefing, "is: how high up at Universal did a discussion of this problem go? McWorth? Fletcher Cross? Was it ordered? Did Grimshaw kill her? If so, did he do it on his own?

283

Lord knows, there are any number of thugs that hang out around the water-front who might have been involved."

"But Spinker said he actually saw Grimshaw and Laura together the night she was killed. So if we assume Universal *was* involved, he'd be the logical suspect," Beau said.

"Do you think it would do any good to try to talk to Spinker again? I have made a dozen attempts to reach Grimshaw by phone. I've shown up at his office, I've waited for him on the street. Nothing. He has managed to stead-fastly avoid me."

"This whole thing is smelling like a rat," Beau said. Eleanor nodded, brushing a curl from her forehead and sipping her coffee.

"I'll call Grimshaw again myself and I'll call Spinker too. It's time to set some fires, if for no other reason than to create smoke," Beau said.

"You know, I'm getting more and more curious about this whole thing. The D.A. doesn't seem to give a tinker's damn about what we know. You'd think that after we ran the story on Laura's letter he'd at least want to see what we turned up."

Beau nodded but remained silent. He believed he knew the answer to that question from what he'd been told by Blount, McWorth and his father. The D.A. was going to work out a nice little settlement so nobody got prose-cuted. They would downplay the publicity, erase the stink and avoid a scan-dal. That was the way things worked in Bienville. Beau, of course, had told Eleanor none of this, and it racked and nettled his professional and ethical soul.

"Maybe we should go over to the D.A. ourselves. Just march in and demand to be heard, and if that doesn't work, write a story saying he is refusing to consider evidence."

"I've thought about that," Beau said. "It's a possibility, but I'd like to think about it for a while."

"Well, with your friend Sheilah around here, I wonder if we shouldn't do it now," Eleanor said. "I'd expect the *Times* or the Washington *Post* to be getting on the bandwagon pretty soon too. I'd hate to see the story get away from us."

"Yep, I worry about that too," Beau said. He didn't realize that it *had* gotten away from him. Sheilah saw to that the next day.

"United States Congressman Daniel Whittle, chairman of the House Foreign Affairs Subcommittee, has been linked to a series of payments from an oil drilling, import and export company in his own hometown of Bien-ville."

This was Sheilah's lead-in for the nightly news report the following day.

On camera in front of the Bienville Courthouse, Sheilah recounted the information gleaned from the *Courier-Democrat* stories and added a twist of her own—namely, that Whittle had been lobbying heavily behind the scenes in Congress against deregulating domestic oil prices, a fact which neither Beau, Eleanor nor any of the others working on the story had taken the trouble to find out.

Sitting in his office watching the news report, Beau cursed himself for failing to realize this link. Whittle served on half a dozen committees, most notably Armed Services and Foreign Relations, where he had seniority. But Sheilah's researchers in Washington had uncovered some damning evidence.

"Whittle, a six-term member of the House," Sheilah continued, "has lobbied successfully during the past two years for retention of fixed price controls on domestic oil, a position opposed by the major oil companies.

"The controls have been crucial in maintaining prices paid by oil companies for oil produced within the United States at a low level of about ten dollars a barrel, while foreign oil can be sold in the States for up to three times as much."

"Damn!" Beau said, and cursed himself again for failing to appreciate Whittle's influence. Now he had the whole picture. What Sheilah didn't know, of course, was that Universal was pretending to import oil, which they sold for a huge profit, when it was actually oil that came from wells right here in the state. If the price controls were removed, domestic oil prices would rise, but not to anywhere near what was now being paid for foreign oil. With the increase in U.S. oil prices, foreign oil prices would drop too. So keeping the status quo was very important to people like Fletcher Cross and Gordon McWorth and the other investors in Universal Oil—and apparently it was to Dan Whittle too.

Eleanor was off somewhere and the newsroom was busily preparing the morning edition. Beau sat in his office and gave only perfunctory notice to the layout sheets being brought to him by the various desk editors. He knew he was between a rock and a hard place, that whatever idea he might have come up with to try to save his old man was shattered by Sheilah's news. Given what was already known, there was no way he could avoid running a damaging story on Dan Whittle. It was a case of official misconduct and bribery, pure and simple.

Just then the phone rang and the operator told him that he had a call from Katherine Whittle. He sighed and told the operator to put it through. Katherine's voice sounded shaky.

"Beau—I need to talk to you. Can we meet someplace?"

"You're in town?" he asked.

"Yes, we came home last night. They're asking a lot of questions in Washington. And Dan has a speech to give tomorrow to the Rotary Club here."

"I don't know if it's such a good idea for us to talk right now," Beau said. "I'm sorry about what's happening, but it's part of my job."

"Did you see the news tonight?"

"Yes, I saw it," he said.

"She's trying to hang him," Katherine said. "I just can't believe it. He thought he could handle her."

"Then he doesn't know Sheilah," Beau said, wondering anew at how Dan Whittle could be so stupid.

"Please," Katherine begged. "I've got to see you. Just for a few minutes."

"Yeah, okay, how about Gallory's?" It was the remote and secluded bar Gordon McWorth had suggested for their meeting. She wasn't familiar with it, so he gave her directions and put on his coat. He knew this was going to be unpleasant. Perhaps traumatic.

"Oh, Beau," Katherine said, "I don't know what to do. I'm just completely lost. We're going to lose everything."

"I'm afraid it might be out of hand," he said, "but you have each other and you have . . ."

"No—no, it isn't," she interrupted, pulling at her hands. "Dan says the district attorney can do something. They've already worked out a deal."

"They can't work out a deal with Dan," Beau said evenly. "Do you have any idea what's been going on?"

"Well, not—not really. I know Dan was getting some money. It was a fee of some kind. It was . . ."

"It was a bribe, Katherine, or worse. Nothing less. Dan took money from Universal Oil for influencing votes a certain way on the oil and gas issue. He's going to have a hard time proving that he didn't."

"Oh, damn, Beau," she said. "Dan always voted the way he felt was right. We talked about it. He always believed that these price controls were a good thing. He told me so."

"And what about the oil producers here in Bienville County and the rest of the state? They lose money every time they sell a barrel of oil—maybe they don't lose it outright, but they could be making three times as much as they are, but instead Universal Oil and its rich investors are making a bloody fortune. The state loses taxes. It's corrupt."

"Maybe, Beau, but I know he had his reasons."

"Yeah, two thousand dollars a month."

"Well, we *needed* that money." Beau stared at her, his mouth open. "Do you know how hard it is to live in Washington on a congressman's salary. Sure, you get sixty-thousand dollars a year, but you can't get a decent home for less than a hundred and fifty thousand, and two kids in private schools soon—do you know how much that costs?"

"And shopping trips to New York, and fur coats and diamond earrings and . . ."

"Stop it," she said. Katherine had lowered her head and was wiping her eyes. "I never knew it was anything really illegal. And I don't think Dan did either. It was nice, that's all. They were just showing Dan their appreciation."

"He knew, Katherine," Beau said, leaning forward to grab her shoulders.

"Beau, you've got to help us," she pleaded, tears welling in the corners of her eyes. "Please. I don't want to beg, but . . . please."

"Help you how?"

"Don't print any more of these stories. Just let the district attorney handle it, Beau."

"I don't think that's going to solve your problem," he said. "Other people are interested—at least one network. And pretty soon the news magazines and national papers are going to be after him. Dan's a congressman, for God's sake. That's going to bring on heat."

"But, Beau—you—it was your newspaper that started it all. If you hadn't printed the first story . . . Could you print a retraction?"

"It doesn't work that way, Katherine. I won't lie and I don't think I could stop it now if I tried. Not all of it. With what's been made public, I think the D.A. is going to have to open this thing up or the FBI will come down and do it for him. He's no fool, he has to understand that."

"Well, maybe they won't," Katherine said. "If you don't print anything, maybe it will just sort of fade away."

"Katherine," Beau said, "I've got my own personal problems with this whole mess. I don't know what I'm going to do, but I'll tell you this—I'm not out to get your husband. I hope you believe that, and I hope he believes that."

"He doesn't," she said slowly. "He thinks you're out to ruin him—us."

"Do *you* think that?"

"No, but—well, I guess I can understand how he feels," she said quietly.

"And why would I want to ruin him? What possible motive could I have."

"Sheilah, me, I don't know," Katherine said. "He's very upset. He's not himself. He's afraid of losing his reputation, his job."

"But I'm not the only one on the trail of this thing," Beau reminded her.

"Yes, yes, I know that. She came to see him—at our *house*. Did you know that?"

"No."

"It was very hard on me and I wonder how she got involved," Katherine said, a tinge of suspicion in her voice.

"I don't really know," Beau said. "I'd guess that our story came to somebody's attention up there, and they sent her down. Maybe she asked for it. She came to see me a few days ago, but I didn't ask her how she got onto the story. I think I was too flabbergasted to even ask."

"I can't believe *she's* doing this to him too," Katherine spat. "You'd think there'd be some sense of, of—loyalty or friendship. Don't those things count anymore?"

"I don't think Sheilah feels like she's doing anything wrong," he said. "Any more than I do. I feel badly about it, but this is my job."

"Yes, but she went to *bed* with him, and now, to come down here and try to hurt him . . . and then there's our history too."

"Katherine, did you tell Dan about New York?" Beau asked.

"Yes," Katherine said distantly. "I wanted him to know two could play the adultery game. He's a changed man where Sheilah's concerned, but he's been pretty down lately. I just thought I'd ride it out, Beau. I'm sorry."

"Listen," Beau said, wincing, "if we print something, I'll try to go easy on him. But I can't promise you anything."

"Thank you, Beau," she said softly. "For me, and my children, and Dan. You don't know what it means. I don't think I could take it if . . ."

"It doesn't do any good to worry about it," he said, but he was only trying to reassure her. He knew that what was happening would probably lead to wreckage and humiliation in her life.

"Just take it as it comes," Beau said.

Katherine stood and straightened her dress. "Yes," she said, "I will. And thank you." She walked out with her head held high.

Beau walked out with his shoulders slumped. He was a very worried man.

Finally, two days after his talk with Katherine, Beau had it all nailed down—or just about all.

Tim Harte returned from Haiti with confirmation that the story the sailor had told Pacer was completely true. Universal Oil *was* shipping barrels of crude to a tiny refinery in Port-au-Prince and, after having it processed there, was returning it to the United States for sale on the spot market.

Thanks to Spinker, Beau had evidence that Tommy Brodie did not kill Laura Katts, and other evidence that her death was probably connected with her threat to expose the goings-on at Universal Oil.

There was evidence that Universal had been bribing public officials in Bienville—and Katherine herself had confirmed the payments to Congressman Dan Whittle, in exchange for favorable votes in a House subcommittee, when she talked openly about how welcome that money had been to them.

He also had information on the well-connected Bienvillians who had invested in this scheme, including his own father.

Last, but far from least, he had information that the district attorney was planning to downplay the criminal aspects of the case and settle it internally. A cover-up.

The fact that the D.A. had not phoned him or subpoenaed him said a lot. To Beau, it meant the D.A. was waiting for his move. If Beau and the paper kept their mouths shut, so might the D.A.'s office, in which case Universal and its investors would probably be required to sign some sort of consent decree with the government and pay back the money, and no one would ever be the wiser. The information about Dan Whittle was harder to dispose of, but possibly it would be explained away as a consultation fee. Whittle would have his hand slapped and it would all fade into oblivion if no one connected Universal with illegal dealings. As long as Tommy Brodie remained the prime suspect in the killing of the girl, there would be no need to investigate further, and the case could be closed.

Provided, of course, that Beau and the *Courier-Democrat* kept their mouths shut, and provided Sheilah hit a lot of dead ends and didn't bring the rest of the national media down on their heads. Beau knew from his own experience that the national media, Sheilah's network included, wouldn't stick it out for any length of time if they weren't getting regular breaks. It cost too much to keep correspondents on the road without any breaking stories. Perhaps Katherine was right, after all; perhaps if he just sat on it, it would evaporate.

If it did, Beau's father would be saved from the loss of a reputation he had spent his life building and Katherine might be spared as well. Beau and the paper would have blown the story of the decade—if not the century—in Bienville, and Beau knew he would want to resign. He could not go on as editor knowing he had sacrificed his and the paper's principles. It was against this backdrop that he was forced to make a decision. It was Friday afternoon and the paper was quiet. More than anything else, Beau wanted to go someplace and have a drink. A nice big golden scotch and soda and another and another and fade into the mist of drunkenness and forget about the decision that faced him. But he didn't. He pulled out a sheet of paper and put it in his typewriter. He wasn't sure what he was going to write, but he wasn't going to run to a bottle. If nothing else, he thought to himself, I have licked *that* problem. At the top of the paper, Beau wrote: "Universal Oil—Katts Murder." Beneath it he typed: "By Eleanor Campbell."

It was three in the morning by the time Beau finished the story, and it contained everything he and his staff had learned. The only missing link was who had actually killed Laura Katts, and he suspected that would surface soon enough if the story ran.

If it ran.

About midnight, Beau had gone out to the front desk and told the news editor, who was responsible for page makeup, to save a slot at the top of the front page of the Sunday edition and leave a large news hole inside. He didn't say why. When he finished the story, Beau put a note at the bottom of the page crediting every reporter who had worked on it, including the Sob Sisters. He read the story over once, corrected a few mistakes and leaned back in his chair. From beginning to end, it was Pulitzer Prize material and he knew it. Then he locked the story up in his desk drawer and went home.

What he was contemplating publishing gnawed at him for the remainder of the night and into the morning too. When he got to the office, Eleanor was waiting for him and she was in a chipper mood.

"Well, chief," she said, "what are we gonna do?"

Beau shook his head and smiled. "I still ain't decided."

"Yes, you have," she said. "Rumor has it you're holding a big news hole for tomorrow's paper."

"I can hold anything I want," Beau said testily. "I'm the editor."

"Well," she said, "you'd better give me some time if you want me to put this thing together. There's a lot of stuff."

"I'll let you know," he said in a tired voice, rumpling her hair. "Now, why don't you run along an' chase a fire truck."

She stuck out her tongue and left him alone. The rest of the morning Beau could see her through his partition, sitting at her desk, glancing his way every so often—happy as a puppy, nervous as a cat. Waiting for his word. It never came.

Just before noon, the phone rang from the reception desk. Sheilah Price was downstairs and wanted to see him. He said to send her up.

She walked into his office as though she had just won an election.

"Look, Beau, this is ridiculous. We ought to be helping each other on this thing."

"I thought that was unilateral," he said. Sheilah was sitting with her legs crossed and a short skirt showing just the amount of thigh she thought would be useful.

"Not anymore," she said. "I've found something out."

"Oh, what is it?"

"Will you tell me what you've got if I tell you what I've got?"

"What if it's something I already know?"

"Then you don't have to tell me," she said.

"Well, I still can't answer that until I know what you've got."

"Okay," Sheilah said, "I'll just have to trust you, then, won't I?"

"That's the way it goes," he said.

"Then try this. The Katts woman who was murdered was *not* killed by Brodie. I've found an alibi witness."

"Spinker," Beau said flatly.

"Yeah, Mr. Spinker. He came to me yesterday. He's been watching my stories. He said he'd already talked to you, and that you haven't printed anything."

"That's right," Beau said, "because he didn't want me to use his name. But you still haven't told me anything I don't already know."

"I know that," Sheilah said sweetly, "but I'll bet you don't know who did kill that girl."

"Do you?" Beau asked.

"Not really, but I think I know who *does* know."

"Spinker?"

"Nope."

"Then who?" Beau asked impatiently.

"The sheriff's department."

"The sheriff's . . ."

"Yes, because the day he died, Tommy Brodie left a letter or suicide note or something and I've been poking around the jail. One of the custodians let it slip that this note exists, *and* the sheriff's department confiscated it immediately after they found him dead."

"So what does it say?" Beau asked.

"I don't know, but apparently it was so important that the sheriff phoned up the D.A. immediately after he got it and the D.A. had him send *two* deputies over with it—*under armed guard.*"

"So if you don't know what it says, how do you know Tommy Brodie didn't kill the girl?"

"Because the custodian who told me about the note had been cleaning up in the sheriff's office and he overheard part of the conversation. The sheriff said something to the D.A. like 'We've got a real problem—Brodie was the wrong guy. What the hell are we going to do about it, because now he's dead?' "

"Well," Beau said, "that doesn't . . ."

"Oh, but it does," Sheilah said. "It means the sheriff *knows* they had the wrong man. If they *knew* that, then they also know who the *right* man is— don't you see?"

"Unless the sheriff knew they had the wrong man all the time," Beau said.

"That wouldn't make sense, though," Sheilah said. "If the sheriff knew it all along, why wouldn't he have just destroyed the note and let it go?"

"That's a good point," Beau said. "But it's not *proof* of anything."

"C'mon, Beau," Sheilah said impatiently. "This is enough for a story! Now, I know you've got that letter Laura Katts wrote before she died. And I'd like to see it and your other information too."

Beau settled back and looked at her. She still had the same deep blue eyes, the same squintish downturned smile, the same marvelous body and peaches-and-cream complexion that had helped him fall in love with her all those years ago. He was too drained to think further about that. It was done, gone, and he had other things to face.

"All right, Sheilah. You've kept your part of the bargain," he said wearily. Beau unlocked the desk drawer and took out his story and handed it to her. He waited fifteen minutes, watching as she read it. Twice she gasped. When she was through she put the papers back on his desk.

"So you've really got it cracked, don't you?" she said solemnly. "And I suppose you're going to run this tomorrow?"

"I don't know," he said.

"You don't know! Why, this is one of the hottest pieces of news reporting I've ever read! How could you sit on it for one single minute?!"

"Well, I'm going to tell you, Sheilah, and I trust what I say will be between the two of us. There is one name I have left out of that story; my father is among the investors in Universal Oil."

"Your father . . . !" she stammered.

"Oh, if we run it, I'll pencil his name in, of course. I have no choice. Hell, they'd find out in two seconds anyway, once the cat is out of the bag. But it's the hardest decision I've ever had to make in my life. If this comes out, it will ruin him. It will kill him. He's eighty years old and he's led an exemplary life. And now this."

"But you've got to report this, Beau. I mean, how can you not?"

"Well, as you've read in the story, the district attorney is working some deal with them, trying to keep it under wraps, and at the same time satisfy the issues raised by the Katts girl's letter."

"He has *told* you this!"

"No, of course not. He's too smart for that. But he has *not* come to us to ask us about our stories. By just ignoring us he is sending a message that we hear loud and clear: cool it and maybe it'll just go away."

"Surely he can't expect to keep this investigation under wraps. Who else knows all this?"

"A couple of our staff, the D.A. and the principals."

"So if you don't say anything . . ."

"Exactly," Beau said.

"But why . . . why did you show this to me, then?"

"Well, we made a deal," he said, but in truth he knew he wanted someone to force his hand and Sheilah was just the person.

"And you don't plan to run it?"

"I don't know," he said. "I told you I haven't decided."

"Well, Beau, there's someone else who knows now," she said, pointing a perfect red nail at herself.

"It's up to you, Sheilah. You know what kind of mess I'm in. You can use what you've just seen, or you can pack up and go back to Washington."

"That's not fair, Beau. You showed it to me. I don't want to hurt you, but you can't expect me to just ignore a story like this."

"It's up to you, Sheilah. We go back a long way. I can't tell you what to do. I only hope you appreciate my position."

"I do, Beau. It's a terrible one to be in. I don't know what to say."

"Think about it, just think about it, and do what you believe is right."

She stood up and smoothed her skirt. "I don't suppose you'd let me copy that story, would you?"

Beau sat up straight in his chair and looked at her. Their eyes locked across five years of stormy romance. Finally Sheilah turned and walked to the door.

"Good luck, Beau." He nodded.

As soon as Sheilah had left, Beau summoned Eleanor to his office.

"I want you to go over to the sheriff's department right away and ask them what happened to a letter that Tommy Brodie wrote before he died. Tell them you know about it. See if you can get a copy if they have it."

"Did she tell you that?" Eleanor asked. She sounded hurt.

"Never mind that now," Beau said. "We need to act fast on this."

An hour later Beau's phone rang. The operator said that Congressman Dan Whittle was on the line.

"Beau, this is Dan Whittle," a stiff voice said. "I understand you're planning to run a story on me tomorrow."

Beau was irked that Sheilah had gone running straight to Whittle with what she knew, but he kept his tone even. "I don't know what I'm going to run tomorrow, Dan. We haven't laid out the paper yet."

"That's not what Sheilah Price told me." Whittle's words trembled over the line. He sounded like a man barely in control of himself.

"Look," Beau said, "Sheilah just left here. I had a talk with her over this Universal Oil case. I showed her a story that we might possibly run—in some form. I haven't decided yet."

"She wanted me to comment on it," Whittle said.

"Did you?"

"Hell no, I didn't. Just what are you trying to do to me!"

"Nothing, Dan. We've known each other for thirty years. I'm not trying to *do* anything to anybody. But I've got a newspaper to run and I'm going to run it the best way I can. You must appreciate that the Universal Oil story is news."

"News, hell!" Whittle cried, slurring his words a little. "There's more to it than *news!* There are lives and careers at stake here."

"There always are."

"Look, just tell me what you want," Whittle's voice sounded deflated now, tired. "Whatever it is, we can help you. I'll do anything you say."

"It won't matter. There's nothing you can do. It's gone too far. Too many people know about it."

"It's *not* too late. There are people who can control this situation."

"I doubt it. Besides, you can't control Sheilah. It's impossible."

"I believe I can."

"You'd be the first person. Anyway, as I've told you, Dan, this is my decision. I've got to make it the best way I can."

"Don't run any story, do you hear me? Just don't run it. We can talk about it on Monday—or tomorrow even. Just give me a chance to tell my side of it."

"Tell me your side now, if you want. I can take it down right here."

"Goddamn you, Gunn!" Whittle shouted. "You're not going to trick me into some statement. I'm not stupid, you know. I've been dealing with the press for fifteen years!"

"Dan, I was just offering to take down your version. That's all."

"Don't run that goddamn story!" There was a click, and the phone went dead. Beau shoved his chair away from his desk and looked out into the newsroom. It was less than six hours before the closing of the first Sunday edition.

Eleanor had come back into the office and was standing beside her desk talking animatedly into the phone. She glanced up and saw Beau watching her and motioned him over. She cupped her hand over the mouthpiece and whispered, "Tommy Brodie's father!" After speaking with him for a moment or two she put the phone down.

"He's got the note," Eleanor said breathlessly. "He's coming in with it! He's . . ."

"Wait a minute," Beau said. "Slow down. Tell me what happened."

"I went to the sheriff's office and nobody would tell me anything. Then I went to the D.A.'s office and it was closed, of course, because it's Saturday. So I went back to the sheriff's office and I asked a deputy what the procedure was, what happens to the personal effects of people who die in jail, and he said they send them to the family. And so—well, it was just a hunch—but I decided to try Tommy Brodie's father—and it's, well, it's sort of confused, but Brodie wrote his father a letter the day before he died. He told him everything he knew about the murder. And then, the day he died, he left another note saying he'd written a letter to his father telling him everything."

"Hot damn," Beau said. "I knew this thing would come together. What's the letter to his father say?"

"I don't know, but I've talked him into giving it to us. He's coming right now—from Tallahassee."

"But that's . . ."

"About a four-hour drive. He wants to talk with you personally."

"Okay, good work. Now, I want you to come in my office and get a story that I've written. Go over it carefully and make sure we've got it all down. Save a hole for a new lead when Mr. Brodie gets here."

It was 2 P.M. and the Sunday edition crew was just beginning to arrive. Beau thought about his father, and some of the fishing trips they'd been on when he was a boy. The old man used to cook him breakfast at the Still River camp and get him dressed. He showed his son how to tie flies and clean fish and then, later, the two of them pan-fried big bass at night for supper and his father told him stories of other hunting and fishing trips decades before, in the twenties and thirties, when the land was much wilder. He was preparing to repay all of this, and so much more, by humiliating that eighty-year-old man. Beau shook his head and closed his eyes and the time flew past like dandelion flowers on an autumn breeze.

At six-thirty it was already dark and Beau was still sitting with his hands folded in his lap, staring at the clock on the wall. The deadline for the Sunday-morning edition was in half an hour and the news editor was getting impatient. He had already checked with Beau twice about the news hole, and Beau had put him off. It was indeed the biggest, most difficult decision Beau had ever made. He had watched the five o'clock news, but there was no report about events in Bienville from Sheilah's network. Either she had decided not to go on the air with the story or she had chosen to give Beau first crack.

If he waited, he might be able to save his father's ass. Dan's plan might work. He would have to face Eleanor and the others, but he could go home and try to forget this. Of course, if she *did* decide to go with the story tomorrow, or the next day, or the next, he'd still have his own ready, and all they'd lose would be the scoop and a little face. Beau was trying to cope with the churning in his stomach when Eleanor appeared at the door with Tommy Brodie's father. Beau showed him to a chair. He was still sad-eyed, a little like Tommy, a rotund man in his early seventies, perspiring even though the weather was cool.

"I appreciate your coming, Mr. Brodie. I really didn't mean for you to drive all the way over here, though."

"No—I wanted to," the old man said. "I thought it was important. I've thought about this for weeks, and well, I want you to have this." He reached in his shirt pocket and pulled out a wrinkled letter and handed it to Beau. Eleanor was standing beside him as he opened the envelope and unfolded the pages.

Dear Daddy,

When you read this, I will probably be dead. Believe me, it is easier for everyone concerned this way. My life has not been a happy one, and I am grateful to leave it.

I did not kill that girl, but I believe I know who did. It was a man called Grimshoe or Grimwall, someone the girl worked for and dated. I know because my friend told me. I will not mention his name because I do not want him associated with my life in any way. I have not told you this before, but I am a homosexual. As you know, in this part of the country, that is still a thing that brings disgrace on a person and his family and his friends. I could not bear to do that to you, because I have already brought enough pain into your life.

The night the girl was killed I was in a bar with my friend and the girl. The man who killed her was there too. Mr. Grimshow called my friend over and they talked and then my friend and I left and I went back to my apartment. My friend had something to do, so he came over later. When he arrived he had a paper bag and he had something in it that he put under the sink. I asked him what it was and he wouldn't tell me. He said to stay out of it. But I looked and it was a knife and my friend said that Mr. Grimshoe had paid him to hide it for him and get rid of it the next day.

Beau looked up at Eleanor. "Spinker," he said quietly, and resumed reading.

The police came and arrested me the next day and I could not tell them what I knew because it would get my friend in trouble. I love him and I had always promised him I would never let anyone know about him. But as the days go by I realize that I am going to have to tell the truth to save myself. If I do, I am going to bring an awful shame and disgrace to our family and betray my friend. I do not believe my friend knew he was being used. He was, of course, so someone knew about us and someone thought nobody would question another murder rap that was blamed on me. I hope by doing what I am going to do I will end all the years of anguish I have brought upon you and I want you to know that I love you very much.

Your son,

Tommy

Beau's hands were trembling as he finished the letter. He looked at Mr. Brodie, who had begun crying softly in his chair. "Times haven't changed much down here," Beau mumbled. It wasn't much to offer, but it was all he had.

"He was never a bad boy," Brodie said. "Things just started going wrong for him after . . ."

"I know," Beau said. "I think I could have been a better friend. We all could have. I suppose we were too busy with our own lives to see what was happening."

"He never got over the stain," Mr. Brodie said.

"And we didn't help him much. We just let him slip away from us."

"No, Beau. He always said you were there when he needed you."

"I was too far away when he really needed me."

"Could I get you something—a cup of coffee—a drink?" The old man looked at him, and Beau turned to Eleanor.

"Go out to one of those desks in the newsroom and poke around. I know somebody's got a brown bag with a bottle in it hidden away. Get a paper cup from the water cooler too, okay?" She hurried off.

"Do you mind if we use parts of this letter in a news story?" Beau asked.

Mr. Brodie shook his head. "That's why I wanted you to have it, Beau. I don't trust that district attorney with anything that's said in this letter. I called him up after I got it and he said that an 'investigation' was underway and for me to send him the letter. 'Don't say anything about this to anybody,' he told me, and so far, I don't see that he's doing anything."

"He's not," Beau said, "but I am."

Eleanor returned with a paper cup and a pint of rye whiskey.

"I found it in one of the Sob Sisters' desks," she said.

Beau smiled. He poured Mr. Brodie a drink and told Eleanor to get him a hotel room at the paper's expense. After a while Brodie decided to leave and Eleanor walked him to the door.

"All right, there we have it," Beau said when she came back. "Write it up."

"Do you want to see it first?"

"No, there's not that much time. Bring me a copy when you're done."

Beau sat with his feet on his desk while Eleanor wrote furiously at her typewriter. People came and went in his office, leaving him proofs and pieces of copy, but he did not read them. For the first time in weeks he felt relaxed. He knew what this story was going to do to his father and to Katherine, but even if he'd waffled over it, even if he'd actually entertained the idea of sitting on it, in the end he didn't. At some point a bell rang in the newsroom, signaling that the copy was in and the presses had started. He could hear the rumbling two floors below. Beau was thinking of poor old Tommy and the days of enchanted boyhood summers and of Eleanor and his little house in Buck Hollow. He knew he'd made the right decision coming back here, away from the false and elusive glamour he'd known for the past ten years. He was interrupted by Horace Moulton tapping at his door. Behind Moulton was a man wearing an overcoat. Moulton apologized to Beau as he ushered in Congressman Dan Whittle.

"Beau," Moulton said. "He just showed up out there and said he had to see you."

Beau stood up. He hadn't recognized Whittle's haggard face or bloodshot eyes or the way he walked a little unsteadily and stopped in front of Beau's desk with a lurch. They stared at one another.

"Thank you, Horace," Beau said. It was a signal for Moulton to leave them alone.

"I know what you're trying to do," Whittle said thickly.

"Please sit down," Beau told him. He could see Whittle had been drinking. Whether he was drunk, Beau couldn't tell. He hadn't counted on this visit. He'd hoped the phone conversation would be the end of it.

Ignoring him, Whittle continued. "I've got a wife and two children, but I suppose you know that already."

Beau nodded. "Yes, I do."

"And you—you and I, we go back a long way, don't we?" Whittle asked.

"Yes, Dan, we do," Beau said.

Whittle wiped sweat off his upper lip with his sleeve. "All the way back to Singer, right? All the way back to that time when you got caught lying, isn't that right, Beau?"

"Yes, that far."

"And you've held that against me all these years, haven't you?"

"Well, Dan, maybe I have to some extent," Beau said.

"And Sheilah—you hold that against me too, don't you?"

"No," Beau said calmly, "No, Dan, I don't. You're welcome to her."

"Don't get smart with me, damn you," Whittle said, his voice rising. "Sheilah called me a while ago. She says you're going to run the story in the morning. I want you to call it off."

There was a sudden tap at Beau's door and the news editor was outside. Beau looked at the clock and waved him off.

"Call it off," Whittle snarled. "Call it off, goddamn you."

"I can't do that, Dan. The presses are already running. It's done. Why don't you sit down."

Whittle reached slowly into his coat pocket. His hand came out with a pistol—a .45 Army Colt—and he pointed it right between Beau's eyes.

"Dan, that's not . . ."

"Shut up," Whittle spat. Beau heard the hammer click as the weapon cocked.

"All right, Dan," Beau said placatingly. He reached for the phone.

"No, you don't," Whittle said.

"Now, Dan, look," Beau said. He felt his voice tremble and suddenly it began to come back to him, that terrible night of the interrogation. Cold, wet. The night of the attack on the Fake. He had cocked the pistol and aimed it at the Vietnamese's head. And the boy had stared at it, at the black hole of Beau's .45. His eyes fixed on the hole, his mouth drawn in terror. . . .

"You've ruined me!" Whittle whispered.

. . . and the dream. That was in the dream too, except it wasn't Beau then, it was the sergeant. Beau hadn't killed anyone in the dream, but it kept coming back. In the dream Beau had never been the one to shoot—he was always the one to scream, "Stop!" Never the one who shot . . .

"You've ruined my wife and children!" Whittle snarled.

"Dan, this won't help. What about Katherine?"

"Katherine!" Whittle said. "What the hell do you care about Katherine? You'd destroy our lives and I'm going to destroy yours."

Katherine in the dream.

The play too.

My God! Beau suddenly thought this was the ultimate end of his dream.

Now, staring down the dark, terrible barrel of that gun, staring at that obscene black hole, he realized that for over fifteen years he had been facing his own death in those dreams. It was *him! Him!* He was the one who died.

"Dan, you've got to listen. I wasn't . . ."

Beau never got to finish the sentence. He might have seen the slight orange flame of the pistol in that split second before the slug tore into his head and he might have seen the painfully simple solution to the troublesome scene in his play, but of course we will never know the answer to either.

Dan Whittle stood immobile over Beau's body, slouched lifelessly in his chair, arms flung back, mouth open, the prize-winning story still clutched tightly in his right hand. He was still standing like that when Horace and the others rushed to the door.

"My God!" someone said as Whittle let the gun clatter to the floor.

"He was a liar," Dan Whittle said. "Once a liar, always a liar." Then he began to sob. He stumbled backward until he touched the arm of a chair, and then he collapsed into it and continued his low, racking sob. It was the only sound among the stunned little crowd that had gathered by the door. Eleanor was bending over Beau, cradling his head in her arms, unable to speak.

Later, Dan pleaded not guilty by reason of insanity, but the jury never believed it.

Out in the newsroom, the bell rang again, punched by some unknowing person, someone two floors below in the pressroom. The bell meant that the press run was finished. The edition was closed.

Epilogue

Beau didn't die that night, though by all medical opinions he probably should have. He lived on for two more years, but never regained consciousness. The bullet had lodged deep in his brain, gouging away the thoughts and emotions that make a man human. He spent most of those years in a nursing home, living, as his attendant put it, "pretty much like a vegetable."

The *Courier-Democrat* ran the Universal Oil story, and just as Beau predicted, we got our Pulitzer Prize. Beau's daddy was named in the story, and was indicted by the district attorney along with the other investors, but nothing ever came of the indictment. In a few years the case was practically forgotten.

Every day Beau's old man would visit him, sit by his bedside and talk to him. He even bought a little television set and put it at the foot of Beau's bed. They left it on day and night, but I doubt Beau ever knew it was there. Eleanor Campbell visited too, once or twice a week.

About a year and a half later, Beau's father died peacefully in his sleep. I went over to see Beau and sat by his bed and told him. I thought I saw one of his eyes blink, but I'm not really sure. I guess it didn't matter anyway. I sat there with him a long time, and after I left, I never went back.

Beau finally died early one Sunday morning. He was buried in the family plot next to his father and mother and grandparents and great-grandparents in a magnolia-shaded cemetery. They gave him a military funeral and we did a real nice obituary in the *Courier-Democrat*. I wrote it myself. Six months later I sold my interest in the paper—for a nice profit, of course. After all that had happened, I guess I just lost heart in the thing. It wasn't the same. But

Beau had definitely made it a fine newspaper and we found a good editor to take his place.

Eleanor is the new managing editor and it wouldn't surprise me a bit if she becomes the editor one day. It had always occurred to me that she and Beau would have made a nice couple, but who am I to say?

Not long after that, Sheilah became the White House correspondent for her network and recently I read in the paper that she got married to a businessman in Washington.

Fletcher Cross, Gordon McWorth and others intimately involved with Universal Oil went to jail on fraud charges, but they're all out now and back in town. I'm told Cross got religion in jail, but I'm damned if I believe it. Dan Whittle received five to seven years for bribery and attempted murder but he's out now too. After Beau died there was talk of indicting him for homicide, but nothing came of it. I guess everybody just felt it wasn't worth the trouble. Katherine stuck by him through it all and they're living out in Texas, I hear. Ben Grimshaw was convicted of murdering the Katts girl and is doing life without parole.

Beau's house in Buck Hollow, by the way, remained unfinished. Like Beau's life, it had a lot of promise but was never completed. The sheriff got re-elected the next year and the D.A. became, of all things, the first U.S. senator from Bienville.

Just before Beau died I got a call from his agent, Toby Burr, who told me a repertory theater had put on Beau's play *In Fields Where They Lay,* and that it had gotten good reviews. Later an Off-Off-Broadway group had staged it and now it was running in several of the smaller theaters around the country. Burr said all the notices were good except that nobody liked the shooting scene. The critics were pretty much in agreement that it just didn't work.

Oh, and one more thing—the bear.

A couple of months ago there was a photo in the paper of a game warden kneeling next to a large black bear he had shot in the delta swamps north of Bienville. According to the caption, the bear had been raiding people's trash cans, and since it was too old for a zoo and too incorrigible to relocate, they figured it was a hazard and decided to kill it. I suspect it was Beau's old boy.

The story said the bear was one of the largest of its species left in Bienville County and, like Beau Gunn himself, I imagine it was the last of its line.